VENGEANCE CHILD

VENGEANCE CHILD

Simon Clark

This first world edition published 2008
in Great Britain and in 2009 in the USA by
SEVERN HOUSE PUBLISHERS LTD of
9–15 High Street, Sutton, Surrey, England, SM1 1DF.
Trade paperback edition published
in Great Britain and the USA 2009 by
SEVERN HOUSE PUBLISHERS LTD

British Library Cataloguing in Publication Data

Clark, Simon, 1958-
  Vengeance child
  1. Horror tales
  I. Title
  823.9'2[F]

  ISBN-13: 978-0-7278-6705-6   (cased)
  ISBN-13: 978-1-84751-104-1   (trade paper)

All Severn House titles are printed on acid-free paper.

Typeset by Palimpsest Book Production Ltd.,
Grangemouth, Stirlingshire, Scotland.
Printed and bound in Great Britain by
MPG Books Ltd., Bodmin, Cornwall.

For Janet

Prologue

This midnight rain did not whisper. It struck the big house hard. Rain clattered at windows. Drops hit the patio table in a salvo of violent bangs. Heaven's bullets. A sound like war. As if the earth had been invaded from above. *Take no prisoners. Batter the house into the ground . . .* Balls of water exploded against a sign on the wall until the force of it dislodged the board announcing Badsworth Lodge. The board's fall revealed the old sign beneath: Badsworth Orphanage.

The vicious crack of rain against glass had roused the children in the dormitory. Ten boys, aged between eight and eleven, tore along the corridor, laughing, shouting, pushing one another, and hell-bent on making the weird kid's life a misery. Normally, they'd know better than to torment Jay, only this wild weather got into their blood. These were categorized as 'problem children'. Their file notes bore headings such as Learning Disorder, Conduct Disorder, OCD, and a whole clutch of other phobias and compulsions. They'd get themselves into a storm of temper at the best of times. Now this ear-busting cacophony of rain bashing against the building cranked up their aggression levels so much they forgot all about words like consequences, recklessness, danger, and that all-important rule they learned from day one in Badsworth Lodge: don't mess with Jay.

Jay had his own bedroom. He'd only been in the boys' dormitory three days when the rest took to sleeping in the corridor. Although he'd got his private sleep zone it was only a partial fix. The other kids rarely spoke to him. Today he'd spent the day in bed with a comic in his hands. The care staff recorded notes in his file. *Since 10 a.m. emotionally withdrawn. Marked lack of physical movement. Unresponsive. Skin clammy.* Jay: eleven years old, slightly built, with large brown eyes that made strangers look at him in surprise, as if there was something amiss that they just couldn't place. Jay had skin the colour of lightly toasted bread: a pale gold. Jay was dangerous.

'Little witch!' A rubber mat pinched from the bathroom struck Jay in the face. He didn't react. Nor did he appear to notice when ten boys, howling like demons, shot through his door. Some bounced on his bed. The tallest grabbed Jay's jet-black hair and yanked his head sideways. 'Little witch! Hey, piss face, get out of bed.'

Raindrops snapped against the glass. Like the rattle of claws as if some night creature tried to rip its way through.

'Comic . . . shitty comic,' sang another boy. A second later pieces of it fluttered in the air. 'Hey, it's snowing!'

One kid lost his balance as he jumped on the bed and landed on Jay's lap.

The boys sang, 'Ricky loves Jay! Ricky loves Jay!'

The storm outside caused the patio table to topple with a crash.

'Open the window. Stick his head out!' Ricky scrambled away from Jay. 'Get the little witch outside.'

'I'm looking for chocolate . . . I bet he's got chocolate!' A tiny boy, with a face old beyond his years, ransacked a bedside cabinet. 'If I find it, it's mine.'

'Yeah, Archer, you eat it. You'll catch what he's got.'

All through this Jay never seemed to even notice the boys running riot in his room. The biggest there pushed open the window. Rain sprayed on to Jay's head. The water roaring in the storm drain could have been a monster's bellow.

The kids shouted, 'Grab his head.'

'Get him by the arms, push him out. Mess the little shit up!'

'Out by the ankles.'

Screams of laughter made the air electric, as if the force of emotion charged everything it touched. Lights flickered. And with the outburst of mischief came a dangerous blaze of hysteria. One child who warned the others they might drop Jay to his death was loudly ridiculed as a 'crybaby'. By the time they'd got Jay into a standing position by the window, the rain had soaked his face. His expression altered. When he all of a sudden spoke it was in soft tones, almost too soft to be heard, but it stopped the kids as suddenly as if a bomb had exploded.

A silent pause then: 'He said something.' Alarm flashed across Ricky's face. 'What did he say?'

Nobody else could bring themselves to speak. They stepped back from Jay. His elfin face unnerved them. Their eyes flashed with uncertainty; not sure whether to cover their faces, so they wouldn't see what awful thing Jay would do next. Meanwhile, the rain fell faster. A frantic drumming sound. Ten boys stared in horror at Jay as they waited for the inevitable. Then he began to murmur slowly. It was the same word over and over.

Ricky hissed, 'He's doing it again. I know it's a name.'

'Which one?'

They all started to speak, the words bursting from their lips like sobs.

'Is it my name?'

'It better not be me!'

'Nor me!'

'I said it first.'

'Make him stop.'

'Can you hear what name it is?'

An adult voice cut across theirs. 'What's all this then? You know you should be in bed.'

Ricky turned to a woman of around forty in the doorway. She had the pleasant figure of an earth mother.

Despite the scolding tone, she smiled warmly. 'What's the problem, sweetheart?'

'Maureen, it's Jay. He's doing it again.'

'Doing what again?'

'Saying a name.'

The smile froze. 'You're not telling me fibs?'

'No . . . listen to him.'

The way Maureen tensed a panther might have just crept into the room to bare its wicked fangs at them. She took a deep breath. 'It's OK, boys. You run along back to bed.' Her eyes fixed on Jay as he murmured the name. 'It's all right, sweetheart,' she soothed. 'I'll dry you, then you pop back under the covers.'

Ricky tried to sound tough, but it came out scared. 'What name is he saying?'

'Boys. Get back to bed. *Now.*'

They clamoured anxiously.

'We want to know what name it is.'

'Tell us, Maureen.'

'*Please.*'

One sobbed, 'You know what happened to Tod . . . you've got to say.'

They began to shout, 'Please, tell us,' until the words fused into a howl of noise.

'Boys! Enough!' The second adult voice had enough authority to stifle the clamour instantly. Nurse Laura Parris added, 'Thank you,' in a gentler tone. 'Back to bed. I'll be along in a minute.' Obediently, they returned to their dormitory. Laura shot Maureen a weary smile.

'One day they'll realize I'm all bark and no bite, then I won't be able to do a thing with them.' She noticed Maureen's troubled expression. 'What's wrong?'

Maureen swallowed, then nodded at Jay who stood by his bed, murmuring. 'It's Jay . . . he's doing it again. Saying a name.'

'Which name?'

'I can't make it out.'

Laura shut the window, then plucked a towel from a shelf and put it round the boy's narrow shoulders. 'Everything's all right, Jay. We'll get you dry and settled back into bed. What's that you're saying?' She leaned closer.

Maureen's composure was evaporating. 'It's a name, isn't it?'

Laura tried not to let her expression betray what she'd just heard from his lips.

Maureen flinched. 'Oh, God . . . it's my name, isn't it?'

'I don't—'

'It's my name!' In sheer panic Maureen fled the room. Laura heard her repeating, 'My name, my name, my name . . .' as she raced down the corridor.

But Laura knew, just as Maureen knew, and all the kids knew – running away wouldn't save her.

One

'Ouch.' Victor Brodman understood this fact: *unless I do it now, in five minutes he'll be dead*. And there was one more thing. The wire had sliced through that web of skin between Victor's first and second finger. Blood ran into the fur of the fawn's neck, which he gently supported. From there, the blood dripped into the river to form little clouds of scarlet. Giving himself the luxury of one more, 'Ouch,' he blanked the pain from his mind, then focused on saving the infant deer from drowning. The black-faced, blue-eyed deer, of the species known as the Saban Deer, had been feeding on kelp in one of the beach gullies when it had got itself caught in a tangle of steel wire. Now the tide had begun to sweep in, the water reached its neck. In another five minutes, its head would be underwater. The island's uniquely precious herd would be reduced to 281.

'Take it easy,' Victor said gently as the fawn began to panic. 'I'll get you out in one piece.' He glanced back over his shoulder. A shingle beach, bushes, then a grassy bank rising to a spine of stones. This, the remotest part of the island, boasted no houses. There was nobody out walking, either. 'It's down to just you and me, son. How we going to do this without cutting your leg off?' He knelt in cold river water that now reached his waist. Carefully, he used his injured hand to keep the animal's head clear. With the other hand he steadied himself against a sign that blazed DANGER! DEEP CHANNELS. QUICKSAND. FAST CURRENTS! Already the river pulled at him. Further out, the brown water formed pyramid shapes as an angry current powered over submerged rocks. Once Victor was sure of his balance he used his free hand to tug off his Island Warden's green fleece. He hung it over the danger sign. The dry garment would come in useful if – when – he freed the animal.

From the undergrowth another black face with blue eyes peered out. 'Try not to worry, Ma. I'm going to bring your baby back just as soon as I can.' He pulled his knife from its sheaf. *Now or never.* Using his free hand, he felt his way down the fawn's leg until he found the wire again. Someone had slung the kind of line used in grass-strimmers into the River Severn. Eventually, it had been washed here, then waited in one of the beach gullies; as lethally effective as the old-time poacher's snare (something demonstrated when he sliced his own hand when tugging at it). String he could have cut easily. This stuff had a toughness that resisted snapping, or even cutting.

'Nothing for it.' He took a deep breath. A second later he plunged his face underwater. The fawn struggled, its furry flank pressing against his face. A roar of bubbles filled his ears. Though he couldn't see much through the murk he glimpsed the white of a pebble. Quickly he grabbed it, then used it as a makeshift chopping board. This was his last chance to save the animal that he devoted himself both professionally and emotionally to protecting. He managed to hold the wire taut against the stone. That done, he used the knife to saw at the steel line. By this time the water must have been over three feet deep. For all he knew, the fawn's head might be submerged, yet he couldn't afford to check, just in case he couldn't find the stone again. Underwater, he heard the muffled scrape of blade against wire.

Come on . . . you can do it . . . press harder. Harder! The words beat in his head. The infant deer twitched. *Damn it . . . convulsions? You get no points for delivering a dead animal back to its mother.* From the depths of this huge, ancient and pre-eminently dangerous river came a bass rumble . . . a sound of primeval voices . . . anger at the intruder. The sound always sent shivers along his backbone. He knew the cause of the rumble – the current rolling boulders along the river bed – but even so, he found himself glancing out underwater, half-expecting to see a dark shape torpedo toward him.

Got you! The second he cut the wire he surfaced, the fawn in his arms. He dragged his fleece from the danger sign, wrapped the animal inside, then waded back to the shore, panting. As he paused in the shallows to catch his breath the sound of applause greeted him . . . a somehow sarcastic handclap. He wiped the water from his eyes.

A man of around fifty, dressed in a dark blue business suit, clapped him without enthusiasm. 'Bravo, Victor. Bravo.'

'Good afternoon, Mayor Wilkes.' Although Victor would have preferred to substitute Mayor with 'Pompous fart-bag'.

'You've cut yourself.'

'So I have.' Victor adopted a deliberately understated tone when what he'd like to have done was lobbed the man into the river.

'I'd give you a hand but –' Wilkes smiled a political smile – 'you can see I'm not dressed for the job.'

'Another golf club lunch?'

'Don't start that again, Victor. I take my role as the island's guardian very seriously.'

'Seriously enough to rip up meadow for a fairway.'

'It would have brought new income to the island. And jobs.'

'We need income. We need jobs. But that's not the way.' To the fawn Victor said, 'Take it easy. There.' He set the animal down on the shingle then gently dried it using the fleece. He caught the pleasant scent of its fur. Rose pelt, as it was called, had been popular in years gone by. Aristocratic ladies would have a pinch of the fur sewn into the corner of their handkerchief so they could delicately inhale its fragrance as they walked down the fashionable streets of Cheltenham.

'Pleasantries aside.' The mayor's voice became tart. 'I'm here to do you a favour.'

'So you're agreeing with me that we introduce a grass management programme? Good. That'll help restore the butterfly numbers.'

'That still has to go before the committee, Victor. As you know.'

'You also head the committee.' Victor checked that the wire hadn't cut the animal's legs.

The mayor eyed Victor distastefully. 'You'll find they still have two at the front and two at the back.'

'It became entangled in a line. If it's broken the skin it'll need a stitch.'

'My God, you really do love those creatures. Thirty-five, aren't you? Pulling beasts out of the river – is that a proper career for a grown man?'

'It's the Saban Deer that bring the tourists.'

'And I know the old wives' tale as well. They're people in animal form.'

'Do you believe it, Mr Mayor?'

'Do I hell, but I happily believe in the money they generate. If the National Trust allowed us to sell their stuffed heads as souvenirs I'd be even happier.'

When Victor was satisfied that the animal hadn't suffered any cuts he took away the fleece. It shook itself, then trotted to the undergrowth where the other deer stood. From a black face its blue eyes closely watched the return of its offspring before both mother and fawn slipped silently away.

'You know . . .' The mayor looked thoughtful. 'Maybe a book . . . it could tell the story of the Saban Deer. How does the legend go? A thousand years ago there was another island out there in the river.

It sank underwater but the gods took pity on the islanders' children, turned them into deer, and they all swam across here to live happily ever after. We could turn the story into a colouring book. Parents would go for that. We could sell them over the Internet.'

'You're the man to do just that, Mayor. Don't you still own a print works in Bristol?'

'You think I'm only interested in making money out of the island?'

'Didn't you say that you'd come here to do me a favour?'

'I did.' He eyed Victor, as he stood there dripping river water. 'You're expecting a batch of orphans tomorrow.'

'From Badsworth Lodge. They're coming down for the week. But we no longer call them orphans, Mayor.'

'Orphans, waifs, inmates, I'm not interested. They're a negative drain on the island. They don't generate cash revenue.'

'You could always train them up as golf caddies.'

That touched a nerve. The man flinched before stating coldly, 'The visit's been cancelled, so you'll need to rearrange your schedules.'

Victor shook his head. 'You politicians and your funding cuts.'

'Not this time.' The mayor smiled. 'One of the orphanage staff took it upon themselves to stand between two buses. One reversed into the other with the clueless mare in the middle.' He clapped his hands together as if crushing a fly. 'Now, go home and get changed. You're going to catch your death of cold.'

Two

Despite it being May, gusts of cold air made it feel like the approach of winter. In the grounds of Badsworth Lodge the children played on the swings. Usually, there'd be laughter. Today, they were so quiet it made the staff glance apprehensively at one another. Meanwhile, Nurse Laura Parris was determined to work a miracle. Age thirty, blue eyes, wearing casual clothes, strands of blonde hair being mussed by the breeze, she talked into the phone. 'What happened to Maureen was a tragedy. Everyone here's in shock. Yes . . . the funeral's tomorrow. Eleven o'clock. You're going to authorize permission for Lodge staff to attend?' Laura paused as the Director of Child Care Services ummed, then tried to add provisos. 'No, Miss Henshaw. Nobody will use it as an excuse to slip away for a long lunch. Maureen was extremely popular with both children and staff. So, I'll have your written permission for us to go to the funeral, and that personnel cover will be provided? Pardon? I don't know how long. As long as it takes to say goodbye to a dead friend.' She struggled to keep her anger under control. 'Another thing. Don't cancel the children's holiday. Postpone it a few days, but do not cancel. After what happened the children are traumatized. Yes . . . what do you think? There's bed-wetting, emotional outbursts, bouts of social withdrawal. A couple of teenage girls have been self-harming. Yes, I really do believe that the holiday is essential. Goodbye.'

Laura scanned the children on the swings. Listlessly, they swung to and fro. Their faces were so lacking in normal youthful exuberance they could have been plastic mannequins. A girl of fifteen sat on a bench. She appeared to be scratching an itch on her forearm. Laura knew better. Catching the attention of one of the carers, she nodded to the girl, then touched her own forearm. The carer understood and went to chat to the girl to distract her from inflicting another wound.

A middle-aged man with a security pass clipped to his lapel appeared on the patio. He pretended not to notice the eerie appearance of the children who played as if someone had hit the mute button. 'Nurse Laura Parris?' He gave a sympathetic smile. 'I'm Robert Cole, Human Resources. I've come to collect Maureen Hannon's personal effects. We're sending them on to her family.'

'Of course. I'll take you to her room.'

'Terrible weather for May.' Despite pretending to shudder at the cold he lingered on the patio without following Laura. 'Absolutely arctic. They're forecasting hailstorms for this afternoon.'

'Really. I'll get Maureen's things before the children go to lunch.'

'You're doing amazing work here. It can't be easy.'

She sensed he was building up to say something of more importance. 'Is there anything else I can help you with?'

'You've a boy here—'

'Several, as you'll have noticed.'

'Absolutely.' He laughed. 'But they all aren't as famous as . . .' He scanned the children, trying to recognize a face. 'Jay, isn't it?'

'Ah.'

'The Miracle Moses Boy. The newspaper headline still sticks in my mind after, what is it now? Seven years.'

'The children will be going to lunch, Mr Cole. If you'll follow me.'

He didn't follow. 'So he'll be eleven now, won't he?'

'Mr Cole—'

'Imagine what he went through. Four years old. A ship full of refugees sinks with the loss of over three hundred lives. There are sharks, storms and he's there alone. A four-year-old boy in an inflatable dinghy. It makes you think, doesn't it?'

'The newspaper must have paid you plenty if you're prepared to risk your job.'

'N-Newspaper,' he stammered. 'I'm nothing to do with any newspaper.'

'No?' Laura glared at him. 'The guy who came to fix the roof tiles swore he had nothing to do with a television company, but he had a video camera in his tool bag. Something told me he wasn't going to use it to bang in nails.'

'I was just intrigued about Jay.'

'Really.'

'I am here to collect Mrs Hannon's personal effects.'

'OK, do it and get out.' Laura turned to where a burly man dug a flower bed. 'Mr Holt, would you do me a favour? Escort this gentleman to Maureen's room to collect the box on her bed, then make sure he leaves the premises.'

When she was alone again Laura crossed the lawn to where Jay sat on a bench under a tree. The breeze sighed mournfully through the branches. As always, the boy was by himself. Before speaking to him she paused. Laura took pains to avoid having favourites. However, she often found herself thinking about Jay. He always seemed so alone and so fragile. Once a carer commented that he looked like 'a changeling'. Laura had googled the word. The search had revealed myths about human children being stolen soon after birth by goblins. Then the goblin family replaced the human child with one of their own. It wasn't a happy fairy story. The changeling child looked different to other children – Jay certainly did with those uncannily large eyes – and brought unhappiness to its human hosts. Bad luck would haunt them. Other children in the household might become sickly. Crops would fail. The parents finding themselves with a changeling substitute might be advised to treat the goblin cuckoo in the midst badly, either by beating, starving or even placing on a shovel and holding over a fire. The theory being the real parents would snatch the changeling child back to prevent further suffering. In order to maintain the supernatural balance the real human child would then be returned to their mortal parents. *But Jay doesn't face the prospect of a he-lived-happily-ever-after ending.* She'd been standing behind Jay. He'd not turned back once. When he spoke it took her by surprise.

'Do you hate me too, Laura?'

Smiling, she sat beside him. 'Of course I don't. What makes you say anything as daft as that?'

He regarded her with those huge dark eyes that were wise as they were mournful. She, too, remembered that face seven years ago, when it looked from every television and newspaper in the world. The Miracle Moses Child, cast adrift on the high seas. Three hundred and ninety refugees died when their ship sank in the Atlantic. Only one inflatable craft had been found amid shoals of hungry sharks, and on that craft had sat a solitary boy. All this flashed through her mind in a second, but the look in her eye must have told Jay a lot.

'Why am I different to everyone else, Laura?'

'We're all different from one another.' She ruffled his hair. 'That's what makes us individuals.'

He sighed. 'I'm *too* different. I frighten people.'

'Nonsense.' She tried to sound cheerful. 'Now . . . Jay. I haven't told anyone else this, but I've asked my boss to rearrange our holiday.'

He gazed at her. 'The others are blaming me for what happened to Maureen.'

Air currents whispered through the tree. Laura found herself glancing up into the branches half-expecting to see a frightening face. She brushed the disquieting notion away. 'Why should they blame you?'

'You know, Laura. It's happened before.'

'Coincidence. Nothing more. Come on, time to eat. There's apple pie today.'

His eyes became even graver. 'Maureen knew something bad would happen.'

Laura tensed. 'Did you say anything to her?'

'The others told me I was saying her name – over and over.' Gusts shook the branches. 'But I don't remember doing that, Laura. Only what I did later.'

'And what was that? What did you tell Maureen?'

His eyes became vast, dark pools. 'I went to her room. I told her I was going to take her for a little walk.'

'A little walk?' she repeated. 'Why would you do that?'

His voice appeared to merge with the breeze. 'I wanted to make her happy before she died.'

'It was an accident. Nobody could possibly guess. How did you know that she was going to die?' She took his hand. 'Jay, tell me how you knew.'

At that moment a piercing scream rang out. In the play area everyone stopped to stare at the teenage girl who clutched her arm. A boy raced across the lawn toward Laura. 'Ruth found a knife. She's cut her wrist again!'

Three

When the school party, comprised of a dozen fifteen-year-olds, reached Chapel Hill Victor Brodman hung back as the teacher, a dark-haired beauty with scarlet nails, delivered the lesson. 'Class, listen up. This is one of the highest points of the Isle of Siluria. Just a hundred yards away from us across that channel is England. Over there is Wales. This is one of the largest river islands in Britain. Until 1875 it had its own parliament and referred to Queen Victoria as the "foreign dame". Being surrounded by the river means it rarely drops below freezing point, allowing more exotic species of insects to survive the winter.' From time to time Miss Hendricks caught Victor's eye. 'The Isle of Siluria is named after which ancient kingdom? Gary?'

'Wales.'

'Very good. Siluria is indeed the old name for Wales. Tricia, what are the deer called?'

'It's in the fact sheet, miss.'

'Humour me, Tricia. I'm the educator, you are my acolyte.'

'You what?'

Miss Hendricks shot Victor a smile, then fixed a steely eye on the girl. 'Tricia, I ask questions, you answer them. So, dear, give me the name of the deer, dear.'

The students laughed. They clearly liked their teacher.

Tricia read from the sheet. '"Saban Deer. Growing no larger than a Labrador dog . . . they have golden body fur, black fur to head and distinctive blue eyes. Said to be a unique species, but probably a mutant variant of roe deer."'

'Thank you, Tricia. The name alone was what I wanted.'

A boy with an Afro hairstyle pretended to be scared. 'Mutants, miss. You mean like with ten eyes and tentacles.'

'No face-sucking monsters here, unless you include yourself, Theo. Seeing as I noticed you smooching with Pippa at the back of the bus.' More class laughter. Miss Hendricks was a hit. 'The deer are mutants in the sense of being a biological offshoot of the common roe. So, no bloodthirsty rampages today.'

The children took advantage of the teacher's discourse being interrupted. 'Can the island ranger take the class?' asked one. 'I bet he knows all kinds of stories.'

'And what time the pub opens,' Tricia added.

Miss Hendricks took it in her stride. 'You've juice and sandwiches so no need to waste your time in some stuffy tavern.'

'We don't mind, miss.'

Theo eyed the channel between the island and the mainland. 'I bet I could swim there and back in twenty minutes.'

Tricia shivered. 'In this weather? It's f-f-fu-fur-freezing.' The class laughed.

Victor enjoyed the lively banter. 'Swimming isn't a good idea. There's a current running at over ten miles an hour round the island. Not to mention whirlpools and rip tides. You'd be safer playing with a hand grenade.'

'So that's why there are a million signs with *danger* plastered all over. Cool.' Theo was impressed. 'Anybody drowned recently? Have you ever seen a drowned man, Victor?'

'Mr Brodman to you lot.' Miss Hendricks' eyes twinkled at him.

'No, Victor's fine. I insist.' He smiled back.

Tricia tapped him on the arm. 'So – Victor – what's this about your Saban Deer being the ghosts of drowned children?'

'And isn't it true,' asked a boy in a bush hat, 'that the population of the deer always matches the island's human population, which currently stands at two hundred and eighty-two?'

Victor was surprised. 'That's not on the fact sheet.'

Tricia wore a pained expression. 'Please excuse Greg. He always researches a place before we visit. Hormones, I think.'

Theo winked. 'He's never kissed a girl.'

'All right, class,' Miss Hendricks announced. 'More walking, less talking.'

They moaned.

Miss Hendricks advanced on Victor. 'So, how long will it take us to walk from this end of the island to the castle at the other?'

'It's just over two miles, so I reckon we can do it in forty-five minutes.'

'If them mutant deer don't gore us to death,' Theo added with a huge grin.

'If they do –' Miss Hendricks pointed the way along the path – 'interpose your youthful frame between the savage beasts and us.' As they walked the teacher dealt out the facts. 'At its widest the island is a mile, narrowest just a hundred and fifty yards. Access is by the ferry you dear children arrived on. Its main settlement is the village of Penrow. Tony, pick up your gum and deposit it in the bin provided yonder. Siluria derives its income from tourism, farming and some cottage industry such as pot-making, weaving, and baking.'

Victor nodded. 'And there are some locals working in website design, PR and we've even got a couple of television script writers.'

Tricia piped up as they walked along the shoreline path. 'Miss? Miss, a word please, miss.'

They continued to stroll along as the teacher waited for Tricia to catch up. Victor led the way as Theo asked if there was shop that sold rolling tobacco. Even though Tricia and the teacher were now at the back of the group Victor could hear the young girl's excited whisper. 'I saw how you were looking at Victor. You fancy him, don't you, miss?'

'Tricia, that's not an appropriate topic of discussion.'

'He's really dead good-looking, miss. You like him. I can tell. When we get back to the hostel why don't you invite him to the pub?'

'Thank you, Tricia. I'm perfectly capable of arranging my own romantic liaisons.'

Victor took a moment before glancing back. When he did Miss Hendricks shot him a winning smile.

Once more Laura Parris found herself fighting a battle to protect the children at Badsworth Lodge. The self-inflicted cuts on Ruth's wrist had been minor ones, not much more than scratches really. Nevertheless, Laura knew the warning signs when she saw them. The teenage girl grieved for Maureen even though she hadn't so much as shed a single tear. A lot of the children at Badsworth Lodge did that. They'd conditioned themselves to repress emotion. Because in their old homes emotion equalled weakness. Weakness invited bullying. So, as she peeled off the latex gloves smeared with Ruth's blood, she headed to her office where she telephoned City Hall.

'Miss Henshaw, have you rearranged the visit to the island?' Laura sighed as she heard a negative reply. 'The reason I sound ill-tempered is that I'm angry because a friend and colleague of mine has been killed. I'm angry because one of your staff came here today and started asking questions about Jay Summer, leading me to wonder if the press have found out if Jay's now living here. All the more reason to get away for a break.' In the heat of the moment she steamed on. 'Badsworth Lodge is a volcano that's about to blow itself sky-high. Our children are self-harming, and they're either not sleeping or having nightmares when they do. Come down here, feel the tension for yourself. Everybody's wound up so tight you'd swear this place will be torn from its foundations when the shit finally starts to fly.' Lights in the building flickered. It didn't take a leap of faith to believe this was a sign of an emotional conflagration building. A child shouted in anger in the corridor. Another symptom that nerves had been rubbed raw. Barely suppressed rage simmered in the air. 'A holiday, Miss Henshaw. Fix it today.'

The voice wheedled in her ear. 'It's not possible to rearrange one just like that. Maybe in a week or two?'

'Today, Miss Henshaw. Give me confirmation today.' A crash sounded from the corridor.

One of the carers leaned in through the doorway. 'John's throwing chairs down the stairwell again!'

Before hanging up Laura shouted into the phone, 'Today, Miss Henshaw – or lives are going to be lost!'

They were bright kids. Full of energy, too. Victor Brodman had escorted them to the castle at the far end of the island. They'd been interested in the Giant Men of Siluria's Graves, the name given to slit-shaped pits dug into one of the beaches where boats had been kept in years gone by. One pupil had been reluctant to surrender the notion that there weren't really men thirty feet high, striding round the island centuries ago.

'It's just a colourful name for holes in the beach,' Victor told him. 'They didn't have the resources to build a proper harbour. But those trenches kept the boats safe when storms struck.'

'Only they do look like graves for giants.' With a wistful expression Greg photographed them. 'Any chance I might get shots of the Saban?'

'They're shy animals, but you might catch a glimpse.'

Miss Hendricks strolled up. 'Greg, go remind Theo to read the danger signs. He's getting too close to the water.'

Once Greg had jogged away down the beach Miss Hendricks flicked back her raven-black hair. 'So, Victor, we've seen the wildlife, what's the night life like round here?'

He smiled back. 'Not what you'd call red-hot.'

'Really?'

'There's the Three Impostors pub.'

'Oh? I wondered what it would be like. But it won't be much fun for me drinking alone.'

'I'd ask you to join me for a drink tonight, Miss Hendricks, but what about your class?'

'Oh, they can do with a break from me for a while. The hostel staff will make sure they don't wreck the place, so, what do you say to—?'

'Miss?'

'What is it, Greg?'

'It's Theo.'

'Oh, Lord, he's not fallen in the river, has he?'

'No, he's feeding the fishes.'

'Pardon?'

'Feeding the fishes,' Greg repeated. 'Throwing up, puking, vomiting, barfing . . .'

'Yes, yes, I get the picture.'

'Lots of others are feeling ill, too, miss. It must be those cheeseburgers.'

'Damn.' Miss Hendricks' sunny disposition turned all of a sudden cloudy.

'I'll help you get them back to the hostel,' Victor told her.

She gave a regretful smile. 'I'm sorry, Victor. It looks as if I might miss that drink tonight.'

'Some other time. Oh, best stand back. Greg's starting to look off-colour.'

By the time they had got the kids back to the hostel even Miss Hendricks had started to wear a distant expression. When the hostel manager asked if she'd like a coffee she dashed through the door marked bathroom.

'It looks as if we'll be on mop and bucket duty tonight,' commented the manager as he eyed the hiccuping kids with displeasure.

'I can stay and give you a hand?' Victor offered.

'We can manage, thanks anyway.' The man paused. 'There's one thing you can do.'

'Fire away.'

'The Badsworth Lodge visit's back on again. They're arriving tomorrow evening. We make special arrangements for them to stay at the islanders' houses rather than the hostel – it's more homely for them. Would you call at the addresses on this list and let them know when the children will be arriving?'

'No problem. Are you sure you don't want me to—?'

Gurgling sounds came from the bathroom.

The manager grimaced. 'I guess it's best to let nature push outside what man put inside, if you see what I mean.'

Victor grinned. 'You paint a vivid picture, Dave. I'll leave you to it.'

Four

'Marry a man, not a job.' The carer, an amiable Jamaican woman of fifty, took the towels from Laura as they met in the corridor. 'I'll get these down to the laundry.'

'Thanks, Lou. While it's quiet, I'll check if Jay's ready for bed.'

The woman's face became serious. 'I'm not joking, Laura. You should get some love in your life – I'm talking about man love, not a love affair with this place – otherwise you'll end up haunting the Lodge when you're in your box.'

Laura smiled. 'I wish I had the time.'

'Make time, honey. Or you'll wind up like me. Fifty. Two failed marriages. A face like an old prune.'

'You're here because you're an angel. We couldn't manage without you.'

'Yes, you could – one day you will. Laura, girl. Don't get left on the shelf, pretty young woman like you. Catch yourself a man.' She sighed. 'Lord, isn't it ever going to stop raining? We've got a lake for a playground.'

'I'll think about what you said. About man love.'

'Plenty of man love. Make it soon, or I'll put a spell on you that'll make you fall for the first man you meet.'

'Best do that, Lou. It's going to be the only way I'll find romance.'

'You asked for it, honey. I'm going to put your photo in a bag full of rabbit bones tonight.'

Laura shot Lou a startled look.

Lou chuckled. 'I can't even cook Jamaican food never mind put a love spell on you. Go put an ad in the paper. "Lovely blonde, thirty, seeks handsome man. GSOH." Now, I'll drop this off, then my time to watch some television in bed. See, told you I'm a lonely shrivelled old prune!' With a hearty laugh she sailed away down the corridor.

Laura checked her watch. Other members of staff would be switching off dormitory lights in the wing that accommodated the younger children. After a fraught day a silence had finally crept over the building. Good silence? Or a bad silence? Only time would tell. Sometimes when it got quiet like this in Badsworth Lodge it was like sitting on a time bomb. At least she had good news for Jay.

She found him sitting on the bed in his pyjamas. Rain clicked at the windows. A brittle sound that tugged your nerve endings until you wanted to shout, 'Stop that!' Jay stared at the picture of a ship in a comic. *Maybe he's beginning to remember?*

'Jay,' she sat beside him. 'Good news. I've just had confirmation from my boss: the trip to the island is back on. We're leaving tomorrow afternoon.' She refrained from adding 'after Maureen's funeral'. 'You must be pleased about that.'

He stared at the picture. A red ship sliding across the ocean.

Gently, Laura added, 'I haven't been there, but I've heard it's a nice place. It's an island in a river, not the sea. We can have barbecues. They tell me there are otters, deer and even wild mink.'

Without letting his eyes wander from the ship picture he asked, 'Will I meet new people?'

'Some.'

'That's frightening.' A simple, matter-of-fact statement.

'You're going to be frightened of people on the island. Why?'

'No . . . I'm frightened of what I'll do to them.'

'Jay.' She put her arm round his shoulders. 'That's nonsense. You're the kindest, most considerate boy I've ever met.'

'Nobody says Maureen's name in front of me. They know I killed her.'

Laura had overheard what the children were saying to each other. *Jay's done it again . . . the little witch made the bus crush Maureen . . .* She leaned forward so he could see the smile she now wore. 'You mustn't say that. It was an accident. What happened was tragic, and it makes us all hurt inside because we loved Maureen, and we miss her.' Laura made a point of talking about feelings to the children. They were accustomed to suppressing grief until it festered dangerously inside of them. 'Do you want to talk about Maureen?' she asked.

'Do you think she ever went on a boat like this?'

'I guess so. What made you ask that?' *Maybe he's having flashbacks of when he was on the ship.* With that thought came memories of seven years ago when the news was dominated by the sinking of the *N'Taal*, taking hundreds of refugees with it. Just one four-year-old boy had been picked up from an inflatable raft.

Slowly, he shook his head. 'Grown-ups won't talk about Maureen in front of me, just like they don't talk about Tod Langdon.' He turned those large brown eyes to her. 'Tell me what really happened to him.'

'Well . . .'

'You can tell me a made-up story; that's OK if it makes you sad to tell the truth.'

Her mind whirled back six months. Just hours after Jay arrived at Badsworth Lodge she had found him in the kitchen. The eleven-year-old sat on his floor with his back to the fridge door. Emotionally withdrawn, face clammy enough to shine beneath the fluorescent lights, he could have been a mannequin sitting there. A fragile one with jet-black hair, and large – strangely large – eyes that were dark as a shadow. And then Jay began to speak from the depths of his trance. She had to crouch down to hear properly. 'Tod . . . Tod Langdon. Tod Langdon. Walk . . . going for a walk.' The syllables pulsed with their own unsettling rhythm. At first she thought Tod had bullied the younger boy. But no. Not Tod. He obsessively cut pictures of animals from old magazines. Many children here related better to animals than people. These pictures he carefully filed away in an old filing cabinet in the cellar. Love was too tame a description for his interest in wildlife. So there was no obvious reason why Jay should repeat the teenager's name. 'Tod Langdon . . . Tod . . . Tod . . .' And that peculiar comment: 'Walk, go walk, walk him.' A mantra? A spell? Or a curse?

Laura picked up the story of what happened all those months ago (without mentioning she'd found Jay in the kitchen, almost comatose, and uttering Tod's name). 'Tod Langdon had reached an age when he felt he was growing into a man. We should have realized that he'd outgrown Badsworth Lodge. One day he ran away. I think he wanted to prove that he was independent. That he could find a job.'

'Animals. He loved animals.'

'That's right. I'm sure his plan was to go to a zoo and ask for work there, so he'd be close to them. Only he met some people . . . unpleasant people . . . who wanted to use him. They tricked him into stealing things from shops. From what I hear they secretly put drugs into his food so it would stop him realizing what he was doing was wrong.' Jay appeared to be digesting what she told him so she continued. 'Only there was a lot of anger in Tod. He kept it stored away in the back of his mind for years. You know, like something nasty pushed into a drawer, where you hope you'll forget it, but never do. Anyway, the drugs let it out.'

'They say he went crazy.'

'It wasn't madness. It was all those memories of bad things that had happened to him. He got so angry because it seemed to him everyone in the world had ignored the cruel things his father did to him, so he took his anger out on the world that was around him at that moment. Tod smashed windows in shops, which was very frightening for him and the people near him at the time. Then he hurt himself badly with pieces of glass.'

'You've told the truth.'

She realized he wasn't asking a question. 'How did you know?'

'Tod told me.'

'He can't. Tod's . . .'

'He's not dead.'

'That's right.'

'It's a place like this. Only there are bars on the windows. They don't let him outside. Mostly he's very tired because of the medicine they give him. The walls are painted green because the doctors say that colour helps keep the patients calm.'

'Jay, has one of the children told you about Tod?'

'I'm right, aren't I, Laura?'

She nodded, mystified. 'But how do you know?'

'I've said already. Tod told me.' He closed the comic. 'Sometimes I take Tod for a little walk.'

She tried to quell the shiver, but there was nothing she could do to suppress its creep up her spine. 'I liked Tod. He didn't deserve that.' A more recent memory brought yet another shiver. 'Yesterday. When we were talking about Maureen. You told me you took her for a little walk. What do you mean by that?'

He said nothing. Exhaustion had drained the poor kid. *Shame on me. I shouldn't be interrogating him. He's been through hell, too.*

'OK, young man,' she said brightly. 'Time for bed.'

His face darkened as a troubling thought struck him. 'When we go to the island, will we have to cross the water by boat?'

Five

Why didn't you keep your mouth shut? Haven't you heard what happened to the cat when it became too damn curious?

Laura Parris turned down the quilt ready for bed. At midnight Badsworth Lodge could have the dead silence of a tomb. She pictured all those empty rooms downstairs. Vaults filled with darkness. Damn the local authority for housing troubled kids in a creepy old pile like this. Savagely, she started to brush her hair. A tangle made her hiss. Damn it, she was really angry with herself. When Jay had asked about crossing the river by boat she'd made light of it, telling him that she heard it was just a short ferry ride. That had made him happy enough to make a light-hearted comment about them needing a boat to cross the lawn if it didn't stop raining soon, so carelessly she'd asked the question that had been bothering her. 'Jay. You've told me that you took both Maureen and Tod for a walk. Will there be a day when you take me for a walk?' His shoulders had scrunched as if he'd been doused in cold water. Trembling he'd climbed into bed and pulled the sheet over his head. She'd wished him good night, while cursing the looseness of her own tongue. *What made me ask that?*

She dragged the brush through her hair. 'What's got into you, Laura? You looking for a death wish?' Grimacing, she set the brush down. 'It's fine. Don't get all superstitious. You need a break, too.' She leaned to the mirror to study her eyes. 'Look at those bags. Big enough for the week's groceries.'

Quickly she climbed into bed, then switched out the light. Outside, the rain fell with a steady murmur. Through her mind streamed the kind of night-thoughts that keep sleep away. She needed to collect the flowers for Maureen's funeral. A temporary team of carers would arrive early to cover while the permanent staff were at the chapel service; they needed briefing on meal and medication requirements. Also she had a list of numbers to call to confirm the children's arrival at the island. *And don't forget the children's cards for Maureen. They're collected at 10.30.* As she lay in the darkness, the rain finally stopped with a suddenness that made the silence heavy against her ears. Then soft footsteps in the corridor. Puzzled, she sat up in bed. Her door swung open to reveal a figure in the gloom. Its eyes glinted, sparks of unearthly flame.

Then a voice. 'Laura. I've come to take you for a little walk.'

'Jay? Is anything wrong?'

'It's time for your walk.'

'Jay, it's gone midnight. You should be in bed.' Quickly, she donned her dressing gown and slippers. 'Give me your hand. There . . . come on back to your room. We've got a busy day tomorrow.'

Again, he spoke in a whisper. 'It won't take long.'

When she took his hand to walk through into the corridor she flinched. Drops of rain struck her face. A breeze sighed through the trees. They walked beside a high wall topped with razor wire.

'Jay . . . no . . . *no!*' A sense of cold dread filled her. 'I didn't see where . . .' Confusion swirled her senses. 'Jay, how did we get outside?'

He glanced up at her. His normally golden skin had turned white as bone. In the darkness all she could make out of him was a face that blazed like a skull, the huge eyes dark as midnight. Suddenly, the boy dragged her by the hand.

Dear God, how did he bring me outside without me knowing? 'Jay. No, I don't want to go. Don't make me . . . please . . .' Fear scrambled her senses. She could barely see, only confused images of trees that towered over her with all the menace of giant men. The sense of the *masculine*, a raw *animal* power was so overwhelming she staggered before it. She'd never felt so vulnerable. *Someone's waiting out there for me. They're going to hurt me.* Air currents in the branches hissed . . . an impression that they murmured suggestions. *Come into the bushes, Laura, dear. We're waiting for you.* Still being dragged along by Jay, her gaze was drawn to a seething mass of hawthorn. A figure in a bright blue dress stood there. 'Maureen . . . Stop Jay! I don't know where he's taking me.' Maureen wore an absurdly cheerful smile, only her mouth had been daubed so thickly in crimson lipstick it resembled the fixed grin of a clown. 'Maureen?' *But Maureen's dead. Crushed between two buses. Her body reduced to a sack of jelly. Every bone broken. Teeth squeezed from their sockets. Eyes ruptured . . .* 'Jay, stop this. I don't want to walk any further.' Terror became a peal of church bells. Panic, fear, distress, dread – all had a different note, but all clanged mercilessly inside her skull.

All of a sudden they were running hand-in-hand across a lawn to a forbidding building. Its windows gazed coldly at her. Through one window a man and woman in green uniforms that suggested medical care writhed together on a sofa. Quickly, frantically, they were stripping one another. The man pushed up the woman's top to reveal her bare breasts. Dark nipples against brown skin stood out as they hardened. The man kissed her nipples before moving down her stomach to a smudge of hair. When he worked her with his hungry tongue she writhed on the sofa in pleasure.

Even though Laura closed her eyes she still felt herself slip through solid brickwork like a ghost.

'Here,' Jay whispered.

She swayed in a bedroom with green walls; vertigo tugged at her. A steel door with a peephole stood firmly shut against the outside world. Stuck to one wall, a huge poster seemed to act as a window to the Arctic. In the picture a polar bear swam in deep blue ocean.

'Why haven't you visited me before?'

A grey-faced figure sat on the bed with the edge of the blanket grabbed in his two fists. One eye was swollen from a punch; his face had bloated since she last saw it, but she knew the identity of this teenager.

'Tod? Tod Langdon? What happened to you?'

He stared at her with blazing eyes. At last he choked out, 'Laura . . . Why haven't you visited me?' His voice got louder. 'I don't like it here. I don't!'

She backed from him as his fear turned to anger.

'Don't leave me! Don't you dare!'

As he stood up on the bed, still holding the blanket in front of him, Laura tried to push Jay behind her to relative safety. She knew the crazed youth had reached breaking point.

'You're not leaving me again!' He leapt from the bed. As he did so he threw the blanket over her like he would net a wild animal. 'You're going to stay and see how they torture me.'

She cried out as she fought to free herself from the blanket. The light that struck her so forcefully made her blink until her room came into focus. For a moment she lay there, savouring the tranquillity. Sun shone through the curtains. She heard the gardener whistling as he trundled the wheelbarrow across the patio. The nightmare image of Tod Langdon hurling the blanket over her head came back so strongly she kicked her bedding off her entirely. For a moment she lay there, the cool morning air on her bare legs, just thankful to be free of the dream. Such a darkly terrifying dream, too. A shudder ran through her as she recalled it: Jay's appearance with the promise he'd take her for 'a little walk'. Then the stroll through the forest to the mental hospital where had Tod sat in his room, his face bruised from beatings and mad with fear.

'Stop it,' she told herself. 'You're having bad dreams because you're stressed.' Chasing the remnants of the nightmare away, she headed for the bathroom.

Lou suggested they take her car to the funeral so they could pick up not only the flowers but three dozen flip-flops, assorted sizes.

'Knowing these kids,' she said as Laura sat beside her in the car, 'they'll be in and out of the water all day. Their shoes will get ruined.'

For a moment they chatted about everyday things, especially arrangements for the stay on the island. Then, when they pulled up at the red stop light and they both had a clear view of the hearse containing Maureen's coffin in pale brown wood, they fell silent. Laura knew that Lou must be thinking about Maureen, too. The usually happy-go-lucky Jamaican woman sighed; a tear ran down her cheek. Laura didn't like the silver handles on the coffin. The way they shone seemed far too bright. Nothing had the right to glitter cheerfully on a day like this.

As the cortège pulled away, Lou shook her head. 'Maureen was younger than me. Married to the job like you and me. Remember to learn from our mistakes.' After a pause Lou spoke again. 'They're burying her in that dress she liked so much. Remember the one at the Christmas party? Electric blue. Whoa, girl, I told her. Wait until I get my shades before you go exposing that dress to the public. That fabric's giving the Christmas tree lights an inferiority complex.'

Laura tried to sound as if she was making conversation, but when she asked the question Lou shot her a surprised glance. 'Pardon?'

Laura repeated it. 'Do you ever visit Tod Langdon? He's at that secure unit on the other side of town, isn't he?'

Lou clearly wondered why Laura was so suddenly interested in one of their – let's face it – failures. 'From time to time. Since they committed him six months ago.'

'Does he know who you are?'

'Not really. One of the nurses there said, "You've heard the term brain-dead? Well, he's mind-dead. Does nothing. Doesn't interact."' Lou shot her a probing look. 'Why the sudden interest in Tod?'

'Oh . . . I found myself thinking about him this morning.'

'Because Jay did that thing? Repeating his name, just like he did with Maureen then – pop. Bad thing happens out of the blue.' She pressed her lips together, annoyed with herself. 'Pay no heed, Laura.

I've been thinking a bunch of nonsense about Jay. Huh, I've found myself surfing the Internet looking for stuff about curses, prophecies, portents of doom.' The funeral cortège crossed a railway bridge. 'In the end I helped myself to a glass of gin with sugar in it. My grandmother always said if you add sugar to booze then it's medicine not liquor.' She read Laura's expression. 'What happened to Tod is bothering you, isn't it?' She gave a world-weary sigh. 'Have you ever been to the secure unit?'

For a moment Laura nearly poured her heart out about the nightmare. All about seeing Maureen in the bright blue dress, the medical team making whoopee at midnight, the dour corridors, the cells with steel doors all firmly in lockdown. Instead, she gave a tiny shake of the head. 'I've seen it from the outside. Razor wire. High walls. It looks grim.'

'Yup, it's no sweeter on the inside. All the walls are painted green, a dull, dull green. I used to go along with Maureen to visit Tod. We always feel responsible for our charges. Success or failure. We could do nothing for the boy, but we couldn't let go. Story of our lives, huh? They locked Tod in his green cell, all so damped down with tranquillizers he could barely move. All he did was stare at nothing. Maureen hated the idea of him staring at a blank wall so she bought a poster. A huge one. Once it was up there on the wall it could have been a big picture window on the outside world.'

Laura tingled. 'Good idea. He loved animals.' Images from the nightmare shot back with such a pungent reality that she clenched her fists so tightly her fingers ached. For a moment she stood in the green cell again, steel door locked, a drugged Tod Langdon cowering on the bed, the only homely touch a poster on the wall of his favourite animal.

'More than anything –' Laura heard her voice as if it came from some other place – 'he loved polar bears.'

'And that's what Maureen bought him. A big poster of a polar bear swimming in a bright blue sea.' She sighed. 'Well . . . here we go.' The line of cars followed the hearse through the gates to the chapel. The handles on the coffin flashed silver, as if they sent out a warning: *danger ahead. Take care . . .*

Six

Siluria is such a small island, with a permanent population of just two hundred and eighty or so, that when a large party of visitors arrives a good chunk of its residents pitch in to help. When the party from Badsworth Lodge arrived it was dusk. Victor Brodman helped his neighbours carry the children's holdalls from the boat on to dry land. As the tired-looking party disembarked from the ferry he counted ten girls aged between eight and eleven. Twelve boys in the same age group. Then four girls and four boys in the twelve to sixteens. Add five members of staff and that cranked up the island's population by a decent percentage. The kids from Badsworth Lodge had been coming here ever since he could remember. They were kids that tended not to be fostered for various reasons. Most had behavioural problems. But the custom of them spending a week on the island worked surprisingly well considering. Instead of staying at the hostel like the school parties, they were shared out amongst more than a dozen homes. Childcare specialists advocated a homely environment for a few days each year to help prevent them becoming too institutionalized. Victor liked the children from the Lodge. Despite what they'd gone through they tended to be better behaved than school parties and they took a greater interest in the animals. The guy who'd been the island ranger before him insisted that they formed a bond with the Saban Deer. 'These animals share the same kind of quality as dolphins. Do you follow what I'm saying? The deer have a calming effect on troubled souls.' The ranger had believed in that absolutely, especially when one of the carers explained that children from the Lodge often developed a deep mistrust of human beings. Animals didn't steal, trick them, lie to them, or use their heads as punch balls. Animals could be trusted.

The sun was setting as the exhausted group moved ashore. As he took one carer's bag she confided in a melodic Jamaican accent, 'Poor lambs. They're all shattered. They've been through a terrible ordeal over the last couple of days, Mr Brodman.'

'The mayor told me you'd lost a colleague. I was sorry to hear about it.'

'It was a shock, Mr Brodman. Here, don't carry too many bags.'

'Lou, remember to call me Victor or I'll make sure they hide the cider.'

'You'll do no such thing – *Victor* – that's the elixir of life. I've been promising myself a big, big glass tonight. Heck, no, just fill a bathtub: I'll leap in naked.'

They laughed. Victor remembered how Lou had the knack of infusing the entire island with her good-natured presence. Staff like that at the Lodge must be as precious as rubies. He scanned the faces as they disembarked on to the jetty. He recognized some of the children from last year. These he greeted by name. The others he helped ashore with 'Hi. Welcome to the island. My name is Victor. I hope you enjoy your stay.' Behind him an assortment of fishermen, craftspeople, and even a TV scriptwriter helped divide the party into smaller groups so they could be taken to their new homes for the week. A boy with such striking brown eyes that Victor had to look twice stepped off the ferry. His elfin face seemed to radiate an uncanny glow in the dying light of the sun. 'Here, let me help you with that holdall.'

'I'll see to that.' A carer he didn't recognize spoke sharply enough to suggest he keep his distance from the boy. She had blonde hair, and a face that, while being extremely attractive, had the drawn appearance of someone living on their last reserves of nervous energy.

'No problem.' He shrugged. 'Is there any more luggage on board?'

'No, we've got it.' She seemed on edge.

'My name's Victor Brodman, the island ranger. I'll be helping out generally and will be your guide while you're here.' Despite his burden of half a dozen holdalls he freed a hand, then held it out to her.

For a second she eyed him suspiciously, then extended her own hand. 'Nurse Laura Parris.' The woman flinched as if not liking the steely sound. Softening it, she gave a tired smile. 'Call me Laura. I'm in charge. Thanks, by the way. You've got everything organized.'

'We're well rehearsed now,' Victor said. 'We've been taking parties from Badsworth Lodge for years.'

'Ever since it was known as Badsworth Orphanage, no doubt?'

Is she always this prickly? He nodded. 'We enjoy having you. The whole island prides itself on making sure the children have a good time.' She appeared not to be listening but was scanning the crowd of faces instead. 'So, Laura, I've still got to learn some of new children's names. This will be . . .' He nodded to the fragile-looking boy

with the elfin face. When she didn't make the introduction he did
it himself. He held out his hand to the boy. 'My name is Victor.
Pleased to meet you.'

Laura quickly drew the boy away. Guiding him to a gangling boy
of eleven or so, she said, 'Billy, Jay is your holiday buddy. He'll be
staying with you at Mrs Miller's house.'

Billy immediately let fly with a howl of protest. 'No damn way!
I'm not stopping with that little witch.'

'Billy—'

'What if he starts saying my name? I'm not going like Maureen
and Tod. I'm bloody well not!'

Lou stepped forward. 'Let's not wage a war about this.'

Billy trembled. 'You can't make me. I'm not staying with Jay. I'm
not, I'm not, I'm—'

'OK. We'll shuffle the deck,' Lou told him. 'Calum, if you swap
places with Billy, then—'

A freckled boy reacted exactly as Billy. Flinching back, he yelled,
'Not with Jay! I'm not being anywhere near him. Never!'

The other children retreated from the elfin-faced boy as if he'd
burst into flame and burn them to cinders. All clamoured that they
wouldn't stay with him; that it wasn't fair. What struck Victor so
forcefully was that they weren't being merely stroppy, they were
absolutely terrified of Jay.

Mayor Wilkes had been overseeing the arrival of the party in his
usual manner – hands behind his back, pointedly announcing that
his status was far too elevated to actually help with the mounds of
luggage. He scanned the adults from the Lodge.

'Who's actually in charge?'

Laura Parris turned to him. 'That would *actually* be me.'

'You can find that boy another child to stay with?'

'Don't worry. I'll work something out.'

'That's how the system operates for your party. They stay in groups
of two with carefully selected local residents. We can't have children
chopping and changing.'

Laura glared. 'The children are worn out. We can deal with this
in the morning.'

'But where does the boy stay?'

'He can stay with me at the hostel.'

'The terms of the visit don't allow that. Besides, there's no room
at the hostel. The dormitories are being redecorated. There's accommodation for your staff, that's all.'

Laura snapped back. 'What do you suggest? That he sleeps under a bush?'

'I'm suggesting that he returns on the ferry.'

Victor saw the blaze of anger in Laura's eyes. *Watch out Mayor Wilkes, she's just about to go for your jugular.*

The mayor added breezily, 'If that boy doesn't get along with the others then it's clearly a recipe for disaster if he stays.'

Laura closed in. 'All these children have been through hell. Not just last week, but for every week of their lives. They all need a holiday. I won't stand by while people I care about are run off the island like two-bit thugs.'

From his Mr-High-and-Mighty stance, Mayor Wilkes huffed. 'I merely said that in the interests of harmony—'

Victor interrupted. 'He can stay at White Cross Farm. There's plenty of room.'

'You mean, stay with you?' Laura turned that glare on Victor – a glare that reminded him of a lioness ready to attack anything that threatened her cubs.

'We have rules relating to children's accommodation.' Mayor Wilkes wore a smug expression. 'The boy must return on the ferry.'

Victor smiled. 'More precisely, I'm suggesting that Jay stops with my sister and her husband. Both have childcare clearance checks. They've experience of fostering children as well.'

Laura still resisted. 'I won't have him staying by himself.'

'Then you stay with us, too. There are spare bedrooms.' He read her expression. Grinning, he added, 'That's right, although my sister runs the place I'm the lunatic sibling who they keep chained up in the attic.'

Lou grinned too. 'That's perfectly true, the man is a lunatic. But Victor's the kind of lunatic you can trust with your life.'

He put his arm round her shoulders. 'Thank you, Lou. I'll take that as a compliment.' He glanced at Mayor Wilkes. 'Well?'

'Look, I'm fine with this if Nurse Parris is. Besides, I'm late for a meeting.'

Victor nodded, 'Say hello to the golf club guys for me.'

Scowling, Mayor Wilkes marched on to the ferry, while gesturing to the crew to cast off straight away.

Victor took in the view of the stars coming out in the sky. 'It's going to be a beautiful night.' He added another holdall to the six he already carried. 'Lou, I'll see you in the Three Impostors at nine. First cider's on me.'

Chuckling girlishly, she followed her party in the direction of the village.

Laura didn't appear impressed. 'So you can charm Lou.'

'Lovely Lou. I'm sure she's an angel in human form.' He paused. 'Only us three left. You can accept my offer to stay at my sister's farm, or there's always the ferry back to the mainland.' Its motor coughed into life.

Laura scowled. 'For one night *only*. I'll sort out a place for Jay tomorrow. The children are just overtired.'

He acknowledged the statement with a nod. 'Follow me.'

For the first time the boy spoke. 'Where's he taking us?'

When Laura smiled her face turned from winter to spring. 'To a farm. That's where we'll be staying.'

Victor led the way along the shoreline path. He dropped off holdalls according to the address labels as he went. Behind him the boy talked quietly to Laura, thinking Victor couldn't hear.

'Laura. I'm frightened.'

'There's nothing to be frightened of. There might be animals at the farm. You'll like that, won't you?'

Jay's reply was so odd that it kept coming back to Victor for the rest of the night. '*I'm not frightened about where we're staying. I'm frightened that I'll do the same to you as I did to Maureen.*'

Seven

The boy known as Jay beamed with pleasure as he fed the goat slices of bread. A group of ten children had walked up here in the morning with Lou to get acquainted the animals and to meet with the island ranger. The children kept clear of Jay. There was none of the name-calling from last night; they just excluded him from their play as if it all came as naturally as *not* sticking your hand into a fire. Lou showed them how to feed the chickens. Victor kept an eye on the goat. When the bread ran out the animal tended to butt the hand that fed it.

'The goat doesn't frighten you?' Victor asked.

'He's like me,' Jay spoke casually. 'He keeps himself to himself.'

'The other children weren't kind to you last night. That didn't seem fair.'

'They're scared.' Again, the casual manner. 'I'm creepy.'

'You don't seem at all creepy to me.' Victor kept it light-hearted.

'I sometimes have these episodes.'

Victor didn't pry. 'Hold the bread by the crust, right at the edge. Wilkes tends not to bother about the difference between fingers and food. Just look what happened to me.' Victor held up a hand with two fingers curled in to make it look as if they'd been bitten off.

Jay laughed. The sun shone down warmly for the first time in a week, and it seemed to bring out a sunnier mood in the child.

'Jay, what happened to Laura this morning?'

'She had to talk to the mayor.' His grin broadened. 'Mayor Wilkes. The goat's called Wilkes. You named the goat after the mayor, didn't you?'

In mock horror Victor threw up his hands. 'Promise me you won't tell. He'll blow a fuse.'

The boy skipped from subject to subject. 'Laura isn't always like that. You know, arrrr.' He growled as he hooked his fingers into claws.

'She's being protective of you all. That makes sense to me.'

'Yeah, she's nice. Only I had one of my episodes.'

'Oh.'

'I took her for a walk . . .' The large, brown eyes glittered.

'A walk doesn't sound a bad thing to me. I thought we'd all take a walk along the shore later.'

'Not that kind of walk.' Perspiration formed on the boy's face. 'I can't help it. I took her to Tod. And I showed her Maureen in that dress she wears in the coffin. Even though I couldn't stop myself I hoped it might make her happy to see Maureen and Tod again. But I'm scared that Laura might be next.' Wilkes licked breadcrumbs from Jay's fingers. The damp rasp of the tongue distracted him from what must have been troubling thoughts. 'Is that the last slice of bread?'

'We have to ration Wilkes. He'd eat all day if he could.'

'We've got someone like that. Ricky could eat chocolate until he explodes.' Jay pulled a camera from his pocket. 'Will you take my photo with the goat?'

'I'm sure it wouldn't hurt to get a couple of shots while we've got the bread.'

'I saved pennies in a jar for the camera.' The boy's mood lightened. 'It took ten months, three weeks, six days.'

'Your commitment is a credit to you. I'll crouch down as low as I can. Hold the bread higher so Wilkes lifts his head. That's it. Hero shot!' Victor took a couple of photographs as the goat curled its pink tongue around the crust. 'Superb. I'll ask Lou if we can put these in the farm's album.'

'You won't be allowed.' He chuckled as the goat nibbled his shirt cuff.

'Oh?'

'I'm supposed to be a secret.'

Though Victor's curiosity was teased he knew better than to pry into the personal lives of the children who came here, especially from such a sensitive establishment as Badsworth Lodge. 'That's the last of the bread. We best get Wilkes back into the pen or he's going to gobble the shirt off your back.'

Jay frowned. 'Why does the island do that?'

'Do what?'

'Make things different inside your head.'

'It's very relaxing here.' Victor grinned. 'Sometimes too relaxing. When a warm wind blows from the south you could fall asleep on your feet. It's inspirational, too. There are a couple of islanders who write scripts for—'

'Ghorlan. I can take you to see Ghorlan.' Tremors ran through Victor. 'Come with me to Ghorlan.'

Victor recoiled. 'What made you say that?' He snapped out the words with an equal measure of shock and anger.

The boy's eyes glistened. 'I told you. I'm creepy.'

Victor took a deep breath. 'You're not creepy.' He tried to put Jay at ease again. 'Put your arm around Wilkes. I'll get another photo.'

'You hate me.'

'I don't hate you. What you said surprised me, that's all. Now put your arm round his neck. OK. On the count of—'

'Hey! Stop that!' Victor turned to see Laura Parris bearing down on him with a furious expression. 'No one gave you permission.'

'I'm just taking Jay's photo with the goat.'

'You don't have the authority to photograph Jay.'

'It was Jay who asked,' Victor protested in bewilderment. 'There seemed no harm—'

'I'll be the judge of whether or not there's any harm.'

'There's never been a problem in the past. Lou didn't mind last year.'

'It's my professional duty of care to mind.'

'OK. Not a problem.'

'Jay,' she said in gentler tones. 'Go join Lou. I'll be right over.' The boy obediently trotted across the yard to where children fed the chickens.

Victor held out the camera. 'Jay, you forgot something.'

Laura snapped, 'I'll take it.' Her face flushed a fierce red. Shrugging, he handed her the camera. Once Jay was out of earshot she hissed at Victor, 'Which paper's got you in its pocket?'

'Paper? I don't—'

'A newspaper would pay you a fortune for a photograph.'

'Hey, Nurse Parris! I don't know about any newspaper. I'm the island ranger. I do it to the best of my ability, that includes respecting the privacy of my visitors.'

'And I respect the children I care for. They deserve my protection.'

'So you're protecting them from me?'

'Yes, you bastard!'

His jaw dropped. 'Pardon me? Bastard?'

'I'm sick of every rat who finds where Jay is living and thinks they can earn easy money by selling his photograph.'

'You're not listening to me, Nurse Parris. I don't know what's so special about Jay, why the press are interested in him or why you think you're so high and mighty you can speak to me like I've committed the crime of the century.'

'When I'm protecting those kids I've got every right.'

'The right to be permanently angry, foul-mouthed, judgemental, always bawling everyone out?' He paused as he noticed something in her expression. 'Wait, you're not angry, are you?'

'Go to hell.'

'You're not angry. It's fear – you're frightened.'

'You're saying I'm scared? Who of? The mayor? Billy goat gruff here? You?'

Victor rubbed the goat's back. Angry shouting made it jittery. 'You are frightened.' He lowered his voice. 'No, not of me. You're scared of Jay.'

She began to walk away.

'Nurse Parris. I'm right, aren't I?'

She froze mid-step. Slowly she turned to face him. From her expression he sensed her shift in mood. He continued. 'I don't know exactly what's bothering you. You may never tell me. But can I confess a problem that's bothering me so much right now that, quite frankly, I want to go to my room and gulp down half a dozen whiskies?' He rubbed the rough fur on the goat's neck.

Her eyes flicked from his face to where Jay stood near the children. 'A confession?'

'Yes, a confession.'

In a quiet voice she said, 'OK, go on.'

'A few minutes ago Jay offered to take me to Ghorlan.'

'Ghorlan? I don't know where Ghorlan is.'

'Ghorlan's a person, not a place.'

'You mean Jay offered to walk with you to find Ghorlan?' The colour drained from her face. 'Mr Brodman, who is Ghorlan?'

'My wife. Ten years ago she drowned in the river.'

He saw the way she reacted, as if she'd clumsily hurt someone. 'I'm sorry.'

'I didn't mean you to feel bad about it. I guess there's no delicate way to explain how my wife died, even if it was a decade ago.'

'But she and you must have been so young when you got married.'

'Both twenty-three. We'd been married fifteen months, when . . . ah.' He stopped himself from going into more detail. 'That's by the by. Jay offered to show me Ghorlan. What bothers me is how does Jay, who I only met yesterday, know about my late wife?'

'Victor.'

'Nurse Parris.'

'We seem to have got off to a bad start.' She gave a ghost of a smile. 'And please call me Laura.'

He nodded. 'Laura. We've been at cross-purposes, haven't we?'

'A downright muck up, if you ask me.' Her face became serious again. 'Victor. Now for my confession.'

'Oh?'

'I think I must be going mad.'

'Why?'

'You've had a conversation with Jay. He knew Ghorlan was in your life. When he said her name did it feel like you were losing your grip, and you could feel yourself slipping into some big, dark hole in the ground?' Her eyes were glittery. 'Because, sometimes, when I talk with Jay, that's how it feels to me.'

From the chicken enclosure came a shout. Lou called Victor while pointing at her own watch.

He checked the time. 'We should have set off ten minutes ago.' Quickly, he ushered the goat into its compound. 'Look. Can we talk about this later?'

'How about tonight?'

'OK, meet me at the village pub at eight. The Three Impostors – you can't miss it. You look as if you need a friendly ear.'

She held out her hand. 'So we agree to press reset button and start at the beginning.'

Smiling, he shook her hand. 'Laura. I'd like nothing more.'

Eight

Victor Brodman walked alongside Lou as they followed the path to the castle at the southern tip of the island. A tiny boy accompanied them. His hair was a mass of blond curls, yet his face seemed far older than his proud boast that he was 'eight years, three months'. Behind them, the rest of the group, about twenty in all, their ages ranging from eight to sixteen. One teenager slouched along. His miserable face said it all; as one of the oldest from Badsworth Lodge he'd been detailed to help look after the group. An adult carer guarded the tail of the crocodile.

From the mop of curls the adult-looking face peered out at Victor. For some reason Victor found himself reminded of a high-court judge just about to gravely announce a life sentence.

'Victor?' said the boy.

'Yes, Archer.'

'What's the river called?'

'The Severn.'

'So there are at least six of them?'

'No, the Severn is spelt different to the number. It's S-E-V-E-R-N.'

'I see.' The tiny blond boy walked with his hands clasped behind his back. 'Why's that, then?'

'Two thousand years ago the Romans invaded England. They gave places names in their own language. They called this river Sabrina after a magical woman. Down through the years the name Sabrina eventually became Severn.'

'I see. My name is Archer. An old kind of soldier who fired a bow. Have you ever fired a bow and arrow, Victor?'

'A few times. My father made me one when I was your age. The arrows weren't pointed. Even so, I broke the glass in the greenhouse door. My dad took the bow and arrows away. He said I could have them when I was more responsible.' Victor smiled. 'I never saw the bow again. Maybe he still thinks I'll only go and break more windows with it.'

'My dad's dead.'

'I'm sorry to hear that.'

'He stole money from a bank, sold lots of drugs, cheated his friends so –' Archer gave a little shrug – 'they shot him.' Then he added cheerfully, 'I watched them do it. Blam-blam.'

Victor glanced at Lou for a lead. She gave a look that said don't worry. She held up her arm to signal to the children to stop. 'Victor's guiding us around the island today. Just now he wants to tell us something interesting about this beach.'

Hearing the tiny boy's cheerful admission of watching his drug-dealing father being gunned down derailed Victor. He raised his eyebrows, hoping Lou interpreted it as quick, give me a clue.

'It's really interesting,' she said. 'It involves sharks. Victor? Over to you.'

Instantly, he was back on track. 'Sharks. Right.' He pointed to a stone slab at the low-tide mark on the beach. 'See that square of stone. Seventy years ago the island's doctor had it put there. We won't go down there because it's too dangerous.'

'Why's that?' asked Archer.

'Quicksand.' He made a sucking noise. 'Anyway, Dr Evans believed that sharks swam up the river to breed in shallow water. So he bought himself an old diving suit. One of those with the iron boots and a big brass helmet that fitted over his entire head. He'd a bad leg, which meant he couldn't walk in it, so he'd put on the diving suit, connect a hose to an air pump higher up the beach. Then he'd sit in a chair fixed to that stone slab. He'd wait until the tide came in and covered him. That's when he could look out underwater.'

Archer nodded wisely. 'And the shark ate him.'

'Uhm, no, it never did. No sharks come up this far, as he was to find out, but he did make developments in underwater photography and the doctor became famous for his pictures of fish as they swam underwater.' The kids weren't hugely impressed. 'We can see the diving suit in the visitors' centre at the castle.' They still weren't impressed. A couple threw stones at the stone slab. Archer pretended he had a machine gun. He blasted everyone at point-blank range.

They continued walking. By this time a heat-haze made the outline of the castle ripple. Often the River Severn was a muddy brown; today, however, bright sunlight turned it golden yellow. Archer fell behind to talk to another boy. From the way he made a pistol out of his hand with the barrel/finger pointing at his own head Victor guessed the topic of conversation.

'I like to picture your old Dr Evans.' Lou grinned. 'Going out there to sit on the chair in his diving suit, then waiting for the water to get higher and higher up his body until it reached his helmet. Back then, to sit underwater must have been like travelling to another world.'

'It's this island. It inspires people to think in unusual ways. Sometimes crazy ways. But it can make us inventive.'

'What an amazing little heap of rock this place is. It gets inside your head. You think thoughts here that you don't think back home. I remember that story about the shepherd who arrived here a hundred years ago. He suddenly got this wild idea he wanted to write a play even though he could hardly write his own name. *The Value of Man.* That's the title, isn't it? Didn't it persuade the government to introduce old age pensions for the first time? Now what's the guy's name? Victor, you're not listening to a word I'm saying, are you?'

'Sorry. I was thinking.'

'I'll say. You look like you're sleepwalking. Too much cider last night?'

'No,' he said with a laugh. 'It's just what you said about the island getting inside your head. Jay told me the same thing this morning.'

Lou tensed. 'Did he say anything else?' She glanced back at Jay. He seemed lost in his own world.

'Oh, this and that. He enjoyed feeding the goat.'

'But there's something bothering you, Victor.'

'If anything, I'm concerned about the kids. They seem different this year. They just come across as . . . edgy? Scared?'

'Maureen's accident was a shock.' Lou called back to the children. 'Keep up, people. We've got to reach the castle by one.' She walked faster. 'I want to see that diving suit if you lot don't.'

Victor liked Lou. An open, honest, warm-hearted woman. But she'd changed. There was something she wanted to stay hidden. He hung back to point out to the group a lizard sunning itself on a wall. Even so, he found himself thinking about what Laura might tell him later. Oddly, despite the heat, his blood all of a sudden ran cold. When he started walking again he found himself in the company of the little boy with the blond curls.

'Cool lizard,' Archer told him. 'Can you get them as pets?'

'It's not a good idea. They're better off in the wild.'

'They bite?'

'No, there's nothing to be scared of. But they're happier living a natural life.'

'I'm not scared of lizards, but I *don't* like him.' He scowled at Jay. Luckily, the child was out of earshot. 'Nobody does.'

'Oh?'

'Not even grown-ups.' Archer became angry. 'If he starts saying your name again and again it means something bad's going to happen to you.'

'How can someone saying your name hurt you?'

'Jay said Tod's name and Maureen's, and look what happened to them.' Archer shuddered. 'One day he's going to say my name. I know he will. Then I'll be like my dad. I'll be in a big black coffin and shoved into the ground.'

Before Victor could say anything the little boy retreated down the line so he could hold the hand of a carer.

Jay approached with a smile on his face. 'Victor . . . Victor.'

Victor couldn't help himself. He felt cold shivers race through his body. The boy had spoken his name. For a moment he stared at those big brown eyes that seemed so other-worldly.

'Victor.' Jay pointed to a clump of trees. 'Are those Saban Deer?'

With a gush of relief that embarrassed him with its intensity he went to join the boy. *He repeated my name . . . I don't believe what Archer told me, do I?* As he pointed out the deer to other children he tried to push away the sense of superstitious dread. Even so, he remembered Laura's words when Jay had referred to Ghorlan: '*When he said her name did it feel like you were losing your grip and you could feel yourself slipping into some big, dark hole in the ground? Because that's how it feels to me.*' He shuddered. That's exactly what it felt like to him. A huge, dark pit of nothingness opening beneath his feet.

Nine

'Adventure.' Archer stood on a tree stump. 'Red alert! I want adventure now!' In his mind's eye he was no longer eight but a man. A tall man with muscles bulging in his arms, a pistol strapped to his belt. Something about the island excited this boy with a face that was more like that of a world-worn adult. An urge gripped him to be reckless. He eyed the trees beyond the fence. Climb one of those, then yell in a voice as loud as thunder, '*I am Archer!*' This wasn't like Archer at all. Back at Badsworth Lodge he was one of the timid boys. He avoided climbing frames. Swings made him nauseous. But now he was on this island . . . damn . . . damn! Excitement buzzed through him. He wanted to climb trees, then yell swear words.

He surveyed the island, pretending it was all his. The other kids had gone into the barn for fruit juice. But he was too wired to waste time sucking at stupid cartons. There was the river. What had Victor said? A goddess lived in it. Waves ran across its surface. In his mind's eye, he saw a beautiful woman swimming underwater with long hair wafting back, her kicking legs would make those waves. Maybe the goddess fought monsters in that wide stretch of water?

Archer studied the field. Nothing here to do. Nothing exciting anyway. Over the fence were massive trees. Wasn't it time he climbed one? He felt his biceps. There was a bulge of muscle, he was sure of it. He remembered his father's big, hard muscles. His father used to have a gym at home. There he'd work out with weights until it felt hot as a furnace. Sweat would drip down his dad's face as he hoisted those big metal dumb-bells up and down. '*Archer . . . get your skinny body down here with some water. Make sure it's cold. Archer. I'll give you to the count of ten . . .*' His father had an argument with his friends. They had killed him. The grave in the cemetery had been like a big oblong mouth that had swallowed the black coffin . . .

'Adventure! Damn to danger, damn to danger!' Whooping, Archer jumped down from the stump and raced across the field to the fence. He glanced back. No one about. No one to stop him! Archer climbed through the fence rails. Rotten trees. They'd be tricky to climb. No branches lower down to use like ladder rungs. But surely there'd be one that he could climb. Almost straightaway he saw it. One of those funny creatures with the blue eyes. Saban Deer. He grinned. Knowing the name of the animal pleased him. Getting smart as well as strong. The moment the deer caught sight of him it slipped away into some bushes.

Great! The hunt is on! He grabbed a stick from the ground. This would serve as a spear. The hunter's spear! He rubbed his thumb along the rough bark. The other kids would be amazed when he caught the animal and brought it back. Laughing with sheer excitement, Archer plunged into the bushes, gripping the stick like a huntsman handling a weapon. When he spied the deer again he'd zoom the stick right at the animal. Then – pow! Knock the animal out. He smiled as he imagined the way the kids would be impressed. *That's great, Archer. Will you show us how to hunt? Can I hold the spear?* Blood thudded in the boy's ears. If he could have seen his face he'd have been startled by the wild expression. He was drunk on the thrill of the chase. The branches smacking into his chest didn't faze him as he sped deeper into the wood.

Soon the afternoon sunlight vanished as the tree canopy grew dense, shutting out the sun's rays. Within minutes he ran in near darkness. With the gloom came silence. All he heard was the thump of his feet and the rush of his breath through his mouth. Every so often he caught a glimpse of gold fur. The animal fluidly weaved around the tree trunks. Oddly, it had the appearance of sliding along the earth rather than running.

'Here, boy, here, boy.' Archer panted the words as if calling a dog. 'Then ready with the mighty spear, O warrior.' He laughed as he recited a line from a comic he'd once read. 'I will smite you . . .' Then in a darker, more savage voice, he added, 'I'll rip off your face and stuff it down your throat.'

The deer bolted down a tunnel made out of tangled bushes. Archer followed. When he saw what was there he cried out. What was more, when he stopped dead he tumbled forward on to his knees. Instantly, the excitement bled out of him. Archer no longer felt like the powerful warrior – all muscly arms and fierce as a lion. From where he knelt he stared in shock at a face that gazed at him from the shadows. Its eyes possessed hard, glittery flashes that radiated pure menace.

'Archer.'

Archer forgot all about hunting the Saban.

'Archer.'

The boy shuffled round as part of his plan to run away, only his legs had gone so watery he couldn't stand. The face got closer. It seemed to drift out of the shadows, disconnected from any body. A fiery face with burning eyes. A terrifying ghost face.

'Archer.'

'Jay, don't keep saying my name.' Archer pulled his knees up to his chest. 'Don't you dare!'

'I'm going to show you something.' Jay's voice didn't even seem to issue out of those pale lips. Instead it oozed out of the earth. Or so it seemed to Archer. 'You've got to come with me for a little walk.'

'No.'

'Archer . . .'

'I told you not to say my name . . . you witch. I know when you keep saying someone's name over and over, then something rotten happens to them. Look what you did to Maureen. She's dead. You killed her.'

'We're going for a little walk.' Jay spoke in a dull, lifeless way. The face had no expression. It hung there in the gloom. Archer wanted to run back to the farm. He needed to be back with his friends so much he ached inside. Because he knew Jay would do something that would be so horrible that he, Archer, would be sick with terror. Jay took a step forward. Now there was enough light to reveal the boy's delicate build. His arms hung loose. The fingers seemed so long that they stretched down toward his knees in a way that couldn't be natural. Archer knew that Jay wasn't normal. Then he had no doubt that Jay wasn't even human. Those ghastly things he did to people. He repeated their name one day then the person would suffer an accident the next, or go so crazy like Tod that the police locked him up.

Jay gazed down at Archer. 'You never told me about your dad.'

'Why should I?' Then he added with a desperate attempt at defiance, 'Witch.'

'You told the others.'

'I'm not saying anything to you. Creep.'

'Archer. You hate me.'

'That's dead right. Now, I'm going back to the others.'

Jay shook his head. 'We've got to go for a walk first.'

'No!'

Jay didn't seem put out by the refusal. 'Your father died.'

Archer got more angry than scared. 'He got shot by his friends. They robbed money from a bank to buy drugs. My dad cheated

them. They came to the house. When he opened the door they –'
Archer pointed his finger at Jay's face – 'blam-blam. Satisfied?'

For a moment there was silence. Neither of them moved. The
gloom grew more intense, the smell of damp soil became stifling.
Archer found himself suddenly wondering if it smelt like that when
you lay buried in your coffin. Like his dad. Listening to the coffin
lid creak under the weight of the soil. Archer wanted to vomit. The
taste of soil filled his mouth, then it slid down the back of his tongue.
All Jay was doing was staring. A stare as if he was reading words on
Archer's face.

'Let me go,' Archer pleaded.

'First, I've got to show you something.'

'I don't want to see it.'

'Archer.'

'Don't say my name. Please, Jay, I haven't hurt you. Don't do
anything bad to me, Jay!' The eight-year-old was close to tears. A
breeze stirred the leaves into a chuckle. As if the forest would take
pleasure in witnessing whatever fate befell Archer. 'Please, Jay. It isn't
fair . . .'

'Archer.'

'No, please don't.'

'I'm going to take you to see your dad.'

This shook Archer. 'You can't; he's dead. I saw him open the door;
then they shot him.'

Jay murmured, 'Keep next to me. Don't stop walking.'

Archer looked down at his feet – they were traitors. He hadn't
even realized he'd stood up, let alone started walking. Jay led him
through the undergrowth.

'You can see yourself, can't you, Archer?' The voice could have
been a whisper of cold air coming from a cave.

Close to panic, Archer snapped, 'I don't know what you mean!'

'You can see yourself coming down the stairs at your house.'

'Course I can't. You're being stupid.'

'You can see yourself walking down the steps. You're wearing a
green T-shirt.'

'You're making it up.'

'Your mother bought you that T-shirt earlier that morning.'

'You witch. You're trying to scare me.'

Jay continued in the monotone as they walked down a soil bank.
'You're on the stairs and you're looking down at your father. He's
standing in the hallway. Someone's banging on the front door.'

'Liar.'

Archer ran down the banking. He'd had enough of this. What mattered now was to get back to the farm. Only the soft dirt under his feet became hard steps. When he reached the bottom he saw the bushes had gone. He couldn't see Jay. There was no smell of dirt. Instead he could smell the bacon his father had fried.

Archer blinked. Somehow – and he didn't know how it had happened – he was standing in the hallway at the foot of a staircase. He was back in his old home again. He knew his mother was upstairs. Now it was *that* day again. The one when his father's friends came to call after they'd discovered the money had vanished. His father had shiny black hair, brushed back from his face. His face was always tanned and he wore a thick gold chain round his neck. 'My freedom ticket' was how he described it as he fingered the heavy links. Always he looked pleased with himself. Even cocky.

Except today. His face had gone ugly with fear. The knock on the door grew louder.

'Archer, come here, son,' he said. 'That's it. Don't be scared. There's a good lad.' He tried to smile but his lips curled oddly as if he might start crying. 'Go to the door, Archer. Don't open it. *Whatever you do, don't unlock it.* Just shout through that you're home with your mother but your dad's out of town.'

'I want to get Mum the facecloth.'

'Later.'

'Her nose is bleeding.'

'Archer, you little runt, do as I tell you.' Even as he spoke he rubbed his hand against his trouser leg to wipe away the red smear. 'Tell them, I'll be back tonight. I'll phone them then.' Then he said to himself, 'Some chance. I'll be long gone.'

'Dad—'

'Just fucking well do it. OK?'

Archer nodded.

'You see you do it right. If you screw up, I'll rip your face off and stuff it down your throat.' With that threat he backed through the basement door, and Archer heard soft footsteps descending.

Archer noticed drops of his mother's blood on the floor tiles. These days when she cried she made it silent. Dad didn't like weeping noises.

The thuds on the panel grew impatient.

Archer went to the door. He remembered what his father had instructed. '*Go to the door, Archer. Don't open it. Whatever you do, don't unlock it. Just shout through that you're home with your mother but your dad's out of town.'*

The thud of fist against wood got louder.

Archer took a deep breath. Then he unlocked the door and opened it to three men in leather jackets, they had gold rings on every finger. He always remembered those huge gold rings.

One of the men started to speak. Archer interrupted, 'He's down in the cellar. You'll find him hiding behind the washing machine.' When they looked at him blankly he added, 'He made a secret space in the wall behind the washer.'

For a moment Archer thought he was waking up in bed. He realized he stood in the forest with Jay. He gasped as if in pain.

Jay's face held no emotion. 'You saw your father.'

'It wasn't like that,' Archer protested. 'I didn't tell them where he was! He opened the front door and they shot him. I didn't tell. I didn't!' A muscle seemed to tear inside Archer's chest. The pain freed him from standing there. He fled through the trees. Rabbits scattered in panic. His breathing came in hard, moaning sounds. Something between weeping and angry shouting. All his feelings were mixed up inside. For years he'd genuinely believed he'd seen his father shot on the doorstep of the family home. Now, it had changed. The truth had been revealed to him by Jay. Now he remembered what really happened. His mother had laid on the bed with a bloody nose. The words he'd uttered to the men in their heavy gold rings came back so powerfully they roared inside his head. '*He's down in the cellar. You'll find him hiding behind the washing machine.*' What if the men hadn't shot his father? What would his father have done to him if he had found out that Archer had betrayed him?

Sunlight falling through the branches dappled the ground. Where now? He was lost in the wood. A breeze moaned through the trees. Timbers creaked. A sound like a coffin lid opening. Oh, how he'd dreamed about that happening. How his father would escape from the cemetery to find him. To get his own back. Archer knew all about his father's anger. Death wouldn't be enough to stop it.

Archer circled a clump of brambles. Then he stopped running. His father stood in the shadows. Archer saw where the bullet had smashed through his cheekbone. The force of the impact had thrust the left eye from the socket so that it hung out to gravely regard the ground. The right eye, however, glared with hatred at Archer.

His father snarled, 'You told on me, Archer. I'm going to rip your face off and stuff it down your throat.'

Then a strange thing happened to the boy. He could still move. Yet his limbs seemed to turn stiff as wood. Although he couldn't run he turned away from the man with the bullet hole in his face, then he started walking. His rigid legs carried him back into the trees. At that moment he couldn't shout, or even turn his head to see the monster.

'Archer . . . stay there . . .'

Instinct told Archer to keep walking. Even his mind had jammed up now. No thoughts went through his head. Just walk. Maybe everything will turn out well. Footsteps sounded behind him. They grew louder. He reached open ground. A shadow fell on him, a big black stain that spread out on the grass in front of him. His father always cast a huge shadow. Now it engulfed the child as the man got closer.

'Archer. Don't run away from me.'

A hand clamped down on his shoulder. It stopped him from moving. He found himself being turned round to look into the face from the grave.

'Archer . . .'

The boy's knees gave way. Everything had gone faint.

'Archer, what's wrong?'

He looked up into the man's face.

'Victor?'

Then the world went away.

Ten

Victor had been surprised by his effect on Archer. The child's entire body had seized up tight. Then he'd slowly walked away through the trees. Victor would have needed all the sensitivity of a concrete block to miss the fact that something had gone badly wrong with him. He'd gone after the boy, calling his name. When he touched one of Archer's narrow shoulders the boy had dropped down in a faint. As Victor picked up the boy, marvelling at how light he was, he noticed the dead stare of the eyes. Immediately, he returned to his sister's farm at a run. At that moment he believed the boy would die in his arms. Yet the jog of being carried revived him.

'Put me down,' Archer insisted.

'Don't worry. I'll get you indoors, then we can get someone to look at you.'

'Put me down.' The voice rose. 'Let me walk.'

Victor gently set him down. 'What happened back there?'

'Nothing.'

'You might be coming down with a bug.'

'I'm not. I'm fine.'

Before Victor could say anything else the boy raced across the field to join the other children at the barn, where they still tucked into snacks. What now? Report Archer's fainting spell to Laura? Had the shock of seeing Victor in the woods caused some kind of blip that made him keel over? Of course, he knew what he had to do. He decided to find Laura.

Laura was busy in the farmhouse kitchen with a teenage girl who complained loudly that she had a headache. When Victor signalled he needed to speak to her she mouthed, just give me a minute. Then she broke a couple of tablets out of a blister pack. The girl kicked up a fuss. 'Is this all? My head's splitting. It's my period!'

Victor returned to the yard. There Archer held a juice box in his hand as if it had just dropped down from another planet. He stared at the carton, eyes glassy.

He doesn't know what to do with it, Victor told himself, the kid must have had one hell of a shock. From twenty paces away, Victor checked the boy over the best he could. His clothes weren't dishevelled, no sign of physical injury. Maybe he'd got himself lost in the woods and given himself a scare. Victor knew he'd be overstepping the mark if he interrogated the boy so he decided to stay put until Laura emerged.

There were around twenty children standing outside the barn. Most were dropping their empty cartons into a box that had been provided for refuse. Often school parties would squirt what remained of the juice on to other kids, however the children from Badsworth Lodge were not only well behaved but there was a sense of stillness about them. They could be so uncannily quiet at times. Maybe it was just because Badsworth Lodge was a specialist centre for troubled youngsters. These kids today were unusually subdued. It didn't take long to recognize the source of their unease. Jay stood near the barn. Although the kids didn't make a fuss about it they quietly gravitated to the other end of the yard to keep their distance. Jay, meanwhile, did nothing but watch them with those large eyes of his.

'Victor? Did you need me?'

He turned to see Laura. The breeze toyed with her hair. 'Can we speak?'

'Weren't we due to meet up at eight? It's just we've got to get the children back to the lodging houses by three.' She shrugged. 'I don't know what it is . . . some are out of sorts today.'

'We don't have much in the way of transport on the island, but I can borrow a tractor and trailer.' He smiled. 'That passes for a limo service round here.'

'The walk back might be just what they need, so I'll pass on your limo service this time. Thanks though, I appreciate it.'

'No problem.'

'Sorry if I sound like a clock-watcher but I can only spare you five minutes.'

'Can we go into the field? We best chat out of earshot.'

'What's wrong?' Concern appeared on her face.

'It might be something and nothing . . .' He opened the gate to the field. Lou noticed where they were going and pointed to her watch.

'We run a tight ship.' Laura sounded apologetic. 'We try to get them into a routine.' She gave one of those little shrugs again that Victor found heart-warming. 'You see, at Badsworth Lodge spontaneity is too close to chaos for the children's liking. Generally, they've led unstable home lives so routine, such as meals at set times, is comforting.' When they'd put distance between them and the children she said in a businesslike way, 'So, what have you got?'

'About twenty minutes ago, I saw Jay go off into the woods alone. He doesn't know the area so I decided to bring him back to the yard.' This time it was Victor who shrugged. 'I didn't find Jay, but I found Archer. When he saw me he reacted like he'd seen a . . . I don't know . . . a monster. He just froze in shock. It was as if he was so scared he could hardly move his legs. When I caught up with him he just fell in a heap. Out cold. Like a lump of dead meat. He came round a few minutes later, even so, I have to admit to being worried about him.'

'I'll check him over. Thanks for telling me.'

Victor reacted with surprise. 'You aren't going to ask him what happened?'

'Not yet.'

'But—'

'Victor, children at Badsworth Lodge aren't like the ones you normally meet. You've heard of planets out there in the solar system, where gravity's so powerful a bird would weigh the same as a cow. Or it's so cold that the atmosphere has turned to ice. Well, Badsworth Lodge is another world. Normal rules of human behaviour don't apply there.'

'It wouldn't hurt to ask Archer what—'

'But it might cause more damage than you can imagine. I have to tread carefully. We are a specialist unit, just like some hospitals specialize in cardiac care. We treat some of the most troubled individuals in the country. Listen, when something unpleasant happens to one of those children –' she nodded at the group – 'they invariably clam up. They repress emotional hurt. It's second nature. Because being emotional is seen as weakness, which invites bullying. It's not pleasant, Victor, but those children learnt that one way to survive abuse is to lock away the truth.'

'Point taken. It's just that when Archer collapsed I thought he was dying.'

'A typical Archer response. He saw his father murdered. If things get too much for him, even if it's a violent cartoon on television, he just shuts down.' She smiled. 'OK, I know what that look you're giving me means. I will talk to Archer, but it will be softly-softly, you follow? A word here, a hint there.'

Victor acquiesced with a nod. 'Though I don't think you need to look far. From the way the children are avoiding Jay it would be my guess he's what frightened Archer.'

A breeze from the river blew Laura's hair out in rippling strands. 'Ah, Jay. Of all those we've seen at Badsworth Lodge he is unique. We've had troublemakers of course. A while ago we had an episode that we refer to as the Green Dragon Winter. Children were terrified. They said a green dragon lived under the floorboards. What's more, they claimed they were shrinking in size and were frightened that they'd fall through the gaps in the boards to be eaten.'

'Now that is surreal. But Jay?'

'No, nothing to do with Jay. The green dragon frenzy took place before Jay arrived. It took us a month to discover that a fifteen-year-old was spiking meals with LSD. The kids were tripping on acid. Now that kind of trouble we can understand – eventually. Yet with Jay he doesn't really do anything. Normally, he's just so passive.'

'He tells the children things,' Victor said. 'He gets under their skin.'

'And Jay is our responsibility. He's been through all the care homes. Frankly, we're his last hope. After us, there's nowhere else for him to go.'

'But he's clearly freaking the others out.'

'So what do you suggest?' Laura's eyes flashed with anger. 'That we tie a rock round his neck and chuck him in the river?'

Victor met her glare. 'You know I'm not suggesting that. But it's clear the other children are frightened of him.'

'Like I'm frightened of him?' She fixed him with those bright, defiant eyes. 'Like you're frightened of him?'

'I'm not frightened. I'm—'

'He knew about Ghorlan.'

'Not frightened, though I'll admit to a burning curiosity.' Victor felt a creeping unease. 'I'm going to break my own rule about not asking questions. What is it with Jay? What's he done?'

'He's done nothing.'

'Oh?'

'No, it's what the world did to him.'

'You've lost me.'

Laura's expression was grim. 'Do you remember, about seven years ago, a news story about a ship called the *N'Taal*?'

'The *N'Taal*? That's an unusual name. I'm sure it rings a bell.'

'It ought to,' she told him. 'There'd been religious persecution of a minority faith in West Africa. After a church had been burned with dozens of the congregation still inside there'd been an exodus of refugees. There's the usual conspiracy theories. The main one being that the government of this country wanted rid of this tribal group so they provided the ship. Of course, it was a tub of rust that barely floated.'

'I remember something about a shipwreck, that's all.'

'There's more to it than that. The *N'Taal*, with almost four hundred refugees on board, sailed round the northern hemisphere for weeks. At every country where they sought refuge they were turned away. Nobody wanted to help. All these developed nations insisted they'd exceeded their quota for refugees for that particular year, so this sorry spectacle continued. The ship tried to enter port after port. Each time they were denied access. In increasingly desperate straits the freighter with this human cargo struggled across the Atlantic. There was a storm, the ship sank . . .'

'And they all died,' Victor added in a quiet voice.

'All but one.'

'Jay?' Astonished, he glanced at the boy in the farmyard; he stood alone as any marooned sailor on a desert island. He radiated solitude.

Laura nodded. 'The story ran for weeks. Remember the Miracle Moses Boy? Found in an inflatable raft a week after the ship sank. He was just four years old.' She gave one of those little shrugs that seemed to convey so much. 'Nobody has been able to identify him. He was named Jay by the captain of the ship which rescued him. His age is just guesswork. He's mixed race. He didn't speak at all until he began speaking English, which he picked up from his carers.'

'So he's a mystery?'

'And we keep his presence at Badsworth Lodge a secret. The press are eager to know what he's doing now. If they found out the kind of trouble that surrounds him the media would besiege the house. The damage to Jay and the other children doesn't bear thinking about.'

Victor said, 'I won't breathe a word. You can trust me.'

She looked him in the eye. 'Yes, I believe I can. Now, if you'll excuse me.'

'Wait there's more, isn't there?'

'We can leave that for later.' She gave a tired smile. 'I'll see you at eight.'

With that she walked back to the farm where Lou was gathering the children together.

Eleven

'The pub's a no-go.' Victor Brodman met Laura with those words in the village street. The church clock chimed eight. Across the span of the river its waters blazed the colour of gold as the sun sank toward the horizon.

Laura was taken aback. 'The islanders haven't turned against us already, have they?'

'No, but Mayor Wilkes has commandeered it for one of his planning meetings. The public are barred until nine.'

'Oh, well, a pleasant evening for a walk. That is, if you want to walk with me?'

'What is it about your line of work that makes you so touchy?'

Her demeanour cooled. 'It's not working out, is it?'

Victor sighed. 'Why do you try so hard to take offence to everything I say?'

She marched away, down the path that led to the jetty.

Victor walked alongside her.

'You still here?' she asked.

'You'll be annoyed at me saying this again. But I see fear.'

'You see fear? That's up to you.'

'Not just fear for your own safety, fear that the children you devote yourself to protecting might be harmed.'

Laura stopped at the river's edge. 'Damn right I'm scared. Listen, we've been through hell at the home. I thought we'd leave all the crap behind when we came here. We haven't. It's getting worse. The kids are jumpy. They're getting ready to explode. And we can't do a thing about it.'

'There's nobody you can call?'

'We're the behavioural emergency team. We are the ones that other people call when they have children who are psychologically self-destructing.'

'Jay?'

Tight-lipped, she nodded. 'OK, I'll tell you this, Victor. Because if I don't I'm going to end up jumping in that river. Right now doing something crazy is preferable to doing nothing.'

Victor began with, 'What you need is—'

'What I need is to get this off my chest! Only I don't know you, Victor.' She searched his face, as if hoping to find some clue there to his character. 'Lou adores you. You care for the island's wildlife, so you might rank alongside St Francis of Assisi. So I'm going to tell you the truth. After that, you might never speak to me again. The bottom line about Jay is this. He isn't a mere boy. He's an instrument of a force . . . a power . . . I don't know what exactly. No, please, Victor, hear me out. Listen. Every so often Jay withdraws into himself. It's like he goes to another place mentally. When he comes back he repeats the name of someone he knows. Then that person suffers an accident — an injury, or even death. This happened to one of our staff. He repeated Maureen's name over and over. A few hours later she was killed by a bus. The other children believe Jay is a witch. Even though my team try to rationalize what's happening, we all believe, deep down, that he's . . . well . . . he can inflict a curse, for the want of a better word. When he goes into that state and repeats a name it's as if he attaches bad luck to that individual.' A gull cried out to the dying sun. 'OK, slap me. Tell me to stop being hysterical.'

'Remember, he told me about Ghorlan. How does a child I've never met before know that my wife disappeared into that?' He nodded at the river as its colour morphed from gold to blood red.

'Victor, one of the reasons I've been a bitch is that I want you to keep your distance. I don't want Jay to say your name.' Shivering, she folded her arms. 'Oh, God . . . it's not as if Jay is a bad child. He's not got a spiteful bone in his body. He's sensitive, he cares about people. He hates to see them suffer. That's why he offers to take people on one of his little walks.' She injected the words 'his little walks' with an unsettling timbre. 'He took Maureen on one of his little walks before she died. He told me he did it to make her happy one last time.' A shudder ran through her.

'You're cold,' he told her.

'Colder than you can believe. All this about Jay . . . it's a burden I'm carrying, Victor. For the first time in my life I can't find a solution to a problem. There've been times when I picture myself standing by Jay's bed at night with a pillow in my hands.' Then she whirled round with such savage speed he thought she'd do something reckless. In a way, she did. She threw herself at him. Then kissed him hard. Gulls cried out across the mighty Severn, yet she didn't take her mouth from his.

*   *   *

How it happened, Archer wasn't sure. He'd been in a daze since that encounter with Jay in the wood. However, he realized that he was back at White Cross Farm again.

Lou said to him, 'Are you sure you're OK being Jay's holiday buddy? After all, it's only fair he has a friend staying with him.'

'Yes, Lou.' In Archer's topsy-turvy life yes sometimes meant no. And vice versa. *Was it Brian that gave you a black eye? 'No, Lou. It wasn't Brian.'* Because if he told on Brian, or whoever it was that had punched him, the bully, would hurt him ten times worse next time. In any event, Archer found himself in the next bedroom to Jay's at White Cross.

Max, one of the fourteen-year-olds, had carried Archer's bags from the village. Max was one of the evil ones. When Lou had been distracted he'd nipped the skin on Archer's neck on the walk up here. That had given the bully a lot of pleasure; his grin had been one of fierce delight as he'd dealt out the sadistic pinches. At the farm they found Jay in the goat's enclosure. It consented to lie there like a cat as Jay had stroked its rough pelt. While Lou talked to the man and lady who ran the farm, Archer and Max entered the enclosure.

Max's lips curled into a cruel grin as he watched Jay with the goat. 'Hey, Jay . . . hey, witch, look at me when I'm talking to you.'

Jay looked up with such large dark eyes.

Max chuckled. 'Have you ever had a monkey kiss?'

Jay didn't answer. He seemed miles away.

Archer saw that Max was in a reckless mood. Then everyone had been reckless today. Even Archer.

Max bent over Jay. 'This's a monkey kiss.' He pinched the skin on the side of Jay's neck just under the ear. Even by Max's standards it was a particularly sadistic pinch. When he released his grip on the flesh, Jay's neck was briefly a bloodless white before turning a sore-looking red. Strangely, Jay hadn't even flinched.

Despite his usual timid demeanour Archer protested, 'Max, you shouldn't have done that.'

'You going to stop me? You're only as big as a mouse. You couldn't stop nothing.' Max gripped the skin of Archer's neck then crushed it hard. Archer whimpered. 'Crybaby,' Max sneered.

Jay stared into space, his hand resting limply on the goat's flank. 'Max.'

'What, witch boy?'

'Max . . . Max . . .' Jay's voice had a lifeless quality. There seemed to be no strength behind it, but at that moment it seemed that no power on earth could stop him repeating the bully's name. 'Max . . . Max . . . Max . . .'

Victor found himself in the grip of some force not unlike gravity. He couldn't resist wrapping his arms round Laura. He returned her kiss with a fierce passion. Although they stood by the river he could have been a million miles away from the island – lost in a cosmos of scintillating lights. His heart beat harder as she buried her face in his chest. At that moment, a mood of recklessness electrified the very atmosphere around him. He couldn't remember feeling like this for years.

'Now you think I really am mad,' she panted.

'No. Not at all. I needed that, too.'

'A safety valve.' Despite her earlier near panic-attack a smile reached her lips . . . such soft and pretty lips too. 'Do you think we released some dangerous pressures there? Or are we inviting more danger into our lives? I don't know, I feel in the mood for crazy adventures, or . . . wild encounters.' She grinned.

He touched her hair. Its softness sent his pulse racing. 'You know, I'd forgotten what it felt like to be alive.'

'You're starting to sound a lot like me. I can't remember the last time I kissed someone with . . . I don't know . . . anything that can be described as passion. It must be this island. It affects people, doesn't it? Makes them act out of character. You find yourself longing to do things – extraordinary things.'

'I hope I was partly responsible, rather than a few acres of dirt in a river.'

She kissed him on the cheek. 'Will they let us into the pub for that drink yet?'

He checked the time. 'Right about now.' At that moment he wanted to hold her again. 'Although what we did just then was nicer than being in the pub.'

She laughed as if a burden had been lifted. 'I'll buy you a drink. We've got all evening to find out about each other.' Her eyes twinkled. 'Verbally.'

They headed back up the lane to the only village on the island. At its centre there was a church at one side of a tiny market square and a thatched pub at the other. Men and women in business suits were briskly emerging through the door. Most gave hurried goodbyes as they made their way to the ferry.

'There goes Mayor Wilkes' planning committee.' He grunted. 'Seeing them always fills me with foreboding.'

'I take it you and Mayor Wilkes don't always see eye to eye?'

'He'd like to run the island like his own personal empire. Fortunately, there are a few people who refuse to let him get his own way. Otherwise you'd be standing in the middle of a golf course right now.'

'People like you?' She squeezed his arm in hers. 'You know, I'm starting to warm to you.'

In the dusk, gazing up at him like that, she was so extraordinarily beautiful. As the voices of the committee members faded on the warm air he found that gravity exert its pull. His face drew closer to hers.

'Victor! I'm glad I caught you.'

'Mayor Wilkes. Good evening.' Victor nodded at the man who emerged from the shadows.

'Can I have a word?' Wilkes asked. 'If you've got a moment?' He glanced at Laura. 'In private.'

'Excuse me, Laura,' Victor said. 'I'll just be a minute.'

When the mayor had considered they'd put sufficient distance between themselves and Laura he began to speak with an abruptness that hinted at sadistic pleasure. As if he'd been waiting a long time to say these words to Victor. 'You've been our island ranger for a long time.'

'Over ten years.'

'So you will appreciate me speaking plainly, Victor. You might as well hear it from me rather than some inaccurate tittle-tattle.'

'Go on.'

'You'll know that revenue streams aren't what they were and the council have been forced to trim budgets?'

'Ah, you've found a financial justification for your machinations, then?'

'Meaning?'

'Meaning, whatever you're going to reveal now has the backing of the committee and it isn't just something you've thought up on the spur of the moment.'

Mayor Wilkes eyed Victor in a way that suggested he wished to commit violence. Then in times past wasn't it the mayor's privilege on Siluria to deliver beatings with a boat paddle? Victor sensed a blow was about to fall, but not from a wooden oar.

Wilkes spoke as if addressing a meeting rather than an individual. 'We have to cut back on expenditure across the board.

School transport, library opening hours, road maintenance. We're also streamlining the island ranger service.'

'I thought you might.'

'We're not doing away with it. Saban Deer are of national importance, but we're looking to contract out the ranger service to a company off-island.'

'Figures.'

'The service won't be compromised, but we must cut costs.'

'If you cut costs the service will be compromised.'

'Don't fight me on this, Victor.'

'Why not? You're firing me.'

'Nothing of the sort.'

'Oh?'

'The job can still be yours. You just have to reapply for the position.'

'And you're really going to consider keeping me on as ranger? You do know I'll fight you every step of the way over the golf course development.'

'Don't get unpleasant with me, Brodman. The fact of the matter is, that the work will be contracted out to—'

'One of your own companies. Nice move, Mayor. Then you'll choose the new ranger. Go the whole hog, hire a yes man. They'll know fig all about the island's wildlife, but they'll know how to say "Yes, Mayor, of course, Mayor, anything you say, Mayor."'

'Listen, you—' Wilkes grabbed Victor's arm.

'You warning me, Mr Mayor? Go on, see what happens.'

'What's that?' The shout came from Laura.

At first Victor thought she'd heard the two men's angry exchange. However, she stared up the lane that ran along the island's spine. A noise grew louder. Almost like a wailing siren.

'Oh, no.' From her body language she knew there was trouble.

Moments later a teenage boy came barrelling out of the gloom. It was his yelling that sounded so much like a siren. A cry filled with alarm and dismay.

'What the hell's wrong with the fool?' Mayor Wilkes hissed.

Victor ran forward as Laura caught hold of the screaming youth.

'Max, what's wrong . . . ? No, stop running. Tell me, what's the matter?'

Max's eyes were wide with terror. 'Laura . . . that little freak . . . he's saying my name.' Tears coursed down his face. 'Now I'm going to die!'

Twelve

In the lane Mayor Wilkes stood with a face like thunder. 'Nurse Parris,' he snapped. 'Can't you shut that child up?'

'That child, as you put it, is Max. He's scared out of his wits.'

'Because some other boy said his name?' Wilkes sneered. 'If hearing his own name has had that effect then he needs some form of care beyond what you offer.'

'He's frightened.'

'Of his own name? That's not fear, that's schizophrenia.'

Victor waded into the argument. 'Mr Mayor, let Laura handle it. This situation is more complicated than you might think.'

'If you knew what I really think . . .' He shook his head, disgusted. 'I'll leave you to sort this out, but I warn the pair of you – if you can't stop that child screaming the place down he'll have to leave the island.'

Laura was ready to launch a physical attack on the mayor. 'It's after nine o'clock at night. Where do you expect him to go?'

The mayor glanced at his watch. 'He's disturbing the residents. Whatever the problem is, deal with it. OK?' With that he marched away down the street.

'He's insufferable,' Laura seethed. 'Dear God, it's all I can do not to throw rocks at him.'

Victor gave a grim smile. 'I like the sound of rocks. You and I have more in common than I thought.'

Together they took Max to the cottage where Lou was staying. As Lou did her best to soothe the sobbing youth Laura and Victor walked back out into the garden.

Victor glanced up at the bedroom window of the cottage. 'Max is beyond scared, isn't he? He's genuinely terrified.'

'I'll say.' She sighed. 'Lou will do her best to calm him. I don't see she'll make much progress, though. He's in pieces.'

Standing in the light falling through the window, Victor saw how vulnerable she looked. As if at any moment she expected the sky to fall on her. 'Laura, if Max is saying that Jay repeated his name, what does he expect will happen?'

Her face darkened. 'Max will expect the worst.'

★　★　★

'Archer, come with me.'

Archer opened his eyes. If it wasn't for the light on the landing his bedroom would have been in total darkness. Numerals on the clock radio burned at him from the gloom: 10.03. All he could see of Jay was a silhouette.

'Archer. Listen.' His voice had that near-silent quality. Like a draught blowing through the gates of a tomb. 'Archer, you've got to come.'

'Go away.' Archer pulled the bedclothes over his head.

'There's something you've got to see. It's important.'

Archer tried to hold on to the bedding so Jay couldn't tug it from his face, only his fingers seemed to lose all their strength. He felt the bedding being hauled from his body. He closed his eyes. *If I don't see Jay that might be enough . . . I'll be all right . . .* Yet the cold night air touching his skin brought him up into a sitting position. The sharp outdoors smell had appeared with an abruptness that shocked the boy.

'Why aren't I in bed? What have you done to me?'

Jay gazed at him. His eyes glowed in the darkness. Archer reached out for the bedding but all he felt were the pyjamas he wore. The bed had become hard now. He groped for where the mattress should be. Instead of soft fabric, a block of cold matter.

Archer's heart beat hard. Where was his bedroom? How had Jay brought him outside?

Jay's witchcraft, that's what it is! Was Jay taking Archer to see his dead father again? No way! He jumped up then began to run across the damp grass. His bare feet skidded as Jay caught hold of him.

'Please don't say my name, Jay,' Archer pleaded. 'I know you did it to Max. You said his name twenty times. I heard you. More than twenty. More than fifty! You're going to make Max die. He's a bully. But he doesn't deserve a curse.'

As Jay gripped him, his face was strangely impassive. Really, it should have been too dark to see. Yet it glowed; the skin itself generated its own light. The elfin eyes grew larger.

'Archer, there's something wanting me to do bad things to people. I don't want to. I'm trying to stop myself, but it's getting too hard. Listen . . .' His voice became a whisper. 'Things are different here. I think I might be able to change what I am. But I've got to keep looking all over the island for it. A secret. There's something here that will help me. So I go out looking. I can search all kinds of hidden places without leaving my room. Do you understand? My mind can move through all the houses and even the ground. Now I've found something under the castle.'

'Leave me out of it, then,' Archer gasped. 'You find it yourself. I'm frightened.'

'I can't do it myself. You've got to help. You're my hands. You can pick things up. I can't.'

Archer struggled. 'I don't know what you're talking about. Let go.'

Jay tugged him toward a grassy slope. Above it, the castle wall where a tower reared up, a fist of stone to threaten the moon. 'I've found a hidden place under the castle. There's something in there you have to get. It's precious. You've got to find it for me.'

By now Archer's bare feet skidded across the grass as if he were skiing. In front of him a bank of earth loomed closer as Jay dragged him toward it. He didn't want to go. He sensed a dark terror in that bank of soil. An object that had been hidden because it was too terrible for people to see. Jay did not stop. Archer felt himself falling through the earth. Beyond it lay death in all its dark essence.

'Bite. I want you to bite.'

Victor felt Laura pull his face toward her bare breast. The dark nipple had become engorged. Her skin had become bumpy with gooseflesh.

'Bite me, please,' she panted.

When he closed his teeth round her hard nipple she moaned with pleasure. They were on the bed back at his apartment above the garage at White Cross Farm. They'd been talking about Max, about how he'd calmed down as soon as the tranquillizer had entered his bloodstream. Now some detached part of Victor wondered how it had all happened. The magic of the island? Maybe. From a whispered conversation beneath the stars to this. They'd been talking calmly. Then Nurse Laura Parris, the steely woman who had looked as if she could cheerfully beat him with her fists just a few short hours ago, had kissed him again with as much ferocity as passion.

After that had been a blur. Mouth on mouth kisses. Once inside his apartment they'd wrenched at each other's clothes, becoming a writhing pair of bodies. As their limbs entwined they made love with such force that it was more than sex. This passion drenched their emotions in erotic sensation. This was a way of forgetting all about Max, about Mayor Wilkes, about the whole insane world.

When fears about what tomorrow would bring began to intrude

Laura had begged Victor to bite her. 'Bite them hard. Don't be afraid. You won't break me.'

So he gripped those dark tips of skin between his teeth. With a sigh, this naked beauty melted into an ocean of pure creature feeling. A place where the waking nightmare that was Jay couldn't reach her.

For long moments Archer was certain the black earth would suffocate him. Jay had dragged him through the soil as if they were moving through a mass of bed sheets hanging on a washing line. A stream of material flapped against his face. The stench of moist dirt filled his nostrils. Thick fleshy worms with sticky, pink bodies squirmed in the blackness around him. Then he was alone in the room.

But what kind of room? Eight-year-old Archer had seen nothing quite like it. Straightaway he saw the car. However, this was no garage. The walls were made of blocks of stone. There were pillars like those you find in old churches. Even though he could see there were no lamps, no windows, nothing to allow light into the room.

'Jay?' The whisper died on stagnant air. Jay had gone. Archer was alone in a room with stone walls and the car. He took hesitant steps toward it, looking around him as he did so. At any moment he expected his father to appear. Jay had made his dad appear before, even though he had a bullet hole in his face. Jay could make healthy people die. Now he knew the boy could bring people back out of their graves. Archer remembered what really happened now to his father. *Dad used to hit Mum. He made her face bleed the day the men came to the house. So I told them where Dad was hiding. I did that. I wanted Dad to be killed. I as good as murdered him myself. No one else knows I did that. I got away with it.* But if his father returned? He'd get hold of Archer then enjoy exacting a painful revenge. Archer's senses began to shut down as he sensed danger approach. This was his way of protecting himself. He detached himself from reality. At that moment he seemed to see himself as if he watched from a distance. *There goes little Archer. He's got stick-thin arms. He's wearing green pyjamas. If he gets his face punched now, or his throat squeezed, it's nothing to do with me. I won't feel it. Because I'm not in Archer's body.*

Even so, Archer marvelled at the strange place Jay had taken him. The stone vault was several times bigger than a domestic garage. From the ceiling tree roots had grown through to hang down like monster tentacles. The place was full of spider webs. Spiders had even spun white shrouds over the car.

So why park a car here? He couldn't even see an entrance to bring the vehicle in. *Like me, the car's a prisoner here.* The eight-year-old approached it. Pulpy white bags adorned the tyres. Mushrooms? Archer sniffed. Indeed, an aroma of mushroom tainted the air. Paintwork had turned as dull as old rhino skin. Archer didn't recognize the model. And why leave it sitting here in the underground vault?

Now curiosity got the better of Archer. He tried the door handle. For a moment it stuck. However, after a good tug the door opened with a squeal. And, pooh! The car smelt bad inside. Red fungus had grown out of the dashboard like fingertips pushing through the plastic from the other side. Archer slid on to the driving seat behind the wheel. Green gunge covered the windscreen. Spider webs covered the speedometer in a rippling white membrane. Weird. Why had Jay shown him this? An old car buried underground? Who'd be crazy enough to entomb their car? The cold air made him shiver.

The vehicle shifted on its springs. A suspension that hadn't moved in years gave a deep groan. To Archer the sound embodied both pain and loneliness.

'Jay,' he whispered, 'get me out of here. I don't like it.' But there was no Jay. Only him, frail young Archer with the face of a haggard adult. Creeping shivers advanced up his back. Alarm bells rang deep inside of him. Get out, Archer, they could have been saying. Get out fast. Something's in here with you.

Rats, maybe. He looked down at his feet. They were pale blobs in the gloom. If rodents had made their home here they'd attack. He imagined the pain of rat teeth crunching into his bare toes. Although he couldn't make out any animals he could see that the carpet had been messed with black stuff. He touched it with his toes. It was crusty. A bit like spilt soup that'd dried into carpet pile. Deeper shivers ran through him. Something was badly wrong with this place. Terror folded round him. He panted hard. White mist billowed from his mouth. Despite his growing sense of panic he noticed little details. Like a pen that lay in the black gunge on the carpet. In the compartment that normally held things like cups and sunglasses there were a handful of coins. Dead spiders lay on top of them.

Wait! The car rocked again on its suspension. Archer froze. He'd not been moving. So why did it move? Holding his breath, he didn't twitch so much as a finger. Yet the car wobbled again. *There's someone in the back seat . . .*

Jay? No, it wouldn't be Jay. Jay's gone. Without moving any other part of his body, as he sat there at the steering wheel, Archer's eyes turned to the rear-view mirror. Despite a ghosting of spider web over the glass he could still see. Heart pounding, mouth dry, the boy watched as a dark, rounded shape rose upward from the seat. Watched as he saw the brown blanket that covered it begin to slip down. It seemed to take place in slow motion. Archer stared as the dull fabric slipped from the figure. He knew when that figure was finally revealed it would be too much for him. He couldn't foresee a time 'after' its exposure. When he saw what had lain in the back seat for years there could be no future for him. Time would end.

The blanket slipped away in a cloud of dust. Swathes of black hair. The gaunt face. A mummy face. It had echoes of female beauty. But the flesh had shrivelled. Skin had cracked across high cheekbones. The mouth was a slit framed with black lips. White teeth glinted. As if it grinned with pleasure at finding this diminutive companion.

No longer alone . . . Someone to keep here for ever and ever. These thoughts slid through Archer's head. At that moment the overload of terror produced a dreamy effect, as if he'd fallen into a doze. His eyelids grew heavy. All that existed now was the face framed with long black hair. *She has no eyes . . .* He gazed sleepily into a face that had a beautiful sculptural quality, only it had been sculpted from withered skin and bone. Instinct drove him to push open the door. In a moment he could walk away from the car. Where would he go? He didn't know. But to simply get out of the car would be a start. Without taking his gaze from the mummified face in the rear-view mirror he slid sideways on the seat.

The moment he began to exit the car the creature in the back moved. A pair of scab-like eyelids snapped open to reveal a pair of bright eyes. They were a beautiful blue. Ocean blue on a summer's day.

Archer gurgled with fear. He swung one leg out of the car. Then the creature struck. A pair of brown arms that were hard as polished wood lashed at him. Hands gripped his shoulders. With a cry of fear he was dragged back into the car by its monstrous occupant. The door slammed shut to seal him inside. Once more he tried to cut his senses off from reality, so he wouldn't experience what happened next to him.

This time, however, he couldn't retreat from the real world. With absolute clarity he saw that pair of bright – blazingly bright – blue eyes as the creature dragged him from the front of the car into the back seat.

Skin tingling, a luscious sense of relaxation pouring along his limbs, Victor Brodman lay on the bed. In the light of the lamp he saw Laura Parris smiling at him. Two hours of love-making had made her so young-looking. The cloud of exhaustion she'd brought with her to the island had been dispelled. A youthful glow transformed her into a woman of such beauty that Victor could only stare.

She murmured, 'Does this island always make people do crazy things?'

He smiled as he stroked her hair. 'What we just did was crazy? I rather liked it!'

'Me, too. It's just . . .' She shrugged. 'Even five hours ago I couldn't imagine doing what we just did in a million years.' She wriggled round so she could lie alongside him, skin to skin.

'Feel good?'

'I feel brand new again.' Then she groaned.

'What's wrong?'

'I'm going to have to take Max back to Badsworth Lodge tomorrow.'

'Are you sure?'

'He needs to be back in a familiar environment. If he doesn't see his own things and sleep in his own bed he'll never get better.'

Victor experienced a pang of anxiety. 'You'll come back?'

'I can't promise. I'm sorry.'

After that they lay there as the weight of real life, and all its pressures, settled back on to them once more.

In the car Archer fought for his life. All he could see were a pair of huge blue eyes. They burned with the ferocity of flames. He tried to scramble away but a hand gripped his wrist. A second hand pulled back his fingers that he'd bunched into a fist. Then a sharp object – a fingernail? A knife-blade? – was forced into the soft skin of his palm. It dug deep. A cruel pressure.

'Stop it! You're hurting!'

Those blue eyes burned without compassion. Swathes of cold hair from the skull flooded his face. Strands filled his mouth. His lungs burned as if he was drowning. The pain in his hand was incredible. It seemed as if a red-hot spike had been driven into the skin. With a desperate effort he twisted sideways.

A breeze hissed through trees outside the bedroom window. Archer blinked. Glowing in the darkness, the clock radio read 2.17. In the post-midnight air an owl hooted.

The car? The dead woman? Archer desperately wanted to say it was a dream. Only he knew better. Jay had taken him to a real place. How, he didn't know. Fear still rang through his body as if it was a bell sounding out doom-laden chimes. He sensed an impending disaster. What he'd experienced had been bad. It was only the start though. He was sure of that. When he switched on the bedside lamp he checked his arms for bruises. There was nothing there, yet his skin itched as if it had been touched by something unpleasant. When he put his hands under the sweaty pillow to turn it over in the hope the cool side would help relax him something pricked his finger. He recoiled, thinking an insect had stung him. When he checked he saw a bracelet in yellow metal. The chain had snapped so it presented a sharp piece of broken link. That must have been what pricked him.

With a shudder he remembered the woman driving a sharp object into the palm of his hand. It took a moment for him to pluck up courage. Eventually, however, he picked up the chain bracelet. Adorning it, a flat strip of gold. Black specks were unpleasantly stuck to it. Even so, when he held it to the light he could read what was engraved there. *Ghorlan~Victor.*

Thirteen

Victor Brodman carried Max's bags to the jetty. Laura walked beside the boy. Max's eyes glittered as if made of glass. Barbiturates damped down his jangled nerves. Yet his expression oozed nothing less than naked dread.

Victor tried to catch Laura's eye. *How long are you going to be away? Will you leave me your phone number? Can you come back soon? Did last night mean as much to you as it did to me? Will we be together again?* These questions were the ones he longed to have answered. That morning he'd tried to grab a few words with her. But after a hurried departure in the early hours from his apartment at White Cross Farm Laura had been busy making arrangements to get Max back to Badsworth Lodge. If the boy put distance between himself and Jay maybe the panic attacks would abate. *Some hope.* From what Victor had gleaned, once Jay had done that thing of chanting a person's name, like a mantra, then to all intents and purposes they were cursed. Of course it must be psychological, he told himself. Jay couldn't have supernatural powers. However, if an individual believes they really are cursed then bad things generally follow.

Down on the jetty Mayor Wilkes performed his busybody routine. He bossed around the man who'd moored the ferry to the jetty when it arrived. Some children from Badsworth Lodge had come to the riverside to wave off their friend. Although most appeared to be there out of morbid curiosity. These children Wilkes chivvied away from the water's edge with comments like, 'If you fall in nobody will get you out again. This current is a killer.' *Charming.*

The children muttered amongst themselves.

'Did you hear that Jay has been saying Max's name?'

'God, he's for it.'

'I wonder what will happen to him?'

'Whatever it is, I bet he doesn't make it till the end of the week.'

'Max's a bully anyway. He deserves everything he gets.'

Constantly Laura spoke softly to Max. Mainly reassurances that everything would be fine.

Mayor Wilkes prowled the jetty. From his expression you'd have thought he'd bitten a lemon thinking it a strawberry. 'What the hell are they doing?' His sour tone intensified as he stared across the water at the mainland. 'Look at the idiots.'

'What's wrong, Mr Mayor?' Victor enjoyed a brief but satisfying image of pushing Mayor Wilkes into the river.

Wilkes fumed. 'The ferry should have been here ten minutes ago. It's still moored to the pier.'

'Perhaps your committee have cut sailings to save money.' Victor spoke with an innocent tone, but he knew full well it would irritate Wilkes.

'That's utter nonsense, Victor. The crew'll be sleeping off a hangover.'

Victor glanced at Laura. He'd decided to tell her what she meant to him – as soon as he grabbed an opportunity. Only it wasn't looking good. Another child was running down the lane calling her name. Nurse Laura Parris wasn't just popular with the island ranger. Everyone loved her. For a moment, he stood beside Mayor Wilkes as the man grumbled about the tardiness of the ferry. As a breeze whipped tufts of white cloud across the sky part of him planned the day out. He needed to check the shoreline to make sure no deer had snagged themselves again as they grazed on the kelp. Also, he intended to take the children to the castle tower. They loved the climb up the spiral staircase to the very top. He shot another glance back at Laura. Just a minute alone with her, that's all he needed. His perseverance was rewarded with a smile. From her hand gesture to Max she was telling him to stand there. In a slow sedated way the teenager answered with a nod. At last! Victor'd get his chance to speak to her. He'd already decided to give her the carefully composed note that was in his pocket. Maybe it was a bit schoolboy-ish but it just bore a few words, thanking her for her company, then he'd added his telephone number. Come to think of it, handing her a note on the jetty, would it seem weird? Damn. Regarding the dating game, he was seriously out of practice.

They were within six paces of reaching one another when a boy raced along the jetty shouting, 'Laura . . . Laura! You've got to come to the hostel.'

'I can't,' Laura said. 'I'm catching the ferry back to the mainland.'

'You've got to. It's important.'

Her expression became serious. 'Why? Has something happened?'

'The manager's sick. Big sick. All over the stairs.'

'Go find Lou. I have to take Max back to Badsworth Lodge as soon as possible.'

'Well, you're not,' Mayor Wilkes told her as he pocketed his phone. 'The ferry's going nowhere.' He glared at the vessel as it sat in its dock across the span of water. 'My guess is the hostel manager has the same as the crew. They're all sick, too.'

'We're stranded here,' intoned Max, glassy eyed. 'With Jay.'

I must do something about the bracelet. But what? The question perplexed Archer. There were other dilemmas too. A man and woman ran White Cross Farm. Every morning they rang a gong to announce breakfast was ready. Archer would hurry downstairs, his stomach rolling hungrily as he sniffed grilled bacon. This morning he'd waited until half eight. No gong. No delicious bacon aromas. Just a strange silence. Even though the hunger pangs had started he decided it was important to show the gold bracelet to Laura. He must tell her the circumstances of the find or his head would burst. Laura would listen sympathetically when he described the underground car, and his fight with the mummy creature. For a moment, the eight-year-old stared at the bracelet on his bedside table. Touching it was creepy. Even to look at the dirty gold links made him remember all too clearly those dead features, the mane of black hair, and, worse, the blue eyes. They were beautiful, but they were terrifying, too. The way they blazed out of that mummified head. Archer gulped. His hands turned clammy while his heart thudded hard.

'Laura,' he told himself. 'She'll know what to do.' Archer carefully slipped the bracelet into the pocket of his shorts then went to Laura's room. After knocking he looked inside. Alarmingly, it was empty. What's more she'd taken her clothes. Panic jolted him. 'She's left without us!' Where now? Jay's room? No, Jay might start repeating his name. Or announce he was taking him for a little walk again. No, thank you. He'd had enough of Jay's 'little walks' to last a lifetime.

Archer hurried downstairs in the hope he'd find Laura at the breakfast table. 'Bloody Laura,' he said loudly to the empty room. 'Bloody hell. You're not allowed to go. You can't leave us.' His scared voice echoed back from the farmhouse kitchen walls. 'Bad Laura.' He flinched at how babyish he sounded. 'I'm going to be brave. I've been given some jewellery. It's important.' When he spoke the words aloud, he realized that the gold chain *was* vitally important. It had to be. That dead woman with the blue eyes had come back to life to give it to him. She'd fought to push it into his hand so he wouldn't let go of it. She needed him to take it, to keep it safe, then to give it to someone. But why? And who should he give it to? Archer sat by the table. Nothing was cooking on the hob. However, the cereal bowls were already out. In the middle of the table were boxes of Frosties and cornflakes. The notion of there being no one there to make breakfast troubled him almost as much as knowing that gruesome corpse had come back to life. He glanced at the window, suddenly fearful that the monster face would be staring in. A pair of eyes did watch him. He cried out before he realized it was only the fat old Siamese cat that lived in the barn. Archer decided to fend for himself. He switched on the radio which was perched atop the refrigerator. A DJ announced cheerfully that it would be breezy today with sunshine. Then he played a sad song about being alone.

'I'm OK, I'm brave,' Archer insisted to his reflection in the spoon he'd picked up. 'I've been given an important job.' He continued to address his distorted reflection in the spoon. 'The woman knew I'm big enough to keep the jewellery safe.' He took a deep breath. 'I'm going to tell Laura about the underground car, too.' He recalled the detective shows he'd seen. 'Something's not right. The car's been deliberately hidden.' He chose the box of Frosties. 'The woman was hidden in the car. Back seat. Blanket over.' Chuckling, he relished the role of brainy policeman. 'Clues. They tell me . . .' He froze in surprise at his deduction. 'Murder. The woman was murdered.' He poured a stream of cereal into the bowl. 'The woman was *brew*-tally murdered . . . the gunge stuck to the car's carpet is –' he spoke with relish – 'blood. Dried blood. All poured out from the wound, as she lay screaming. Bleeding. Bosh, bosh.' He brought the spoon down on the tiger's face on the box like he was beating it to death. 'Bashed out her brains. Bosh!' Hysteria grabbed hold. 'Bosh, bosh, bosh, brains and blood, and—'

'I'm sorry.' A woman with wild hair lurched forward. Her hands slammed palm-down on to the tabletop. 'Uh . . . I feel like death.'

The corpse-woman's back for the bracelet! Archer screamed.

With an effort, the woman straightened. 'I'm sorry, Archer. I didn't mean to frighten you. I'm . . . uph . . . I planned to . . . tell you that Laura had to leave for . . . ferry . .' The woman grimaced. 'Lou's supposed to be here . . . I don't know . . . sorry about breakfast. Only I can't face . . . cooking.' Shuddering, she pulled her dressing-gown collar up toward her throat. 'We're both down with a bug. Graham can't get out of bed. You know my brother . . .' She rocked unsteadily. He stared, not knowing what to say or do. 'Victor. You know Victor?' She gulped. 'I need the bathroom.' As she fled the kitchen she managed to say, 'Archer. Tell Victor. Ask him to—' The rest of the sentence disintegrated as she rushed to the toilet.

Archer realized the woman wasn't the corpse-monster from the car after all. It was Victor's sister. Only she looked a lot different from yesterday. He thought hard. 'Dishevelled.' That's it. Dishevelled. First things first. He'd eat his Frosties, then he'd go find Victor. Archer was pleased. He'd been given another very important job to do. It made the eight-year-old feel grown-up. As he spooned cereal into his mouth he sensed the pressure of the bracelet in his pocket against his thigh. He recalled the words inscribed on the bracelet. Ghorlan~Victor. Might that be the same Victor as Victor Brodman? Had he known the dead woman in the car? *Were they family? Or did he murder her?* This made Archer freeze mid-chew. *If Victor bashed out the woman's brains, will he do the same to me?* The gold bracelet had changed now. Before it had been valuable, something of importance. Now it had become a curse. It made his skin crawl. Like a metallic parasite, it seemed as if it wanted to bore into his leg. *If I'm not careful I might wind up dead in the car, too. Dead men tell no tales . . . the same goes for little boys, too.*

Fourteen

'Congratulations.' Mayor Wilkes addressed Laura Parris in his best officious weasel voice. 'Your children have managed to infect half the island.'

'I beg your pardon?'

The others on the jetty saw her anger. They watched in anticipation, wondering how she'd respond to such an accusation.

'Whatever those kids brought with them,' Wilkes snapped, 'they've passed it on to our people.'

'If they have, then it's no fault of theirs.' Laura's eyes blazed. 'How dare you say things like that, as if they're unclean! Is that how you see them? Lepers!'

Wilkes snarled, 'I've just heard that the ferry won't be sailing for at least two days. That means we're confined to the island. Do you understand? We're marooned.'

Max groaned. 'I want to go home.' Tranquillizers gave his voice a leaden quality. 'I don't want to stay here. Jay's going to hurt me.'

'What a mess,' Wilkes fumed. 'What a bloody awful mess.' He took another phone call. During this he fired out what amounted to news bulletins for everyone's benefit on the jetty. 'It's our GP. He says that fifty people are infected . . . vomiting, cramps, fever. Great, just great.' He finished the call. 'Nurse Parris. I'll be making a formal complaint. This is the last time those . . . *people* . . . from Badsworth Lodge set foot on this island.' Sheer loathing slurred his words. 'You're not managing an orphanage. It's a bloody zoo.' He shot a look of disgust at Max.

Laura ripped into Mayor Wilkes. 'I can't believe how crass you are. Badsworth Lodge isn't an orphanage. We are carers. We're attempting to rebuild lives.'

'In the most squalid, unhygienic surroundings. Nurse Parris, you and your horde will be off this island within forty-eight hours. For good. And if I had my way—'

'Wilkes. Shut up.' Victor had heard enough. 'It doesn't matter if the bug *had* come from these children. But do I have to remind you that the school party earlier this week came down with the same symptoms? Vomiting, fever. They were sick before anyone from Badsworth Lodge set foot on Siluria. Give these children a break.'

Laura nodded a thank you to Victor, though she hadn't finished with Mayor Wilkes. 'I don't know what you did with your soul, you arrogant bastard. But you've lost it somewhere along the way. I've never known such an uncharitable, uncaring little shit in my life.'

Max groaned. The raised voices unsettled him.

Victor stepped in again. 'OK, so we've lost the ferry for a while. What we must do now is return to our usual routine. Otherwise the children will get upset.'

'Exactly,' Laura agreed. 'I'll check if any of our children have symptoms. I'll need to speak to the GP, too.'

'Don't you listen, Nurse Parris? He's busy. There's an epidemic.'

'You, yourself, used my title. Nurse. If the island's hit as badly as you say by this bug I'm qualified to help out.'

Mayor Wilkes, sour faced, marched from the jetty in the direction of the village. Laura started to usher the other children back to the houses where they were staying. 'I'll be round shortly to tell you the plans for this afternoon. The castle, isn't it, Victor?'

'We'll be climbing the tower.' He smiled to reassure them. 'You'll enjoy it.'

Laura caught his eye. 'Thanks for taking my side. You know, I could cheerfully strangle that man.'

'You'll have to join a very long queue,' Victor told her with a grin.

Archer had almost completed the ten-minute walk to the village. In his pocket he carried the Ghorlan~Victor bracelet. He would tell Laura everything as soon as he could. When he entered the village he paused. It all looked very strange to him. Even though it was mid-morning, with the sun shining down, a lot of houses had curtains drawn shut. He passed some people in gardens who sat on benches with their heads in their hands. The way they were so droopy reminded him of how Victor's sister had been as she'd staggered to the bathroom. A woman in yellow rubber gloves tipped water from a plastic bowl on to a garden path. Her expression wasn't a happy one. She called back through her door. 'Tammy. You sit there with the bucket. Don't move away from it. OK?'

Archer scurried down Main Street. This morning the river shone silver in the sunlight. Gulls rode the breeze, screeching their heads off like gulls do. Then he saw Laura with Max. The teenager moved in a zombie shuffle. Archer knew it was pills. He'd seen kids like it before at the Lodge.

With his heart leaping with joy at seeing Laura he ran toward her. 'Laura!'

She waved, 'Hi, Archer.'

'I've got something to show you.'

'In a minute, I've got to get everyone back to the houses.'

'It's important.'

'Archer. Patience please.'

'No, look at this. Someone gave me it. It's really important.' He dug down into his pocket to retrieve the bracelet. It had become tangled up in the threads of cotton. He struggled to free it. Only it just wouldn't come.

'Archer. I'm sorry, sunshine. But I'm busy.'

'Why don't you show it to me?'

Archer started back. It was Victor, the island ranger. Instantly images of both the Ghorlan~Victor bracelet and the living corpse in the car sped through his head. The woman had been murdered. It might have been Victor who'd murdered her. He glanced at Victor's hands. Big hands like that could easily bash your brains out.

'What is it, son?' Victor asked. 'I might be able to help.'

'Nothing.'

'Nothing?'

'I haven't got anything.' Suddenly the once friendly man became a looming, ominous figure. Archer backed away.

'Are you all right?' Victor asked. 'Nothing's bothering you, is it?'

Archer stuttered, 'No . . . I've been sent. Mr and Mrs Knowles are poorly.'

'Thanks for letting me know, Archer.' He turned to Laura. 'Archer's just told me that my sister and her husband are down with the bug. I'd best check on them.'

'Everyone's probably got the same. Drop by the GP's surgery first. If he's identified what it is he'll have printed out an information sheet on dos and don'ts.'

Victor smiled at Archer. 'We'll need help feeding the animals. Do you want to walk back to the farm with me?'

Archer shuddered.

Laura said, 'It's best he sticks with me. All this excitement might get too much for him.'

Victor headed in the direction of the farm. Archer didn't like the look of his hands. Skull breaking hands, they were. Laura had been walking with her arm protectively around Max's shoulders. But Kate and Tina were bickering, so she had had to go do her peacekeeper thing. Archer took the opportunity to talk to Max.

'It was rotten what you did to me, Max. It really hurt when you kept nipping my neck. But I don't want you to die.'

Max just stared.

'I know Jay was saying your name.' Archer gave him an appraising glance. 'Has anything bad happened to you yet?'

Max said nothing, but he started swallowing.

Archer started to back off. 'After it happens to you, you won't come back to Badsworth Lodge, will you? I saw Maureen after the accident. She came into my room. Her face was all . . .' He gulped. 'I don't want to see you when you're dead, Max. Promise to stay away.'

A growl, starting in Max's throat, morphed into a howl of terror. 'Jay!'

Archer followed Max's line of sight. Jay walked along Main Street, face expressionless, arms hanging limp by his sides. Even from here, Archer could see that he mouthed a word over and over. Laura ran back to Max. However, the teenager had already fled. He raced down the hill to the jetty. He didn't stop when he reached the end. Legs still running frantically through God's own sweet air he flew off the end of the boards. A second later he vanished into the river with an almighty splash.

Fifteen

Victor had covered perhaps one hundred yards in the direction of his sister's farm when he heard frantic shouts from the jetty. He glanced back to see people surge along its boards. They were pointing, shouts rose in volume. Victor knew enough from their body language to realize that someone had fallen into the river. This sent shivers down his spine. The currents in this part of the Severn were lethal. He should know, these vicious waters had made a widower out of him. As he raced back to the jetty he tugged the fleece off and flung it aside.

'Stay out of the water,' he shouted. 'Don't go in after him.' Laura had already kicked off her sandals. 'That goes for you, too, Laura.'

'It's Max.' Her face was the essence of panic. 'He jumped in. He's so frightened he's trying to kill himself.'

Victor shielded his eyes against the sun. The teenager lay face down in the water, not moving, perhaps unconscious, or perhaps forcing himself not to swim. If you're so inclined, he thought grimly, this is the perfect place to die by your own hand. Whirlpools, ice-cold pockets of water, turbulence, cross-currents. A death trap.

'Victor, do something,' Laura pleaded.

'The flow's running at around eight miles an hour. I can't catch up with him.' He checked for boats . . . damn, no boats. He would have to go in there after the boy.

'You're going to stand there, watching Max drown?'

Children began to weep at the sight of the still figure being swept away.

Victor shook his head. 'I need to gauge where the current will take him, then try and swim there when he's carried past.'

'Oh my God!' For a moment it seemed as if Laura would start crying, too, but when she noticed Jay standing in the lane her mouth hardened. 'Don't do this to him,' she hissed. 'Don't you dare.'

Victor had to blot out Laura's reaction. What mattered now was getting Max out of the water. He turned his attention back to the river. If he swam for a point fifty yards downstream of Max, then he just might intercept . . .

A shadow flashed past him, brushing his arm. A split second later there was a huge thump as a body hit the river hard. Victor stared in astonishment.

'Did anyone see who that was?'

Nobody had. Victor was just as perplexed when the figure surfaced then swam after Max with so much power that they left a creaming wake in their trail.

'Do you know him?' Laura asked.

'Never seen him before.' Victor shielded his eyes as the stranger blazed through water like an Olympic swimmer. All he could make out was a dark-skinned man with a shaved head. In fact, the skin was so dark it was like gunmetal – a blue-black. 'I only hope that guy knows what he's doing. Those cross-currents are a killer.'

By now the children cheered the would-be rescuer. Adults, too, were praising the man's prowess to one another loudly enough to express their relief that someone else other than them had taken the risky plunge.

Around a hundred yards offshore the man grabbed hold of Max, raised his head above the water, then swam back to the island with big muscular strokes that cheated the current of another victim. Even so, the flow was strong enough to carry the pair away from the jetty so the man was forced to make for the beach, to avoid having to fight the current head-on. Victor, Laura, and the rest, ran across the shingle to help the man carry Max back on to dry land. Laura held the teen's head so she could check if the boy was alive. However, he sobbed hard enough to prove he was breathing normally.

After the crowd of islanders had gathered round to slap the stranger on his drenched back, his white shirt clinging to him like a second skin, he wiped his face with his hand then jerked his head back at the Severn.

'I'm full of praise that this river's got no hippos. I don't like crocodiles. Let me tell you, hippos are worse.' He grinned. 'A hippo will bite a man in two. Crocs only take your feet. If you've got the Lord on your side.'

Laura shook the man's hand. 'Thank you, Mr . . .'

'Constable.'

Laura glanced at Victor, puzzled, then thanked the man again.

Victor shook the man's sopping hand, too. The grip was a powerful one. But then this man was a human speedboat. 'I didn't know we were expecting a visit from the police.'

'You are and you aren't.' His smile was a bright one. 'I'm not British police. I'm from the West African Republic. My baptism name is Solomon Constable. I came here to see Laura Parris and a boy she's caring for.' His smile faded as a grave expression took its place. 'You see, it's important I talk to her. I know God wants me to be here to help her, and her brethren.'

Victor eyed the man standing there in pinstriped trousers and a once crisp white shirt. Water dripped from the clothes until a pool formed around him.

'You are Nurse Laura Parris, aren't you?' The man scrutinized her face. 'You care for Jay. So you know what he does to people.'

'I'm not speaking to you. You're from the press.'

'No, I'm not. Humbly, I claim to be from God. Because though you know Jay destroys people, you don't know why. Or what he is.'

'I'm not interested.' Firmly, she steered Max away through the crowds.

Solomon Constable gave Victor a rueful look. 'I came all the way from Africa for that?'

'You're not a reporter?'

'That I'm not, sir. I'm a retired police officer. Constable by both name and rank. And I have one last case to close before I'm done with the world.'

Victor said, 'Come with me. I'll get you dry clothes and a towel.'

'You are a good man, sir. So I will speak with you then you can convince Nurse Parris to hear me.'

As they strolled to the village Victor asked, 'What makes you think she'll listen to me?'

'She loves you. You love her.' The man smiled warmly as Victor paused mid-step. 'I was a police officer for forty years. And I love my Sherlock Holmes books. So I made a most elementary deduction.' The man's sing-song voice suggested gentleness and wisdom. 'Sir, I make deductions all the time. They're second nature to me. Many married men remove their wedding rings when they go out on the town. Your fingers have an even tan, so when I see an indentation on the third finger of your left hand I have to ask myself why you reverse this habit of certain other men? I think the answer is that you wear the wedding ring when you're alone at night. I mention this deduction because it reveals you are deeply loyal . . . intensely loyal.'

Victor's eyes were drawn back to the river that took Ghorlan away. They had matching wedding rings. Hers must now lie on the river bed. With what remained of her.

'I don't wish to pry, sir. Or cause you sadness.' Solomon Constable's brown eyes held genuine compassion. 'My experience as a police officer tells me you have a good, honest heart. Not like your Mayor Wilkes. Now there's a man who has secrets running through every part of him. Secrets flow in his veins like blood. I did my research before I came here. Even though he has no criminal convictions there is something amiss. He is a businessman as well as elected mayor, isn't that so? Yet though he makes deals his name doesn't appear in legal contracts, even though that would be perfectly normal. It suggests to me a man who is habitually secretive to the extent he conducts legitimate business as if it were a criminal act. Moreover, he employs ex-prisoners in his construction company. These men would normally find it hard to get work. Mayor Wilkes claims he does this because he is being kind. I consider that he has ulterior motives. Former convicts will have to be loyal to Wilkes, because they'd find no work elsewhere. So Wilkes can make them bend the rules; they might even help him bury his secrets, too. And men who build bridges can bury secrets very deeply indeed. Have I been able to convince you that we should talk?'

'Of course we can talk. First, though, you need some dry clothes.'

The grave expression returned on Solomon's face. 'I must give you this warning. You won't like what I have to say. Because once you hear it, you will have to do something about the boy they call Jay.'

Sixteen

Mayor Wilkes watched Victor Brodman from the apartment over the village post office. From a harsh blue sky the sun shone on the island ranger. For some reason he walked in the company of a short, muscular man who had skin the colour of cobalt – a striking blue-black. The stranger dripped water as the pair headed in the direction of the youth hostel.

'Dear God.' Mayor Wilkes shook his head in disgust. 'Where does Brodman find these strays? It used to be just animals. Now he's collecting people, too. Fishing them out of the river by the look of them.' A middle-aged woman, sitting at a computer, began to answer but Wilkes spoke over her as if her presence in the room was merely incidental. 'The times I've seen Brodman mooching across the island with some wretched beast in a cardboard box, because he was going to fix its leg or rub ointment into its rump ulcers. Now, it's strangers. The sooner I get him replaced with our people the better.

'I've had to endure Brodman for more than a decade. Victor-the-beasts'-guardian-Brodman. Do you know what it's like to have that man on the island? It's like walking with a thorn sticking in your foot. I'm trying to push forward plans, but I can't because he's making me limp along like a cripple. Conservation – it's a mantra with the man. What really sticks in my craw is that the locals respect him. Dear God, I wish I could dynamite all their houses. Then we'd have real progress here. But you're probably one of the Victor Brodman fans, too, aren't you?' He awarded the woman with a sneer.

'You promised you wouldn't hit me again.' She pushed back a fringe, prematurely streaked silver. Her right cheek glowed an angry red.

'Well, you promised not to annoy me again. You did, so you were the first to break the promise.'

'I work for you. That doesn't give you a right to knock me around.' She touched her cheek. 'It really hurts.'

'Don't expect me to kiss it better for you.' He eyed her with disgust. 'You've really let yourself go, you know that, don't you?'

'Bastard.'

'Don't push your luck, June.'

June pointed at her face. 'I look twenty years older than I really am because of what you did to me.'

'Did to you? I let you live in an apartment rent-free and pay your wages. That's hardly an exercise in cruelty, is it?'

'To think I lied to the police to save your neck. And you stood by and let me be prosecuted for fraud, when it should have been you in court. Not me.'

Wilkes shook his head. 'Self-pity isn't noble, June. Cry if you want but set up the meeting with the planning officer first.'

'Why don't you give him his bribe money yourself?'

'Don't be ridiculous.' Wilkes turned back to the window to watch Victor again. Slapping June again tempted him more than words could say but there was no point in dispatching her on errands with her face puffed up. Besides, the woman was still useful to him. He had her in his pocket. Because she'd served time in jail for fraud she was unemployable. Charitably, he had publicly forgiven her for her wrongdoing. Then he'd offered her a home (as hers had been repossessed by the bank when she couldn't afford the mortgage repayments). Now June did all those awkward chores that might expose him to criminal prosecution.

He realized June had still been speaking . . . well, bellyaching, he told himself. Maybe dealing her another stinging slap would be in order.

'You know,' she said, her voice faltering. 'I don't feel well. I've come over really hot.'

'You do look flushed,' he conceded. 'You must be coming down with that ruddy bug everyone's getting. Whatever you do, don't give it to me.'

'I've never met anyone as cold as you,' she hissed. 'Now I'm trapped in this . . .' She grimaced. 'Oh, no.' Quickly she hurried to the bathroom.

'It's not all bad.' Mayor Wilkes laughed. 'The quack says that infection drives the body temperature up so much that people will have hallucinations. You might hallucinate that you're sunning your old bones in St-Tropez.' He wrinkled his nose as he heard sounds coming from the bathroom. 'I'll let myself out. Bon voyage!'

Seventeen

With the hostel manager indisposed, Victor and Laura used his office so they could talk to the stranger in private. A staff member had also lent the African a tracksuit in a rather too vivid yellow while the washing machine soaked away the river water from his clothes. Victor sat on the desk as the late afternoon sunlight streamed in. Solomon Constable sat in a swivel chair. Laura chose to stand by the door with her arms folded and her face set to distrust.

Laura fixed Solomon with a hard stare. 'I gladly thank you for saving Max's life today, but that doesn't give you the right to exploit Jay. Tell your newspaper friends they're getting nothing from me.'

'I've not travelled five thousand miles to get anything out of anybody.' Solomon settled into the chair. 'God willing, I'm here to give, not take.'

'Jay's been through hell. He was the only survivor on a ship full of refugees. He has behavioural problems. I won't allow you to talk to him, or—'

'I've no need to meet with Jay. In truth, ma'am, I should be very afraid of the boy if I did.'

'I'm too busy to play your game.' She gave an impatient sigh. 'Victor, I've promised Dr Nazra I'll help with his patients.'

'So now there's an epidemic?' Solomon wasn't surprised. In fact, for some reason it seemed as if he expected it. 'There's disease on your island?'

Laura scowled. 'A virus that causes upset stomachs. Hardly a plague.'

'And it has a name, this virus?'

'I have too much work to do to stand around talking.'

Victor knew that Laura was ready to leave. 'Laura, we should listen to what Mr Constable has to say.'

'Solomon, please,' he insisted.

'Victor, you can listen to stories if you wish – I'm going.'

Solomon Constable knitted his fingers together, then announced in grave tones, 'The boy, Jay, does not exist.'

'Fine, believe whatever you want.' She opened the door.

'Don't bad things happen to those near him? Doesn't he sometimes say that he'll take people for a little walk? Only he takes them to places that seem to exist purely in nightmares or to visit friends that have died a long time ago. Am I right, ma'am?'

Grim-faced, Laura shut the door then faced him, arms folded. 'Go on.'

'First, why I'm here. I'm a retired police officer. I always hated not being able to close a case. This is one that I must close if I'm going to make my peace with God.'

'You're talking like you're an old man,' Victor said. 'Anyone seeing you swim today would agree that you're probably the strongest man for miles around.'

'Thank you, sir. That's a heart-warming compliment,' Solomon said. 'I am fifty-seven years old. By rights, I should be dead. Six months ago I helped my neighbour. She's an old African widow who likes to keep chickens; she says they hatch the souls of her ancestors. It might not be a Christian thing to say but she's a good woman, so I helped her mend her chicken coop, and I managed to put a nail right through my hand.' He held up a pale palm. A circular red scar dominated its centre. 'As a follower of Jesus I appreciated right at that moment the pain of such a wound. Anyway, it became infected. My kidneys failed. A priest gave me the last rites and they got ready to move me to the mortuary. But God gave me my life back.

'In three days I was out of the hospital. But every night I dreamed about the refugee ship that sank, and those people that my coun-trymen drove off their own land. Those refugees belonged to a clan that claim they're the descendants of the Carthaginians. You recall Hannibal and his elephants? Out of a desire of vengeance he marched the elephants through the snowy Alps with the aim of destroying Rome. Only the God-given weather defeated him. The Cathdran worshipped the old city gods of Carthage. But that wasn't what angered my people. The Cathdran owned rights to freshwater springs. They made money from piping the water into town.'

'So they weren't persecuted for their faith as the newspapers claimed,' Laura said. 'It was all down to money?'

'Isn't that always the root of all evil?' Solomon let out a long sigh. 'Now let me get to the core of why I've travelled from Africa to see you. A quest that tested me. Even when I'd come all this way there was no ferry to bring me to the island. I had to rent a motor boat so I could cross the water to you.'

Victor listened to the voice of the man. It had a hypnotic tone. Even though he heard every word he seemed to find himself in a world between sleep and wakefulness. The rise and fall of the voice washed over him as he gazed out at the river as the tide turned. Wavelets crept up over the beach. In the turbulent waters some lithe creature slipped across the surface before diving down into the depths where it would be so dark and so cold, and where all those years ago he knew his wife, Ghorlan, must have found herself being drawn down to the river bed. In his mind's eye, he gazed on white bones held prisoner by the cold, oozing silt. Poor Ghorlan. And in his imagination Victor swam down through thirty feet of river water to that hidden place where sunlight never penetrated.

'Five years ago,' Solomon told them, 'I was taken off my beat in the city. My commander put me to a desk with a computer. He ordered me to compile a register of all those refugees on the ship. Dates of birth, addresses, marital status, occupation. All those kinds of facts. Then against each name I was expected to add information about criminal convictions, and when that failed I would record any suspicions of illegal activity connected with those dead people. It wasn't hard to find my countrymen that would testify that the Cathdran contaminated the water they piped into the city. Or even gossip about the Cathdran indulging in witchcraft. All that was expected of me was to list everyone on board that death trap of a boat, and then present so-called proof that they were all criminals anyway. This would ease the conscience of my people, and the rest of the world, which turned the refugee ship away from their ports. These refugees were all thieves and wrongdoers we could say. If you'd let them into your country they would have wreaked carnage. So . . . as you know, the *N'Taal* sank. Only one survivor was found on a raft. The rescuers called the boy Jay. You keep him safe at Badsworth Lodge. Now he is here with you on this island. Don't look so surprised, you'd be amazed what can be found on the Internet, just by typing names into a search engine. I know about your sad loss, Victor. During my research I found reports about the tragedy concerning Mrs Brodman.'

Victor felt himself still drifting between being awake and some shadowy borderland. The room was warm, with the sun shining in . . . he felt drowsy . . . in fact, drowsier than he had ever felt before. That mellifluous voice of Solomon's had such a relaxing quality. That woozy sensation left him with the impression he was floating. After the anger of earlier, Laura stood calmly, her eyelids drooping, yet she listened with close attention.

Solomon's speech flowed on. 'I finished my register of names, with its truths, half-truths and downright lies. My boss was satisfied. The only hitch that stopped me from believing I had completed my task was that one person didn't appear on the list. Jay. He was four years old at the time, or as far as the rescuers could judge. However, I find no trace of him being born in my country. We have perfectly competent civil servants, plus a strict procedure for registering births. Jay doesn't appear on registers. Nobody from the Cathdran village remembers seeing him. Yet he turned up on the ship, and he was the only survivor. That always unsettled me. After my accident I dreamt, as I've told you, about the refugees, about how the ship fell apart, and most of all I dreamed about the four-year-old boy surviving for days in an open raft. Even though I'd retired by that time I tried again to find a record of the boy, so that he might be reunited with any surviving family. What I did discover is that wherever Jay stayed afterwards, whether in children's homes or with foster families, bad things happened. It was as if the boy was cursed. Or . . .' Solomon dabbed at his forehead where perspiration beaded. 'Or the boy was the instrument of that curse.'

'Jay had bad luck . . .' Laura began. 'People blamed him. It's not his fault.'

'No?' Solomon took a tissue from a box on the desk so he could dab his glistening face. 'Even discussing this makes my heart beat faster. Please. I'm here to impart facts. This boy does not exist, at least as far as the public records show. The boy is dangerous. He is like a lightning conductor, but instead of lightning he conducts tragedy and death.' Solomon plucked another tissue from the carton. 'Just as I dream of the refugees and of Jay, I also dream that this is my last year on earth. I know God has given me the chance of redemption by putting right the wrong committed by my people, your people, and by myself. I compiled a register of lies against innocent men, women and children. That is my evil act. I must atone, so I've travelled here to tell you what I know . . .'

'What you've said wouldn't help us. Or Jay.'

'Maybe not. But I have information that will help. If you do as I advise you will have a chance of stopping the suffering, the fear, the deaths.'

Victor still gazed drowsily at the Severn. In the river a shape swam beneath the surface. It seemed so ominous. A predatory shark? Or one of the old river gods? He rubbed his forehead. The heat in the room made him dizzy. He was thinking such strange, troubling thoughts.

Solomon continued in a calm tone. 'Imagine I'm here to warn you about an earthquake. You will respond with "there are no earthquakes in this part of the country, don't be ridiculous." Nevertheless, I'll explain as much as I can about Jay. On the surface you won't believe me, yet deep down I'm sure you will. Remember my words if Jay puts more lives in danger. Then maybe you will act on them and innocent people will be saved.'

Laura bit her lip. To Victor it seemed she was making a decision whether to step over a threshold. And once crossed, there would be no way back. This was one of those pivotal times. Like signing a death warrant. Or accepting the risk of dodging bullets in order to cross a battleground. A sudden resolve took hold of her. Nodding sharply, she said, 'OK, Solomon. Tell us what we need to do.'

'In most cultures there are legends of changelings. You know how it goes, a baby is born to a family. Then one morning the mother notices the baby is different. The eyes are a different colour. Maybe it doesn't cry any more but growls like an animal instead. The parents realize that during the night a demon, or troll, or some such sprite has stolen their baby and put one of their own offspring in its place. The family know they are cursed, but they continue to care for the demon child, even though it grows up to be ugly and wicked. Crops fail. Bad luck dogs them, but they're afraid to cast out the child in case they never get their own flesh and blood child back home again.'

'You're saying Jay is a changeling?'

Solomon didn't answer the question directly. 'Sometimes the demon child would be a changeling. Sometimes it would be a foundling. The family believe they are doing the decent thing by taking in an orphan child. Only it turns out to be the son or daughter of a devil. Whatever the details are of the adoption by the human family the evil foundling or changeling has a purpose. That purpose is to punish the family. Someone in the family might have sinned. That sinner might already be dead but when the world of magic is involved that doesn't matter. It's as if whoever has the sinner's blood is punished. So brothers, sisters and cousins suffer. Vengeance is visited upon those who share the wrongdoer's blood. The Cathdran believed in the Vengeance Child. If they lost a war they would conjure a foundling into their enemy's town to exact revenge. Whether you believe it is neither here or there, just as you might not believe in the story of Moses or reject the existence of heaven. My purpose is to tell you what I know. So I ask you to imagine that you are back on that ship, the *N'Taal*, as it breaks apart. You see the panic of the refugees. They know they will drown. Mothers cradle babies. Fathers weep in frustration at not being able to save their families. They have been hounded out of their homeland. When they sailed the Atlantic looking for a safe haven they were turned away. Not one nation helped them. As the vessel sinks, the men, women and children are crying, but the Cathdran are a fierce people. You can imagine as the water gushed in they all screamed – but this time it was a scream of fury. And as one they cursed the blood of my people, they cursed the blood of your people. As one they directed their anger at you and me, at all our people, at mankind. All those different individuals united in the moment they died to direct their collective willpower at us. To curse us, to wish that we suffer like they suffered. When the ship vanished underwater nothing remained. Except one life raft. In that raft was a child. He is the vessel of their fury. His purpose on earth is to inflict suffering. It doesn't matter to who. Because our elected governments did nothing to help Jay's people then we are all guilty of murder. At least in the eyes of the Cathdran.'

Victor realized his muscles had grown tense. A pain burned behind his eyes. Part of him wanted to tell Solomon to shut up, but a deeper, primeval part longed to know which weapon he could use against Jay. Again, he felt that current of unease as strange thoughts plagued him. There was an ominous sense that violence would erupt at any moment. For some reason he was gripped by the urge to yell. Then maybe lash out. Was that fear? He clenched his fist, trying to control his racing heartbeat.

Solomon wiped perspiration from his face. 'My mouth is so dry. It's hard to tell you this. It goes against my oath to uphold the law and protect the innocent.' He patted his neck with the tissue. It came back as a damp wad. Grimacing, he dropped it into the bin. 'The old remedies for dealing with a changeling or evil foundling are this. Expose the child to danger. In times gone by families would even lock the child in a hot oven . . . or put it in a barrel into which they'd pour water. Imagine those desperate men and women. They put the changeling in so much danger that they hope the demon parent will take pity on their offspring then snatch the child back.'

'Let me get this straight.' Victor ran his hand through his hair. 'You're saying that we put Jay in peril? We do something so bad to him that his life is put in danger?'

For once, Laura couldn't even bring herself to speak. She looked guilty at even hearing such a measure.

Solomon stood up. The man's hands were shaking. 'I told you that on one level you wouldn't believe me. Deep down, however, you do. If you have the courage to stop Jay causing any more deaths you will have to act. You must put the boy in so much danger – genuine danger, mind – that he is taken back to those who made him. I believe in God, I believe in heaven. I also believe that in the moment of their dying those hundreds of men, women and children aboard the *N'Taal* willed Jay into existence. A Vengeance Child. A boy who would have the power to send us, the guilty, mad with fear before destroying us. This kind of vengeance might be blind, but like a wounded lion lashing out to anyone who comes near it's still lethal.' Solomon glanced at the wall clock. 'I've done what my God wanted me to do. I've explained about Jay, I've advised you of a method to stop the killing. What you do with that advice is up to you.'

Solomon nodded to Laura and Victor, then he left the room. As for the pair they could only stare wordlessly at each other. For a moment Victor thought Laura would go after Solomon to harangue him. Instead, she went to Victor and made a whispered plea, 'Hold me.' When he put his arms around her she sighed as her head rested against her chest. But he saw the way she stared out at the river. She was thinking hard.

Solomon Constable left the hostel thirty minutes later. His clothes were now dry enough to wear, despite a little damp clinging to the shirt collar. The weight of that guilt he'd experienced for years slipped away. That sense of redemption made his step lighter. He felt such pure relief at completing his mission. Softly, he sang a hymn under his breath. 'Onward, Christian soldiers . . .' On his walk through the village to the beach, where he'd left the motor boat, he noticed that an outbreak of illness was taking hold. Men and women sat in their gardens, their heads in their hands, and the colourful fallout pooling on lawns and patios. Jay brought the plague, too. Then a Vengeance Child had many powers.

It was dusk when he reached the red motor boat pulled on to the pebbles. The sun glinted on its Perspex windshield.

Solomon eyed the river. 'Thank goodness there are no crocs or hippos. Especially hippos. I hate hippos.'

His heart still pounded. Telling the couple, and such a lovely couple, that they would have to act in an extreme way to preserve life was hard. He wondered if they would have the courage to do as he suggested. If anything, his heart clamoured even faster as he untied the rope from an old tree trunk lying in the mud. Nerves, he told himself. Is there any wonder? Sweat dribbled inside his shirt. His mouth tasted bad. The sooner I get away from this island the better, he thought. When the boat was afloat the current pulled it quickly downstream. Before he'd even started the motor it passed a headland. At the tip of that headland stood a young boy. One with elfin eyes. He stood, feet apart, completely motionless.

The man's heart lurched. He recognized the boy from the photographs his Internet searches had revealed. The boy watched him drift past. The ex-cop met his gaze. Inside his chest his heart went berserk.

'Solomon . . . Solomon . . . Solomon.'

Even though Solomon didn't hear the name he knew that Jay mouthed it over and over. The moment he managed to start the engine his heart rammed against his ribs with enough force to make him grunt. Then that fist-sized block of muscle that had driven blood through his veins for more than five decades stopped dead. Solomon Constable collapsed backward across the boat's seats. Sightless eyes gazed heavenward. Still hopeful, always hopeful, of ascending there when his day was done.

With no one to guide it, the boat surged down the estuary toward the ocean where it dwindled to a speck and eventually disappeared from human sight.

Eighteen

'Archer . . .'

'Go away.'

'Archer. I hurt people. I know that. I hurt the policeman today. He fell in the boat. The river took him out to sea.'

'Go away.'

'Archer, I'm frightened.'

'Why should I want to know that, Jay? Go tell Laura.'

Jay stood in Archer's bedroom at the farm. Archer had been in bed ten minutes when Jay appeared in the door. Archer hated Jay. He talked in that weird way again, sort of dull sounding, his arms hanging down all limp. When he told Jay to go back to his own room he didn't seem to hear, he just kept talking. Archer didn't want to hear. *What if he starts saying my name? Or if he takes me for a walk?* Archer remembered the last time with a shudder. The car in the cave-place . . . the dead woman in the back seat . . . how she'd got hold of him . . . then stuck the gold bracelet into his hand so hard that it hurt. Tears welled in Archer's eyes. *Jay's a witch. He does bad things to people. He's done bad things to me!* Jay took a zombie step into the room. Archer moaned in fear. He pulled the blanket up so only his eyes peered over the material.

'I don't want to hurt people, Archer. But there's this thing inside of me that makes me do it. It's like being hungry. You can't help it when you're hungry. Your stomach aches until you put food in it. This begins with me hurting inside. I know I start to look strange to people. I just keep staring and muttering and I don't move. You see, I've got the power to do bad things to people. But I try to make good things happen for them. If I concentrate really hard I can do nice things instead of bad things . . . or at least I try. Because sometimes it turns out wrong. I took Laura to see Tod Langdon, where he was locked up, but she became frightened. I thought Laura would be happy to see Tod again but it was nasty.'

'You made me go into that room with the car. There was something horrible inside it. It scared me, Jay, 'cos I thought the dead woman would kill me. That wasn't to make me happy it was to frighten me to death, you bloody witch.' Archer knew he risked provoking Jay, but the memory of the body in the car still tortured him. 'You did that to be evil to me, and I've done nothing bad to you, Jay.'

Jay continued in monotone. 'That wasn't meant to hurt you. I wanted to do a nice thing for Victor. Victor's OK. I like him. He worries about Ghorlan. I knew I could bring something back for him. The bracelet. You're going to give it to Victor.'

'No fear.' Archer buried his face in the blankets. Even looking at Jay made him feel sick with terror. He didn't want to be in the same house as him, only with everyone falling ill on the island he'd been forced to stay here with Jay. Laura was in the room down the hall. Victor had an apartment in a different building across the yard. *If Jay wants me to take the gold bracelet to Victor then he's dead wrong. Victor might have put the woman in the car. If he finds out I know about the body he'll put me in the car, too. For ever.* There was silence for a moment. Archer began to hope that Jay had gone. When he peered over the blankets he saw Jay had come closer so he could look right down at Archer. *Or do something awful to me.*

For a moment Jay did that zombie stare at Archer, then continued. 'Archer, this island has done something to me. My power is different here. I can make it do more. Something inside me wants to hurt you.'

Archer whimpered.

'It wants me to hurt you, Victor, Laura, Lou, Max, Trisha, Ben, Carol . . . and everyone on the island. It wants me to kill everyone I can. It's what I'm supposed to do. But this island is strong. It's made me stronger too. I'm changing. I feel different inside. If I try as hard as I can I'll be good.' His eyes shone in the gloom. 'Tonight I'm going to do magic. I'll make nice things happen for everyone.'

Jay wants everyone to be happy. That night he went across the island. He longed to help people, not hurt them. So he strived to make wishes come true. Of course, everyone whose wish came true the night the epidemic took hold blamed it on the fever. They insisted they dreamt it. But the scars they received, both inside and out, told a different story. Because sometimes what you wish for can so easily become your curse.

'You're getting cold. Come back to bed.'

The church clock chimed midnight. Tonya Fletcher continued to stare out of the window, hardly daring to believe her eyes. Her naked body rashed with the faint puckering of gooseflesh.

'See? You're cold,' said her husband. 'Aren't we going to finish what we started downstairs?'

Tonya shivered. That wasn't the cool air. She shivered because she saw something that excited her.

Richard sat up in bed. 'What's out there?'

'Oh, it's nothing.' Don't come to the window, she thought. If you look you'll spoil it . . . like you've managed to spoil everything else.

He laughed. 'It must be an interesting *nothing*. You can't take your eyes off it.' He swung his legs out of bed. 'Are you going to let me see, too?'

Tonya hid the powerful emotion that must show on her face by keeping her face to the blind. 'It's the Saban. They're back in the street again.'

Richard smiled. The foreplay had put him in a good mood. 'You know what they say? When the deer come into the village then miracles happen.'

'I don't see any miracles yet,' she lied. 'Just a bunch of animals munching flower beds.'

'Speaking of munching . . .' He patted the mattress.

Tonya Fletcher continued to look out of the window. In the moonlight she saw about twenty of the Saban Deer. A little bigger than Labrador dogs, they were moving slowly along Main Street; they resembled a dark stain seeping over the road. The peculiar sight that first caught her attention wasn't the rare appearance of the Saban in the village, but that a boy stood down in the garden. He gazed up at her as she'd gone to the window just moments ago. Aged about eleven, he had large almond-shaped eyes. The way they caught the moonlight in such an uncanny way had held her attention. Tonya saw him mouth a word as he locked his eyes on hers. At that instant she felt such a tug of vertigo she thought she'd tumble forward out of the window. Then she saw an impossible sight. Andrew sat astride his motorbike in the middle of the deer herd. There, her first love gazed up at her. It was just the same as when they'd dated each other. Andrew would arrive on the motorbike, then wait patiently until she looked out of her bedroom window back at her parents' home. Her heart would leap with excitement when she saw his face. Then she'd hold up three fingers. *I'll be down in three minutes.* One minute to change. One minute to apply lipstick, spray perfume. One minute to brush her hair. Then she'd dash downstairs with a hurried, 'Mum, I'm going out. See you later.' Seconds later, she'd kiss Andrew – a heartfelt kiss. Then she'd swing her leg over the

pillion, pull on the helmet that he held for her and . . . whoosh
. . . they'd roar away through the suburbs.

But here there were no city suburbs. Her parents were long dead.
She'd not seen Andrew in twenty years. Yet all those issues she should
be considering rationally evaporated. The conundrum of the past
suddenly gatecrashing the present was blocked by the sheer pulse-
racing excitement of seeing twenty-year-old Andrew Derby waiting
astride his BMW bike. Her heart filled with a warm tide of pure
love for the man again. Other than the child there was no one else
about. Only her first boyfriend sat astride the motorbike as deer
ambled by them. Normally, they were so shy they'd flee at even a
glimpse of a human. Tonight they were unperturbed. As the fable
goes: if the Saban enter the village they bring miracles on their
horns. Tonya smiled down at Andrew. He returned it with a heart-
warming grin of his own. As always, still so completely patient. He'd
wait hours for her without a word of complaint.

'Tonya, I'm jealous. You've found something more fascinating than
me.' Richard walked toward the window, clearly intrigued by what
fascinated her.

'The deer?' Her mind was racing. 'Oh, they've gone now.'

'But what are you looking at?' He closed in on the window.

She gave him a smouldering look. 'I'm looking at you, handsome.'
*God, did that sound false or what? But whatever you do, don't let
Richard see Andrew.* Despite the impossible scene outside, and all the
questions that threatened to burst her bubble of happiness like 'how
can Andrew be on the island?' and 'why hasn't he aged in the last
twenty years?' she fiercely suppressed any doubt. Come to that, she
crushed rational thought entirely. Seeing Andrew out there on the
bike, just like old times again, had gifted her the happiest moment
in years. *If Richard sees Andrew everything will be spoilt.* As Andrew
smiled she held up three fingers. *Give me three minutes.*

'If those animals become a pest they'll have to put cattle grids
in the roads,' Richard said as he reached out to pull back the blind.

Before he could look out and ruin everything Tonya turned to
him. With her mouth on his she desperately pushed him back to the
bed. Breaking the kiss, she panted, 'I thought we were going to
finish what we started?' For a moment she feared Richard would
insist on looking out. However, the rub of her hand soon aroused
him enough not to give a damn if even the Welsh national choir
was marching down the street, singing at the tops of their voices.
With a grunt he settled back on to the bed. Tonya glanced at the

clock. Three minutes past midnight. Richard stroked her nipples. They were still hard from the attack of goosebumps when she saw Andrew. Now she knew what she must do. Before her husband could roll his masculine weight on to her she sat astride him, her inner thighs clamping against his hips. Quickly, she positioned herself so she could slide on to him. She needed to control the pace of sex tonight. The sooner this miserable, life-deadening man climaxed, the sooner she could leave the house.

Tonya rocked against him hard. She made all the right noises. She moaned when he kneaded her breasts. When he came with that pretend roar of his that normally annoyed the hell out of her, she closed her eyes in bliss as she pictured Andrew waiting so patiently for her. In twenty seconds Richard had turned over. Soon he began to snore, his legs twitching every now and again. Tonya didn't want to hurt the miracle by thinking it through in a logical way. In a silent whirlwind of activity she slipped on her jeans, zipped shut a pink leather jacket over her naked top half, applied lipstick, added a spray of perfume, then brushed her hair. So, it had been more than three minutes. But then good things take a little longer.

Elsewhere on Siluria Jay visited more residents. A bright moon turned the River Severn to liquid silver. Trees on the island were hunched beast-like shapes that seemed to gather pools of moon shadow to them. Nearly all the houses lay in darkness. Jay, the boy with the elfin face, reached into these quiet homes like a child reaching into boxes full of delicate butterflies. He tried so hard to do the right thing and not cause damage, but like a child touching fragile wings his innocent intervention wreaked an ugly carnage.

When Gerald Moore closed the mirrored door of the bathroom cabinet he saw the boy in the reflection. At seventy-five, Gerald still had pinpoint sharp vision. *So what on earth's a child doing in my bathroom at midnight? Such an odd-looking boy, too. Surely, I've never seen anyone with eyes as large as that, have I?*

As Gerald turned round he was struck by vertigo. Just for an instant he seemed to be in a hospital room and in his bathroom simultaneously. *And the symptoms of senile dementia are?* His attempt to make light of an increasingly disturbing vision. The boy had vanished. Instead, his wife stood there in the centre of an otherwise empty hospital room. She was connected to a machine by tubes that pumped vivid red fluids into her neck.

'Lydia?' He stared. There was a youthful freshness about her. Since his wife died three years ago he always pictured her as a young woman. Not the exhausted figure that had lain as limp as an empty nightdress on the bed. 'Lydia, you know this isn't right. You mustn't come back here.'

Gerald swayed as she smiled warmly. Around him the walls fluctuated between those of his bathroom and the hospital room where he held his wife's hand as she died. By now she looked all of twenty-five.

Brightly, she announced, 'Darling, I'm better now. I wanted to make you happy by showing you how well I am.'

'The symptoms of dementia are . . .' He swallowed. 'Damn, I can't remember what the symptoms of dementia are.'

'Now, Gerald . . .' Crimson fluids raced through the transparent tubes into her neck. 'I know you yearned with all your heart that I could be unhooked from this awful machine, which distressed you so much. And for me to say with a big, bright smile, "Look, Gerald, I'm all better." You pictured me saying that, didn't you?'

He groaned. 'More times than you can imagine.'

'Well, then, look, Gerald, I'm all better.'

He whispered, 'You're not, my dear. Your heart muscle wasted away. The doctors couldn't do anything. I wished they could – oh, how hard I wished.'

'Your wishes have come true.' Vivacious, she clasped her hands together. 'Aren't you pleased?'

'You are dead, Lydia. I've come to terms with that. Now, I'm either dreaming or my mind has gone.'

She reached up, grabbed the tubes that carried fluid into her neck, and pulled. 'Just as you wished for. I don't need these any more.'

In the background the boy with the large eyes watched them. Gerald felt he'd seen him somewhere before. The school trip to the island? Or the party from Badsworth Lodge? With a sucking sound the plastic tubes parted from the incision in his wife's neck.

He shook his head. 'Lydia, what's dead is dead. Despite what I wished for, you mustn't come back to me.'

'I thought I could make you happy for one last time before you die.'

Gerald frowned. The voice wasn't his wife's. It seemed to come from the boy, standing there in the shadows.

Then his wife's voice returned with the clarity of a bell. 'Gerald, you asked about my heart. There's nothing to worry about. Look.'

Then, as if she lifted a T-shirt from the bottom by its hem to show her bare chest, Lydia pinched her skin on her midriff then raised it. Up over her bare ribs. Then she parted the bones like she was opening a jacket. It exposed a beating heart: fresh, healthy and red from which veins sprang. 'Look,' she purred. 'Good as new.'

Gerald recoiled. His heel caught the corner of the bathtub. When he slammed down backwards the top half of his head crunched against the china lavatory bowl with so much force both ceramic and bone shattered. He'd always joked that he'd hate to be found dead in the bathroom. Now there was nothing he could do to change just that.

Tonya Fletcher wrapped her arms round the leather-clad torso of Andrew. The island lanes were a blur. Andrew wove the machine skilfully through the twists and turns. The wind blew through her hair. She knew she should have donned a helmet but tonight she didn't care. She was blissfully happy. In fact, so happy she refused to question the reality of the situation. Her old boyfriend was back. They were riding his bike just like when they were twenty years old. That's all that mattered. Life blazed through her with all that wonderful excitement she'd not felt in a long time.

'I love you,' she shouted over the roar of the motorbike. 'I love you! And I'm never going back there! This time we're staying together for ever and ever!'

Now Cynthia Huddleston was confined to a wheelchair she wished she could go swimming with her school friends in Horseshoe Bay again. As the hoot of an owl sounded on the night air she found herself standing ankle deep in the river.

'Horseshoe Bay,' she murmured in wonder.

Moonlight twinkled on waves as the tide drew the waters down to the sea. Fallen branches from upstream raced by. An otter surged with the rapid current, then let itself enjoy the high-speed ride. Nearby, a boy regarded her with an air of expectation.

He expects me to speak, so I will. 'I am eighty-five years old. My dearest wish is to swim with my friends again.' Cynthia frowned at her legs. 'Of course, I can't really be here. For one I can't walk. Oh, well, at my age if one experiences a dream as authentic as this one, I should make the most of it.' In the moonlit waters she saw a pair of fifteen-year-old girls laughing and splashing one another. 'Joan. Harriet. Wait for me!' Cynthia hurried toward her old friends. Within five paces the water reached her waist. 'So refreshing,' she said, surprised, 'and so unlike a dream.' After another five paces the water supported her body. Another step deeper, the current caught hold and rushed her away into the night.

'I wish my uncle would stop looking at me.' The thirteen-year-old island girl confided in the boy who found her hiding in the barn. 'I know he watches me through the keyhole in the bathroom door.' Chelsea shuddered. 'Lately he's come into my bedroom to stare once he thinks I'm asleep.' Her eyes moistened. 'He scares me. I know he wants to do something wrong.' The church clock struck the half hour. 'He'll be coming home now. I'll hide in here until he's gone to sleep.' The shudder ran through her again. 'I just wish he'd stop looking at me.'

The door of the barn banged.

'Chelsea!' Her uncle's soused voice echoed from the walls. 'Chelsea, stop running away from me. I just want to talk to you.' A man lumbered through the barn. Strangely, he seemed to be pursuing a figure she couldn't see in the gloom. And he'd mistaken that figure for her. 'Chelsea, come here. I need to talk!' He lurched past where she hid behind the bales of straw. She saw those gleaming eyes of his that always made a point of fixing on her these days. That stare was like being touched by slimy hands. 'Chelsea. There's something on my mind.' He lumbered to where implements lay on racks at the far end of the barn. And just as he did seem to see *a* Chelsea running from him he appeared unable to see those racks of farming tools. For the first time those hard, gleaming eyes of his let him down. He raced full pelt into a pitchfork that jutted from the rack. Its two prongs found his eyes with uncanny accuracy.

By the time he'd staggered, screaming, into the farmyard Chelsea realized those eyes would stare at her no more.

As Tonya rode pillion behind Andrew, her breasts pressing luxuriously against his back, she glimpsed many a strange sight. Despite it being after midnight dozens of people were out walking. Most were in their nightclothes. A few even gleamed nude in the moonlight. *When the Saban come to town they bring miracles on their horns. These people are having their wishes granted.*

Being so close to her first love again made her so relaxed she found herself slipping into a warm, drowsy state as he powered along the island's narrow lanes. She saw Bessie Gwyllam dressed in white

pyjamas. Tonya Fletcher knew that Bessie had been searching for
her late father's will for ten years. The woman was adamant one
existed. Until she found it she couldn't prove that the house she
lived in was really hers. For the past decade she'd been forced to
pay her half-sister rent for the property. Bessie believed a will would
place the ownership of her home securely in her hands. Then she
could tell her detested half-sister to go to hell. From the back of
the motorbike Tonya saw Bessie dancing on the lawn in the moonlight. In her hand was a sealed envelope, no doubt covered with
fluffy cobwebs from being hidden away. And no doubt the envelope would bear in grave black print: Last Will and Testament of
Robert Allen Gwyllam.

Though the words were lost in the engine's roar, Tonya called
out joyously. 'It really is a night for miracles. We're all having our
wishes granted.' She patted Andrew's firm back. 'Look at Mr Henry.
He convinced himself there's a box of gold coins buried under the
beach. Now he's going to find it.' Old Mr Henry, with a coat over
his pyjamas, a shovel in one hand, and a lantern in the other, followed
a boy down to the shore. It was the same boy she'd seen before
with the almond-shaped eyes.

Tonya luxuriated in being so close to Andrew once more. All
those thousands of times she'd thought, I wish I was back with
Andrew Derby again . . . Tonya blinked. She realized the sound of
the motorbike's engine had vanished. She blinked again. The bike
had gone. And Andrew, too. For some reason she stood in a garden,
one overgrown with nettles and brambles. Right in front of her was
a window to a living room. A man had slumped in an armchair
with a bottle of vodka. He was as untidy as the lousy room. Clothes
dishevelled, hair stuck up in greasy spikes from being unwashed for
so long. Stubble covered his blotchy jaw.

Tonya noticed a slight figure in the moonlight beside her.

'It's you again,' she said to the boy. 'You're doing this, aren't you?
You're making everyone's wishes come true.' A chill spread through
her. 'So why are you showing me this? Where's Andrew?'

The boy said nothing. In the moonlight his eyes appeared to burn
with an eerie fire. A dangerous fire that could cause untold harm.

Tonya shivered. 'I know you've brought me here. Just like you
found Mr Henry's treasure for him, and you showed Bessie Gwyllam
where to find her father's will.'

'I took them for a walk,' murmured the boy. His expressionless
face gleamed with perspiration. 'Just a little walk.'

'You made their dreams come true.'

'I can do that. But it's not my fault that it goes wrong for them. Miss Gwyllam's crying. She found a letter that gives the house to her sister. Mr Henry dug the hole in the beach. He found a box full of money, then thought there'd be another one further down, so he wouldn't stop digging. The sides of the hole were all wet and sloppy. They fell on him. He can't get out.'

A flood of shivers cascaded down her spine. 'But you did a good thing for me. You brought Andrew back to me, didn't you?'

'Yes, I did.' A powerful emotion worked inside the boy but his expression didn't so much as flicker. It was all in his eyes.

With a growing sense of dread Tonya held on to her lovely miracle. Andrew was back. She'd leave Richard. Andrew would love her all over again. Memories of those sex-filled nights with her first boyfriend made her heart beat faster. Think about all those soft kisses. Focus on those and this ominous sense of dread will go.

Forcing a smile, she said, 'So, what have you done with Andrew?'

The boy glanced toward the window.

Tonya found herself looking at the shambles of a room. The man there sucked on the vodka bottle. 'No, don't you dare. That's not Andrew. He's younger than that, he's . . .' *But what's the use?* Disappointment plunged through her. *Of course the man is Andrew. It's twenty years since I've seen him.* She regarded the drunken wreck of a forty-year-old Andrew Derby. She recognized the tattoo: his initials entwined with hers on the back of the paw that held the booze. He'd gone crazy with the tattoos. Red lines like badly drawn serpents entwined his bare arm.

'Why did you show me Andrew like this?'

The boy's eyes burned.

'What a cruel . . . *monstrous* thing to do. Do you know the harm you've caused?' Tears rolled down her face. 'I wanted to remember Andrew as he was. Did you do it to punish me? Because I had this rose-tinted memory of him? So now you hurt me by showing him as a middle-aged piss artist!' Anger made her voice rise. 'My husband would love this, you know. Seeing me cry like a baby because yet another dream I had has been ripped to shreds.' Bunching her fists, she glared back through the window. The bloated alcoholic slumped in his chair. A burned-out loser that nobody loved. So what happened to the wife? Probably fled the marital home when his boozing got out of control. Tonya searched the figure for some hint that the old Andrew remained. The fine line of Andrew's jaw that made him so handsome had degenerated into hanging jowl. The nose had become blotchy. Only his grey eyes hadn't aged. Despite the vodka binges, they were still clear. But what possessed him to have those weird serpent tattoos done? Only when she looked again she realized they weren't tattoos. They were streaks of red . . . some liquid, maybe. She moved closer to the glass so she could see the arms more clearly in the light of the table lamp.

Tonya caught her breath. They weren't tattoos at all. Those red streaks were trickles of blood. Each time he sucked on the bottle he smudged the marks. Had he cut himself? She almost pressed her nose to the pane so she could examine the arm as he sat there. Even though blood smeared his skin, with more staining his jeans, she could see no wound. Her gaze travelled round the room's interior. Magazines littered the sofa. In the doorway were a pile of clothes. A blaze of wet crimson besmeared the white-painted door from the living room to the hallway.

Wait . . . She rewound back to the clothes on the floor. There was more than a sweater and a skirt there. In the ruffled garments lay a figure. Tonya saw blonde hair, a face . . . oh God, just part of a face. Half of it had been destroyed. Gashes in the flesh leaked blood on to the carpet. While in a growing pool of crimson lay a hammer.

'Is this real?' The words almost choked her as she asked the boy the question. 'Are you showing me the night when Andrew killed his wife?'

The boy didn't answer.

'Talk to me, you little monster.' In frustration she smacked her hands against the window.

Instantly, her former lover turned to the window. When he saw what would be, to him, a stranger peering at the scene of the crime, he began to move. Something shrivelled inside of her. Because with a furious speed he snatched the hammer from the pool of blood, then ran over the corpse of the woman to the door.

'What have you done?' she hissed at the boy. 'In God's name what have you done?'

Clouds had obscured the moon by the time she started to run. But where could she go? The house door clattered open. A drumming of feet. Tonya fled along an overgrown path that smelt of mushrooms. A pungent smell that made her want to gag. Now she did question the reality of this. Yes, it would be a dream; that's all. 'So wake up, Tonya, wake up!' She blundered through straggly bushes. The wild growth of lawn tugged at her feet, slowing her.

'Come back here,' Andrew barked. 'I want to know what you're doing here.' His heavy body surged through the undergrowth. 'Wait till I get my hands on you.'

Tonya wanted to wake up. She'd be next to her husband again. Richard wasn't so bad, was he? They'd had fifteen years together that had been safe, stable.

'Come here, you bitch.'

The vegetation closed in on her. Branches had tangled together so she couldn't get through. The last of the moonlight had gone. She struggled in utter darkness. A hand gripped the collar of her leather jacket. The first blow that fell didn't hurt. In fact, she found herself remembering what a wise soul had once warned: '*Be careful what you wish for.*'

In a gloating voice her first love purred, 'Gotcha.'

Andrew shoved Tonya to the ground. The hammer head glinted above her. *Dying like this won't be painful.* She wished with all her heart that would be the case. Only this time Jay did not grant her that one last wish.

Nineteen

The morning after the night Jay had tried so hard to make the islanders' wishes come true, Victor, Laura, and the still-healthy volunteers, emerged from the meeting at the doctor's surgery to find an astonishing sight.

Victor estimated around fifty men and women of all ages shuffled into the square near the church. Some people wore assorted nightwear. A few were clothed after a fashion in mismatching garments. At least three wore nothing but dazed expressions. The day had begun under a cloud, a cool breeze jetted from the river. In his fleece Victor felt the chill. These people would end up with hypothermia.

A silver-haired man who'd been at the doctor's emergency meeting watched his neighbours walking by. 'It's like the Village of the Damned,' he breathed.

Victor appreciated the spirit of the reference, even if it wasn't accurate. It really did look as if the villagers were bewitched in some way; they shuffled like they were sleepwalking.

Laura hurried to the nearest. A woman of around thirty in a flimsy nightdress. Her feet were bare; one toenail bloody from stubbing it during this weird stroll through the village. 'Madam, can you hear me? Can you tell me your name?'

'Hmm?' She appeared to be distracted by her own thoughts.

'Your name?'

The woman's face had frozen into an expression that suggested both delight and bewilderment. 'I went for a walk on the beach with him last night. The boy took me to him . . . sunny day at midnight. Mac brought a picnic. He liked chocolate cake and cream.'

Laura rested her hand against the woman's face. 'Just as I thought. Burning up.'

'The boy took me to Mac,' insisted the woman. 'It's marvellous what they can do these days. Because Mac died six years ago. That factory accident. Took his hands right off. Both of them. So how could he pick up the cake?'

Laura turned to Victor. 'We've got to get everyone indoors.'

Victor took the arm of an elderly man who was saying, 'I went back to school again. We played football in the field. I haven't been so happy since . . . oh, I can't remember when.'

'Zombies,' intoned the silver-haired volunteer. 'Just like zombies.'

Laura snapped, 'It's this infection. It's pushing their temperature up so high they're hallucinating.'

The old man beamed. 'The boy took me back to school. He said to me, "Come on, we'll go for a little walk."'

At this Laura shot Victor a telling look, and mouthed, 'Jay.'

The man chuckled as he allowed himself to be led by Victor to a cottage. 'I saw the headmaster again. Old Master Grice. If I'm ninety he must be a hundred and fifty years old. He still chased us with his cane. Swish, swosh, swish.'

Victor could feel the heat of the fever through the man's pyjama sleeve. Glancing back, he noticed Mayor Wilkes leave the surgery with Dr Nazra beside him. Neither was happy with the other's company.

Wilkes stormed, 'Look at these bloody people, they're wandering the streets like a herd of stunned mules. Now's the time to bring in outside help.'

The doctor tried to be patient. 'Mayor Wilkes, there are three villages on the mainland affected with the virus. Like them we're obliged to quarantine ourselves.'

'And fend for ourselves? From this plague?'

'There is no plague, Mayor. The disease has yet to be identified, but it's probably just a mutated version of gastric flu. People will experience high fever and vomiting for a few days, then it will pass. The health authority is keen to contain the illness where it possibly can. It should burn itself out within a week.'

'I have business meetings. I can't sit about, watching the whole place go insane.' Wilkes back-stepped from an elderly woman in a dressing gown. She appeared to be plucking objects out of the sky. The mayor barked, 'Mrs Fielding, will you get yourself back home? Don't you see, you're making a fool of yourself!'

'Look at all these gold butterflies, they are all around you. I'm taking some home to Daddy.'

'Good grief.' With a face like thunder, Wilkes stormed away.

Dr Nazra called after him, 'We need every able-bodied person we can muster. Can you volunteer your time, sir?'

Victor was sure that Mayor Wilkes muttered, 'In your dreams,' before shouting, 'Too busy. Far too busy!'

'What a charming man,' Laura said to Victor.

The doctor bustled round. 'Make sure they all get home as quickly as you can. The cold won't be doing them any good. Here.' He handed Victor a sheaf of papers. 'These are dos and don'ts for the patients. They should avoid dairy products but drink plenty of water. Go on ahead, please, and leave one sheet by the bed of each patient, or with an occupant of their home, if there is one. Let those who care for the sick know that they must help get fluids inside of them. Water is best.' He gestured to the silver-haired man who'd made the Village of the Damned comment. 'Mr Lees, you take Victor's patient so he can go ahead and distribute the leaflets.'

Victor whispered to Laura, 'When you get a break come up to the farm. I'll make lunch.'

'Realistically, by the time we finish here it might be supper.'

He smiled. 'Supper it is then.' Then he added seriously, 'You heard it, too, some of these people say that a boy took them to meet friends and family that died years ago.'

Laura nodded, her face grave. 'It's time to talk about Jay.'

'You know what Solomon told us we must do?'

Laura started to reply, but the man who'd made the crack about the Village of the Damned sat down on a wall. 'I don't feel so good myself now,' he said. Then his shoulders heaved.

Laura grimaced. 'We'll talk later, Victor.'

Later would have to be a lot later, Victor decided by midday. He'd distributed leaflets giving advice on dealing with the infection. Clearly, however, two-thirds of the island were down with the illness. Where houses waited the return of the wandering occupants, under the guidance of the volunteers, he left leaflets on bedside cabinets along with jugs of water and a cup. He also checked properties belonging to those who'd wandered off to make sure stoves or electrical appliances hadn't been left on that might become dangerous. Though the work kept him busy he still replayed what the African policeman had told him. All of it troubled him. Not just the part about Jay, either. True, Victor long suspected Mayor Wilkes of shady dealings. Solomon had shrewdly made a compelling deduction about Wilkes' methods. Then there'd been the comment about the wedding ring. Victor glanced at his left hand. During the day he didn't wear the ring that Ghorlan had given him. A casual observer wouldn't notice the slight groove in his otherwise unmarked skin but sharp-eyed Solomon Constable had spotted a slight indentation. A year after Ghorlan had vanished into the river he'd stopped wearing the ring by day, but every night he slipped it on before going to sleep.

'So,' he murmured, heading for the next house. 'Solomon told you how to deal with Jay. Do you act on that information? Ignore it? Or do you meet this head on and damn the consequences?'

By five that afternoon Victor could take a long-needed break. For once his charges were human ones, not the island's wildlife. He'd checked in with Lou. Fortunately, she was fine, as were the children from Badsworth Lodge. None of them had come down with the bug, but some of the people providing accommodation for the children were sick, so Lou had brought three children up to White Cross Farm where there were spare rooms. Victor was relieved to see that his sister seemed to be over the worst; what's more, she hadn't been one of the zombie-like wanderers. With Laura still down in the village he grabbed a hot shower then decided to spend twenty minutes at the computer. What Solomon had told Victor about Mayor Wilkes had intrigued him so he decided to fish for some facts of his own in the Internet search engines of the world.

It's amazing what you can find out about people on the Internet, he mused. Just enter their name into the search engine. You can even find out details of their ancestors, not to mention photos, videos, resumes. You name it. It can have consequences though. Once he'd searched under his own name. There were still filed reports about not only his conservation work on the island but how the river took Ghorlan. Reporters had devoted a lot of text to the lovely young bride who'd walked down to the shore one evening. Then never returned.

Victor rubbed the groove on his wedding finger before snapping out of his darkening mood. Quickly he tapped at the computer's keyboard, entering 'Mayor Wilkes Siluria business deals'. As Solomon had told him, Wilkes kept himself at arm's length even from wholly innocuous commercial deals. Victor had to admit that suggested habitual secrecy; as if it was second nature for Wilkes to conceal even innocent projects. Victor typed: 'Mayor Wilkes ex-prisoner rehabilitation'. Now, a blizzard of websites filled the result's page. Even though many a business in nearby towns had only a tenuous link with Wilkes he seemed to be instrumental in finding employment for men who'd recently served prison sentences. These were companies that did everything from running fleets of ice-cream vans to construction to road haulage to crop picking. The picture painted by the media of Mayor Wilkes was of a charitable man, who believed in giving former lawbreakers a second chance. Then, when in public, he adopted an extremely charming persona. Victor, however, knew the man behind the affable mask.

The African policeman had told Victor such ex-con employees would be loyal, for the simple reason they'd not find well-paid work elsewhere. What's more Solomon had said, 'They might even help Mayor Wilkes bury his secrets, too. And men who build bridges can bury secrets very deeply indeed.' What Solomon had told Victor helped the jigsaw pieces click into place. Suddenly, Victor saw the whole picture. Wilkes sat like a spider in the middle of his web. The different strands were the different companies he ran through puppet figures. In every company would be a former prison inmate, who'd turn a blind eye when necessary, or bend the rules or even dig a hole to bury one of Mayor Wilkes' mistakes. Perhaps even a literal hole in the earth if need be. Not that all ex-convicts would voluntarily return to a life of crime, but by then they were stuck in the web that Wilkes had spun. Victor gazed out of the window as the low sun turned the river a copper colour. A flock of Saban Deer ambled on to the beach to feed on kelp. As he watched the animals nibble the salty, brown fronds he cast his mind back to the many building projects on the island.

'So just what have you managed to bury here?' He recalled renovation works at the castle. There were thousands of tons of rock tipped on to the northern tip of the island to prevent erosion. But also a convenient dumping ground for Mayor Wilkes' problems. Almost flippantly Victor asked himself, 'So is that where the bodies are buried?'

Victor typed another name into the computer: Jay Summer. This yielded a truly amazing crop of results. Thousands of them. Victor hadn't appreciated what a huge story it had been at the time. He flicked through newspaper reports from all over the world: *Miracle Moses Child. Sole survivor plucked from shark-infested sea. One lives out of hundreds. Refugee ship that died of shame.* There were plenty of photographs of Jay when he was four years old. That fragile elfin face with the large eyes was just the same. Nations blamed each other for turning the rusty tub of a boat away from ports. Photographs of the thing, even weeks before it sank, revealed a ruin of a vessel that listed to one side. After the initial splurge of rescue reports the media were clearly still fascinated by Jay. Efforts to track surviving relatives in Africa drew a blank. He was the miracle boy who'd appeared floating Moses-like in his basket, albeit an inflatable one.

Victor zipped through dozens of reports at random. When he

saw a news story online with a photograph of an older Jay Summer he stopped. His heart gave an uncomfortable lurch in his chest. The newspaper carried a huge black headline: MIRACLE MOSES CHILD CHEATS DEATH AGAIN. The photograph was of Jay aged seven. Victor read on.

> Yesterday the sole survivor of the *N'Taal* disaster survived yet another tragedy. Neighbours woke to find the house of the Clancy family to be in the grip of an inferno that tore through rooms in minutes. Jay Summer, who'd survived alone in shark-infested seas, was found in the garden unscathed. All four members of the Clancy family perished in the flames. Jay had been their foster child for six weeks.

A report five days later quoted the police emphatically ruling Jay out from any involvement in the fire. The blaze had started in the basement when a faulty boiler had caused a gas pipe to heat up until it exploded with enough ferocity to demolish the house internally. Yet the reporter also quoted the child of a neighbour who claimed Jay had spoken to her the day before the fire.

> Alyssa Bartley, 13, told our reporter that Jay had tearfully made this confession: 'They've got to die. You've all got to die for what you did to the ship. I've been put on earth to get revenge.' Police maintain that this alleged statement made by seven-year-old Jay Summer cannot be corroborated.

'Good God,' Victor breathed. 'Death and disaster follows you around, doesn't it?'

'What's that?'

Startled, Victor turned in his chair to see Laura Parris standing in the doorway.

'You were miles away. You must have found something fascinating.'

'Oh, this?' Victor switched off the computer so Laura wouldn't see Jay's picture. 'It was something that Solomon said about Mayor Wilkes. I thought I'd do some research on our illustrious politician.' He looked closely at Laura. 'You look exhausted. Grab a seat. I'll get you a drink.'

'Thanks. Sorry about just appearing at your apartment like this. Your sister told me to come straight up.'

'You're always welcome.'

'Am I?'

'Sure, we're partners in adversity now.' He headed for the kitchen area at the corner of the room. 'Coffee, or something stronger?'

'Coffee for now, but I'll take you up on "stronger" later.'

'Everything under control in the village? You've rounded the wanderers up?'

She dismissed his question quickly. 'It's fine now.' Something more important demanded their attention now. 'Victor, I need to talk to you.'

'I know. I've been thinking about Jay non-stop.'

'There's Jay. Absolutely. But there's an important question I have to ask you, Victor.'

Twenty

Victor put the kettle on to boil. 'You want to ask me a question?'

Laura sat down on the sofa. 'Can you guess why?'

Victor was mystified. Laura's attractive face was unreadable. It seemed as if she had some secret of her own to reveal. He spooned coffee into a pair of mugs. 'OK, fire away.'

'We find ourselves in this situation, but we don't know one another, do we?'

'My name's Victor Brodman, age thirty-five, the island ranger. I live here, the former chauffeur's apartment at White Lodge Farm, Siluria.'

'Great, just great.' Laura spoke politely. 'You've given me information I could find in one of your educational handouts.'

'Am I missing something?' He frowned.

'My name is Laura Parris. My parents ran a care home for the elderly. When I was seven I found one of the residents, a man of eighty, lying dead in the greenhouse. He told me often that he loved the smell of tomato plants. The day I found him he'd taken a drug overdose. I've never told anyone this before outside my family. My first boyfriend liked to massage oil into my breasts as he made love. He was horrified when I suggested oral sex might be nice. When—'

'Whoa, Laura. Why on earth are you telling me this?'

'When I qualified as a nurse I got the job of preparing corpses before they went to the morgue. I used to go back to the nurses' accommodation block every night and wondered how I could deal with it. You know, moving the arms and legs of dead people like they were just the plastic limbs of a doll. Those noises they made after death? They made you want to rip your own ears off. I started to drink vodka. It works best with sugary drinks. Pow! A liquid right hook. But you know how I stopped going mad from handling dead men and women? Like pushing my fingers into mouths to pull out their false teeth? You know how, Victor? I discovered a taste for erotica. I read sex stories in magazines. Then I graduated to reading erotic novels. I haven't told anyone else about that, either. No . . . don't make the coffee yet. I want you to listen.' She spoke in a cool, purposeful way. 'Reading about people having sex – full penetration, lots of different positions – it all helped. People enjoying the act of creating life chased away this fog of death that surrounded me. Before that I'd look into a mirror, then all those dead faces, with staring eyes and blue lips, would flow through my reflection. Reminding me I'm mortal, that we all die anyway.' She took a breath. 'I haven't told anyone else this either: Before I met you I hadn't had sex for fifteen months.'

'Oh.' Victor didn't know what to say.

'There, I've put my trust in you with all these facts.' She tilted her head. 'You've given me your biographical details that appear on the handout. Funny that, hmm?'

'It's been a difficult couple of days.'

'Difficult in what? About Jay or what Solomon told us? Or difficult that you haven't been able to give me even one sentence about what attracted you to me? Or that we made love, or maybe it was just sex? I don't sleep around, Victor. But you've made me feel disposable. Now you expect me to trust you with everything I know about Jay, or what *we* should do with him, or *to* him when he's my responsibility. I don't even know you, Victor. You know nothing about me. Even though you took a heck of a lot of pleasure in screwing me.'

'Hey, that's not fair. We haven't had time to—'

'What was wrong with making a time just to say you feel something for me, and that being in bed with me was at least OK.'

'Laura—'

'You've made me feel like a piece of gum that's had the flavour chewed out.'

'Laura, you're wrong about that. You're wrong to take this attitude, too.'

'I thought you'd repressed all memory of us being together.'

'Laura, you're exhausted . . .'

'I'm angry. Incredibly angry. You don't want to even make a start about discussing us.'

Victor shoved the cups into the sink. 'You better go back to your room.'

'I trusted you. I came here tonight to see if there's the start of a relationship we could develop. But you've built this great big wall around Victor Brodman – no one can see the real man. What we get is an island ranger, with a sunny disposition, but with less heart than one of those little lizards you stand guard over here.'

'Laura, this isn't—'

'Working. You're so dead right.'

'Laura—'

'Good night, Victor. I hope you're so damn well pleased with yourself.'

She left without slamming the door. For some reason that sudden silence was an even more eloquent expression of her contempt for him than words or noise ever could be.

Twenty-One

Victor opened his eyes. Far away the church clock struck two in the morning. He lay there in the darkness as echoes of the final chime lingered on the warm air. A moment later a human voice called his name to the rhythm of the bell's chime. 'Victor . . . Victor . . . Victor . . .' Rather than sound it seemed a ghost of a sound.

Victor sat up in bed, hopeful that Laura had come across the yard from the farmhouse. Her accusations yesterday had pained him. Just what had made her flare up like that?

Now this call. It possessed a shimmering quality that suggested a voice emerging from the river waters. He went to the window. 'Victor . . .' When he looked out it wasn't what he expected. First of all the farmyard had vanished. Instead of an area surrounded by fences, with the block-shaped farmhouse standing at the far side, there were trees. He licked his lips. A usual dryness made his mouth feel like paper. The person calling his name wasn't whom he'd hoped for. Jay stood beneath the trees, arms limp by his sides. Jay gazed up at Victor as he uttered his name: 'Victor . . .'

Victor pushed open the window. Only it wasn't there any more. His hands brushed against leafy branches rather than glass.

'Victor. I'll take you to meet someone.'

'It's late,' Victor told him. 'Go back to bed.'

'Like I promised before, I've come to take you to her.'

'No doubt you are in bed.' Victor gave a grim smile. 'Just like I'm in bed. Because I'm dreaming all this, aren't I?' He glanced back at where his bedroom should be. In the moonlight he saw trees. Through the trunks he glimpsed silver glints of the Severn. He checked his hands. There was a scab on the stretch of skin between his fingers where he'd cut himself while freeing the fawn. 'In great detail,' he told Jay. 'But I'm still dreaming this.'

'I'm going to show you Ghorlan.'

'Correction. My subconscious is going to show me Ghorlan.' Victor grimaced. 'She drowned in the river. They never found the body. So don't go showing me any horror pictures, will you?' Victor realized this wasn't so much a dream as the beginning of a nightmare. He sensed the approach of something ominous. 'I'm not going to like this, am I? Tell me why am I questioning a dream version of Jay Summer?'

'Follow me, Victor. I want you to be happy.'

'Happy before I die?' Moonbeams pierced the branches. 'Laura told me what happens. You're taking me for one of your little walks.'

Jay moved through the forest ahead of him. A herd of Saban parted to allow him through. Their blue eyes regarded Victor with such deep sorrow. They had the eyes of human babies. 'So the legends are true . . . these animals are the souls of children . . . then I'm dreaming this, aren't I?' He pricked his hand as he pushed a branch aside. When he pulled out the black thorn from his palm a bead of red welled out. 'Ouch. Boy, does this dream have verisimilitude.' He sucked the wound clean. 'Good word that: *verisimilitude*. Authentic. The substance of truth.' He licked his dry lips. 'I see accurate details: you, trees, moonlight, the river, the Saban, nettles, this purple foil from a chocolate bar in the grass. I felt the thorn prick my hand. See? Still bleeding. It tastes like real blood. Everything indicates reality. Only I'm in bed sleeping. So, therefore, I dream.'

'Nearly there, Victor. You'll see her soon.'

'Please God, don't make it a nightmare. The times I dream she's lying on the river bed . . . in such a mess . . .' He swallowed.

Jay continued in a monotone. 'Victor . . . you see yourself walking through the forest. It's that day the new ferry replaced the old one with the yellow funnel. You're going to find Ghorlan; the sailing times have changed; you have to leave earlier, so you don't miss the ferry; you're going to visit your parents . . .'

'Jay, I don't want to do this.' He tried to stop. However, his traitor feet kept him moving through the wood. A fox watched him. 'Mr Fox, you know something I don't, don't you?' Despite shivers cascading through his flesh he chuckled. A light-headed sensation disorientated him.

Jay walked toward a moonlit clearing. 'You're wearing the ranger fleece.'

'It's our first wedding anniversary. It wasn't like this. I didn't walk through the woods in the dark.'

'When you did see Ghorlan, you found her doing something, didn't you?' He moved faster. 'She was doing something you didn't expect at all.'

Victor surged through the bushes into the clearing. A woman with hair as black as raven feathers knelt in the centre. Her actions were exactly the same as when he'd surprised her on that first anniversary of theirs.

Ghorlan glanced up, a look of astonishment on her beautiful face. 'Victor? I didn't want you to see this. You weren't supposed to know.'

Victor approached her. When he'd seen her on that day she'd been wearing the green ranger fleece. Now she wore a white flowing dress, a fairy tale kind of outfit that a child might imagine would be gorgeous to an adult.

Victor's heart clamoured. 'I know this is a dream,' he said. 'I wish to God it wasn't.' He turned to Jay. 'You've been making dreams come true, haven't you? Or at least you've tried. Because this wish-granting thing of yours has been going wrong, hasn't it?'

'It's not my fault. People wish for the wrong thing. They want to see people who've died, but I can't make dead people live again. Not properly anyway.'

Victor watched Ghorlan. When he'd found her on that day a decade ago she'd been planting a tree. It had been her intention to surprise him with it. Then she'd been using a spade and been wearing the fleece. Now, in this dream-version she wore the beautiful flowing white dress as she smoothed soil around the newly planted tree with a shiny hand trowel.

'It's Cedar of Lebanon,' she explained. 'In my village it was a tradition to plant a cedar on the first wedding anniversary. It would grow as the married couple spent their years together. So the hill-side near my home was magnificent with all the Cedar of Lebanon standing there. Big green sentinels. Enduring symbols of love, no?' She smiled at Victor, her lips an outrageous red. 'You weren't supposed to see this yet. It was to be a surprise.'

The sensation made him sway. For a moment it seemed he'd really stepped back all those years to the day he found his wife planting the tree. While in his hand he saw he held a bracelet. Engraved on a gold tag: Ghorlan~Victor.

Victor shook his head. 'Jay. This isn't right. You've manufactured a fantasy version of what happened. Ghorlan didn't wear a dress like that. She never wore scarlet lipstick. You think you're pleasing me by showing me Ghorlan, but you've made her grotesque. This is a leering puppet. Artificial. Lifeless!'

'I did my best. I want to make you happy.'

Ghorlan smoothed down the fabric of her dress with impossibly clean hands, considering she'd just planted a sapling in the mud.

Smiling, she said, 'A problem, Victor?'

'It's time I woke up.'

'Because I'll tell you what the problem is, Victor, dear,' her voice turned deeper. 'The *problem* is you never looked for me.' Her smile became a snarl. 'I vanished from your life. Why didn't you try to find me?'

'I did. I devoted weeks to searching the river. Every inch—'

'Are you blind? I was never there. Never ever!'

Ghorlan fled. Instinctively he followed. Ahead of him, the dress gleamed white as bone as she flitted through the trees.

'Ghorlan, come back. Tell me what you mean.'

'The river!' she cried. 'I was never there!'

'I don't understand. Explain what you're saying.'

As she darted amongst dark tree trunks he strove to catch up. She'd become an elusive phantom now. A flicker of light in the darkness.

I'll catch her, he told himself as his mind whirled with crazy thoughts. I'll hold her so tight she can't get away . . . then I'll squeeze the truth out of her. I'll force her to tell me what she means. Moments later, he burst from the trees. The castle tower loomed in the night sky. Ghorlan's dress shone against the earth mound beneath the castle wall, then she vanished. The ground had swallowed her.

He groaned with frustration. 'I wish I could hold her again. I need to tell her I love her.'

Jay appeared. 'I can take you to her again. That's what she wants.' Jay pointed at the castle mound. 'Just keep walking into there like you're walking through a door.'

'I'll do it. I'll do anything to be with her.' A pain jabbed his stomach.

'You've got to be quick,' Jay told him.

'I'm going.' A metal taste filled his mouth. He took an unsteady step forward.

'Hurry,' Jay urged. 'You want to find her, don't you?'

'More than anything else in the world.' Victor reached out to push his hands into the grassy banking. His fingers pressed against fabric. When he clawed them aside he saw they were his bedclothes. The bedroom walls pulsated. His tongue tasted awful. Victor grimaced as the pain stabbed his belly. 'You thought you'd escape it didn't you, Brodman?' Briefly, he clung to memories of Ghorlan in the dream. The next moment all that mattered was reaching the bathroom.

Twenty-Two

All the next day after *that* dream, the encounter with his dead wife planting the cedar, Victor Brodman lay in bed with about as much vitality as a garden slug. One of the black unctuous kind that slithers across the patio. When stomach cramps didn't keep him awake he slipped into fevered sleep.

'You're down with the same bug as me, Victor. Bloody awful, isn't it?' his sister proclaimed cheerfully. 'I'm feeling much better now, though.'

'My mouth tastes as if a slug died in it; one of those fat, slimy . . .' He groaned.

'Same as me. The muscle spasms were worst, though. Felt as if I was splitting in two. Now, you've got a jug of water. Can I get you something to eat?'

'Ugh . . . that's just cruel. Nothing like a big sister to be chief torturer.'

'It's no worse than what you did when I went down with food poisoning when I was fourteen . . . you'd have been . . . what? Eleven, twelve? You came into my room as I lay there with a bucket by the bed. You were pleased as punch with yourself when you announced the best way to treat food poisoning was by eating frogspawn. You showed me a jar of the stuff that you'd collected from a pond. You said that to feel better I'd have to swallow it all in one go.'

'I was eleven, Mary. It was a joke.'

'Failing that, the next best thing was all the fat and gunk scraped out of a frying pan after Dad had one of those revolting fry-ups of his.'

'Sis, if you leave me alone I'll give you a million dollars, a million euros, whatever it takes for you to stop making me feel . . .' He gulped.

Mary smiled. 'I've been waiting years to get my own back. As they say, revenge is a dish best served cold.'

'Medusa, witch, monster . . .' He blinked. A housefly buzzed around the room.

Mary entered the room with a jug of water.

'Do you feel like anything to eat yet?'

'Uh . . . I dreamt you were here just now asking the same thing. Then you started talking about Dad's cooked breakfasts.'

'Ah, the cholesterol express.'

'It wasn't so much a dream.' He swallowed. 'A nightmare, a horrendous, torturing nightmare.'

'It was no such thing.'

'You actually said those things? About frogspawn and bacon fat?'

She grinned. 'I thought it might cheer you up. But I said all those things over an hour ago. You keep falling asleep at the drop of a hat.'

'Never become a doctor, sis. Your bedside manner's a killer.'

'Speaking of nurses, there's one to see you now.'

Victor perked up. 'Laura?'

'Lou.' Mary touched his forehead. 'We could fry eggs on your face.'

'Thanks for the lovely image.'

'You must be feeling better. Until this afternoon all you did was grunt.'

His sister left the room. The fly remained. That buzz began to drive him insane. With an effort he turned over in bed. Jay stood in the shadows.

'Jay? You shouldn't be here. You might catch . . .' Victor swallowed queasily. 'Makes you feel rotten.'

Jay gazed at him. 'You thought what your sister told you about the frogspawn was a dream.'

'That's right, I did.'

'When you met Ghorlan last night you thought that was a dream, too.'

'Of course it was a dream.' He lay as limp as a wet towel. 'Yes, I love my wife. I also know she's dead.'

'You pricked your hand on a thorn.'

'It was a realistic dream. I'll give you that.'

Jay advanced on him, gripped his hand, then lifted it. 'What do you see?'

Victor's heart lurched. For there in the centre of his palm was a small, black scab. After burning with fever now he shivered as if plunged into ice-cold water.

'What's that in your hand?' Lou bustled in. She fixed him with her dark eyes like she'd found a young boy up to mischief.

'Uh, nothing.'

'You find nothing mighty interesting.' Without hesitation she gripped his hand so she could study the palm. 'Did you get a splinter in that, Victor, from breaking someone's heart?'

'A thorn. I pricked myself last night . . .' He frowned as what she said fully registered. 'Breaking someone's heart?'

'You heard right, Victor.'

'My sister was messing with my mind – and stomach – earlier. Don't you start or our cider drinking days will be over.'

She ripped open a foil sachet then shook white powder from it into a glass of water. 'Drink this.'

'Trying to poison me?'

'It replaces natural salts in the body, restores electrolyte balances and the like.'

'I don't think I can really—'

'Drink!'

'Ouch, not so loud, Lou. I really do feel like death.'

'If you're feeling like death that's an improvement.' She bustled round, straightening his bedding, then yanked the curtains open, which admitted eyeball-searing light.

Victor protested. 'Why don't people leave me to wallow in peace?' Scrunching his eyes against the light, he peered round the room. 'Is Jay still here?'

'Jay? No, he's down in the yard with Wilkes.'

'With the mayor?'

'No, Wilkes the goat. Victor, will you start thinking straight?'

He took a swallow of the cloudy water. 'Hell's bells, that tastes awful.'

'While you were sleeping today the health authority dropped a thousand of those packets by helicopter. They won't cure, but they restore chemical balance to the body.'

'Is the island still under quarantine?'

'That we are. We're prisoners here until the emergency committee lift the order. So far there's a seventy per cent infection rate. The elderly are hit the hardest, young folk like you, Victor Brodman, start to pick up within twelve hours of feeling the first symptoms.'

'Do they know what it is yet?'

'Probably a mutated version of gastric flu. Already there's stupid speculation in the newspapers that like some epidemics of influenza are supposed to arrive from outer space, so this bug flew in by meteor.' She sniffed. 'In truth, the cause of this outbreak is more about hygiene systems rather than solar systems.'

'So it's not that serious?'

'Serious enough to claim two lives already.'

'Really?' This shocked him enough to sit up. 'Who?'

'Two elderly men. Mr Moore. And Mr Henry.'

'Good grief. I've known them for years. So the disease is worse than they thought?'

'The disease wasn't directly responsible. Mr Henry decided to dig a deep hole on the beach. The sides collapsed and he suffocated. Mr Moore fell in the bathroom and struck his head hard enough to cause a haemorrhage. There are also rumours that at least two women have gone missing. I'm sorry to bring such bad news.' She sat on the end of his bed. 'But I'm also here for another reason. An important reason.'

'Lou, is it Laura? Is she all right?'

'So Laura *has* been on your mind?'

Lou was usually such a warm, bubbly character that this chill manner roused him from his lingering drowsiness. 'What's wrong, Lou?'

She plaited her fingers together on her knees. 'Today, Victor, I'm going to test our friendship to breaking point. We've known each other for many years. We respect each other . . . shush, Victor. Let me say my piece.' She took a deep breath. 'You are a fine man, Victor Brodman. Loyal, caring, compassionate. You're also a turtle of a man. By that I mean that whenever you find yourself on the brink of a potentially romantic relationship you retreat into that damn shell.'

'Lou, I'm not like that.'

'Oh, yes, you are. I've watched you with female visitors to the island. They flirt, you might flirt back, then when it seems as if the lady is ready to take it further, back into your cold, hard shell you go. You retreat. You say you need to count ducks, or lizards, or whatever, then vanish into the woods. You might have been Mr Right in the woman's eyes, but within minutes you are Mr Gone, never to be seen again until the woman's left the island. No, shush, Victor. Let me finish because what I've seen over the last few days has made me so angry.'

'Angry?'

'Yes, angry at you. Dunderhead.'

'Lou, what's got into you? I—'

'Victor, let me finish. Listen, Laura is a lovely person. I've never seen anyone devoted like she is to the children in her care. Every

day she fights battles to save them from being locked in secure units
or kept on tranquillizers that would knock down a horse. Just before
she came to Siluria her friend, Maureen, died in a traffic accident.
Laura has been under so much pressure! Her spirit was breaking to
little bits. Then something marvellous happened . . .'

'Oh?'

'She met you, you foolish man. For the first time in months I
saw her like the time we first met. Her entire face changed. Eyes
sparkling. She was happy, happy, happy! I don't know what happened
between you. That's none of my business—'

'You're right, it is none of your—'

'But being Laura's friend and being concerned for her well-being
is my business. It's my business to want the best for you, too.' She
sighed. This wasn't easy for her. 'I saw two lovely people meet. They
clearly like each other. That old magic happened. I saw it in Laura's
eyes and yours. Then you go back into your shell, Victor – your
cold hard shell. A shell that doesn't protect you, no sir. That shell
keeps you isolated from womankind.'

'Lou, I'm tired.'

'Sleep when you're old like me, Victor. Now's the time to fight
for happiness. Defeat your demons.'

'I don't have any demons.'

'You do! They are turning you into a hermit. Kill the demons
now; otherwise you're going to turn into a lonely, miserable hermit.'
She balled her fist. 'Someone must tell you one important fact.
Victor, it is time you buried your wife.'

He flinched. 'Lou, stop right there. You've no damn right to say
that.'

'OK, so hate me. But it's got to be said. I know Ghorlan disappeared in the river. You never could bury her body. But it's time
to bury her in here.' She extended her hand to touch his head.
Furious, he pushed it away. 'Bury your dead wife, Victor, so you can
rejoin the world. You deserve a life. Ghorlan wouldn't want you to
live as if part of you died with her.'

'How can you say what Ghorlan would or wouldn't want? Leave
me alone!'

'You keep Ghorlan alive. She's dead, Victor. Bury her.'

Sweating, he twisted the sheet in his hands. 'Get out . . . *get out!*'

That evening Victor headed into the forest. Lethargy made walking
hard work. He still alternated between sweats and a shivering

coldness; the fever hadn't quit yet. Every so often he needed to pause until a surge of queasiness passed. However, he was determined to get out of the apartment because he churned inside.

This time it wasn't the virus, it was thinking about the last twenty-four hours. Constantly, he replayed what Laura had said to him. Then there were Lou's home truths that had been so very bitter to hear. Add to that the dream of last night when he met Ghorlan in the clearing – if it was a dream. Now, the symptoms of the physical illness seemed almost trivial in comparison. He wanted to yell his fury at the sky. In the last few days it seemed as if some monster had been peeling him alive. His heart had been bared. His nerves exposed. Now his soul that had been sheltering deep inside of himself was being roughly dragged out into the cold light of day.

Instinct guided his feet. Soon he found himself in the clearing. In its centre, the tree that Ghorlan had planted on their first wedding anniversary. Now the Cedar of Lebanon had grown to some twenty feet or so. Its deep green leaves formed distinct horizontal layers. The trunk soared upward, straight as a rod. Beneath the deepening blue sky he moved forward to press his palm against the tree's bark. As he did so he felt the sting of the wound that the thorn had inflicted last night. At that instant he noticed two figures at the edge of the clearing. Jay and Archer stood side by side. Neither wore the carefree grin of a young child out on an adventure. Archer's old-beyond-his-years face appeared to be good company for Jay's eerie elfin face, with those large, almond-shaped eyes. Both watched Victor with gravely serious expressions. Then Jay took a dozen steps toward Victor. Victor glanced round, half expecting to see Ghorlan in the shadows.

Victor was determined to keep a grip on reality. 'How's Laura today?' he asked. 'Have you seen her?'

Jay didn't answer. Instead, he said, 'You hate me. I tried to make you happy last night, but it went wrong.'

'It always goes wrong, doesn't it?'

Jay gave a solemn nod.

'You try so hard to do nice things for people but it ends up hurting them. Why's that, Jay?'

'I don't want to. But that's what I'm supposed to do. I frighten people. I make bad things happen to them. Then they die.'

'Can you say why that is?'

Jay shrugged. 'I do everything *not* to hurt people. I fight what's inside of me. In the end it always wins. I can't stop harming them.'

Victor glanced across at Archer. The eight-year-old had been watching the adult and the boy talking by the tree. Now he gazed up into the clear blue sky. Five miles above his head two jetliners flew parallel to one another, though they must have been miles apart. Jay looked up as well. The two jets drew white lines through that perfect blue.

'It's getting stronger inside of me.' Jay watched the contrails. 'I know all the hurt comes from inside my head. I killed Maureen. I made Max want to drown himself.' Perspiration oozed from his brow. 'It's my job to make everyone die.'

Five miles above the island the two jetliners began to turn.

'There are people on those planes.' Victor's mouth turned dry. 'Men, women, children. Innocent people. They've never hurt anyone.'

The once straight vapour trails now curved. The tiny silvery glints showed that the two planes were changing course. Victor's heart thudded. A sense of the inevitable filled him. A cold, oozing dread. Down here it all seemed in slow motion. Of course, up there in the sky two aircraft, filled with passengers, had a closing speed of a thousand miles an hour.

Archer gasped, 'Those jets are flying right at each other.' With that he fled into the forest.

Victor crouched so as to be eye-level with Jay. 'Don't do this. Please don't. Think of all those hundreds of people.'

'I have to . . . I don't want to. But they've got to die.'

A fist-sized stone lay by Victor's feet. He saw himself seizing it, then smashing the hard rock down on to Jay's skull. Fragile bones would splinter, the brain would bleed. Then all this would be over. For ever and ever, amen.

Above them the planes closed at a relentless rate. Two missiles on a head-on collision course. In little more than twenty seconds from now the contrails would merge in carnage. The boy gazed up at the aircraft. No expression revealed what he was thinking. Those uncannily large eyes did not blink.

Victor searched his fever-ridden mind, knowing he'd have to stop Jay now. If he couldn't find the right words he'd have to wield the rock. Victor scrunched his shoulders as he forced himself to think. Eureka! He shouted: 'Jay. I'm going to marry Laura. Great news, eh?'

Jay's eyes swung from the planes to stare at Victor. For the first time there was shock there. Then the boy raced away into the bushes. Victor could hardly bear to bring himself to look up into the sky. For a moment, he stared upward, his eyes watered, his heart hammered as emotion overloaded every nerve. Five miles above the peaceful island of Siluria the two jet trails were parting. He watched as the pilots guided their aircraft away from danger. Two minutes later, with a safe distance between them once more, the pair of airliners vanished over the horizon.

He thought, by God it worked. But next time I might not be so lucky.

Twenty-Three

The next morning hard gusts struck the building; air currents sighed around the eaves like someone psyching themselves up to broach bad news. Victor checked his reflection in the mirror. Tongue still coated, cheeks flushed with patches of red, dark rings under his eyes. That tenacious bug was determined to make life unpleasant for him. If anything, he longed to rest in bed for a bit longer before he started out across the island. Only he'd woken that morning with a revelation. *Jay is changing. Whatever's inside of him is getting more powerful. Before, he picked off people at random one by one. Now he has the power to destroy entire plane-loads of passengers.* Or would have done if Victor hadn't sprung that lie on him. That he planned to marry Laura. What next for Jay? Bring death to a community and what then? Entire cities. A whole nation? He steadied himself as vertigo rolled through him. This sickness tried hard to keep him at home. But he had to find Laura to share what he knew. That Jay would soon exterminate people by the dozen – then what? By the thousand? The need to speak to Laura burned with that same intensity as the fever. A moment later he flew out of the apartment, leaving the door banging in the breeze.

Mayor Wilkes cursed the cold breeze. He cursed the quarantine order that kept him on the island. He cursed the crappy signal on his mobile phone. A gusty lane was no place to conduct important business. Black clouds shot through the sky. Any second now there'd be rain. He was certain.

'Don't let the asbestos in the mill make you miss the completion deadline,' he told his site manager. This was the biggest project of the year. Now his profit margins were in danger. 'Bring the boys in at night. They'll clear out the asbestos without the need for a specialist team. They're too bloody expensive. What's that? I said have the boys clear the asbestos. Ass-bess-toss . . .' The voice in his ear spoke fractured words. 'Did you hear what I just told you, Heggerty? The signal's all . . . damn it.' His frustration cranked up a notch. For some reason Heggerty couldn't make out the word 'asbestos'. *Crap phone, crap signal, crap island!* Mayor Wilkes raged at the man, 'Get that asbestos out. Did you hear me? Make it vanish. I don't care if it is toxic. Get rid of it. Did you get that?'

Saban Deer trotted by him into town. They regarded him with their bright blue eyes as if he was trying to amuse them as he stood there, jacket flapping, shouting into a little black box in one hand. Even the deer acted out of character. They would never normally get this close. Hell, he was near enough to kick a bristly backside. It might relieve some of this tension. As he debated clumping one with his glossy black shoe a horde of figures came round the bend. He recognized them as the Badsworth Lodge rabble. God, how they tried his patience. They weren't like other kids (who annoyed Mayor Wilkes at the best of times), these kids were weird. They all had old-looking faces. Mostly they were quiet, peculiarly quiet, like they brooded over secret plans. Every so often, however, they'd release an outburst of anger. A kind of rage he'd never seen before. 'Weird little beggars.' he muttered. 'What?' He pressed the phone against his ear. 'You heard that clearly enough, Heggerty, but I wasn't calling you a weird little beggar.' He spoke faster as the children approached. The troublemaker he recognized immediately as Jay walked apart from the group. Lou brought up the rear. They were heading in the direction of the hostel. It must be a rough time for the little swine, he thought sourly. Something that might be a voice crackled in his ear. Mayor Wilkes tried again. 'Asbestos. Ass-bess-toss. Get the asbestos out before the building inspector arrives tomorrow. I don't have her in my pocket yet. If the asbestos isn't gone she'll close down all demolition. For crying out loud, Heggerty, are you getting any of this? If that asbestos doesn't vanish you're sacked. Got that? Sacked.' Random syllables came through the speaker. Dear God, what's wrong with the phones today? But whatever happened he had to get the command through to Heggerty or he'd lose a fortune on the mill project. At that moment, however, the children arrived.

Aged between eight and mid-teens, they had been walking in silence, their faces stony, like only Badsworth Lodge kids could do. Robots without souls. Automatons marching. Right now, Mayor Wilkes wished he had a cattle prod. One of those that dealt out an electric shock. That'd put some life in them. *Clockwork boys and girls! See how you like five hundred volts!* Only at that precise time one of the kids decided this was the perfect location for a hysterical outburst.

'Jay! Why'z Jay gotta come wi' us all the time?' The teenage girl rounded on Lou. 'Why'nt leave him back on ya' farm?'

Speak English, child, Wilkes fumed silently. The voice of Heggerty sounded in his ear. 'Heggerty, I told you to get rid of the asbestos.' Only the girl's shrieking was so loud that he couldn't hear Heggerty's reply. No doubt his site manager couldn't hear Wilkes either. Damn. Wilkes had only trudged all the way up here because he couldn't get a signal at home. The landline was a no-no because he'd become so paranoid that the police might be listening in. Now everything had gone belly up because the kids had gone mental. Shrieking, howling, weeping.

A tiny boy with an unsettling adult-like face protested to the girl, 'Leave Jay alone. He's not said your name.'

'Jay lover, Jay boyfriend, Jay kisser!' screamed the girl.

'Will you be quiet,' Wilkes thundered, 'I am trying to make an important business call.'

Lou bustled up. 'I apologize, Mayor Wilkes. We'll soon leave you in peace.'

'See that you do!' He eyed the children with distaste. 'Any of these sick?'

'No, sir.'

'None from the lodge at all?'

'We've all been fine.'

'Typical,' he seethed. 'Three-quarters of the island are puking but all these are in the pink. And I'm a prisoner on this blasted muck heap.' He tried to speak again with his site manager but the din wrecked any chance of communication.

'Move along, children. Mayor Wilkes has important work to do.'

The little boy with the old face tried to block a girl's way as she went to harangue Jay. The boy with the goblin eyes just stood there in that inert way of his. Not speaking. Not registering any emotion.

Oh, what I wouldn't give for that cattle prod, Wilkes thought again. Five hundred volts. I'll bring the little devils into line.

'You keep out of this! Archer the Jay lover.' She gave the tiny child a muscular shove. Archer fell sideways to smack against the tarmac.

'Enough of that, young lady,' Lou chided. 'We're eating at the hostel today. Best behaviour, folks, let's show them that Badsworth Lodge folk are polite folk.'

As Archer got back to his feet he realized his elbow bled from where it had struck the roadway. Eyes watering, he pulled a tissue from his pocket. Normally, Wilkes had such little respect for these children he found it easy not to notice what they did. Just then, something *did* catch his attention one hundred per cent. When Archer yanked out the tissue an object fell from his pocket. It was flexible, slender and glinted yellow. Archer dabbed his red graze, not noticing he'd dropped one of his possessions.

Even though the voice in the mayor's ear now spoke with perfect clarity that gold object wouldn't let go. For some reason it seemed important. Come to think of it, the apt word was familiar. Quickly, Wilkes picked it up. Gold links . . . a broken bracelet. Dark blobs stuck to the metal. Heart racing, he turned it over. In the middle of the links, an oblong plate perhaps an inch long; inscribed there a pair of linked names. Ghorlan~Victor.

His heart thudded in his chest as he grabbed the boy. 'You, child. Where did you find this?'

Archer stared at the bracelet. The kid's eyes bulged in horror.

'Did you hear me? Where did this come from?'

'S'mine.' Archer glanced back at Jay. Wilkes couldn't tell whether the look was for backup or because he was frightened of the other boy.

'Mayor Wilkes.' Lou advanced through the group of children, her face the picture of astonishment. 'What on earth do you think you're doing to the child?'

'Nothing, he fell . . . I was just helping him to his feet. Look at the elbow. He's skinned it, I'm afraid.' Mayor Wilkes made light of it. 'Worse things happen at sea, huh, young man?'

Before he could react Archer grabbed the gold bracelet from his fingers. A second later he raced down the lane toward the hostel.

'Someone's got an appetite.' Although Wilkes smiled he felt nothing short of fury at the child snatching the jewellery from him. Even so, his memory had caught a perfect picture of the gold bracelet sitting there on his palm. He recalled the links speckled with brown. In his mind's eye were those two engraved names: Ghorlan~Victor. He would remember that boy the next time they met. And there was one thing Mayor Wilkes was sure of. It would be very soon.

Twenty-Four

Victor found Laura serving lunch to the children in the hostel's dining hall. She carried a tray piled high with sandwiches from table to table.

'Laura, I've got to talk to you.'

'And I've *got* to listen I suppose.' She caught the eye of a teenage boy. 'John, drink the juice, don't squirt it at Tricia.'

'Look, I'm sorry,' Victor told her. 'It's my fault. I should have made time to talk to you.' Inwardly, he winced at the memory of the arguments with both Laura and Lou. 'Can we go somewhere private? I've got something important to tell you.'

'All the hostel staff have the bug.' She nodded at the sandwiches. 'Lou's in the kitchen making more of these. I'm going to have my hands full this afternoon.'

Victor felt as if he'd explode if he didn't tell her about what had happened. But where to begin? The night-time encounter with his dead wife? The arguments with Lou and Laura needed resolving. Yes, he was a bonehead. Yes, he retreated into his shell at the first sign of commitment. He saw that now. And, more importantly, they simply had to do something about Jay. Victor felt a deluge of cold, stark fear when he recalled how he'd met Jay by Ghorlan's tree, and how the jetliners had nearly converged. Also, there was the not inconsiderable matter that he'd lied to Jay that he and Laura planned to get married. Right then, he wanted to spill the beans – a vast amount of troublesome beans. Laura, however, was encouraging the sedated Max to eat.

'Laura, this is important . . . hugely, vastly important.'

'Victor, can't you see how busy I am?'

'When can we talk, then?'

'Not now, that's for sure. Also I promised to help Dr Nazra this afternoon. The poor man is making so many home visits he hasn't slept in days.'

'Laura, what are we going to do about Jay?'

Max crushed a sandwich in his hand. Tears ran down his face.

Laura hissed, 'I can't talk now. These children are an emotional time bomb. We're doing everything we can to stop them blowing sky-high.' At the next table a teenage girl burst into sobs. A boy standing by the doorway used a fork to scrape the skin on the back of his hand red raw. 'Please, Victor, let me do my job.' She set the sandwiches down then ran to take the fork from the boy.

Victor stood there for a moment. The words he longed to express seethed inside of him; they needed to erupt from his mouth in a torrent. Yet, he could say nothing to Laura for now. Near bursting point with frustration, he stormed out of the hostel. He knew that very soon he must do something about Jay. At that time the only remedy he could see frightened him. It frightened him badly.

Eight-year-old Archer ploughed his way across the dining hall. The gold bracelet in his hand worried the life out of him. He knew the speckles on it were blood – the dead woman's blood. If he didn't tell Laura about the bracelet he suspected that monster woman would find him. And probably hurt him as punishment. Archer knew that the Ghorlan~Victor bracelet was important. *Evidence.* He chanted the word in his mind. *Evidence . . . Evidence . . . There's been a murder. The woman's corpse has been left in a car that's hidden underground.* He was sick of carrying the bracelet round with him. Always he had to make sure it was safe. That he didn't lose it. This morning Mayor Wilkes had seen it. Archer hadn't liked the look in the man's eye when he examined it. Somehow it reminded him of the look in the eyes of the men that shot his father. A cold, mean look. One that said dirty business had to be done. Archer reached Laura who sat at a table with Ricky. She was using disinfectant wipes to clean a graze on the boy's hand. It was vital he show Laura the bracelet.

'Laura,' Archer blurted. 'Look what I've got.'

'I'm sure it's very nice, Archer, but can't you see I'm busy?'

'It's important. I've got something to tell you.'

'Everyone today has something important to tell me,' she said calmly as she examined Ricky's self-inflicted wound to his hand. 'But it will have to wait.'

'Laura. There's this car, and – and I found this . . . evidence. It's evidence about a crime.'

Ricky jerked back in his chair.

Laura strove to be patient. 'Sit still, Ricky. You've broken the skin. If the fork wasn't clean you'll need—'

Ricky's eyes bulged as he stared across the room. 'It's Jay. He's watching me. I don't want to be the same as Max. I don't!' He

pushed himself away from the table. 'Don't look at me, you witch!'
He ran toward the kitchen door.

'Laura . . .' Archer ached inside, he was so desperate to show Laura
the bracelet. He didn't feel safe with it. At that moment he realized
how dangerous it was to be its keeper. What if the dead/alive woman
appeared in his bedroom tonight? Had Victor anything to do with
the woman's death? Was he the same Victor that was inscribed on
the bracelet? Why had Mayor Wilkes demanded to know where the
bracelet had come from? Whatever you do, give the bracelet to
Laura, then I'll be safe, he said to himself. 'Laura. I found this bracelet!
Look at it, Laura . . . look at the names on it!' But all Archer saw
was a swinging door. Laura had raced into the kitchen after Ricky.

More than anger Archer felt fear. He wanted rid of this bracelet. It
was as if he were fastened to its gold links; they wanted to embed
themselves into his flesh. 'Bloody thing, damn thing,' he muttered
as he exited the dining hall for the hostel garden. Its picnic area was
deserted with the exception of Jay. The eleven-year-old sat on a
bench staring upwards like there were phantoms in the sky that only
he could see. Kids from Badsworth Lodge habitually avoided Jay.
Archer, however, knew he must talk to him. A cold breeze tugged
at the trees, making the big old trunks groan. A sound that seemed
full of pain. Archer shivered. This wasn't good. Jay had gone into
one of those trances of his, just like he did before he started repeating
someone's name. And bad, bad things would happen to that someone.
Archer knew the score all right. He knew exactly how Jay's evil
power worked. Air currents tugged Jay's black hair like ghost fingers
ruffled it.

'Jay,' Archer began awkwardly. 'I don't want it any more.' He held
out the Ghorlan~Victor bracelet. 'I want you to have this now. It's
scaring me.'

Jay didn't respond.

Archer continued. 'I've tried to give it to Laura, but she's busy
with the other kids. She hasn't got time to talk to me, and I hate
it, it's not fair.'

Jay focused on the hand. 'Take it to Victor.'

'Victor? Not likely. He probably killed the woman in the car.
Laura's the only one I want to tell.'

'When I was watching the planes in the sky, when I knew they'd
crash into each other, Victor told me he was going to marry Laura.'
Jay seemed to be thinking aloud rather than addressing Archer.

'I was sure the planes would meet in the sky, then there'd be fire, and dead people all over the fields. But when Victor told me about marrying Laura something switched off in here.' He touched his head. 'In a way I wanted the planes to crash, they needed to crash, it would have felt good if they had.' He swallowed. 'All those people . . . What Victor said stopped me making it happen. The planes flew away without anyone being hurt.'

Archer was stunned. 'Victor's going to marry Laura? What if he does the same to her as he did to the woman in the car?'

'I like Victor.'

'Jay, don't trust anyone, except Laura . . . and Lou's OK, but grown-ups . . .' His face burned with anger, 'they pretend to be nice but then they hurt you. My dad said he loved my mum but he used to punch her.' That anger turned into a dark vengeful fury, just like it did when he told the gunmen where to find his father hiding in the cellar. That was such a good feeling when Dad got shot in the face – blam, blam – he'd never hurt Mum again. So Archer hardly knew he was uttering these dangerous words, 'Jay, you know what will happen if Laura marries Victor?'

Jay murmured, 'They'll be happy. I want them both to be happy . . .'

'No, no, no,' Archer screeched. 'If they get married Laura will go away. She'll leave. She'll stop living with us at the Lodge. Do you want her to go? Someone else will get her job; they might do rotten things to us. Remember Miss Pryke. When I was having a bath she used to hold my head under the water. Listen to me, Jay.' He gripped the boy's thin wrist. 'Jay, you've got to stop 'em getting married.'

Jay shook his head.

'You must!' Archer experienced a sudden revelation. 'I know how you can do it. Jay, look at me! This is what you've got to do. Keep repeating Victor's name. Say "Victor" over and over again. Then you put your curse on him. He'll get killed. Laura will stay with us, and everything will be all right.'

'Victor?' Jay appeared dazed.

'That's it,' Archer gripped Jay's wrist tighter. 'Keep saying his name: Victor, Victor, Victor . . .'

Jay's face grew shiny with perspiration. A tremor started in his cheek. Archer snarled his satisfaction. All the signs were there. This was just how Jay acted when he put his curse on people.

Archer urged him, 'Stop him taking Laura from us. Say his name: Victor, Victor . . .'

Jay's lips moved, forming a name, yet still utterly silent.

'That's it, Jay. Victor's name. Keep repeating it.'

When Jay began to chant a name the one he uttered wasn't the one that Archer expected at all. In horror, he backed away, his hands firmly clamped over his ears. 'Don't say that one . . . not that one.'

Twenty-Five

Mayor Wilkes strode along Main Street to the home of his PA. Heavy black cloud boiled in the sky. Gales whipped the river into angry waves that seethed white on the shoreline. Gulls screamed.

'Damn these kids,' Wilkes fumed. 'The quarantine's bad enough, now this.' Sight of the gold bracelet this morning had shocked him. He knew exactly who the bracelet belonged to. He'd read the name inscribed on the oblong piece of gold: Ghorlan~Victor. Now he needed to investigate this further, then find a solution to this new problem. Despite his anger, he grinned. 'Problems make me perform better. Give me obstacles: I get better results.' He rammed open the door, then thundered upstairs to June's apartment.

Victor Brodman watched Mayor Wilkes march along the street as if he owned the whole island. What on earth drove a human being to act in such an arrogant way? Victor shook his head as he stood on the jetty. A cold breeze jetted against his hot skin. Spray from waves, smacking against the wooden structure, speckled his clothing. The tang of salt told him that the ocean winds were carrying a storm this way.

Archer listened in horror as Jay repeated the name. The boy's lips moved to a deadly rhythm. 'Laura . . . Laura . . . Laura . . .'

To Archer, hearing Laura's name uttered by Jay, the witch, the curse boy, the monster with a child's face, was overwhelming. Archer knew the outcome. He'd witnessed Jay chanting Maureen's name. And all the rest of those people that had been doomed by this little boy with the devil inside of him. 'Laura . . . Laura . . .' The soft voice had all the dark power of a tolling bell that foretold impending disaster.

Waves of fear rolled through Archer. That fear had the power to plunge him back into vivid memories of the day he told the gunmen where his father hid in the cellar. Blam, blam, blam. Bullets had exploded the face of the man who'd treated Archer and his mother so cruelly. Memory hauled him back to the dormitory at Badsworth Lodge when he'd seen Maureen loom over his bed just hours after she'd been crushed between the buses. Then he was back in the vault under the castle again. The gloomy place where it was always night-time. Spiders. Cobwebs. Fungus smells. The car with the thing in the back. The woman with the mass of black hair. Her face had been shrivelled like an old peach, yet she had beautiful blue eyes. Archer's muscles locked tight. Yet, instinct drove him to walk away from Jay . . . bad Jay . . . witch Jay . . . because Jay chanted Laura's name.

He should warn Laura. Nasty . . . bad . . . awful things would happen to her. Archer loved Laura. If she died he doubted if he would survive without her. The eight-year-old made it as far as the dining hall where he collapsed on to the floor tiles, dead to the world.

Mayor Wilkes glared at June. 'This isn't a social call,' he hissed. 'I'm not here with a bunch of grapes and to enquire if you're feeling better.'

'I never expected you would.' June's face bled nothing less than complete resignation. Her hands were shaking. 'Damn, I thought I was getting better.'

He eyed her with distaste. She wasn't an A-class employee; she was, however, loyal. Then she had to be. Without this job she'd be homeless. No one was going to employ a convicted fraudster. Just another lousy crook who had got caught.

June sipped water from a glass. 'What do you want me to do?'

'Nothing too arduous.' He grinned. 'It'll be like taking candy from a baby.'

She stared blankly at him.

Damn idiot of a woman. Irritably, he said, 'A child, one of the Badsworth Lodge creatures, has something of mine.'

'Something of yours?' Her dull eyes gazed up at him.

'Yes, a boy called Archer. You can't miss him. He's tiny, almost a dwarf. Lots of blond curly hair. Only his face . . . you'd think he was forty, if he was a day. Peculiar-looking kid. Then that lot from the orphanage always are.' He grimaced. 'What makes them like that God alone knows. Anyway, this specimen has a gold bracelet. I want it.'

'A bracelet?'

'Yes, can't you follow what I'm telling you, June? It's blindingly simple. Archer has a gold bracelet. Go get it for me.'

'How?'

'Use your initiative. Offer to help out across at the hostel, they're short-staffed so they'll welcome even a dried-up husk like you. Get in there, find Archer. The bracelet's in his pocket. Take it from him.'

The stare became even more glassy.

Wilkes debated whether a slap across her face would sharpen her wits. Tempting . . . Instead, he slammed his hand down on the tabletop. 'Wake up, woman. Surely you're over this wretched bug. Now, once you have the bracelet bring it to me at my house. Don't let anyone else see it. Don't tell anyone about it . . . Dear God, June. Snap out of it. This infection only lasts twenty-four hours at the most. Don't go faking being ill.'

She rubbed her forehead. 'I'm . . . uh . . . sorry. I thought I was getting better. I'm finding it hard to . . . think properly.'

'June, take the bracelet from the boy. Where do you think you're going?'

'I need to lie down for a while.' Unsteadily, she walked down the hallway toward her bedroom.

'Heaven preserve me from imbeciles,' he barked in the direction of the bedroom door. 'I'll do it myself. But don't get too comfortable. As soon as the quarantine's lifted you're out of this place. Do you hear?'

Wilkes marched out into the street as the wind roared past the houses. He couldn't delay this any longer. It was time for him to find Archer. Then take the bracelet. And no more Mr Nice Guy. His lip curled into a grin. *As if I was ever such a thing.*

Twenty-Six

That old tingle ran through him. One that told Mayor Wilkes the hunt was under way. Sometimes it would be the hunt of the commercial deal, or a strategy to crush a political competitor. This time the tingle came upon him as he walked briskly along Main Street in the direction of the hostel. With June, his PA, confined to her sickbed he'd find Archer himself. Then he'd get hold of the bracelet. That promise of action was enough to get his adrenalin flowing. In the hostel's dinner hall he found commotion. Laura shepherded children out into the garden through the hall's rear doorway. Lou sat cradling a boy on her lap. It was the boy with the middle-aged face. He appeared to be asleep. However, the concern on Lou's face suggested there was more to this than met the eye.

'Lou,' Wilkes said, 'is Archer all right?'

'Mayor Wilkes? You remembered one of the children's names?'

He smiled his best political smile. 'I'm not made of stone, you know. Archer had a nasty fall out on the street earlier. I thought I'd look in on him.'

If Lou was surprised by his sudden concern for the Lodge children she kept it hidden. 'Oh, that little graze. He's fine.' She hugged the boy. 'Archer's got his own way of dealing with the world. When things get that bit too much for him he closes down for a while. It's like a trip switch on electrical equipment.'

'He'll get well soon?'

'Archer will be fine, Mr Mayor. We're going to get him to bed for a while.'

'Here?'

'No, something more homely. I'll take him to the place I've been staying.'

Mayor Wilkes went to pick Archer up. Already he glimpsed a twinkle of something gold in the child's pocket. 'Here, let me help you, Lou.'

'Thank you, but no, Mr Mayor,' Lou said pleasantly in her sing-song voice. 'He needs to be close to someone familiar right now.'

Wilkes tried not to show it but inwardly he seethed with

frustration. 'Of course. Just you give me a call, though, if you – or Archer – need anything.'

She smiled her thanks. One of the teenage children arrived carrying a Burberry pattern blanket. The girl helped Lou wrap the comatose Archer in it. Then Lou, still holding Archer, got to her feet without any difficulty. The boy must be as light as a feather, thought Wilkes with a modicum of surprise. At least extracting the bracelet from him will require no effort at all. What I need is just a minute alone with him. Still smiling, Wilkes adopted a helpful persona. He opened the door to the street then held up his hand to stop a couple on bicycles so Lou could safely cross.

'Sure I can't be of help, Lou?' Wilkes asked.

'I'm fine.' The woman carried the boy easily. 'Besides, I'm staying at that cottage just over there.'

'The one with the lilac door?'

'That's the one,' she answered. 'Thanks anyway.'

Wilkes watched her go toward the snug cottage with a weeping willow in the front garden. Still smiling, he made a mental note of the address. He'd call back later. When there was nobody around to interfere with his plans.

Archer heard everything. Like when you listen through a rolled-up comic it all sounded funny, sort of echoey, faraway, yet he heard each word distinctly. He knew that Lou carried him. He'd heard her conversation with Mayor Wilkes. Archer remembered that Jay had repeated Laura's name. That meant he'd put his curse on her. For now, while in this state of seizure, that knowledge occupied another part of his brain. He knew it was bad. Only he was detached from that sense of danger. Archer could not move, or talk. He'd remain like this for a while. Eventually, he'd fall asleep. When he awoke he'd be back to normal again. Until the next time. Archer felt Lou carry him upstairs. Then more voices . . .

'Oh. Lou, what happened to the little chap?'

'He's fine, Agnes. He just needs to rest a while. How's William?'

'I'm perplexed, dear. He seemed to have got over the bug this morning. He ate a huge breakfast. Then by lunchtime he came over all drowsy, and forgetful like. Not him at all. About an hour ago he said he'd have to go back to bed. Thing is, he couldn't remember how to find the stairs. Funny that, isn't it?'

'William could still be dehydrated. Have you called the doctor?'

'He's on his way.' A bell rang. 'Oh, that'll be him now. By the by, can I help you with the little chap?'

'No, I'll be fine. You concentrate on getting William back on his feet again.'

Within moments Archer lay on a soft bed with a quilt over him. He felt its protective touch. Lou bustled around him; a window opened a fraction for a healthy dose of fresh air. Water poured into a glass on his bedside table. Motionless, he gazed at a white lamp-shade against the red ceiling. More voices:

'Oh, Victor.' It was the old woman's voice. 'I thought it was Dr Nazra.'

'I saw Lou carrying Archer and wondered if she needed any help.'

'Go on up, Victor. First door on the left.'

Archer could not move. The clump-clump of Victor's feet on the risers grew louder. Lots of things went through Archer's mind. The Ghorlan~Victor bracelet. The dead/alive woman with the bright blue eyes. She'd risen from the back seat of the entombed car. Archer suspected Victor had put her there . . . after bashing her to death with his fists first. And that bracelet was evidence. Evidence of murder.

Footsteps grew even louder. A sound of breathing. Archer knew that Victor approached. He couldn't move a finger. Paralysis gripped him. A shadow moved in the room. Then Victor's face loomed over the bed. The eyes locked on the boy's face. Concern? Or the moment before the man smashed his fist into Archer's face? Cold spread through Archer's body. A deathly cold . . . just like the dead/alive woman would feel as she lay in the car.

'Archer. I wanted to see you.' Victor smiled.

Heart pumping, Archer tried to scream out. Not so much as a sigh escaped his lips. With all his might he tried to leap from the bed. He must get away before Victor reached him. Only he had no power of movement. He might as well have been carved from dead wood.

'Victor?' Lou's voice. 'Were you looking for me?'

'I saw you carrying Archer. Do you need any help?'

'I'm fine. All Archer needs is rest.' She chuckled. 'My, my, everyone's being very considerate today. Mayor Wilkes wanted to help, too. He was most concerned about Archer's well-being.'

'Really?' Victor's voice suddenly became deeper. 'Talk about miracles.'

'Are you over the bug, Victor?'

'I think I'm just about back to normal.'

'You sure? You look as if you've got something on your mind.'

Archer heard Victor start to speak but another voice echoed on the stairs. The old woman called, 'Dr Nazra, come on up. William's taken to his bed again.'

The doctor's soft tones resembled chimes on the air. 'That's been the pattern today. Those who contracted the virus appeared to make a complete recovery. Now some are starting to display signs of confusion and lethargy. Unfortunately, that's prevalent with influenza. You may suffer bouts of mild depression for months after. I hope this germ doesn't do the same to us.'

With Lou nearby to comfort him Archer found himself drifting into sleep.

Mayor Wilkes faced the breeze coming in from the river. Mountains of black cloud were marshalling themselves over the Welsh hills. He knew this was a sign that Siluria would be attacked by a storm. Attack was the right word. When bad weather blew in from the west it could be hurricane force. For ten minutes Wilkes had watched the cottage where Lou had taken Archer. As soon as Lou returned to the hostel he'd nip in quick. He knew Agnes Davies. Suavely, he'd explain he'd dropped by to find out if old William had recovered yet. Then he'd track down Archer. Only things didn't go to plan. Within seconds of Lou entering the cottage, she'd been followed by Victor (*bane of my life, that man, always in the way*); moments later, Dr Nazra had entered the cottage, too. Wilkes needed to get his hands on that bracelet. This wasn't a chore he could delay until tomorrow. A cold wind blew up the street. It seemed to carry with it another of the Badsworth Lodge misfits. A thin boy marched along, as if matching the pace of the breeze. He swung his arms as he walked. His huge, elfin eyes smouldered with something that approached excitement. As if he anticipated wonderful events.

He chanted to the rhythm of his stride. 'Laura, Laura . . . Siluria, Siluria . . . Laura, Laura . . . Siluria, Siluria . . .'

Why mutter the name of the nurse and the island? Then again, the behaviour of these kids to Wilkes was inexplicable. They were screwed up. And this was the boy that caused the trouble when the group arrived here. For some reason, the boy put the fear of God into all the other children.

Air currents screamed through tombstones in the churchyard. Wilkes watched dark cloud racing over the hills. The storm had begun its march on the island. Little Siluria was going to be hit hard.

When the opportunity for Wilkes to enter the cottage didn't arise he decided to check on June. If she dragged her bones off her sickbed she could visit Archer on some pretext. It should be simple for her to separate the strange little boy from the bracelet.

When he opened her bedroom door, he paused. 'Well, well, well,' he murmured in surprise. 'You managed to escape after all.'

Stretched out in bed, the sheets twisted around claw-like hands, June stared at the ceiling. Without a shadow of doubt the woman was utterly lifeless. Already the eyes were sunk into her dead face, while her lips had turned a delicate shade of blue.

Twenty-Seven

Mayor Wilkes found the doctor sitting on a garden bench, staring at a phone in his hand. From the expression on Dr Nazra's face he might have expected the device to turn into a spitting cobra at any moment.

Instead of beginning with a greeting, Wilkes barked, 'You know that pad of death certificates you keep in your safe? Get one. June Benyon has just died.'

Dr Nazra's face had turned a washed-out grey. 'I need more than one.' He inclined his head to the cottage. 'Mrs Hollander died ten minutes ago. Before that I'd been in Mr Kowalski's house. He's passed away, too.'

'This epidemic's got nasty, then?'

The doctor nodded, exhausted.

Wilkes clicked his tongue. 'You've called in more help?'

'Yes, I've just spoken to the director of emergency planning.'

'Good, because this is more than we can handle.'

'No . . . *bad* is the relevant word here. It seems as if the island has been struck by a mutant version of the virus that's been infecting people on the mainland. There, sick people are getting better. Here they become worse. Much, much worse.'

Wilkes fumed. 'My God. All the medical expertise we have is you and one qualified nurse, the woman from Badsworth Lodge.'

'And that's all we will have until the virus is identified. At the moment, the infectious diseases specialist doesn't know what this is. Or how it can be treated. Until they find a treatment for the condition we remain under quarantine.'

'Surely they can send medics in those bloody space suits you see them wearing when they're playing out their biohazard scenarios?'

Wearily, the doctor shook his head. 'Too risky, even for protective suits. We're a code red. Nobody is allowed on to the island, or off. We're locked out of the rest of the world. We might as well have been exiled to the dark side of the moon.'

'Surely this can only be temporary?'

'How long we're isolated here, I cannot say. Medical specialists have seen nothing like it . . . I've seen nothing like it. Not in all my thirty years as a medical man. You've heard of pneumonic plague and bubonic plague, Mr Mayor? Well, this is a psychoactive plague. It starts in the digestive system then it attacks the brain.'

Wilkes began to understand. 'I wondered why June Benyon couldn't comprehend a thing I was telling her.'

'It begins with vomiting,' the doctor said, 'with a high fever, episodes of hallucination, then it appears to vanish from the body. The patient feels much better. Only the virus is in the process of occupying brain tissue. Within hours the patient experiences lethargy, confusion, forgetfulness; the condition worsens until they lapse into coma. Ultimately, the virus switches off the part of the brain that governs respiratory function.' His bloodshot eyes were grave. 'Its victims stop breathing. They suffocate. They die.'

'Wait a minute, June was only forty-two. We're not talking about geriatrics croaking here, are we?'

'That we are not, Mr Mayor. Every single person on this island is at risk. We must assume, also, that everyone who suffered the first stage of the disease will enter second stage within hours. That's everyone, whether they be elderly or young.'

Victor had been to White Cross Farm to check on his sister and brother-in-law. Mary was her old self. However, Graham had tried to do too much farm work after leaving his sickbed. Now he was so weary that all he could manage was to mutter a word or two here and there.

Shaking her head, Mary had complained, 'Can you believe he'd forgotten that we're supposed to be celebrating our wedding anniversary on Sunday? Now he's taken himself back to bed, just as the animals need feeding.'

As Victor took the shoreline path back to the village he felt much better. The queasiness had vanished. Before leaving, he'd been able to help his sister out by feeding the goats and pigs. On the beach the Saban Deer were grazing on kelp now it was low tide. Few land animals could stomach the salty estuary weed but then the Saban weren't your regular animal. Few creatures in the animal kingdom have blue eyes. Some humans do. Siamese cats certainly, but the Saban have eyes that are electric blue. Despite the gloom, due to thick cloud, he caught flashes of sapphire as they lifted their heads to watch him pass, still munching on leathery kelp fronds as they did so. In his role as island ranger, Victor habitually scanned the terrain for anything amiss. As he passed the Saban he noticed specks of silver at the water's edge. Anything that didn't resemble the natural shore required further investigation.

This stretch of beach consisted of brownish pebbles, so those silver glints looked anything but natural. Quickly, he jogged to the water's edge. Lucky I checked, he mused as he bent down to carefully remove what had threatened the safety of the animals, and humans, too, if they chose to paddle here barefoot. For there, tangled in a spray of twigs, was a yellow fisherman's line adorned with a dozen steel hooks. Victor handled the line carefully; the points of the hooks had been filed for extra sharpness, while the barbs would grip their prey with a bloody-minded tenacity. Once that hook slipped into your flesh it wouldn't be coming out in a hurry.

Clearly, the hooks were intended for big sea fish. What's more he counted ten hooks on the tangle of line. Probably a commercial fisherman had left the baited hooks attached to a buoy way out to sea. They'd broken free, then an incoming tide had swept them up the estuary. Victor checked further along the shoreline. Sure enough he found a line with eight more viciously sharp hooks. The havoc these would cause to the soft muzzle of a deer didn't bear thinking about. Victor picked up the line. Dear God, he'd be entering a whole world of pain if he accidentally impaled himself on one of those. He saw the ends of the tough nylon line had been cut. Probably by the propeller blades of a speedboat that had got too close to the fishermen's buoys.

Victor carried the tangled lines, with their barbed weaponry, to one of the bins near the path. Gusts of wind shook the trees by the time he started out again for the village. A pall of cloud obscured the hills. The River Severn rose into angry peaks, as if the water tried hard to form sharply pointed pyramids. At the tip of the island the castle had begun to vanish into a grey murk of water vapour carried by the westerly. As Victor neared the village the path narrowed. Here the beach was narrower, too. The path was raised a couple of feet above the shore on wooden piles. To the landward side a steep-sided mound flanked the path. This constricted section of pathway ran for around two hundred yards until the ground opened out just before the village.

Through the mist he glimpsed a figure almost a hundred yards away. He recognized it as Laura Parris. She headed toward the village, her back to him. He remembered only too clearly the painful conversation with Lou. He hurried after Laura determined to clear the air with her. Damn it, he was so annoyed with himself. Laura was beautiful. They'd got on so well together – both shared the same sense of humour. Then he'd retreated into his shell. You've effectively blown it with her, Brodman, he scolded.

'Laura,' he shouted. If anything, Laura quickened her pace. Had she heard, and decided to hurry away so he couldn't speak to her? 'Laura.' The figure dwindled as it moved along the narrow path between the shore and the bank that rose a good twenty feet to one side. 'Laura!'

At that moment the ground quivered. Victor paused. He frowned. It did it again. The earth shuddered. A deep rumble throbbed through the air. Victor found himself remembering Solomon's words about what to do in an earthquake. An earthquake? Here? That's impossible. He'd barely registered the thought when a huge cry wailed through the sky. Victor spun round to see a vast object racing by the island. This dark mass of steel had no right to be here, or to be so close, or to be travelling so fast. 'The idiots! The stupid idiots!' Victor took a moment to absorb the shocking sight. A huge tanker pounded along the river. Dangerously close to the island, too. The ship must have been seven hundred feet long – and with a displacement of thousands of tons it hurled a bow wave more than ten feet high at Siluria. Victor watched as the foaming wave roared up the beach. The Saban Deer fled before it. Fortunately they were fast, managing to escape the killer wave.

Victor glanced back at Laura. She wouldn't be so lucky. For some reason she hadn't heard the rumble of the ship's engines, or the cry of its foghorn. And because she walked with her back to it she hadn't seen the hulking vessel.

'Laura! Watch out!'

She didn't react. Then again, the roar of the winds must have overwhelmed Victor's cry. His first instinct was to clamber up the banking. He'd make it just in time but that wouldn't grant him the precious moments to reach Laura before the bow wave struck. Already this man-made tsunami had hit the path a hundred yards behind him. Now it raced along this strip of land faster than a man could run. At six feet high that massive body of speeding water would shatter your bones before it swept you into the river. Then a combination of natural current and turbulence created by the ship would ensure that you drowned very quickly indeed. Victor dashed along the compacted shale. At one side of him rose the twenty-foot-high bank. At the other was the narrow ribbon of beach. Then closing in behind him at a furious rate was the tidal wave. The dirty-cream coloured wall of water ripped up the path like a plough blade. The concrete bin containing the fish hooks shattered as easily as a wine glass.

'*Laura!*' Still she didn't hear. Behind him the liquid wall shattered timbers that held the path in place. He knew the wave gained on him. The only thing in his favour was that he'd got a head start. If he could reach Laura, he might be able to save her. Because if that thing hit it would kill her as surely as a bomb. Instead of shouting her name he sank all his energy into running. Vibration shook the ground. To his left the huge black flank of the ship slid past. Water foamed at the bow as the captain broke every safety rule in the book. Victor risked a glance back. The tidal wave was now perhaps fifty yards behind him. When it struck a bush it wrenched it from the ground. Debris in the menacing curl of water would act like a meat grinder if it hit a human being. Ahead of him, Laura walked; she'd got something on her mind that distracted her from the outside world. Once that tsunami struck she'd be gone. Victor, too. He glanced at the river. *Ghorlan's waiting. A cold embrace. Liquid eternity* . . . He drove the thought from his mind. Ahead of Laura a line of bushes concealed steps up the banking. Being a stranger to the island, it was unlikely she knew they were there. If he made it in time, that would be their escape route.

Seconds later he caught up with her. No time for explanations. Nothing but this. He grabbed her. Without slowing he ran with her in his arms.

'Victor? What the hell are you doing? Put me down! Put me down, you . . .'

Then her eyes went wide. She'd seen the ship. The tidal wave, too. Its sheer violence vibrated the earth under them. It thundered. A ripping sound reached their ears as it stripped turf from the banking.

Victor reached the steps. By now, the tidal wave displaced the very air. A hurricane struck them that stank of river mud. The ship's horn cried out again – a lament for dead souls. Bounding up the steps with Laura in his arms, Victor tried to outrun the lethal barrage of water. Bushes writhed to his right as the wave struck.

As he passed the ten-foot mark, halfway up the banking, the crest of the wave smacked against his heel. Then it gouged out a muddy chunk of mound. Half-stumbling, Victor regained his balance, then carried Laura to level ground where they collapsed on to soft grass. Still, with their arms round each other they sat, trembling, as the man–made tsunami roared along the path, channelled by the earth incline. The wave only died when the ground opened out into fields. Even then a wash of brown water, at ankle-depth, swirled its way through stems of wheat.

Twenty-Eight

The cry had woken Archer. Frightened, he'd looked out of the window. A huge ship glided past the island. As big as an office block it dwarfed the houses. The wash from its bows ran up the beach in a big wave to smack against the jetty. In fact, it was so powerful it snatched away a dinghy, which vanished into the foam never to reappear. Archer realized that if it wasn't for the village being built on higher ground the water would have gushed into the houses.

'Jay said Laura's name.' He shuddered. 'He's done that thing to her.'

Sleep had dispelled the effects of the seizure. Even so, he felt unsteady on his feet as he went to pull on his shoes. At least he'd been put to bed in his clothes so he wouldn't waste time getting dressed. What matters now, he thought, what is ultra-important is to tell Laura . . . 'You've gotta know that Jay's put the curse on you.'

Outside, the cold air stank of river mud. A mist made the houses all faint . . . all colours were washed out. All faded, weaker, sickly . . . It was like the village was slowly dying. Normally there wouldn't be wind when it was foggy. Yet a hard breeze pushed the trees. Branches shook as if they protested at the rough treatment. Leaves, stripped from the twigs, raced along the ground in a river of green. And the gales made crying sounds across the roofs. It made Archer think of sorrow and weeping. There weren't many people about as Archer headed toward the hostel. A cottage door had been left open. It banged furiously in the storm. All of a sudden a figure emerged from the murk. It was the island's doctor; he spoke into a mobile with such grave tones they filled Archer with dread.

'Listen . . . I am begging you to send help. Just this morning I've had to issue nine death certificates. I'm on my way now to another patient who is in a coma. At this rate half the island will be unconscious by nightfall. This isn't an epidemic, madam, it is a plague.'

The doctor never even noticed Archer as he swept past. At that moment to Archer the man didn't seem like a human being. He was a fabrication of dark shadows. A seething mass of worries, fears, of problems without solutions, an individual whose role it was to see death in men's faces, to be in the company of the dying, then

to certify their death. Archer couldn't render that intuitive understanding in words. Instead, his imagination turned that figure into
the essence of dread.

These dark emotions made Archer move all the quicker. He had
to warn Laura. Jay had repeated her name. The curse was on her.
How long before the doctor, with all those grim shadows, came to
sit beside her bed?

The boy, however, came to a dead stop. For there, in the middle
of the street, as if waiting for him, was another figure.

'Jay. Get away from me.'

Jay merely stood there. Still as a statue. Green leaves raced by his
feet. Fog swirled round him. Slowly, Archer moved forward. He
longed to flee from Jay, but he had to pass him to reach the hostel.
He needed to find Laura. She must be warned. Meanwhile, the
breeze ruffled Jay's hair. The eyes were bright. As if he was excited
about something. Those eyes tracked Archer as he tried to sidle by.

Then Jay's lips moved. Just a little. Barely a twitch.

'Don't you dare say Laura's name again.' Archer clenched his fists.
'You shouldn't have done that. It's rotten. Laura loves us. She's nice.
You've put a bad thing on her. She'll die now. And it's all your fault!'

Jay's lips parted.

Archer now stood just five paces from Jay. 'D'you hear me? Don't
you dare say Laura's name.'

Jay didn't blink. His stare blazed through Archer. For a moment
Archer glimpsed hundreds of screaming men, women and children
in that stare. A sickening deluge of sound. A ship was sinking into
an ocean. He sensed the panic before it became a surge of rage. A
fury. A distillation of pure anger. That emotion ripped through the
eight-year-old. His nerve endings burned with it. He swayed.
Suddenly it seemed like there was no earth beneath his feet. It was
as if he was slipping downward. *To join Dad in his grave, to smell
wet earth, taste the rot, feel the worm . . .* Then his senses snapped
back to absolute clarity as he heard Jay begin to speak: 'Archer . . .
Archer . . .'

With a howl of despair Archer ran past Jay toward the hostel. Yet
even when he put his hands over his ears he could still hear the
boy's soft, insistent voice.

'Archer . . . Archer . . . Archer . . .'

Twenty-Nine

Victor and Laura followed the wake of destruction. Because the path had been ripped out of the shoreline by the tidal wave they stuck to the top of the banking.

'Damn ship,' Victor growled. 'It was too close to the island. It's a miracle that the captain didn't run her aground.'

Laura had only just been able to find her voice again after the shock of what happened. 'Does this happen often?'

'Rarely, very rarely. The speed that thing was going.' He glared at the ship as it disappeared into the mist. 'It's as if the captain was drunk, or . . .' He grimaced.

'Jay.' Laura groaned. 'I feel as if I'm trapped in a nightmare, and I can't wake up. Tell me I'm asleep.'

'You're as wide awake as I am.' The cold wind seemed to blow right through his flesh. 'Jay took me to see Ghorlan. She's been dead ten years, but I found myself back on the day of our first anniversary, she was planting a tree. A cedar. It's a tradition from her village . . .' The words ran from him faster. 'I saw her. Even though I know she's out there.' He nodded out at the turbulent river. 'She was angry that I hadn't searched for her. But I had, Laura. Month after month. Beaches, the marsh, up and down the river. Every inlet. And two days ago she damn well bawls me out for not looking!' He realized he was shouting. 'What did she think I'd been doing? Watching television? Lazing my time away in the blasted pub!' He shook with anger. 'But how can she have been there, Laura? After ten years in the river there'd be nothing left.'

'Jay can do this. I've seen what he's capable of.'

'He's evil.'

'Little witch is what the others call him. But it's not his fault.'

'It is, Laura! Jay is responsible!'

'He's just a frightened little boy.'

'Yesterday, I stood ten feet from him. He looked up at two airliners. You could see them in the sky, two white lines of vapour. Everything how it should be. As he watched he did something to them, like he did to the captain of that ship, and the planes began to converge. I knew that he'd got into the pilots' heads. He'd make them collide.

Hundreds would have died. I was seconds from picking up a rock and smashing his skull to pieces.'

'Why didn't you?' Laura spoke calmly.

'Why do you think?' A sudden drowsiness gripped him. 'I'm not the skull breaking kind . . . unless . . .' He shrugged as bloody images streamed through his mind of a rock in his hand that dripped crimson. With an effort he focused his thoughts. 'Instead, I told him I was going to marry you.'

'*Marry me?*' Laura registered absolute shock. 'What made you say that?'

'I needed to say something powerful enough to distract him.'

'Do you know what damage you might have caused?' She walked faster. 'Instead of making things better you've made them worse.'

'Hundreds of lives were at stake. Either that or the rock.' Victor kept pace with her. Ahead the village looked sombre as the approaching storm darkened the skies.

Laura paused. 'Most children I care for would be devastated by news like that. They're emotionally dependent on the staff. To them marriage doesn't mean love, it means that somebody they care about will vanish from their lives. If a carer at the lodge plans to leave or to marry we spend weeks gently introducing the children to the idea. We build in reassurances. We devise methods to compensate for the disappearance of the carer.' She began to walk once more. 'Jay's fragile at the best of times. This could push him over the edge.' Grimly, she added, 'Only in Jay's case the devastation goes beyond any trauma he might suffer.'

They moved in silence through the meadows. Victor noticed that apart from the loss of the riverside path, together with a couple of dinghies that had been moored on the beach, the damage hadn't been as great as it might have been. All the houses were built on elevated areas of ground. The flood hadn't touched them. However – a *big* however – a flood of a different kind was poised to devastate Siluria. Whatever was in Jay would deliver a flood of suffering, of fear, of death. Victor had seen it happen. He didn't doubt it was on its way. He shivered as a cold wind blew mournful notes through the telephone wires.

The village streets were empty of people. Leaves swirled like green phantoms. Laura rushed in the direction of the hostel. Angry shouts from children burst from the building with the shocking abruptness of gunshots.

'I told you,' she muttered. 'I told you they'd go crazy if they heard the word "marriage".'

Lou appeared at the doorway to frantically beckon Laura. The normally placid woman was at her wits' end.

'What can I do to help?' Victor asked.

'Stay here. If they see you they'll go into meltdown. And as for Jay, God have pity on us.' Laura vanished into the building.

Mayor Wilkes emerged through wraiths of mist. 'Brodman, have you seen what that bloody ship has done to my footpath? It will cost our entire maintenance budget to replace that. My God, I'm going to find out who is responsible for that ship then I'm going to sue the . . .' Wilkes noticed Victor's expression. 'What's wrong with you? Seen a ghost?'

'You've got to get this quarantine lifted. We need help on the island.'

'In your dreams, Brodman. They've locked us down with a code red health alert. We're not only under strict quarantine rules, we are, as our esteemed GP put it, as good as exiled on the dark side of the moon.'

'What are you talking about?'

'Don't you know? That puke and poop bug mutated. A bad belly was only the first stage. Second stage happens up here.' He tapped his head. 'The virus attacks the brain. People who've had it appear to rally then they start getting forgetful, lose their faculties, they become lethargic, then they fall asleep. Eventually for keeps.' Wilkes stared. 'Good God, Victor. You've had it, haven't you?'

'And Mary, and my brother-in-law.' Victor's blood ran cold. 'Second stage, you say? How long until it starts to take effect?'

'I'm not the quack.' Wilkes shrugged. 'A few hours, maybe.'

'How bad?'

'Today, so far, nine dead. With all this and the ship nearly ramming the island it's like someone put a curse on us.'

Victor rubbed his face. His skin felt strangely numb.

With a degree of satisfaction Wilkes asked, 'Are you feeling unwell?'

'I'm going to stay well until I've finished what I've got to do.'

'Not those flaming animals? Wait . . . Where are you going? Shouldn't you be home in bed?'

Victor fired back, 'I'm going to find Jay.'

'The boy from the orphanage? What the hell for?'

'It's vital I find him.' Blood pounded in Victor's ears.

'You're chasing one of those nutty kids? Dr Nazra said all you infected people would go crazy.' Wilkes was delighted. 'And, boy-oh-boy, is he right!' He chuckled. 'Brodman, you're away with the fairies!'

'One day you'll thank me.'

'Thank you? Yes, I suppose I will but not in the way you expect.' Wilkes grinned. 'By the way, this boy . . . Jay. He appears to have lost his wits, too. I saw him walking down this very street today. His eyes were blazing like he'd glimpsed paradise. And he was chanting names. Barking mad, if you ask me.'

Victor's heart lurched. 'What names?'

'Oh, I can't remember now.' Dismissive, Wilkes waved his hand. 'Totally nuts, though.'

'Wilkes! Which name?'

'I can't remember.'

Victor dashed at the man, grabbed his jacket lapels in both hands, then hauled him until they were nose to nose. 'Which names?'

'Don't you touch me with your filthy bug-infested—'

'*Names?*'

'You've just signed your immediate resignation, Brodman. You're finished here.'

Victor shoved the man back against a garden fence. At last Mayor Wilkes realized that the ranger wasn't playing games.

'OK, OK . . .' Wilkes' lip curled. 'If it means so much to you . . . or to your nasty infected brain. The boy was repeating the island's name: "Siluria. Siluria." Get it? Oh, and the nurse . . . whatever they call the infernal woman.'

'Laura?'

'That's the one, Victor.' His tone suggested he was humouring him. 'Laura, Laura, Laura.'

Victor pushed the man away. A moment later he raced toward the hostel.

Behind him, Wilkes took pleasure in shouting, 'You're second stage, Victor! Go home. Calm that infested head of yours.' He barked out laughter. 'Before you get yourself into even more trouble!'

Thirty

In the dining hall there was pandemonium. The hostel's walls trembled as the children from Badsworth Lodge went berserk. After Archer had heard Jay repeat his name out in the street, the child had dashed in mad panic to find Laura. The other children wanted to know what had scared him so badly. The trouble was, he was so petrified it came out in confused phrases.

'Jay's done it again . . . the witch . . . I fell down here . . . then I woke up . . . and I know really bad stuff's happening! The doctor's got so worried. Nobody's coming!'

A youth grunted, 'Archer, we don't know what the hell you're talking about.'

'Yeah, spit it, or bottle it,' Candice snapped.

Archer stared, unable to speak. At that moment Laura entered the dining hall. Seeing her jolted out a fact that preyed on his mind. 'Laura's getting married.'

'*What!*' All the children flinched at the shock news.

'Archer, how do you know that Laura's getting married?'

'I met Victor. And Victor told Jay that he's getting married to Laura. And another thing . . .' The kids went crazy. They started yelling at each other, at Laura. One boy's face went into spasm, the bottom lip extended so much his teeth were bared in a weird snarl. He punched out at a pair of teenagers who stood next to him. Candice ran to a wall where she beat her own head against the brickwork. While Laura raced to stop her, Lou tried to break up the fighting youths.

Archer cried, 'And another thing. Jay's saying my name. He's saying Laura's. He's put his witch curse on us!' He kept shouting. Only not a single person heard above the racket.

The big room echoed to the barrage of children howling – sorrow mated with rage. Even though no individual words were identifiable, the cacophony all stated the single terrible fact. *If Laura marries she'll leave. What will happen to us? Who will keep us safe?*

The teenager who'd started the fight grabbed a knife from the cutlery box. Lou had to wrestle the boy to the ground, before prising his fingers from the handle.

Archer, meanwhile, shouted himself hoarse, trying to attract Laura's attention. However, she'd wrapped her arms around Candice to stop the girl pounding her forehead into the brickwork. At last the self-harmer collapsed into Laura's hug. There she wailed so loudly it shook the cups on the tables.

Archer tugged Laura's arm. 'Jay's done it to you, Laura. He's saying your name. He's saying it over and over. You gotta stop him!'

Laura indicated she couldn't hear. Then, with both arms around Candice, she walked away – left him, abandoned him. He stared at her. *Laura getting married. Laura cursed. It's happening already. She doesn't want to listen to me.*

A sharp point dug into his upper thigh. He reached into his pocket for the bracelet. He stared at it in his hand. Ghorlan~Victor. This bit of gold chain haunted him. Maybe it was the cause of all this trouble? So great was the din it was hard to think properly. Yet Archer knew this jewellery was important. The dead woman in the car had given it him. Now what seemed even more important was to get rid of it. If he could make Jay take it then maybe all these bad things would go away. Yes, that's it, he decided. Give Jay the bracelet, the little witch. See how he likes having to carry it round. It had more than blood stuck to it: the gold had death glued to it, too.

Archer's problems were too great for the boy to fathom. At that moment they all seemed to be attached to the bracelet. In his juvenile way of dealing with problems the easiest solution was to dump the bracelet on Jay. All panic and horror handed over with it. Of course, in a little while, he'd come to realize that this wouldn't end his woes, instead it would lead him to a face-to-face meeting with death itself.

Thirty-One

He had to get out of the din. That and find Jay. Archer slipped un-noticed through the hostel's side door. 'Jay's gonna get the bracelet. That'll make everything OK.'

He staggered before the blast of chilled air racing up the deserted street. Leaves flew. Mist streamed like smoke from an old-fashioned locomotive. Even though it was mid-afternoon in May the sky had turned black. Gloom filled the narrow streets. Along with the fog it made the houses seem as if they lay in murky depths. Had the river flooded the town? Was he underwater? In that shocked state he wasn't sure. Thoughts didn't run as they should in his head. Constantly, he pictured his father with bullets lodged in his face. Twigs scuttled down the street like spiky-legged insects. In his mind he saw his father's coffin. Only this time he, Archer, lay in the oblong box. All that wet soil pressing down. It would hold the lid shut for ever. Dazed, he pushed on through airborne debris. A newspaper wrapped around his face to blind him. Maybe when he pulled it away he'd find he really was lying in a coffin . . . in the dark . . . alone . . . listening for hungry worms . . . Archer yanked the paper away. A figure stood there in the mist.

'Dad?'

The shadowy form moved closer. 'Remember me?'

Archer stared.

'I'm the mayor.' The tall man smiled down at him. 'I'm glad I've found you.'

'Why?'

'You look as if you need some help.'

'No, sir.'

'Aren't you worried about something?'

'No, sir.'

'Why aren't you back in the hostel?'

'I-I don't want to,' Archer stammered.

'It's going to get all stormy out here. You won't like that, will you?'

Archer was so preoccupied with his worries that he failed to notice how edgy the man seemed. He constantly checked the street as if he expected someone to appear at any minute. The boy strove

to clear his mind of all those jangling thoughts that had no right
to be there.

Mayor Wilkes sidled up. 'You don't look well, little fellow. You've
not had this stomach bug, have you?'

Archer shook his head.

'That's a relief. You know this is a bad sickness. Really bad. People
are dying.'

'Uh?' The word 'die' penetrated the fog of disordered thoughts.

'Oh, yes. Dr Nazra told me so. Victor Brodman's got the disease.
In a few hours he might be dead.' The mayor loomed closer. 'Archer
. . . it is Archer, isn't it? You smiled when I said that Victor is going
to die. Why's that?'

'He said he'd marry Laura.'

'Oh? Well, there'll be none of that now. Victor will be going to
his own funeral rather than a wedding.' The mayor stepped even
closer. 'I told you about people dying because I can trust you. You're
very grown up, you know. I bet you're more intelligent, *brainier*, than
the rest. You know I'm right, don't you?'

Archer hadn't experienced anything like this before. A grown-up
who talked to him like another grown-up. Even though Archer had
an old face, his diminutive stature along with curly, little boy blue
hair made people talk down to him like he was a baby. This he
liked. A big important man that *trusted* Archer. The boy straightened
to make himself taller.

When he spoke he fancied his voice had become deeper, almost
manlike. 'I've got something really important to do.'

'Oh? What?' Mayor Wilkes asked.

'I've got to find Jay. It's important. Most important thing in the
world.'

'I'm sure he'll turn up soon. Look, my house is round the corner.
Why don't we get out of the cold?'

In the window of the post office Archer saw reflections of himself
and the mayor. So that's how people see us, he thought. A big grown-
up man and a tiny boy with curly hair? Archer shook his head,
determined to be grown-up. 'I've got to find Jay.'

The man put his hand on the boy's shoulder. 'I understand. But
first—'

A pair of figures hurried down the street. Mayor Wilkes quickly
stepped back from the boy. The men went to a cottage where a
window shutter had broken loose. It swung back and forth on its
hinges with a metallic screeching.

A woman with long silver hair rushed from a nearby house. 'Mayor Wilkes, have you seen Dr Nazra? I can't wake my Frank up. He's had this bug . . .'

'Try the surgery,' Wilkes told her. As if the wind whisked her away she rushed up the lane. The mayor smiled falsely at Archer. 'I know, we can find Jay together. Now we're friends we can help each other.'

'I dunno,' Archer began doubtfully.

'This Jay, is he the one that the other children don't like?'

'I've got to find him *now*! It's really important. He's said Laura's name and my name, and—'

'Yes, yes, I'm sure the child can be vexing.'

'Now he's gone . . . I don't know where to look for him.'

'You know, Archer, I saw him not five minutes ago.'

'Oh?' Hope surged in Archer's chest.

'Absolutely. He was going that way.' Wilkes pointed into the teeth of the gale. 'He headed up that pathway there, toward the forest. Come on, we'll track him down together.'

Thirty-Two

Mayor Wilkes didn't envisage any obstacles of note. He'd told this odd little child, with the old face surrounded by blond curls, that Jay headed in the direction of the woods. Of course, Wilkes hadn't a clue where the Jay creature had vanished. He didn't care. All that mattered was to lure Archer out of sight of nosey villagers, then he could simply force him to hand over the bracelet. Simple. Then get himself out of this awful weather. The mayor glanced back. The village had almost vanished in the murk. If the boy complained to anyone about Wilkes, he'd merely say he saw the boy find the bracelet on the ground. Seeing as the boy pocketed a possibly valuable item, Wilkes had done the socially responsible thing and confiscated it in order to hand it over to the police on the mainland. And if anyone was damn well persistent enough to enquire about the whereabouts of this piece of jewellery, Wilkes would airily dismiss the question with, 'Oh, it turned out to be a plastic novelty. Utterly worthless. I just dropped it in a bin.' Would anyone accept a child's allegation seriously, especially a strange little child with behavioural problems? Wilkes had absolute confidence that he, an elected mayor and successful businessman, would be believed. The boy would be dumped back wherever he came from.

The pair of them followed a path along the spine of the island. Ahead, the castle tower emerged from shifting rags of mist. Behind them, the village had vanished. Trees creaked as gales wrenched at their limbs.

Here will do just nicely. 'Stop right there.'

The boy turned that old face toward him. God, such a creepy, old man's face. Wilkes opened his mouth to speak again. Just then, he noticed a shape emerge from the fog. The figure hurried toward them. Inwardly, he groaned. This would be tricky.

'Hello, Mrs Knowles,' he said in a friendly way as he searched for some excuse why he should be out in the fields with one of the Lodge children. For this was no other than Victor Brodman's sister. *Damn the family. They must have been put on earth to try my patience.* 'Terrible weather,' he purred. 'I saw this child by himself. It—'

'Can't stop,' she sounded oddly drowsy. 'I'm . . . I've . . . the doctor . . . Nnn . . . I've forgotten his name. It's my husband, Graham. I'm worried. He's so confused. Now he can't even remember my name.' She swayed. 'Don't feel so bright myself. Uh . . . Can't stop.' She lurched away.

'So another one will soon bite the dust. Deary me. Now, Archer . . .'

But it was Archer who turned the tables. 'I don't need Jay,' he announced loudly. 'You're my friend. I trust you.'

'Naturally.' Wilkes got ready to turn out the boy's pockets.

'So I've decided to show you something that's secret . . . top secret.'

This surprised Wilkes enough to make him pause.

'I found something this week. It's been hidden. Jay took me there. I hate Jay, so he can go stink.'

'What did you find, exactly?'

'You won't believe your eyes.' The kid's face shone. 'Promise not to be scared. It doesn't look nice. In fact, it's really horrible. But when you see it you'll know what to do to make everything all right.'

'Just what have you found, Archer?'

'Come on, I'll show you.' With that the boy dashed along the path to the woods. Wilkes followed. His instinct for self-preservation told him to find out what the boy had found. Wilkes knew there were secrets on the island. If they were his secrets he wanted them to stay that way.

Thirty-Three

This is the longest thirty minutes of my life, Victor thought as he waited. He could hear sheer bloody bedlam coming from the hostel. On no account could he help. Laura forbade it. After all, Victor was to blame for this episode. To distract Jay from willing those planes to collide he'd told the boy that he planned to marry Laura. Yes, a lie. Anything to stop those twin contrails meeting in a fireball five miles above the island. So he waited. In a yard nearby an iron gate banged with nerve-jangling ferocity. Leaves torn from trees formed green torrents around his head. A head full of thoughts that were as turbulent as the river. He recalled the near miss with the tanker that had sent a tidal wave crashing on to the shore. Laura would have died if he hadn't reached her in time. Who was to blame? An irresponsible captain with a deadline to meet? No, it had to be Jay. Victor had watched the aircraft turn to fly at one another. Then this epidemic. Islanders had died. Now Victor, himself, faced the second stage of the mystery illness – forgetfulness, lethargy, coma, then . . . he avoided thinking that grim, dark word. As soon as possible he should warn his sister and brother-in-law. So . . . this epidemic . . . this plague. *Who's to blame? Jay. He's the monstrous spider spinning a web of disaster. Each strand a promise of death.* Victor rubbed his face. For a moment he'd forgotten he'd been standing there in the street. Was this the start of the next phalanx of symptoms? How long until second stage really kicked in? How long had he got before he stopped functioning? A day? A few hours? Jay? Where is Jay?

'Victor . . . Victor?'

Drowsily, he searched for the source of the voice.

'Victor, up here.'

He lifted his eyes. Laura, beautiful Laura, leaned out of the hostel's office window on the upper storey. 'Rapunzel, Rapunzel, let down your long hair.' He clenched his fist, feeling betrayed by himself. He was letting go . . . his mind was slipping . . .

'Victor. Hurry. I haven't got long.'

You're not the only one. He bit his lip hard. The pain sharpened his wits again. But for how long? The church clock ticked the seconds down to his own personal zero hour. He crossed the street to the hostel.

'No, not that way, Victor. The children will see you. Use the side entrance.'

Seeing Laura focused his mind. *Now's the time to sort this out once and for all. Today we act on Jay.*

Moments later Laura greeted him at the top of the stairs. Holding her finger to his lips, she led him into the office where they'd be alone.

The shouts of the children downstairs were falling; anger yielded to more subdued, gloomier emotions.

'Close the door behind you, Victor.' Laura's face was the epitome of anxiety. 'The children mustn't know you're here. Especially not alone with me. I've had to come away for a while, too. They get upset when they see me.'

'I had to tell Jay something to stop him. I figured a surprise would distract him.'

'It worked, thank God. It's just the effect on the other children. Hearing the news from Archer that we were getting married has knocked them off kilter.' She gave an expressive shrug. 'These aren't ordinary children, Victor. An innocuous comment can traumatize them. Lou's talking to them now. She's pretending you told Jay that we were getting married for a joke. If she can convince them you were joking, then . . .' She shrugged again. 'We may have averted one disaster.'

He sat on the corner of the desk. 'Now we only have to avert the other disasters then we're home and dry.' He gave a grim smile. 'Nearly being swept away by the wash from that ship this morning might not be the worst thing that happens to us today.'

'You've heard about the epidemic?' Her expression was grave. 'That there's a second stage?'

He nodded. 'And people are dying. I'm sitting here but I know I should be running like hell to warn Mary and my brother-in-law. They've both had first stage.'

'And so have you.'

'So far, I'm fine.'

'But we do have to act quickly.'

'Jay?'

'Jay,' she confirmed. Then she turned an open laptop toward Victor so he could see the screen. 'Remember what Solomon told us about changelings and curses? Well, I already knew about that. When bizarre events started happening around Jay at Badsworth Lodge I did my own research.'

'So you did know more than you were letting on?'

'Absolutely. But how do you go public on something like this? That a boy rescued from a refugee ship has the power to curse people? Look at this.' She pointed at the screen. 'A curse is the opposite side of the coin to a blessing. Just as most religions have rites that bless newborn children, or homes, or harvests then you get the dark side. There are rites to wish harm on others, or actively invoke evil to befall people, whether it's to cause accidents, sickness or blight crops. In voodoo ritual an object, such as a skull or a shoe, can be implanted with the curse. Then the person inflicting the curse would hide the object in their victim's house or even on a path that they know the victim uses.'

'So, like a landmine? Only it detonates bad luck rather than explosive.'

Laura scrolled downward. 'See, thousands of web pages about curses.' She clicked a link. A page appeared showing photographs of strips of metal on which words had been scratched. 'These pieces of lead were found in springs that supplied a Roman bath house.' She read aloud from the page. '"Roman citizens would bathe in the hot mineral springs, which they believed healed skin complaints, arthritis and leprosy. They also believed that the goddess of the thermal spring could drive away the evil eye. Also, if someone had harmed you, you could write the person's name and the damage you wanted to inflict on a lead tablet, then throw it into the water." Here's one that says, "Lucius Praedox took four gold coins from my purse. I beg of Minerva to extract the blood from his heart." And another less specific one, but potentially more destructive. "I wish that Neptune sink all the ships of the Egyptians for men of that race broke my husband's bones in Alexandria."'

Victor scanned the screen. 'So a curse can be as accurately targeted as a bullet or, like a nuclear bomb, cause indiscriminate destruction.' He caught Laura's eye. 'If you believe such a thing.'

'And millions have believed in blessings and curses for thousands of years. Here's a modern curse: "The Toilet Tissue Sting works surprisingly well. One: write your victim's name on a piece of toilet tissue. Two: flush it down the lavatory. Three: tell your victim what you've done. When you do, just watch the expression on their face." Then you have blessings in the form of St Christopher medallions in taxicabs, breaking bottles of champagne over ships' bows. Generally, something like a horseshoe is a non-specific good luck charm. In Northern Europe metal frightened away evil spirits. So often a piece of steel would be put into a baby's cot to prevent goblins stealing the child and replacing it with one of their own.'

Victor nodded. 'OK, type in changeling.'

Laura did so. 'See, thousands more web pages. Belief in the changeling is about as universal as you can get. Globally, parents feared their child would be secretly exchanged for an evil spirit, goblin, demon, you name it. The child initially resembles the parents' child but it slowly changes in appearance, becoming ugly, behaving strangely and soon bad luck starts to dog the household.'

Victor read off the screen. '"Wales. In this ancient Celtic land the changeling child is known as *plenty newid*. Although the child develops physical beast-like characteristics it is noted for its uncanny wisdom. Parents would attempt to reclaim their own child by ill-treating the changeling. This offspring of goblins would be placed on a shovel before being held over a hot fire." Extreme.' Victor rubbed his jaw. 'Very extreme.'

'Solomon told us that Jay isn't a changeling as such. He believed that the doomed refugees on the ship willed Jay into existence to become a Vengeance Child.'

'And his purpose would be to curse people he came into contact with. First on a fairly random basis, and always one at a time. But now he's growing up, he's getting smarter. So now, the aircraft, and we saw what happened with the ship.' He grimaced. 'Add to all that a mutant virus. He's learning new tricks, isn't he?'

'But it isn't Jay that is evil,' Laura insisted. 'An evil force is working through him. Because of this.' She typed *N'Taal* into the search engine. Straightaway, a website appeared. At first it appeared to be a tile pattern. However, each tile was the photograph of a man, woman or child.

'It's a tribute site maintained by people who don't believe that this atrocity should be forgotten. Every picture here is of a person that died on the *N'Taal*.'

Victor read the banner across the top of the screen. '"Turned away from every port. No mercy. Three hundred and eighty lives lost. God help them. God help us for letting it happen." You've looked for Jay's photograph?'

'Solomon's right. He doesn't appear here. Also, his name isn't in the passenger inventories.' She clicked a loudspeaker icon. 'This is a recording of the last radio message from the *N'Taal*.' From the surf-like hiss of static came the voice of the long-dead captain: 'This message isn't directed at emergency services or to coastguard or navies of the Western powers. We have sailed to each of your nations, we have asked for sanctuary. You turned us away from your harbours. When we told you that we needed medicines and food for the men, women and children on board you gave us nothing. When I radioed that the ship had started taking on water we heard, by way of answer, only silence. We, the Cathdran, are poor people. But we are human beings like yourselves – something that you forget. Yesterday, our last pump failed, and water continues to leak through the keel. Today, the ship's engines are losing power. In a few short hours this ship will become our tomb. The passengers and crew belong to the same tribe with the same blood, the same beliefs. We have done with begging. We will not cry any more. Our last few hours of life on this earth will be devoted to our righteous and justifiable anger. Ours is the proud way of the warrior. Our ancestors marched with Hannibal on Rome. Even though we have been a persecuted minority for a thousand years we do know how to strike back. From beyond the grave if need be. Our thirst for vengeance is unquenchable. Our rage, eternal. As you've hurt us, so we will hurt you. We cry vengeance at you. Vengeance!' Victor wasn't sure if he imagined it but he thought he heard hundreds of voices, in a language he didn't understand, join that of the captain. From the speakers pulsed a single word over and over. Although he couldn't interpret it he didn't doubt its meaning: *'VENGEANCE . . . VENGEANCE . . . VENGEANCE!'*

Laura murmured, '"From hell's heart I stab at thee."'

'Those people must have been born holding a grudge.'

'If we were in their position, their children effectively sentenced to death by uncaring governments, wouldn't we do the same? If we could?'

Torrents of air made ghostly sighs through the window. It didn't require much to believe that phantoms from the *N'Taal*, lying at the bottom of the Atlantic, had found their way to Siluria aboard the westerly winds. For an instant, Victor thought he saw shadowy faces peering down through the clouds. *They want their vengeance. Now they're close to getting it . . .* He remembered what Wilkes had told him, that he'd seen Jay repeating 'Laura' over and over. The boy clearly loved her; maybe, however, his compulsion to wreak revenge on behalf of the doomed passengers of the *N'Taal* was stronger. Victor wrestled with his conscience. Should he tell her? Would it benefit her to know? After all, they say that the impact of a curse is psychological . . . if one believes that it is real . . . He watched her closing the laptop. On her face, an expression of pure determin- ation. Should he really tell her that Jay had uttered her name? Maureen died in a road accident after hearing Jay say her name. Max had gone berserk with fear. Fearing her reaction might be one of panic, he nevertheless took the plunge. 'Laura. Mayor Wilkes told me he'd seen Jay in the street. Jay was repeating your name.'

Swiftly, she turned to fix her eyes on his. Had he done the right thing? What if she panicked? This was tantamount to a death sentence.

'Victor.' She sounded shocked. 'You told me that five minutes ago. Don't you, remember?'

Waves of fatigue dragged at his senses. He struggled to keep his eyes open. 'I told you that Jay repeated your name?'

'Yes. You really can't remember saying that at all?'

He shook his head. 'Second stage, I guess. The symptoms are kicking in faster than I'd hoped. Still: work to be done: a goal to be reached.' He breathed deeply as his mind spun. 'Whoa . . . vicious little bug, huh? Just when I thought I was getting over it.'

Laura touched his forehead. 'The fever's back. You need to be in bed. I'll fetch the doctor.'

'No.' Reaching up to where she rested her cool palm against his brow, he took her hand in his. 'We've got to see this through to the end. If I keep myself active, I'll be fine.' He smiled. 'I never could stand being cooped up in stuffy rooms.' He shot a longing glance at the outdoors.

'What are you going to do, Victor?'

'Solomon told us how to deal with a changeling.'

'Victor. Not only is it illegal, but Jay's a little boy. He—'

'Please, listen to me, Laura. I don't have long. You know it, I know it. I'm entering second stage of this infection. In a few hours I'll have lost whatever wits I had. Then after that, coma. Then end stage . . .' He shrugged. 'I just wanted to tell you that you do mean a hell of a lot to me. Only when I get close to someone I start thinking about Ghorlan. *I can't stop thinking about her.* Deep down, I still know I didn't do enough to find her. The thought of her lying at the bottom of the river, it—'

'It's not your fault.'

'The evening she went missing she called me. My phone was switched off because I was giving a lecture. It was only after she'd disappeared that I realized she'd left a message. It was this: "Never mind, Victor. I'll catch you later." There was something about her tone. She wanted to tell me something important. That "never mind" was loaded with so much emotion. Never mind? Never mind! Those seven words she left behind haunt me. It's worse when I meet a woman and start getting to know her. *Never mind, Victor. I'll catch you later.* See, there I go again, being obsessed with Ghorlan.' He sighed. 'Now . . . I'm going to tell you something, Laura. Although I'm not sure if I told you a minute ago and forgotten. It's hard to keep a grip now. Second stage? How can something as devastating as having your mind erased have such a banal name?'

'What did you want to tell me, Victor?' She regarded him with a gentle, caring warmth.

'I like you. I like you a lot. Lou told me I was stupid. I've told myself I'm stupid not to follow up that first night we had together with a long heartfelt discussion, where I should have said you are the most wonderful person to come into my life in the last ten years. That I want to see you again. And try . . . try as hard as I can to develop a relationship with you. You might have decided I'm a lunderhead, then told me to take a hike. But at least I would have put the past behind me, so I could have the opportunity of making a go of it with you.'

'Lunderhead?'

'Old Silurian word.' He paused in thought. 'I was a complete, blithering lunderhead to retreat into my shell and risk losing you. It's important I tell you this now. Because by tomorrow I don't know if I will be capable of even stringing a sentence together never mind telling you how I feel.'

'Thank you.' Laura's smile suggested something had opened in her heart. 'I did want to hear that. Because I like you, too, Victor. The truth is, I find it hard to trust people. And, despite myself, I found I trusted you. When you kept your distance I thought I'd left myself overexposed and downright foolish. Now this feels like starting over.'

The door burst open. 'Oh, sorry, I didn't know you were here with Victor.' Lou eyed him with a fair amount of suspicion.

'How are they?'

'Less volatile, but I'm worried about Archer and Jay.'

'Archer's always been the most sensitive. If I speak to him alone I'm—'

'No, not that, Laura. Both Archer and Jay are missing. I've checked the garden. We've looked in the streets nearby but there isn't a sign. Neither hide nor hair.'

Laura shot Victor a telling glance. Then she turned to the woman, who stood wringing her fingers in the doorway. 'Don't worry, Lou. You keep the others occupied. I'll find Archer.'

Victor nodded. 'You leave Jay to me.'

After Lou vanished back through the door Laura caught Victor's arm. 'When you find Jay, what are you going to do to him?'

'Whatever happens, just remember we didn't have this conversation about Jay today – and especially not anything about what Solomon told us.'

'Victor?'

But Victor ran downstairs without looking back.

Thirty-Four

Archer marched purposefully through the wood in the direction of the castle. Mayor Wilkes followed. Archer had decided to show the mayor where the car was hidden, if he could. Jay had taken the boy there using his weird witch powers. The car had been locked up inside some kind of cellar, the dead woman in the back. But if he explained to Mayor Wilkes where the car was then maybe they could find another entrance. The car, he decided, would be far more important than some old bracelet.

OK, so the bracelet was a clue that would be useful to the police; the car, though, with the corpse in the back, would be big, *big* news. Archer imagined himself being interviewed on TV. 'Yes, I went into the cellar. I got into the car, even though it had cobwebs and blood, and the dead body, all bashed in. No, sir, I wasn't scared.' *Just picture the other kids' faces when they see me talking on television!*

'Much further?' asked Mayor Wilkes.

'Nearly there.'

'Aren't we on the path to the castle?'

Archer nodded. Mayor Wilkes would be so amazed when he saw the car.

The man walked alongside the boy. 'You found a bracelet. That's connected to the castle, isn't it?'

Archer suddenly shivered. Why had Mayor Wilkes decided that the bracelet and the castle were connected? It didn't make sense.

They continued walking up the slope toward the ruin. The big tower punched at the sky; a stone fist bruising the cloud. Now, gales had torn rents in the cloud. Sunlight fell through on to the river and the green back of the island. To Archer the beams of sunlight were blades that knifed the ground. Stab, stab, stab. Archer began to perspire. A taste as bad as dirt filled his mouth. Now he wasn't so sure about Mayor Wilkes. The man had seemed nice. But now he glared at Archer like Max did before he started nipping his neck. Archer glanced round. They were alone here in the forest. Where was Laura? He needed Laura. *This isn't nice. I don't like this grown-up. I know he wants to hurt me.* A beam of light sliced through the forest canopy. Archer screwed up his eyes at the intensity of the glare.

Pain shot through his head. In his imagination he followed the beam that shone down like a searchlight. For Archer it pierced the ground with the intensity of a laser to sizzle tree roots, and scare rabbits in their burrows. Then it would slice through the mud until it reached the castle. There it would illuminate the vault that entombed the car. A great big pulsing explosion of light that would illuminate every detail of the dead lady lying on the back seat. 'A car that's been hidden to conceal the murder victim.' Archer mouthed the words as if he was a television detective.

'What's wrong with you?' Mayor Wilkes asked brusquely. 'Don't go weird on me yet, until you show me what's hidden in the castle.'

Hidden in the castle? Archer flinched. He never mentioned anything hidden in the castle. He'd been careful to keep it a surprise. Mayor Wilkes was supposed to be so proud of him for finding the secret car. Now, somehow, the man had guessed. *It's like him knowing there's a connection between the Ghorlan~Victor bracelet and the castle. That doesn't make sense. The only way he could know those things was if . . .*

Archer murmured the disturbing conclusion aloud just like a TV detective making an important deduction. 'The only way he could know about the bracelet, and something hidden in the castle, is if he knows that's where the car is. And that the bracelet came from the car . . .' That strange mood came over him again. The one that gripped him when he became too worried. Then his emotions would go into shutdown. Catatonia. He'd heard Laura use the word once. Catatonia. It sounded like a disease. Vaguely, he was only half-aware that Mayor Wilkes loomed over him. Above the man's head, trees shook their branches in cold fury. They seemed to rage at Archer. The little boy who knew too much.

'What's that you said?' The man gripped his shoulder so hard it hurt. 'You just said something's hidden in the castle. What is it?'

The stormy gusts must have been noisy enough to prevent the man hearing everything that Archer had muttered. Previously, Archer had feared that Victor had put the dead woman in the car. Now he wasn't so sure. The mayor's eyes bulged. He'd become angry with Archer. *Really angry.* He was shaking the boy as if he were a toy. Not real flesh. Not a human being that could feel pain.

'I'm warning you, you little freak!' Wilkes roared. 'Stop playing the fool! Tell me what you've found in the castle!'

Archer couldn't speak, even if his life depended on it.

'Tell me!' Wilkes bunched his fist. 'Tell me now!'

Archer could only make a gurgling sound.

'Oh, that silly game again. Where you pretend you've gone into a bloody coma. Well, you might fool your imbecile nurses, but you don't fool me.' He grinned. 'You can't kid a kidder.' He pulled Archer toward him. Beams of light stabbed down through the branches. 'Now,' Mayor Wilkes said with great satisfaction, 'in your pocket you've got something I want. Hand it over, or I'll shake it out of you.' To add weight to the words he shook Archer the same way someone would shake dirt out of a rag. 'Bracelet. Give it to me. Or you'll be sorry.'

A loud rustling sound came from the bushes. Mayor Wilkes reacted the same way as when he met Victor's sister in the field. Quickly, he stepped back from Archer. At the same time his features smoothed out, so that gloating expression was hidden behind a mask of normality. The man clearly thought someone would walk through the bushes. Instead, a pair of Saban Deer padded out; a mother and her young fawn. The pair of animals regarded Mayor Wilkes with calm, blue eyes.

'Bloody pests!' Wilkes scooped up a stone then pelted the animals. In a flash of yellow they vanished into the shadows.

Archer knew they had the right idea. As fast as he could he raced away.

Behind him, Mayor Wilkes fired off a vicious response. 'Hey, come back here!'

Archer kept running. A moment later, however, he knew that the big man was chasing after him.

Thirty-Five

The breeze struck Victor the moment he left the hostel. While he still had his wits about him he must find Jay. Solomon had told him what must be done. What he'd read on the websites reinforced the African policeman's recommendation. Expose Jay to danger. Make him fear for his life. Yet Victor had spent his adult life protecting animals. Now this? When he found Jay he wondered what he'd be capable of. By the church he was hailed by their grim-faced doctor.

'Victor—'

'I'm sorry, doctor, I can't stop. I have to find—'

'Victor, your sister is ill. You've heard about this second stage?' Stormy gusts drove leaves along the pavement, ghostly forms that seemed to be searching for something in the maze of narrow streets. Dr Nazra continued, 'Do you understand? The virus attacks the brain.'

Victor nodded. 'How is she?'

'Comfortable, but I have to tell you that she's no longer conscious. She must have been coming to the village for some reason when the illness overwhelmed her.'

'Where is she now?'

'At her friend's house. You do appreciate how critical the second stage is?'

'How long does she have?'

'This mutant strain has no model we can work with.'

'Hours?'

'Hours probably.' Dr Nazra regarded Victor. 'And you, Victor, you've suffered from this, too.'

'I'm feeling OK,' he lied. Already the world had taken on a dream-like aspect.

'My regret is that you won't be for long. Soon you won't be thinking coherently. Memory will fail. You'll become so fatigued that you will not be able to stay awake.' Dr Nazra sighed. 'But my suggestion that you go home will be wasted on you, won't it? I can tell you have a matter of great importance.'

Victor smiled grimly. 'A matter of life and death. If that doesn't sound too melodramatic.'

'Then Godspeed.'

Victor thanked him then headed down toward the jetty.

The doctor called after him. 'And another thing, think twice before you do anything that might cause harm. The fever will cloud your judgement.'

Debris covered the jetty planks: white shards of polystyrene, seaweed, plastic bags and a slimy coating of mud. He wondered why it had been left in such a mess. Then he looked along the shoreline. An upturned dinghy wallowed in the shallows. While on the beach itself were a dozen or so uprooted trees that had been tossed about the beach like a child's discarded toys.

'I should know why it looks like this . . . something happened this morning . . .' He stared at the ravaged coastline. Brown scars revealed where turf had been stripped from the soil. What on earth had caused this? Victor's blood thudded in his ears. He knew the reason. He was sure he did. Only for the moment he couldn't quite . . .

'The ship.' He sucked air into his lungs. The relief at remembering seemed hugely important. 'I haven't lost my wits yet.' Even so, that moment of *not* remembering the incident of just a few hours ago, when an ocean-going tanker had sent a tidal wave blasting along the shoreline, left him trembling. 'You got to keep a grip,' he breathed. 'Because you've got to find Jay. And do what needs to be done.'

He worked his way along the shoreline path. The only figure out in this foul weather was John Newton, a writer of true crime stories, who lived in the cottage nearest the river. The man was clearing away branches left by the ship's destructive wash.

'John,' he called over the roar of the gale. 'John?'

'Victor. Did you see what that ship did this morning?'

'John, this is important. Have you seen a boy around here recently?'

'About ten minutes ago, one of the Badsworth Lodge party headed up that way toward the middle of the island.'

'Can you remember what he looked like?'

John Newton added a dripping branch to the pile. 'About eleven or twelve. Very slightly built. Oh, and his eyes. Very distinctive eyes. Why, what's—?'

'Thanks, John.'

Whatever John Newton's response might have been vanished into the teeth of the gale. Victor raced southward along the path. This wasn't a big place. He'd find Jay, without a shadow of doubt. It was only a question of time.

★   ★   ★

Archer ran. In fact, he ran so fast it didn't seem like running. Dark soil streamed under his feet. Above his head, a green blur of branches. He followed the pair of Saban Deer that flitted through the under-growth; they were more spirit creatures than real skin and fur, or so it seemed to Archer.

Mayor Wilkes chased Archer, roaring at him to stand still. For a moment back there the eight-year-old felt himself slipping into the comatose state that gripped him when the world became too much to bear. But Archer knew the man would hurt him if he stopped, and it'd be a far greater hurt than any bully had inflicted on him in the past.

'You, boy, give me the bracelet!'

Archer kept moving. Because he was so small he could run without stooping under the branches. Not so, the thundering man. They were at chest height for him. However, instead of bending down he punched his way through. Those hard fists snapped the twigs. Every so often he'd encounter a clump of pink blossom. Smack! The fist would strike. Then an explosion of pink petals. Nothing stopped him. What was more, Archer knew the man was gaining on him. Gulping with fear, the boy pushed on through the shadows.

'Come back here, you little wretch!' The voice sounded closer.

And now the forest seemed endless. Archer's legs grew weaker; it was as if the bones had turned as soft as marshmallow. Stitch dug painfully in his side. Hide! But where? The man would find him. They were alone here. Nobody would hear a little boy's screams of pain. For the first time in his eight years Archer found himself looking into the future. Ahead there was only darkness for him. A deep void without light. The same darkness that dominated the coffin of his father's corpse.

His chest tightened. He could barely breathe. The whimper of terror in his throat turned into a crackling sound. Then the light hit him with the abruptness of a slap. He blinked. The forest now lay behind him. In front, the stone mass of the castle on its mound. Its tower loomed above him. He glanced back: surely Mayor Wilkes would be close enough to grab him.

The bushes fringing the forest were at their thickest here. Archer had been able to move freely beneath them. Mayor Wilkes, however, encountered those branches at chest height. His fists still smashed the greenery; yet, here at its densest, it did impede his progress.

'Stay where you are, or I'll make you wish you'd never been born.'

Exhausted, barely able to put one foot in front of the other, Archer slogged his way up the grassy slope to the castle wall. A small doorway pierced the masonry. He prayed the entrance wouldn't be locked. Soon he wouldn't be able to run another step. Then he'd be easy meat for the furious, roaring figure that now emerged from the forest.

Storm winds shook the trees. The tower resembled a fist ready to fall on Archer and crush him into the earth in a mess of blood and bone and hair. By the time he reached the timber door set in the castle wall he saw that Mayor Wilkes had emerged from the forest. Archer sobbed. The man didn't appear tired. If anything, the anger made him more powerful. His eyes blazed – glorying – exulting – in the merciless power he'd soon wield over the child. Archer stumbled. On his hands and knees he struggled to get air into his lungs. Energy drained away from his body. He could barely raise his head.

'Boy! Give me that bracelet. Then, so help me, I'm going to enjoy teaching you a lesson!'

Fists, kicks, biting . . . Archer foresaw all too clearly what the next few moments promised. With a yell he kicked free of the exhaustion that held him back. He staggered to the door. *Don't be locked . . . please don't be locked.*

Mayor Wilkes pounded relentlessly across the turf toward Archer.

The boy gripped the door handle then tugged it down. It turned. Archer pushed the door. It remained firmly shut. He pushed harder. Still it didn't open. It must be locked after all. He groaned in pure terror. Any moment those fists would crash against his head. He pictured the dead woman in the car. The truth was obvious now. Why Mayor Wilkes needed the bracelet was brutally clear.

Weakly, Archer rattled the door. Just time for one more try. He pulled the handle down hard with both hands. A loud click. A mechanism moved. First time around he hadn't depressed it far enough to engage the lever. So exhausted he could barely push, he allowed his body weight to open the door as he slumped against it. Behind him, Mayor Wilkes had stopped running. He was enjoying the luxury of that purposeful, deadly walk toward Archer.

The boy limped through the doorway into the castle yard, surrounded by its twenty-foot-high stone wall. In one corner of the yard stood the timber cabin that served as the groundskeeper's store and souvenir shop. Shutters up. Door locked. Huge padlocks glinted; they held the outside world at bay. Along one wall, a stack of stone blocks ready to be used to repair eroded masonry.

Archer tottered across the cobbled yard. The main entrance gate had been sealed with forbidding padlocks. Huge things, as big as a boy's head. Archer turned round to witness a dreadful sight. A smiling Mayor Wilkes stepped through the doorway in the wall. Firmly he shut the door behind him, then shot across a bolt at the top – a bolt the tiny waif from Badsworth Lodge couldn't reach. Archer looked for open doorways in the castle buildings. There were none. And there was nobody about. Apart from the bad man, Archer was alone.

'Archer. You've got something for me.' Mayor Wilkes grinned as he closed in, his hands balling into fists.

Thirty-Six

Above the castle, torrents of misty air raced in from the west. The turbulence drew a ghostly weeping from the battlements that only underlined Archer's fear.

Boy and man faced each other across the cobbled yard. The grown-up bared his teeth in something akin to a snarl. He knew he'd won.

'Give up, boy, there's nowhere to run.' The adult approached.

Archer searched for a way out. Only the gates and doorways were locked. He was trapped in the castle yard. At that moment a shaft of sunlight speared the cloud. A pool of radiance skated over the stones to where a fence surrounded a metal grid, which had been set into the ground. Archer found himself drawn to follow the shaft of sunlight.

'There's nowhere to run, Archer. Don't waste your time.' Wilkes followed at a stroll. 'Don't you realize it's time to get this over with?'

Archer ducked between the bars of the fence to find a square grille that was no larger than the door of a domestic oven. It covered a circular opening cut into the ground. *This is the castle well.* He remembered Victor had explained its purpose when he showed them round. It used to go a long, long way down but now it had been partially filled with debris. And at this moment the beam of sunlight shone down through a rent in the cloud to illuminate the build-up of dirt in the well. There, foil gum wrappers glinted on the soil plug like so many silvery eyes.

'Game's up,' Wilkes announced as he approached the safety fencing.

Archer saw that the stonework that formed a ring around the well opening had been eroded. A chunk had crumbled away, so there was a gap between the grille, which stopped people falling in, and the edge of the well. As fast as he could the boy used his tiny build to his advantage. In seconds he squirmed feet first into the gap. The iron edge of the grille scraped his chest, while the rough corners of the stone retaining blocks gouged his back.

But he was through.

'Come here, you little cretin.' Wilkes leaned through the fence to grab Archer by the hair. Hooked fingers snagged the curls. The boy forced his skinny torso through the gap. His feet kicked free as he dangled in thin air, hanging on to one of the iron bars of the grille. Then before the man could grab his wrist he let go.

Damp air gusted by him as he dropped into darkness.

When Victor saw him standing on the shore he realized this was how it was meant to be. He'd gone in search of Jay. The boy, however, had waited for the man. The mist had thickened, so Jay cut an ethereal figure there on the beach; a shadowy apparition, rather than a living being. Victor knew he was entering the second stage of the illness, yet at this moment his mental function appeared normal. He remembered, perfectly, what had happened in the last forty-eight hours. The cool wash of air kept his senses alert.

The boy regarded him with the almond-shaped eyes. 'Have people died of the sickness?'

He nodded. 'Completely innocent people that had nothing to do with the sinking of the *N'Taal*.'

'Didn't these people elect governments that did nothing to help the people on the ship?'

'Some will have voted, but they didn't have a say in whether the governments helped those refugees or not.' Victor moved toward him. There was an alien quality about the expression, as if another intelligence occupied the boy's mind. 'You know Solomon was here.'

'The policeman from Africa. He died.'

'Did you . . . ?' Victor stopped himself. Accusations would be futile. He had to take a different approach. 'You are an eleven-year-old boy, Jay. Don't let this thing, whatever it is, use you. You have a right to a childhood and to grow up into a man. It's wrong for you to be used as a weapon.'

'Do you know how many children under the age of thirteen died on the *N'Taal*?' The voice could have emanated from skeletons that clung to each other in a rusting hulk. 'One hundred and seventy.'

Victor's heart pounded. 'Fight this thing, Jay. Don't let it use you.'

'One hundred and seventy children. In all three hundred and ninety men, women and children.' When he stepped backwards, pebbles scrunched under his feet. The sound of bones being stirred by the tide.

'If Solomon was right, then you're a victim of the ship's passengers, just as they were victims of all those countries that prevented them from entering their ports.'

'Do you know how many babies under twelve months drowned, Victor?'

'If it was a million there's nothing you can do to bring them back to life.'

Shapes emerged from the mist. Shaggy, beast–like shapes. For a moment Victor wondered if Jay had conjured something monstrous. Then Victor realized these were trees that had been washed up after the tidal wave. He noticed that amongst the mud–smeared branches there were more fishing lines of the type he'd found earlier on the beach. Hanging from those lines were entire bunches of fishing hooks. Big glittering ones with fearsome barbs. There must have been hundreds of the hooks. One bunch had trapped a gull that hung there lifeless, its beak partly open.

'Keep away from the trees, Jay,' he warned. 'Can you see the hooks? Once they stick into your skin the barb holds it in there. You can't just pull it out.'

Jay retreated along the beach. 'When this is over I'm going to a town, then I'm going to a city. I'm going to keep doing this, Victor. I know how to make people suffer and die . . . lots and lots of them.'

'Do you want Laura to die?'

'She's leaving anyway. You're going to marry her . . . you'll take her from us.'

'So you can control this talent for curses, then.' Victor became angry. 'You have free will. You may be the Vengeance Child, but you can decide who lives and who dies.'

'No . . .' He shook his head, yet Victor saw doubt in his face.

'Come on, Jay. You understand what it means to grow up. You're eleven years old. Growing up means you take control over your actions. When a baby is six months old it can't decide when to pee or take a dump. By the time it's three it can. So, I'll tell you what I believe. OK, until recently you had no control over this power inside of you . . . this power that puts a curse on people . . . a curse that causes bad things to happen. It just happened spontaneously, like a sneeze, but now you do know how to control it. Sometimes, if you like a person, you hold the curse back. If you don't, for example when Max bullied you, then you take out the hex; you wind it up, let it go. You went to town hurting Max, didn't you? You got him so scared, he tried to kill himself. I'm right, aren't I?'

A sheen of perspiration gleamed on Jay's face. He'd retreated into himself as he worked through what Victor had told him.

'Also this other thing, Jay, where you take people into past events of their lives. That's a new talent you're developing, isn't it? You look into our heads and see the big, big things that happened to us, then you exploit it.'

'Ghorlan.'

'Yes, like Ghorlan. You knew she's my wife.'

'*Was* your wife. She's dead.'

'Yes, I know. She drowned out there.' Angry, he pointed at the river.

'No. She didn't go in the water.'

That's what you say!' Victor knew he was losing self-control as he advanced on the boy. 'You're going to torture me, aren't you? How did she die, then? Just burst into flames, I suppose? Are you going to inflict nasty scenarios on me?'

Jay continued to walk backwards. Behind him a tree emerged from the mist. From lines tangled in the branches hooks by the dozen glinted. Jay turned, then he ran full pelt at them. Victor raced after Jay and managed to stop him short of the branches with their arsenal of steel barbs.

'You can stop this epidemic, Jay, like you can stop inflicting all this pain on innocent people.' He caught his breath. 'So, Jay, what do you intend to do?'

'Do?' Jay gave a little chuckle. 'Intend to do?' The boy's expression suggested someone slipping into a trance. When he spoke, it was in a breathy, sing-song way. 'What I intend to do, Victor, is show you things . . . we're going for a little walk.'

Thirty-Seven

Archer thought, I've broken all my bones. I can't breathe . . .

The eight-year-old lay at the bottom of the shaft, on his back, staring up at the metal grille. Each inhalation made him whimper. Squares of light formed by the grille changed as a figure leaned over it. He knew that Mayor Wilkes looked down at him.

'Bigger drop than you thought, eh?' the man grunted. 'You might have just saved me a job.' The silhouette vanished. Archer gazed at clouds through the criss-cross pattern formed by the bars. A shaft of light shone down from the sky to fill the well. Sheer walls rose up all around him, lined with smooth stone. Then the sunlight vanished. It seemed even darker than before. When Archer drew breath his chest ached so much.

Then came loud grating sounds. *Is he opening the grate so he can get at me?* Only when blocks of darkness appeared to blot out part of the criss-cross pattern did he realize what Wilkes was doing. Slowly but surely the man was sliding heavy pieces of masonry over the grille. Especially over the gap that Archer had slid through. These, the hunks of stone stored in the yard for the restoration work, were being used to entomb the boy.

'This will keep you in your place,' Wilkes barked. 'You won't be able to shift these in a hurry. What do you say to that?'

Breathing hurt so much Archer couldn't reply even if he had wanted to. Meanwhile, Wilkes brusquely tossed sentences at the boy. They weren't meant as consolation. Anything but. 'The island's under quarantine. Let me explain. That means nobody can leave the island, nobody can come on to the island. We're cut off from the mainland. Therefore, the castle will be closed to the public for the foreseeable future. I have the spare set of keys. Besides that, my word is law. No one will come here for at least a week.' His eyes burned down through the grille. 'Do you understand what that means for you? You will wallow in that stinking pit of yours, by yourself, for seven days, and seven very long nights. Without food or drink. No doubt you will do a lot of yelling. Go ahead, be my guest. But seeing as we're at the tip of the island no one will hear.' He laughed. 'It looks like rain, too. Did I mention that when it rains the well fills with water again? It's customary to wish a chap in peril good luck, but it isn't good luck I'll be wishing you. Goodbye, Archer.' Footsteps receded across stone cobbles, then the door in the wall slammed shut.

It took a long time. Eventually, however, the pain eased in Archer's chest. He realized he'd been badly winded, that was all. What was more, when he moved his limbs he knew he hadn't broken any bones. From what he could tell, the surface he'd fallen on consisted of old dry leaves. This soft mulch had broken his fall, not his legs.

'Gotta get out, Archer,' he murmured. 'Show Victor the bracelet. He'll know what to do.' *Get out, Archer?* Easier said than done. The walls were smooth. Most of the time he couldn't see because the cloud made it so dark. Occasionally, though, a beam of light would break through. The intense sunshine would reveal the yellow stonework. It also revealed something else that made his heart leap.

He should have been pleased. He should have yelled, 'Yes!' then punched the air. However, dread gripped him in its implacable fist. *You've done this, Jay. You've brought me back here to frighten me.* For there, just at arm's length, half-hidden by shadow, was a chilling sight. A stone archway. One just high enough and wide enough to wriggle through. Not for a second did he believe it led to safety. But he couldn't sit for ever at the bottom of the well. Mayor Wilkes said it would flood when it rained. Archer couldn't swim. Anyway, after seven days, what then? If he was alive the mayor would return to ensure that Archer never told anyone what had happened.

With a deep sense of foreboding Archer crawled through the opening. Ahead it was completely dark. Worse, it didn't open out into a room; instead it narrowed down into a tight little tunnel. In olden times it might have been a kind of water pipe that carried water from the well to stop it overflowing into the yard if it rained heavily. Archer couldn't even crawl. He had to worm his way forward on his belly with his arms out in front, and sort of push along with his feet. He heard them scraping behind him. His back hurt where he'd gouged it on the rough stone when he'd slithered through the grille to escape Mayor Wilkes. Now this. Being here terrified him. His heart pounded. Blood roared through his head. The sides of the tunnel squashed his chest. The pressure made his ribs hurt again. It was hard to breathe. A heavy fungus smell filled his nostrils. The further he wriggled the colder it became. The boy feared the tunnel would narrow to the point he became stuck. *Nobody will ever find me. I'll be trapped for ever . . .* Grimly, he pushed forward. Ahead, it was completely dark. What if he encountered an obstruction? Or rats? They could bite him to death. Trembling, he imagined furry snouts, with bristly whiskers, then teeth munching into his face. He shouted when something feathery stroked his face. Shaking his head to free himself from its clutch, he raked at it with his fingers.

Light soft stuff on his skin? A cobweb, that's all. He struggled to prevent panic engulfing him. At that moment he realized if he started screaming he'd never stop. *Onward, onward, onward . . . that's the only direction.* Now it would be impossible to squirm backwards to the well. He'd have to carry on. Archer believed in all kinds of monsters. What if a hand grabbed his face? It could sink its fingers into his eyes. Archer nearly choked with fear. Even to breathe was difficult. All his body hurt from head to toe. Normally, he'd go into emotional shutdown at times of stress. Only this time even that escape wasn't open to him. He remained clear-headed. He knew the danger he was in. People die in situations like this. *I've got to save myself. No one will come. Not Lou. Not Laura. I'm all on my own.* Taking a deep breath, he squirmed forward. In that darkness it seemed as if he pushed himself down a tube that shrank ever smaller around him. That smell: rich, heavy, a raw mushroom odour. For a long time he struggled forward, his skin chafed from being scraped by stone walls. He moved a hand from side to side as a kind of antenna to get some sense of where the sides of the tunnel were – and what might be lying in wait to bite his face. He knew he'd become weaker. The walls pressing against his body leached their cold through his clothes into his skin. More cobwebs ahead. He didn't see them but he certainly felt them. Probably spiders in there. With big black, bristly legs. He slashed at invisible cobwebs with his hand. When he'd done this before his knuckles had struck the tunnel wall with a painful knock. This time his hand swung outward into nothingness.

Heart beating faster, he pushed forward, feet scraping frantically at the floor. Then the stones under him vanished. He knew he was hanging out into a void. But what lay outside the tunnel? Another shaft? This might plunge down hundreds of feet. He might tumble into it to break every bone in his body. The light that suddenly appeared brought short-lived relief. He groaned. The witch, Jay! This was his doing. For through a ventilation block in the wall thirty feet to his right shone a dozen narrow rods of light as the sun dropped to the horizon. The light shining through the block didn't reveal a lot. But it revealed he'd been here before.

Archer saw that the break in the tunnel opened into a cellar. Tree roots hung from the ceiling. The stink of decay filled the air. In the centre of this vaulted chamber sat a car. Filth covered it. Mushrooms had forced their bulbous growths through the side of the headlight. As he swung himself down on to the floor of the cellar he tried to see through the back window of the car. He knew that was where the vehicle's occupant resided. Only before he had chance to get a proper look the cloud obscured the sun again. Darkness replaced the reddish light.

Standing there, heart pounding, Archer trembled. A cold, cold fear flooded him as he imagined something stirring in the back of the entombed car.

In a shaky voice he cried out, 'I kept it safe. The bracelet's in my pocket . . . you wanted me to give it to someone . . . I didn't know who . . . don't hurt me . . . I did my best . . . please don't hurt me.'

Archer's voice echoed back. This makeshift tomb beneath the castle had just increased its population by one.

Thirty-Eight

'You're going to take me for one of your little walks?' Victor echoed as he stood with Jay on the shore. The sky had grown even darker. Waves rose in angry peaks on the river. 'Where? Back to Ghorlan, when she planted the tree on our first wedding anniversary?'

Jay appeared to be in a trance. Despite the cold, a sheen of perspiration had formed above those dark eyes that held so many secrets.

'You do know this is cruel? You torment people with visions of what they can't possibly change, then you inflict yet more tragedy on them.'

Storm winds blew harder. Steel fishing hooks danced in the trees as the gales tugged at them. Even though the storm had nearly reached Siluria, Victor felt as if he was becoming detached from reality. Branches on the uprooted trees had tapped against the trunks. Only now that tapping had been transformed into a knocking. A fist hammering on the door. Loud. Insistent. *Someone wants in.*

'Here we go.' Jay's eyes appeared luminous in the gloom. 'Here we go. I'm taking you back . . . I'm going to show you something terrible . . .'

A frightened stranger stopped Laura in an otherwise deserted street in the village.

'It's shocking, isn't it?' The middle-aged woman appeared to be in shock herself. 'They say there're now thirty people in a coma. It's this second stage. I've got it, too. I can't even remember my own name.' Her eyes darted with fear.

Laura had problems of her own. 'I'm looking for someone,' she said. 'You haven't seen a boy of around eight with blond, curly hair?'

'People dying. I'm going to be next. I know I am.' The woman's eyes went wild. 'Oh my God! Where do I live? I can't remember how to get back home!' She clutched Laura's arm. 'Help me get home. You've got to help me!' Without waiting for a reply the woman rushed away down the street. Every few yards she'd dart into a garden, then look searchingly at the front of the cottage as if trying to recognize if this was home. 'Where do I live? For God's sake help me!'

Laura's first instinct was to go to the woman. But, no. Archer needed her more. She must find the boy. If he'd gone into emotional shutdown he could be lying out in the open somewhere, so she left the screaming woman. With luck a villager would take her in. Then again, so many were ill now, seriously ill. Laura's anxieties were as turbulent as the weather. Victor had entered second stage. Was he really fit enough to search for Jay? Soon his mental faculties would slip from him. But what else could they do? With the island quarantined they couldn't call in the police. They were alone here. They'd have to deal with this crisis by themselves.

Laura hurried along deserted streets. Doors banged in the breeze. Gales snarled through the trees. The River Severn appeared to be boiling. Mounds of water rose in the channel to explode into sprays of foam. In the hazy distance stood dark woods, beyond those the forbidding mass of the castle. The island was tiny, yet at this moment it seemed an impossibly vast place to search. What drove her was the mental image of Archer lying unconscious in some meadow or copse. As she headed for White Cross Farm she glimpsed another figure walking back through the mist to the village. Victor? She paused, hoping he'd found Jay; perhaps, Archer, too.

The figure moved with nothing less than arrogance. A second later she recognized it. Mayor Wilkes. Damn him, he actually seemed to be enjoying this. During the emergency the island had become his personal kingdom. Before he got close Laura cut off on another path that took her toward the farm. The urgency of her pace intensified. Laura had an overwhelming sense that time was running out.

This is fun. I'm actually having the time of my life. On the path back to the village, Wilkes smiled. He knew why he derived such rich enjoyment from recent events. *It's a sense of power. I'm in control . . . complete and utter control.* He loved problems. Obstacles brought out the best in him. Now all this: the epidemic, the quarantine, the boy finding Ghorlan's bracelet. God, yes, this sumptuous feast of adrenalin elevated him above mere mortals. His spirits soared; his mind enjoyed such clarity of thought.

As he approached his house he saw Dr Nazra. Poor, benighted fool. He'd chased after all his clueless neighbours trying to save their insignificant lives. Now the man had driven himself to the point of absolute exhaustion.

However, Dr Nazra called out in a bright voice, 'Mayor Wilkes. Good news at last. Tomorrow the health authority is sending in a medical team: biohazard suits, field hospital, drugs, the works. It's a miracle.'

Wilkes snapped, 'What about the quarantine?'

'That stands, alas, but we'll have help first thing in the morning. Isn't that wonderful?'

Wilkes stormed up the garden path to his front door. He'd planned to let the boy stew in the well for a few days. Now if people were coming on to the island . . . *that changed everything.* After Wilkes had closed the front door behind him he went straight to a steel cabinet in his study. With a crisp efficiency, he unlocked it. For a moment he gazed at the high quality shotguns neatly arranged in the rack. He found himself enjoying the process of making the selection. Smiling, he chose the twelve-bore pump action shotgun. *Didn't I tell you that I love problems?* Humming to himself he emptied a carton of bright orange shotgun cartridges into his jacket pocket, then resting the gun over the crook of his arm, he left the house. It was time to tie up all those irritating loose ends. Within moments he joined the path that would take him back to the castle.

Sometimes half-light. Sometimes utter darkness. A thick, black fog of nothingness that ate into Archer's soul. The boy had shuffled across the vault as far as he could from the car and its dead husk of an occupant. Half-light. Darkness. The dark periods lasted much longer than those of light . . . yet such a dim light. Every so often the clouds outside would break to admit shafts of sunlight. When these struck the wall outside pencil-thin beams of light shone through the ventilation block. These silver rods would reveal the big gloomy interior of the vault. Archer did his best to seek a way out. Newer bricks, however, filled in the archways where the old doors had once been. He recalled Victor saying that the vaults under the castle had been used by smugglers in olden times. A few years ago it had been decided they were unsafe, so the boss of the castle had ordered them to be bricked up.

Archer began to speak. 'Jay. I know you can hear me, Jay. Please let me out. I'm scared being in here. It's me, Archer. We weren't friends but I never hurt you or was bad to you. Please get me out of here. I'm frightened she'll come out of the car. I'm worried what she might do to me . . .'

Jay repeated the words: 'I'm going to show you something terrible.'

Victor had stood at the river's edge. The branches tapping on the trunks of uprooted trees had turned into an insistent pounding on the door.

'*I'm going to show you something terrible . . .*'

Victor didn't so much hear the words as divine them, as if they ghosted from a world far away. Victor blinked. He no longer stood on a beach but in the hallway of an old house. Traffic droned in the road outside. Horns tooted. City noises. Fried bacon smells filled the air. The knock on the door sounded again. Not just insistent; this was someone who demanded entry.

'I don't know this place,' Victor told Jay. The boy stood an arm's length away. Victor appraised the thin neck. His powerful hands would make short work of the boy. He took a step nearer. At that moment light steps tip-tapped down the stairs.

'Archer?' Victor recognized the boy, though now he appeared younger, perhaps five or six. 'What are you doing here? You should be back at the hostel with Laura.'

'He can't hear you.' Jay regarded Victor with gleaming eyes. 'No one can hear you, or see you here.'

A point proved when a man in his thirties, with slick, black hair, appeared at the doorway to the kitchen. The pounding on the front door continued. The man glared right through Victor and Jay as he addressed the little boy at the foot of the stairs: 'Archer. Come here, son. That's it, don't be scared. There's a good lad.' Fear distorted the man's face. 'Go to the door, Archer. Don't open it. Whatever you do, don't unlock it. Just shout through that you're home with your mother but your dad's out of town.'

Archer trembled. 'I want to get Mum a facecloth.'

'Later.'

'Her nose is bleeding.'

'Archer, you little runt, do as I tell you.'

Even though this fraught conversation continued Victor spoke angrily to Jay. 'Why are you showing me this?'

'I want you to know why Archer is the way he is.'

'Showing off, more like.' Victor shook his head. 'You're like the ghost of Christmas past. Fine, you can inflict sorry scenes like this on me, but do you expect we can change any of this? This is the past. There's no going back. It's dead.'

'Like Ghorlan.'

Victor knew that this walk of Jay's through bygone dramas was just the start. Quickly, he closed his eyes then opened them again in the hope he'd find himself back on the Silurian shore. The hallway remained resolutely in place around him. Floor tiles. Potted fern on a stand. Photographs of sports cars on the wall. Meanwhile, Archer's father angrily told the boy that he must not open the door to whoever pounded on its panels.

'If you screw up,' the man hissed at Archer, 'I'll rip your face off and stuff it down your throat.' Then the bully of a father headed down into a basement.

Archer opened the door to three men in leather jackets. Before they could speak the boy said, 'He's down in the cellar. You'll find him hiding behind the washing machine. He made a secret space in the wall behind the washer.'

Startled, Victor looked at Jay as the boy addressed him in a strangely adult way. 'The morning this happened the father punched Archer's mother in the face. He broke her nose. Archer only wanted the beatings to stop.'

'What's the point in showing me this, Jay?'

'Everyone thinks the men burst into the house. Instead, it was Archer who betrayed his own father to them. Don't you understand yet?'

'Understand what?' Victor seethed with anger.

'I'm trying to make you understand that just because we believe something in the past happened in a certain way, it might not be what really happened.'

The three men, guided by Archer, descended into the basement, where they dragged the man from his hiding place. Victor didn't hear what was said, but he did hear the gunshots when one of the men fired a handgun at point-blank range. Bullets ripped through flesh, exploding bone. Blood jetted from the wounds, then the man dropped lifeless to the floor. Victor noticed how Archer was staring with contempt at his dead father when the house melted away to be replaced by an entirely different location.

Thirty-Nine

'I know this place!' Excited, Victor hurried through a gate into the back garden of a modest suburban house where the sun shone brightly on to red brickwork. 'It's my old home.' With a huge grin, he pointed at a greenhouse filled with tomato plants. 'That's what I managed to damage with my bow and arrow when I was your age. The arrow smashed a pane, then hit a load of tomatoes. Juice and bits all over the inside of the glass. My dad went mad.' He paused. 'But am I here? Can you really take people back in time, Jay? Or is it this virus inside of me? Am I back on the beach, dreaming all this?'

Jay gazed at him. Victor had witnessed the bloody death of Archer's father. Anxiety crackled through his nerves. Had Jay brought him here to show him something awful?

'Jay, why am I here?'

'People are coming,' Jay intoned. 'They can't see us.'

Four youths charged into the back garden. One had a bright orange basketball, which he hurled at the hoop. It bounced back toward the greenhouse. A slender man, with curly black hair, caught it.

'Careful,' he said laughing. 'My dad's only just forgiven me for shooting an arrow through the glass.'

Victor gazed in wonder. 'That's me when I was nineteen. Those are my friends from high school. The guy in the glasses is Benjamin, he studied law; the one in the white shirt is Rajeed, now a computer technician; the one just catching the ball from me is Scotty. The last I heard he ran a hotel in Cyprus.' Astonished, he moved into the centre of the lawn as the four played basketball around him, shooting the hoop fixed to a garage wall. 'Jay, I know what this is . . .' His skin tingled as emotion nearly overwhelmed him. 'This is the last time we were all together. We were all nineteen. My parents threw a party because I'd been accepted on to a conservation programme in Kenya. This was a Sunday. I flew out to Africa the day afterwards. I spent a year working in a nature reserve. We built stock-proof fences, dug irrigation canals, rigged up observation hides for tourists; all kinds of stuff. That's what I'd dreamed of doing since I was four years old. My God, look at my face! You can see how excited I am.'

Victor paused to listen to the conversation. Benjamin was teasing a much younger Victor Brodman. 'When did you lose your mind, Vic?'

'What do you mean?' He shot the ball at the hoop. It plopped smoothly through.

'Good shot. This African thing. Scotty was telling me that not only are you going out to work on a game reserve for nothing, you are actually — *actually* — paying your so-called employer for the privilege. Listen to someone oh-so smarter, my son. When grown-ups go out to work they get paid something called cash. Now cash comes in oblong pieces of paper, or in pieces of metal called coins.'

'Very funny, Benny. Hey, stay clear of the greenhouse.'

'You'll get nowhere working for nothing,' Scotty added.

Rajeed patted Victor on the back. 'Vic's not obsessed with wealth. He loves the world. This charitable work in Africa proves this friend of ours is a noble man.' The four laughed, then sang out, 'Whoa . . . whoa!' when the ball cannoned in the direction of the fragile greenhouse panes again.

Victor turned to Jay. 'We're only half in and half out of this world, aren't we? I can smell roses and feel the sun's heat. I know you can put me into this world fully, can't you? So I can be seen by my friends and talk to them?'

'Is that what you want?'

'But you're not here for that, are you, Jay? You're going to show me something I don't know. Just as you showed me what really happened to Archer's father. That he betrayed him to his killers. So what happens, Jay? Do my friends stab me in the back?'

Jay walked to the house where he vanished inside. Victor followed. He was back in the kitchen he knew so well. That afternoon his retired parents busied themselves making sandwiches. Both wore safari style shirts in keeping with the day's celebrations.

Victor sighed. 'Bless them, they threw an African themed party. Look at the Hippo cake. All that bright green icing. I said to them, "Mum, Dad, I love you but did you have to buy the Hippo cake? I'm nineteen, not nine."'

Jay kept silent.

'Is this what you wanted me to see? Is it connected with what you said about us believing events happened in a certain way in the past? And not realizing that the facts were actually different?' His parents chatted softly, mainly about what plates to use, should they bring out the coleslaw yet, that kind of thing. 'I have lovely parents. My father used part of his retirement lump sum to fund my trip to Africa. They paid my airfare, accommodation, meals . . .' He groaned. 'No . . . I don't want to see what happens next. Jay, please don't do this to me.'

At that moment his mother paused as she sliced the bread. 'You have done the right thing, James. It's a small price to pay.'

'It's not selling the car that bothers me.' He watched the four playing basketball. 'It's that I've lied to Victor.'

'Come on, James, a white lie.'

'Why couldn't we be honest with him? He's our flesh and blood.'

'But there's no need to worry him needlessly. What you've done for James is wonderful. You should be proud.'

His father sighed. 'He isn't a boy any more. I should have told him, man-to-man, that I used the lump sum to pay off that damn loan. He'd have understood.'

'Yes, he'd have understood, James. What he wouldn't have done is allow you to sell the car. You've made this placement in Africa happen. You helped him get the career he's always wanted.'

Victor closed his eyes. 'So that's what happened. I thought my parents had lots of money in savings. I didn't realize they'd made these sacrifices, like selling the car, so I could go work at the reserve. Dear God, Jay, do you know how this makes me feel? Dad told me he'd sold the car because he had a new one on order. I was too full of what I was doing to even ask why there wasn't a new car when I came home. Now I know the truth I feel like some miserable parasite. A sponger. A spoilt—'

He opened his eyes. The kitchen had vanished. Instead, he stood on the deck of a ship at sea. It rolled in the heavy swell. People crammed on its deck had to grip on to the railings. Lightning seared the night sky. Dark-skinned mothers clung to their babies. Victor flinched at the sound that reached him. Such a terrible sound that seemed full of pain and despair. A huge groan rose through the deck of the ship.

Beside him, Jay murmured, 'That's the sound of the keel breaking.'

Victor spun round toward the bridge. Painted in grave black letters beneath the windows was one word: *N'TAAL*.

Forty

N'Taal. The name burned through the fabric of Victor Brodman's being. Here he was on the doomed ship. The rending of metal as it disintegrated told him that he'd arrived in its death throes. Lightning cast rivers of blue light in the sky. With brutal incandescence it revealed the deck of the *N'Taal* in every detail. Victor saw that streaks of rust had corrupted its paintwork. Corrosion-rendered holes in the steel deck. Jay gazed on the scene of imminent tragedy in his customary unfathomable way. Did he sense the panic of his own people? Dozens of men, women and children were struggling through hatches up on to the deck. They called to one another. Mothers passed infants to fathers from the dark pits formed by open hatch-ways. So this was the ship-full of refugees reviled by the world. After Jay's people had been driven from their homes, robbed, beaten, abused, they'd been herded on to a ship condemned by its owners as unseaworthy. Nevertheless, the freighter had been towed out of national waters with its cargo of desperate refugees, then it had begun its grim odyssey. Sailing from port to port around the Atlantic, the refugees had pleaded for asylum only to be turned away by warships before they could even reach dry land.

Laura had told Victor enough of the story for him to know what the grim outcome would be. He watched as desperate crew members and passengers worked together to deploy the lifeboats. The winch mechanisms that would lower the boats to the sea had become so rusted that they'd jammed solid. These lifeboats were clearly decades old. When they were freed from canvas covers the hulls were decayed to the point where the boats simply fell to pieces.

On the deck the men and women were shouting to each other as they tried to launch the lifeboats. This whirlwind of activity turned to weeping and terror when they realized their means of escape was useless. Parents knew that they had no way to save their children. Families sat down on the deck to cling to each other.

Victor adjusted his balance as the ship tilted. 'Jay!' he yelled above the scream of rending metal. 'Jay. I know you can bring me into their world. Do it! Let me help them!' A lightning flash lit up many frightened eyes. 'Fight what's inside of you, Jay. Don't let me stand here doing nothing. You must allow me to fully enter this reality. You've got to give me a chance to help save them!'

At that moment, the mood of the refugees changed. He'd sensed their sorrow at knowing that they and their children would soon be dead. Now, faces became angry. Everywhere men and women clenched their fists. As they sat to await the inevitable they beat their fists against metal decking. Soon the rhythmic pounding rivalled the thunder. One by one they took up a chant. It was in a language Victor didn't understand. Without a shadow of doubt he knew its meaning.

'*Feel this pain . . . everyone who rejected us, feel this pain. Send us the child that can make the world feel this torture. Send us a child that can hurt them . . . like they brought hurt to us.*' The chant grew louder. Filled with rage it drowned out the thunder. The angry pounding of their fists hurt Victor's head; it grew louder and louder until he thought his skull would crack. The faces of the soon-to-be-dead were no longer masks of despair. They were alive again . . . energized . . . a power flowed there. It was hate, it was rage, it was a passionate lust for revenge.

Jay stood amid all those seated people on deck. His face wore the same expression as theirs. His lips moved as if he'd joined the chant.

Victor tried again. 'Jay, let me through into this world. I can save some of the children. See the rafts? Let me through. I know how to inflate them, Jay. I can help!'

The voices grew louder. That pulse of sound was electric with fury. The eyes of the people blazed. The rhythm of the chant and the pounding of the deck grew faster. Blood flowed from torn skin. Nobody felt it. Nobody deviated from the intensity of the chant.

Metalwork in the ship screamed. The flanks collapsed under the weight of seawater. Seconds later waves washed over the deck. Smoothly, the ship began sliding under the surface. Slabs of dark green brine closed over it.

A deluge of water smashed a young mother against a rail, breaking her spine. As the baby she held fell from her lifeless arms Victor dived in the foam after it. Down he swam into the cold body of the Atlantic. Beneath him, the *N'Taal* drifted to its undersea tomb. Heart thundering, pent up breath burning in his lungs, he grabbed the baby. A moment later he was back on the surface. He'd hold on tight to the tiny infant. Whatever happened he'd never let go. It was either survive together, or die together. Victor roared to the universe his defiance at death.

He must keep treading water. With one arm he held the baby tight to him. He wouldn't abandon it . . . he wouldn't.

Victor opened his eyes. For a moment he smelt brine. The rush of surf filled his ears. Then he realized he stood in a bedroom. There wasn't so much as a drop of water on his clothes. Thank God, the baby . . . He felt its body pressed against his chest. Breathing deeply, he looked down. It took a moment for his eyes to adjust to the gloom. What he took to be the shape of the child against his chest was only his arm. At some point he'd gripped his left forearm with his right hand, then pressed it against his breastbone. For a while he'd been convinced that he'd held an infant from the *N'Taal* there.

He gave a grim laugh. It sounded disturbingly maniacal to his ears. Jay stood beside him. 'What are you going to show me next, O Ghost of Christmas Past? But you're no Dickensian ghost, are you? You're a demon . . . OK, you resemble a boy, but you are all monster. You traipse me through a sorry parade of grim events. Ones that I can't change. You can't change them, either, so that's probably what frustrates you. You are a monster with a couple of fancy little tricks: inflicting curses, showing people the past. But, Jay, you don't have the power to do anything else. You're just a neurosis in the shape of a human being. All you're capable of is repeating the same two tricks over and over.' Victor trembled with anger as he added, 'I've worked out what you resemble . . . what you're so dumbly aping. Being with you is like watching television. Does that sound strange? It does, but then I'm in second stage. I'm allowed. The virus is eating my brain. But seriously, do you know why I compare you to a television?' Jay's face was expressionless. No doubt that vengeance-fuelled mind worked behind the mask though. It would be choosing other venues to visit. Victor smiled as the revelation surged through him. 'Being with you is like watching television because, like you, television can show terrible things. Every day we watch murder on our screens, all those endless crimes committed against good people, and all those terrorist atrocities. We watch grim tragedies on television, while we sip our coffees, and we bear witness to all that human suffering, but, we the viewers, can do nothing about it. The news media inflicts scenes of human misery on us, just as you can take me on your "little walk". We are spectators, but we can't do one thing to stop the suffering. And in a way the television curses us. We watch the aftermath of a hurricane on television, say, see dead people in the ditches, think how dreadful it is, then shrug as we hop channels and laugh at some trite comedy show. But deep down all those horrible things we've seen feed our anxieties. We become pessimistic about the world; we worry about how our children are going to cope in the future. Jay, you are redundant. We've all become our own Vengeance Child. And we're doing it so much better than you.'

A door opened to the gloomy bedroom, light spilled in from the hallway.

'So what's this place, Jay? You want to torture me again with the sight of something awful? I can see all man's inhumanity to man simply by switching on my TV.'

A figure stepped through the doorway, then moved silently toward a child in bed. Victor recognized the night visitor.

'Laura?'

Jay said, 'I've told you before. She can't hear you.'

Victor went to block her way, but she bypassed him without any sign she noticed he was there. Laura wore casual clothes; she seemed to carry an object in her hands but Victor couldn't identify it. Stealthily, she crouched beside the bed so she could see its occupant's face.

'Still awake, Tess?' Her voice was gentle.

In bed a girl of around thirteen nodded. The face framed by wispy blonde hair wore the haggard appearance of someone who'd suffered. When she pushed back her fringe Victor noticed the girl's wrists were bandaged.

He turned to Jay. 'This is Badsworth Lodge, isn't it? You're showing me a girl who's tried to commit suicide by cutting her wrists. And here is Laura at work. Is this what you want me to see?'

'If you marry Laura, then she'll go away. She won't look after us any more.'

'Then you really do love her.' Victor watched as Jay gazed with such pure affection at the woman. 'I only said I was going to marry Laura to stop you from crashing those planes. Jay, I've no intention of marrying Laura. Do you hear me? We will not marry.'

Jay didn't respond. He listened in on Laura's conversation with the girl.

'Tess, I know you didn't really want to hurt yourself.' Laura spoke in a soft whisper. 'Now . . . I'm going to try very hard to make life happier here. To do that I've broken an important rule. My bosses will be mad if they find out. But I've bought this.'

She moved the object that she'd carried into the bedroom so Tess could see it. 'His name is Scraps. He'd been put into a rescue home because nobody wanted him. Lovely, isn't he?' Laura held the puppy so Tess could see it.

The girl's haggard face brightened instantly as she saw the bright eyes of the puppy look into hers. When she stroked a floppy ear his pink tongue darted out to lick the girl's fingers. If the wrist wound had bothered her before it didn't now, for the girl chuckled. 'It's a tickly lick!'

'Pets make people happy,' Laura told the girl. 'It might be against the rules to keep a dog here but he's ours.' Although she laughed there was steel in Laura's voice when she added, 'They will have to prise this dog from my cold, dead hands.'

Victor breathed deeply. 'I thought Laura was special. Now you've shown me why.' The room grew blurred. Laura, the girl and the puppy receded to a speck of light. Victor grunted wryly, 'Where now, O Shade? Or can I go home now?'

The world around him snapped into focus again. To his surprise he realized he was in the familiar surroundings of his living room. The television, however, was an older model. The evening sun shone through the window to reveal the same red sofa and a coffee table bearing neatly stacked wildlife magazines. Beside the magazines was a crisply folded newspaper.

Victor smiled. 'That room hasn't been that tidy since . . .' The smile died.

A second later a woman came through the doorway into the room. Her thick black hair fell down over the shoulders of the green ranger fleece that she wore. Clearly she was in a hurry . . . a desperate hurry.

Victor glanced at the date on the newspaper. His blood ran cold. 'I know what you're doing. You're showing me Ghorlan on the day she disappeared.' He shuddered to the roots of his bones. 'Jay, there's no need to do this.'

Without turning to Victor, Jay said, 'You've got to see what really happened.'

Forty-One

Victor knew it would be pointless to talk to Ghorlan as she moved about the living room. It would have as much effect on her as demanding answers from a character in a television drama. This is just a ghost of real events, he told himself. That isn't even Ghorlan. All he could do was bear witness to her phantom actions. She picked up the phone, dialled, then sighed. 'Victor, must you have switched off your phone tonight?' She replaced the handset, pushed back her hair from her beautiful face then got busy. Quickly, she pulled a voice recorder from a drawer in the desk at the end of the room. She clicked her tongue in frustration when she saw that the battery power level was low. Clearly annoyed by being delayed, she opened a fresh pack of batteries, then switched them with the old ones in the Dictaphone.

Victor studied her face with growing perplexity. *Why is she so anxious? But then she seems excited, too, as if she's got to do something that's incredibly important.* Once more she dialled the telephone in vain. She made a tempestuous gesture with both hands as she called out, 'Victor.'

He groaned. 'This must be the last few minutes of her life. I found the fleece on the beach. But why did she go down there at this time of night? And what made her go into the water?' His heart ached beyond belief. 'That last day I was giving a talk to students. That's why my phone was switched off.'

Ghorlan rushed back to the desk again, she opened a notepad, then picked up a pencil. Before she started to write, she checked the wall clock in exasperation. Victor thought he caught the words: 'Can't or I'll miss him.'

Victor glared. *Miss him? Miss who? A man of course.* He grimaced as emotion threatened to overwhelm him. 'Please don't show me what happens next,' he murmured to Jay. 'I don't want to see.'

Ghorlan headed toward the door, then paused before leaving. She seemed torn between rushing to her rendezvous and one last task. After glancing at the clock again she dashed back to the telephone. 'Please, Victor, have your phone switched on.' She hit the speed-dial key. Once more she sighed as she heard the recorded message. 'OK, never mind . . . I'm still going through with this.' The record message tone sounded. Quickly, Ghorlan said, 'Never mind, Victor. I'll catch you later.' After that, his wife raced out of their home for the last time.

Despite what he knew about the impossibility of interacting with anyone in this world he sped after her. At the top of his voice he cried out, 'Ghorlan! Ghorlan!' Her name rang out into the forest. Victor came to his senses as he ran amongst the trees. He knew he was back in the present again on Siluria; even so, he couldn't stop calling out for his dead wife. 'Ghorlan . . .'

Gales laughing through the branches mocked his grief. Ahead of him lay the castle. There was no sign of Jay. Once again, Victor Brodman was completely and utterly alone.

Forty-Two

In the gloom-filled forest Laura glimpsed Jay running through the trees. He ran with a herd of Saban. The animals' blue eyes were like sparks of a flame.

'Jay,' she called. But he vanished into the undergrowth without showing any sign he'd noticed her.

The cloud brought an early dusk. Heavy drops of rain began to smack against the leaves. Tree trunks groaned as the breeze tugged at them. Laura pushed on. Her legs ached; she longed to sit down to catch her breath. But time was running out. When − if! − she found Archer she'd then have to find Victor. The second stage of this disease would addle his senses. In that state he might be capable of anything. And she knew he blamed Jay for the epidemic. Ahead of her stood the castle walls. Even though much of the fortress's interior lay in ruins, the walls were intact. She knew Archer had been fascinated by the castle. There was a chance he'd wandered up here to play in its grounds. Moments later, she broke free of the forest. Raindrops burst against her head. A cold trickle ran down inside her collar sending shivers across her flesh.

The big twin gates to the castle were locked. Standing ten feet high they proved a formidable barrier. Without keys she'd need a long ladder to have even a chance of gaining entry. Wasn't there a small side door? She paused, trying to remember whether it lay in the section of wall that lay to her left or to her right. Storm-force winds howled through the battlements as, shivering, she chose the right-hand flank of the wall. It ran like some bleak cliff face, more than twenty feet high, to a corner tower, then turned at a right angle. In this half-light it made for a gloomy, monstrous place. Laura devoted her remaining energies to searching for the door. Within seconds she'd found it, then came a heart-dropping disappointment.

'Locked.' She turned the iron handle, tugged, pushed, then kicked at the old timbers. 'I don't believe it.' The solid slab of oak was fixed tight into its frame. It didn't budge an inch. 'Archer! Archer!' But if the doors were locked how could the boy be in there? Damn. She'd have to return to the village. Maybe she could find people to help search for him. Then, again, so many of the islanders were either sick or looking after sick relatives. And Victor, himself, might be comatose by now. Laura ran her fingers through her sopping wet hair.

Gusts of gale-force wind tugged at her clothing like vicious claws. A vulnerable child that depended on her wandered the island in a storm. The island was under quarantine, so the police couldn't help. The islanders themselves were dying . . . So wrapped up was she in despair that she ran by it without recognizing what it was. She'd staggered a dozen paces before she realized something strange projected from the castle wall that sat on its grassy mound.

Turning, she peered back through the rain. *Am I imagining this?* For there, projecting three feet from the stonework, and some six feet above the ground, was a slender metal pole. At the end of the pole a triangular pennant in yellow. Laura stared. The pole wasn't fixed to the wall. It protruded through what appeared to be a ventilation block. She took a step toward the pennant as it fluttered. Now she could see that the ventilation block was set in modern-looking masonry, which formed a bricked-up archway the size of a garage door.

The steel rod jerked up and down. *It's not the breeze making that happen.* Laura scrambled up the low mound to the wall. There were no other openings. Just a single block pierced with holes. Through one of them someone had pushed a slender rod with its fluttering pennant.

The moment she stood on tiptoe to try to see through the holes a frightened voice rang, 'Laura! Laura! I can see you!'

'Archer! Are you all right?'

The storm drowned out most of the boy's reply, but she made out the words, 'Stuck here . . . cellar . . .' Then a heartfelt, 'Please, Laura, get me out. I don't like it . . . dark . . . she might come out again. She'll hurt me.'

Frantic with alarm, Laura called, 'Archer! Who's in there with you?'

The pounding rain obliterated his answer. Quickly, Laura reached a decision. 'Just stay where you are, Archer! I'll get you out. It might take a few minutes, so be patient, OK?'

He shouted again. Even though she couldn't make out individual words she all too clearly heard his fear. Once more she tried to see through the ventilation holes. They were way too narrow. What was more, it seemed as if there was no light in whatever place Archer had found himself. She tried to slip her fingers through the holes below where the pole emerged, but the depth of the block prevented her from even wiggling her fingers through at the other side to reassure Archer. All she could do was call out not to worry, she'd be back soon to free him.

Rather than weave her way through the forest, she ran back to the main castle gates. From there a lane ran back along the island to the village. The first thing she was saw when she rounded the corner was Victor.

He approached the castle, calling out as he did so. There was such sorrow in the cry. 'Ghorlan . . . Ghorlan, where are you?'

The rain blurred his image so much he'd become a ghost of a man. Laura ran to him, then grabbed his shoulders. He gazed right past her.

'Ghorlan!'

'Victor. It's me, Laura. Snap out of it.'

'I saw her,' he muttered. 'I was on the ship . . . the *N'Taal* . . . all those people, they didn't stand a chance. I-I held on to the baby . . . I really tried. *Ghorlan!* Where did she go?'

Fiercely, she shook him. 'Victor. Victor! Listen to me. Remember who I am. Remember what you're supposed to be doing. Victor, give me the name of the boy you're looking for.'

He stared as if she babbled a language he didn't understand.

'You're not well, Victor, but I know you can still hold it together. What you've got to do is to want to help me. Then you can start thinking clearly again. Use your willpower, Victor. Want to be well enough to help. You can do it.'

He studied her features. It was as if he saw someone familiar, only he couldn't quite place the face.

'Victor. Who am I?'

As the rain streamed down his face he shook his head.

'Remember this.' She grabbed his hand, then held it to the side of her head. 'Can you remember when you stroked my face, and what you said about the line of my jaw?'

'Soft. Like apple blossom.' He blinked. 'Laura?' His eyes sharpened. 'Laura, where's Jay?' He twisted round. 'Jay was here a minute ago. My God . . . he showed me you. You were at Badsworth Lodge. A girl with bandaged wrists. You had a puppy.'

'Scraps.' She grinned with relief. And, dear God in heaven, it felt such a big, stupid grin. But it was so good to see the man back to his old self. Even if it might only be temporary. 'But he's grown into a big old pooch now. The dog with the bottomless pit for a stomach. The children love him.'

'They love you, too.' He rubbed his face. 'The ship. I stood on the deck. I was there when it sank. At the end the refugees weren't frightened. They were furious. Their anger! It was like standing inside an exploding bomb.' He began to walk. 'We must find Jay. I think I'm starting to make him understand. We've got to persuade him to realize that what he's doing is wrong.'

'Victor.' She caught his arm. 'I've found Archer. Somehow he's got himself trapped in the castle. There's an old dungeon or something.'

'Archer will have to sit it out. Jay's our priority.'

'Victor. Archer's terrified.'

'Jay is the cause of all this mayhem. If we can—'

'No, listen to me. Archer says there's someone in there with him. He's frightened they will hurt him.'

Victor paused. 'Who is it?'

'A woman. That's all I could make out. Please, Victor, Archer's so vulnerable. If we don't get him out the shock alone could kill him.'

'And my sister is in a coma. I'm deep into second stage. Sometimes it's hard to remember even my name. Islanders are dying. Jay is probably already planning to inflict even worse carnage on human beings. What if he decides he can get inside the heads of nuclear technicians and make them detonate a nuclear reactor? Or tricks the army into releasing nerve gas?'

'Archer's a little boy. It will only take a few minutes.' She explained what she'd found emerging from the wall.

Victor inhaled deeply. 'OK. I'm pretty sure I know where he is. It's the old smugglers' vaults.' He hurried toward the castle gates. 'Until a few years ago they were used to store maintenance equipment. Then the structure was declared unstable so the castle's trustees had the place bricked up.'

'Victor, it's no good going that way,' Laura told him. 'The gates are locked.'

'OK, there's a side door that—'

'Locked.'

'It's never locked.'

'It is now. I've tried it.'

'Damnation. No doubt another of Jay's tricks.'

'Victor. Keep a grip.'

'I'm fine. And I know what Solomon told us is true. And that's no delusion on my part. Jay is a vengeance weapon. One that I'm going to stop – or die trying.'

'Where are you going?'

Victor nodded at a tree that grew close to the wall. 'If the gates are locked there's only one way in.'

'You're joking.' Laura watched as the tree whipped around in the storm. Its branches beat at the battlements as if furious at the castle's temerity to dominate the island.

Victor gave a bleak smile. 'Right at this moment I can't see myself joking ever again.' He nodded upwards. 'Use only the branches I use. Stay as close to the trunk as you can. And don't, whatever happens, look down.'

Forty-Three

Victor climbed the tree. At that moment it seemed more animal than plant. Storm-winds made it buck as if it tried to shake them off. Twigs whipped his face. Branches flapped wildly. Leaves, torn away by blasts of cold air, stung his face. Despite his warning to Laura not to look down he shot glances back at her as she climbed those dripping branches. The rain made them dangerously slick. What was more, he expected Jay to manifest himself at the bottom of the trunk. If Laura saw him standing there, mouthing her name, would that be enough to topple her into a bone-breaking fall?

As he inched along one of the bucking limbs to the battlements he also expected to see Ghorlan down in the courtyard of the castle. That image of her as she hurried to meet a man stayed with him. He couldn't stop himself imagining what happened to his wife after that. Perhaps she'd rushed down to the beach to meet the mystery man there? A little while after that she'd gone into the water. Maybe she'd used the boulders as stepping stones to reach the next bay, then slipped off them into the river. But how did that explain the position of her green island ranger fleece? Victor had found it above the high tide mark. Possibly, as Victor had done in the past, she'd left it there to wade into the river to save one of the Saban Deer that had become entangled in discarded wire. Then she'd lost her footing. The currents could be brutal.

'Victor!' Laura had reached the stonework, too, but still remained on the branch because he'd not lowered himself over the battlement on to the walkway. 'Snap out of it. Let me on to the wall!'

As he clambered down on to the walkway he realized that those symptoms had struck again. His mind had wandered. Lately, it had become so difficult to keep a grip on his thoughts. With that, came a creeping lethargy. It would be so good to lie down now.

'Victor! Let me get on to the wall . . . I can't hold on.'

Savage gusts wrenched at the branch. The entire section of tree moved away from the castle so it no longer touched the masonry. Below Laura, a long drop to solid earth. Victor hurled himself, so his upper-half stretched out over the top of the wall.

'Grab my hands,' he shouted as the woman receded through a

fog of driving rain. At that moment it seemed as if the storm was determined to catapult her from the tree.

Laura let go of the branch before running along a lower one as if it were a tightrope. Then she leapt at the wall. Victor grabbed her hands. Rainwater had made one so slippery it shot through his fingers as if it were wet soap. Desperately, he grabbed her wrist.

'I've got you,' he panted. 'I won't let you fall.'

Her eyes met his; they signalled absolute trust.

'OK, when I pull you to the rim of the wall, get one of your arms round the back of my neck. Then I'll haul you over. One, two, three.'

The top of the battlement reached shoulder height from the walkway. So when he dragged her over the rough stones it must have been painful. Yet she didn't so much as murmur as he hauled her to safety. What was more, she didn't pause to catch breath. Instead, she ran for the steps that led down the inside of the walls to the yard.

'How do we get into the vault?'

'It's not that straightforward. The only doorway was bricked up the same time as the archway outside.'

'So how did Archer get down there?'

'I guess that's a mystery he can explain when we've freed him.' He pointed to the groundskeeper's cabin. 'There are tools in there; we'll have to break him out.'

Now they could barely see it was so dark. It took precious moments for Victor to find a piece of masonry that he could use to break a window, then undo the latch to the door. Once inside he could flick on the yard floodlights as well as the light in the cabin. In one corner stood a desk covered with paper coffee cups. At the other side of the room were shelves on which there were power tools, boxes of light bulbs and jars of nails.

Victor selected a couple of lamps that were powered by bottled gas. 'These will give us the best light once we get into the vault.' Quickly, he lit the pair.

'How are you feeling now?'

'If I keep busy I'm sure I can keep all the little grey cells together.' He shot her a smile. 'But if I seem to drift away into my own world again jab me with something sharp. OK?'

'OK.'

Victor handed her a steel bar. 'For jimmying. I'll take this.' He chose a huge hammer with a handle a full three feet long. After that he took a gas lamp, which cast a brilliant white light around the room. Laura held the other. 'Can you feel it, or is it just me?'

Her eyes were grave. 'A sense that time is running out?'

He nodded. 'It's like watching the clock on a time bomb tick down to zero. I can feel the air's different, even the ground is changing. I thought it was part of the second-stage symptoms, but now I'm certain that Jay is transforming the molecules – the very atoms that everything is made of. Back there in the forest I thought the trees would turn into animals.'

She poked his arm with the steel bar. 'Stay focused, soldier.' Her smile was a dry one. 'There's work to be done.'

Victor led the way to a section of inner wall that clearly revealed an area of new brickwork in the shape of a door. Savagely, he attacked it with a hammer.

'Watch your eyes,' he shouted as sparks fired off in every direction.

The concussions were explosive. He noticed that Laura also covered her ears as well as turning her head at an angle to avoid exposing her eyes to shards of brick that shot into the air every time the steel hammer head struck. He worked oblivious to the rain streaming down. For now, he even put aside the memory of Ghorlan rushing to meet a mystery man. Another crash of the hammer knocked a brick inward. From the oblong void the smell of decay oozed. Victor pounded the hammer home again. A brick shattered. He aimed another huge blow at the barrier.

'Stop!'

Laura put her hand on the wall, just where Victor intended to land the next strike. In the nick of time he pulled the hammer back before the block of steel smashed her fingers to pulp.

'Victor, it's Archer!'

When Victor raised the gas lamp to the small hole he'd made he saw a pair of wide eyes staring out.

'Archer, we'll have you out in a minute. Stand right back while Victor takes down the wall. Put your hands over your eyes so no sharp bits hurt them.'

Archer continued to stare out with frightened eyes.

'Please,' Laura said gently. 'Move back from the wall.'

Archer cried, 'No. I've got to give Victor this.' He pushed his bunched fist through the narrow void in the brickwork.

Victor put his own hand under Archer's as the boy opened his fingers. Glittering links fell into Victor's palm.

Victor reeled. At that moment he couldn't have been more shocked if the entire edifice of the castle had tumbled on top of him. He stared at the bracelet.

'Victor. Keep holding it together. You're nearly through.'

'My good God,' he breathed, then louder, 'Archer, where did you find this?'

No reply, just a pair of eyes gleaming through the slot-shaped opening.

'Archer. Did you find this on the beach?'

Then a choked reply. 'From here. From the car. Lady gave it!'

Laura said soothingly, 'Don't panic, we're nearly through. Victor, he's starting to go into shutdown. It's time we got him out of there. Victor? What's wrong?'

'This.' He held the bracelet in a cupped hand. Raindrops sparkled on gold. 'I don't understand where this came from. Archer, tell me exactly where you found this?'

'Don't question him now, Victor. He's near to collapse.' She eyed him as if expecting him to flip out. 'Why? What is it?'

Victor couldn't drag his gaze away from the delicate jewellery in his palm. 'See what's engraved on the link?'

In the light of the gas lamp Laura read out the twin names. 'Ghorlan. Victor.' She caught her breath. 'It's your wife's . . . Victor, careful!'

He called through the tiny opening. 'Archer, stand back.' A strength he'd never known before filled him. In five tremendous blows he felled the wall. Bricks cascaded to his feet. Red dust billowed up into the falling rain. Before the dust had cleared, they picked up the lanterns and rushed inside to find that Archer had already vanished.

Forty-Four

What made Victor stop dead was the car. The old Ford saloon rested on the stone floor. Its tyres were flat. Pale deposits covered its metal-work. Cobwebs rippled in the draught. Fungus growths had erupted around one of the headlights. Meanwhile, tree roots that had broken through the earth banking, on which the castle walls stood, hung down with all the loathsome promise of probing tentacles from some subterranean monster.

Laura held up the lantern as she descended the steps to join him. Its searing light filled the vault. As well as the car a large amount of equipment had been abandoned here, apparently in a hurry. A lawnmower sat alongside one wall. There were boxes of tools. Leaning against one corner beneath the vaulted ceiling were a whole bunch of slender poles topped with brightly coloured pennants. Archer must have managed to push one of these through the ventilation hole to attract her attention. Indeed, the boy had piled plastic crates, one on top of the other, so he could reach the ventilation block. In the shadows she saw Archer, his eyes were dull; fear had driven the boy to hide inside himself.

Victor shook his head. 'A lot of this equipment was in good order. Why brick it up in the vault? Especially the car. It's not as if it had been a clapped-out wreck back then.' He raised the lantern as he tried to see through the windows but they were covered with a white crust of salts that had drifted down from the ancient masonry above. He tried the handle of the front passenger door. The mechanism gave a grudging *clump* before the catch yielded to his pressure; door hinges squealed.

He glanced at Laura. 'You'd think the builder would have asked someone to take the car and all this equipment out before sealing the entrances.' From the vehicle came a smell that made him flinch. This was more than mustiness. Rot had set into the upholstery or something. With the door open he leaned in to inspect the dusty front seats. 'Something got spilt here, but the car must have been in good shape when it was abandoned. Wait . . . there's a pile of old blankets in the back . . . ugh, from the smell I guess the owner left their groceries in here.' The lamplight was so intense in this confined space that he had to narrow his eyes to slits. He reached into the back then pulled back the blanket.

When he was aware of the world again he found himself standing ten paces from the car. Laura rested her hand on his arm.

At last he managed to say, 'So that's how Archer came by the bracelet.' Dazed, he asked Laura, 'Did you see . . . ?' He nodded at the car.

Grim-faced, she whispered. 'It's Ghorlan, isn't it?'

'So she never went into the river. All that time I searched for her . . . when I visited the castle she was right beneath my feet . . . I had a dream; Jay wanted me to walk through the walls into here . . .' Victor felt no emotion. Inside he felt dry; just an empty Hoover bag of a man. Nothing. Only vacuum. 'Shouldn't I be crying, Laura? Or screaming? I just feel empty. Hollow.'

'That's because you're in shock.'

'And we can't even call the police. We might as well be on the moon.' With an effort he recalled what he'd seen on the back seat of the car. It didn't seem much of anything, really. A husk of a figure . . . or at least that's what it had resembled. A shrivelled Egyptian mummy of a thing, only it wore Ghorlan's clothes. He remembered those leather cowboy boots that she'd brought back from a trip to Wyoming. That's before he'd met her. Lots of times he'd been jealous. He thought they'd been bought for her by a former boyfriend. *So there she is now. All dried up.* 'Archer must have found the bracelet here. And did you notice her hair? It's still beautiful. A kind of blue-black, the same as ravens' feathers. The wedding ring's on her finger . . .' His voice grew hoarse. 'But did you notice something else? There's a cut above her eye. That's her blood on the front seat, isn't it? And even though her skin's dried up now, like old newspaper, I could see dark marks on her neck. That's bruising, isn't it? She'd been strangled.' He blinked. 'Murder . . . not in a million years would I have thought murder. All this time I'd convinced myself she'd somehow slipped into the river, then been carried away. That seemed like a peaceful end. Drowning wouldn't have hurt. But the thought of someone with their hands round her throat. Crushing . . .'

'Victor.' Laura touched his arm. 'There's something else. I found this between the passenger seat and the door.' She held up an oblong box in black plastic.

'Ghorlan's voice recorder.' After taking it from Laura he examined it. 'Jay showed me Ghorlan putting this in her pocket the day she died. In fact, Jay repeatedly told me that past events aren't always

what they seem.' He frowned. 'It's been left switched to record.' He
thumbed the play button. Nothing happened. The machine was dead,
of course, the batteries would have become exhausted years ago. 'So
it might have been running when . . .' He clenched the recording
device in his fist. 'And whoever did that to my wife also left her
fleece on the beach to make it look as if she'd drowned.' The ice
in his blood became fire. 'Whoever did this to her I'm going to
find! They are going to wish they'd never been born!'

'Victor.' Laura spoke softly. 'I'll get you and Archer home.'

'No.' He heard the steel in his voice. 'I've got to see this through.
I'm in second stage. In a few hours I'll be in a coma. Not long after
that I might be dead. In the time I have left I'm going to move
heaven and earth to find out who murdered my wife. Stay put.'

'Victor, where are you going? I don't want Archer to be down
here a moment longer – Victor!'

He raced up the steps, then across the rubble of the wall he'd
demolished. Rain beat down in the yard as he ran back to the
groundskeeper's cabin. There he ransacked the desk until he'd found
what he was looking for. A moment later he returned to the vault.
Laura stood with her arm round Archer. The light from her lantern
revealed the entombed car in every detail. And entombed in that
car the woman he'd married. At that instant, however, he felt no
grief. A hunger for vengeance drove him. His mind had cleared.
Exhaustion vanished from his limbs. Ghorlan's killer would face his
wrath.

He held up a blister pack. 'Batteries,' he announced.

'Victor, should you be doing this?'

'Like I said. I might be dead in a few hours.' He held her gaze.
'Will you help me, Laura?'

'You know I will.'

'Thank you. But first I'm going to find out who took her from
me. Then if they're on this island I'm going to rip them apart.'

He noticed the way that Laura looked at Archer. To see if Victor's
hate-filled words had impacted on the boy. But he'd retreated inside
himself. He didn't appear to see or hear anything.

Quickly, as if driven by a power from outside of himself, Victor
snapped the batteries from the pack, slotted them into the voice
recorder, then held it up. 'Here goes,' he said. 'I hope to God it still
works.'

Forty-Five

The thickness of the masonry around them muted the fury of the breaking storm outside. Here in the vault a silence reigned. However, Laura sensed a tension in the air. It was like waiting for lightning to strike. Victor had rewound the tape in the voice recorder; now he pressed play. She stood with Archer hugged to her side. The car squatted there, a loathsome steel coffin. Within it, the dried husk of Ghorlan's corpse. Laura realized that whoever had killed her had placed the body in the back seat, then they'd hidden the car in the vault, which had then been bricked up. By declaring the vault structurally unsound, so as to be far too dangerous to enter, the murderer had been convinced the car and its grim contents would never be found.

Victor stood there in the brilliant light of the gas lanterns that emitted a serpent-like hissing. He held the device level with his eyes, perhaps needing to see it as it revealed its secrets.

Maybe it was the odd sound the tape machine made – a click followed by a whirr as its motor drove the spools for the first time in years – that made Archer suddenly utter, 'Jay brought me here. Then the lady gave me the bracelet. I didn't know who to give it to. Please don't let her hurt me.' Laura tightened her arm around his thin shoulders, the gentle pressure offering some comfort in this frightening place.

Victor locked his gaze on to the machine. The speaker emitted a hiss. At first Laura thought it might be the sound of static, but as it surged, then receded, she realized she heard the whisper of trees.

A woman's voice, pleasantly coloured with a Portuguese accent, could be heard with astonishing clarity. 'Do you have problem with your car? Have you broken down?'

A male voice answered, yet he must have been too far away from the microphone to be recorded properly. In her mind's eye, Laura pictured Ghorlan as she was in life. She must have approached the man in his car as leaves in the trees rustled. Either she carried the voice recorder in such a way that it wouldn't be seen or she'd hidden it in a pocket.

'Oh? Your car is fine.' Ghorlan's voice again. 'I thought it had a fault. This track isn't ideal for driving. Tractor, yes. But cars become bogged the mud. See, already it's starting to rain.'

The male voice again, yet too faint to discern a reply or identify the speaker. Victor's brow furrowed as he strained to hear it.

Ghorlan spoke casually. However, Laura sensed she was pretending to be relaxed. 'May I sit in the passenger seat out of the rain? Thank you.' Rustling; the clunk of a door shutting. 'Thank you. The forecast promised it would be fine tonight.'

Then the male voice cut through the vault with the abruptness of a punch. 'What brings you out on an evening like this, Ghorlan? I thought you'd be with Victor at the hostel. Isn't he telling those students all about the joys of counting speckled newts and tagging stoats or whatever it is the pair of you do?'

Victor knew the identity of the man. The hand that gripped the voice recorder turned white as he squeezed it in cold-blooded fury.

When Ghorlan spoke again it confirmed her male companion. 'Mayor Wilkes, you don't like us, do you? And you hate that as rangers we obstruct your schemes that would decimate wildlife on the island.'

'You and Victor are killing progress. What do the lives of a few deer – ugly little dwarf deer – matter when it comes to bringing wealth to the island?'

'You mean bring wealth to yourself, Mr Mayor.'

'Have you come all this way into the woods to harangue me, Ghorlan?'

'No, I came to stop you using the rifle.'

'Rifle?'

As the voices came ghosting from the machine Laura sensed Ghorlan was building up to reveal some shocking truth. A gentle thud sounded. Laura could picture Ghorlan slipping the voice recorder from her pocket to rest on the seat between her thigh and the passenger door. Out of sight of Wilkes but better placed to pick up the conversation. Ghorlan clearly wanted to record this meeting. It was vitally important to her. But why? What's more, Laura sensed the tension growing. Already she knew how this conversation ended. Clenching her fist, she listened to Ghorlan address Mayor Wilkes as they had sat in that car ten years ago.

'I saw you with the rifle just twenty minutes ago.' Ghorlan spoke calmly. 'You were stalking the deer in the forest.'

'Nonsense.'

'Don't mock me with lies, Mayor Wilkes. I know exactly what

you are planning. The rifle fires darts which vets use to inject drugs into wild animals.'

'Preposterous.'

'No, Mayor Wilkes. I have you figured out. You have obtained a virus culture that causes epidemics in hoofed feral creatures like deer. You know that all you have to do is dart one animal and it will be infected. That infection will spread quickly through such a small herd as this. Nobody will be able to trace the infection back to you. Conservation officers will assume that this was a natural outbreak. Of course, with all the Saban dead the special classification of Siluria will be downgraded.'

'Go on.' Wilkes' voice became cold. He was calculating his options.

'Once the status of the island is compromised it means your plans for commercial development – a new hotel, golf course, lots of new houses – will not be opposed on conservation grounds. In short, Mr Mayor, you will become an extremely rich man.'

'You've no proof.' From his tone Laura could imagine he was smiling. 'No proof whatsoever.'

'I saw you with the rifle.'

'Your word against mine.'

'You have managed to dart one of the animals. As you hoped the dart fell out after injecting the culture into the deer. Then you threw the rifle and the phial, containing the culture, into the river. It is deep, with many underwater ravines, the weapon will never be found.'

'You have good eyesight, Mrs Brodman.' He paused. 'Even if what you allege is true, then it is now too late. The epidemic that will sweep through those animals in the next few days will destroy them. What's your response to that?'

'Then I admit I am too late in preventing you from firing the hypodermic into the deer. But . . .' A note of triumph had raised Ghorlan's voice.

'But?'

'I knew about the virus culture you'd obtained. You've treated your secretary so appallingly – forcing her to act illegally by black-mailing her – that she confessed to me that you'd ordered her to keep the culture in her refrigerator. So, when she told me about your plan I asked her to put the phial, containing the culture, into a pan of boiling water for an hour.'

'You did what?'

'Once the culture was heated to boiling point the virus died. What you've succeeded in doing, Mr Mayor, is inject an animal with a sterile solution. So no epidemic, no extermination of the herd. Your plan is all—'

The sound of the smack made both Laura and Victor flinch.

Ghorlan's voice came one last time. 'So you've succeeded in spilling some blood today, but hitting me won't stop this reaching the police. You've—'

Laura found herself trying to scrunch her senses up tight inside so she could neither hear nor allow herself to imagine what must have been happening in the car. The man had gone berserk. He screamed abuse at Ghorlan. No individual words could be identified but the fury in his voice was nothing less than an assault on their nerves in its own right. It went on for entire minutes. Mixed with the man's insane ranting were the sounds of a scuffle. Then a clunk. That must have been when the recording machine slipped from the seat into the deep furrow between the body of the car below the passenger door and the seat runner. Laura couldn't prevent herself from picturing the final moments. Wilkes' hands around Ghorlan's throat. His maniacal stare. Only the briefest of choking noises before his fierce grasp squeezed her windpipe shut. Then, later, a series of rapid thumps as the woman's death spasm caused her arms to flail against the car's interior.

After that, nothing but the hiss of tape. Eventually that, too, ended with a click.

Victor breathed deeply. 'Part of me wants to – longs to – go to pieces. But I'm not going to let this overwhelm me. I owe it to Ghorlan to keep focused. Then I'll find Wilkes. The man took her from me. I'm going to pay him back. This disease is killing me. So, if this is my last act on earth I'm going to do it right.' An icy calm descended on Victor. 'After killing Ghorlan he drove the car to the vault. Back then it was still used to store equipment. No doubt Wilkes bribed a structural engineer to declare it unsafe. Then Wilkes had some of his men brick up all the entrances: the car safely hidden inside; nobody would ever find it.' He nodded. 'Wilkes employs a lot of ex-prisoners. Not for the love of humanity, but so he can pressure them into doing his dirty work. You can imagine he kept watch over them as they cemented bricks into the doorway, just to make sure none checked what was under the blanket in the back of the car. They wouldn't have known what he'd done. What's more, they knew better than to even speculate about it amongst themselves.

So the wall went up: Wilkes had successfully buried another of his dirty little secrets.'

Applause sounded in the vault; a slow sarcastic-sounding handclap.

'Congratulations, Brodman. It took a decade to uncover the truth, and ten miserable years staring into the river, but you got there in the end.'

Laura spun round to see Wilkes on the steps. His expression was one of such loathsome gloating she shuddered.

'Although, really it was down to Archer, not you, Brodman. Such a brave little boy.'

'Wilkes.' Victor seized the hammer that he'd used to smash down the wall.

'You're outgunned, old boy. And outwitted.' As he descended the steps into the light he revealed what he carried. Instead of aiming the shotgun at Victor, however, he aimed it at Laura as she stood with her arm around Archer's shoulders.

'Victor.' Wilkes smiled. 'Watch me annihilate two people with a single shell.'

Forty-Six

Victor stopped mid-stride. Wilkes remained on the bottom step. Rainwater dripped from his once neatly pressed business suit. The man chambered a round into the breech of the shotgun he aimed at Archer and Laura.

Wilkes curled his lip. 'I thought that would stop you, Brodman.'

Victor lowered the hammer. 'Let them go, Wilkes.'

'Why on earth should I? Remember who's holding the gun.'

'What made you kill Ghorlan? Surely losing some development deal on the island wasn't the reason.'

Wilkes glared. 'Because you, Brodman, and your sort, have always blocked my plans for progress.'

Laura spoke up. 'You don't like being thwarted, do you, Wilkes? Throwing a tantrum at being stopped is the classic symptom of a spoiled child.' She tightened her arm around Archer. 'When it comes down to it, this boy here is bigger than you.'

'Shut up.'

Laura's eyes became fiery. 'You're a spoilt little boy in a man's body. You want to take all the time. I bet you're never satisfied, are you? If someone gives you a cake you go home to brood why it couldn't have been two cakes. If you make a million profit you can't sleep at night because you're angry that it wasn't two million. I'm right, aren't I?'

'I'm warning you.' The man's face turned white with fury.

'I see it now.' Victor picked up the thread. 'All along you've been a problem child in a man's suit. It adds up. You crave your own way all the time. When you can't get it, you plot revenge.'

'Enough of the pseudo-psychology.' Wilkes stepped down into the vault. 'It's time to negotiate a deal, Brodman. You want these two to live. I want you to take the blame for Ghorlan's death.'

'You can't be serious.'

'Deadly serious. You want something. I want something. We can do a deal here. All that's required is to agree the fee.'

Victor's hand tightened around the hammer shaft. All he needed was for the man to be distracted, then he'd slam the hammer through the murderer's skull.

'What kind of fee?' Victor asked.

'Coming to your senses, eh, Brodman? It's about time. You will write a short confession: "Poor me, in a fit of jealousy I killed my wife. All my fault. I confess. Nobody else to blame." You know the kind of thing. You sign it, then I'll let these friends of yours go.'

'What about me?' Victor tensed, ready to deliver a fatal blow with the hammer. All he needed was Wilkes to move a few steps closer. 'Why don't you think I'd retract the confession?'

'Because,' Wilkes said slyly, 'a good contract always contains water-tight clauses to protect the strongest party to the agreement. You've got this disease, Brodman. In a few hours you'll be dead. Detectives will surmise that knowing you're on your deathbed you made the tragic confession that you killed Ghorlan. Of course, the remorse will be too much. With the last of your strength you manage to reach your shotgun. Bang. A merciful end.'

'If I agree,' Victor began, 'then you promise to release Laura and Archer?'

'Victor,' Laura shouted, 'don't trust him. He'll never let us go. Once you've signed the confession he'll kill us all.'

Victor played for time. 'Laura,' he said, 'he's got the gun. What can we do?'

'Not trust that creep for a start.' She glared at Wilkes. 'You know, I've just realized something. This virus that's sweeping the island. It started here first. The ferrymen took it back to the mainland. Somewhere in the river there's another empty phial and a dart gun.'

Victor blinked. 'You tried to infect the deer again?'

'And successfully this time, now there's been no interference from the Brodman clan.'

'If you used a virus that infects common species of deer then you've screwed up.'

'How come?' Wilkes' air of confidence weakened.

'How long have you lived here, Wilkes? You know the stories.'

'That children were magically transformed into the animals when the island sank out in the river? Dear God, man, that's just a fairy tale.'

'The legend indicates they are different to other deer. They're not only a unique species but there are key biological differences. Saban eat kelp as well as grass. Their stomachs have developed differently, and so have their immune systems. They don't catch the same kind of illnesses as other deer types, like certain forms of TB and lung-worm. When that virus of yours went into their blood it didn't make the herd sick. Instead the germ mutated. Eventually people picked it up from contact with kelp and grasses that the animals have touched.' Despite the fact that Wilkes held the gun on them Victor couldn't stop himself. 'You idiot, Wilkes. This epidemic is your fault. You tried to infect the deer herd, but you infected us.'

There was silence as Wilkes digested the facts. 'OK,' he hissed, 'it looks as if it will be a case of third time lucky. Next time I'll poison the damn things with cyanide. Then I'll have the forest ripped down. Just imagine the lovely, valuable building plots I can get out of that. Then if . . .' Wilkes stopped talking. Something had distracted him, yet he appeared uncertain what it was. Taking another step, he peered into the shadows. Victor noticed that Archer had stiffened. He sensed something, too. Laura's eyes roved about the vault. A change had occurred in the place. Victor couldn't identify it, either. Just a suggestion that it wasn't the same place it was five minutes ago. He turned to the car. Had something stirred inside of it? His mouth went dry. Any second he expected the door to creak open.

Dazed, Archer suddenly spoke. 'He's here . . . he's here.'

Wilkes spun round, shotgun at the ready. 'Who's there?' He aimed into the darkness where the light of the lantern couldn't penetrate. 'Show yourselves.'

A figure emerged slowly . . . step by step.

'Jay.' Laura sounded more shocked than relieved that she'd found the boy.

Victor held up his hand. 'Wilkes, don't shoot. He's only a child.'

Wilkes aimed at Jay's face. 'Only a child?' He laughed. 'I've seen him before. This is the creature that terrifies the children, isn't it? He scares them witless.'

Jay stared at Wilkes without a trace of emotion. 'Mayor Wilkes,' he murmured.

'Ha, one of your smarter orphans.' Wilkes tightened his finger on the trigger. 'Maybe I should blow his head off to prove I mean business.'

'You don't have to do that, Wilkes,' Victor told him. 'I'll sign the confession. Just promise me these three can leave.'

Jay's almond-shaped eyes burned in the light of the lamps. A sheen of perspiration appeared on his face. As if only half-conscious he moved his lips. No sound came out.

'Nurse Parris,' Wilkes snapped, 'it seems as if another of your brood have lost their wits. God alone knows what you do to those brats at the orphanage.'

Before she could speak Jay took another step forward. His lips moved again.

Wilkes kept the gun's muzzle level with the child's face. 'Speak up boy, I can't hear you. What's that you're saying?'

Jay began to speak. 'Wilkes . . . Mayor Wilkes . . . Wilkes, Wilkes.'

Archer's voice rang out in a squeal that combined excitement with pure fear, 'He's saying your name! That means bad things are going to happen to you. You're going to die!'

'Shut up!' Wilkes swung the gun to Archer. 'Make him be quiet, or I'll blast the little worm to kingdom come.'

'You're insane, Wilkes,' Victor told him. 'Don't you realize that you can't go round killing people? Have you really lost touch with reality to that extent?'

Meanwhile, Jay continued to repeat, 'Wilkes, Wilkes, Mayor Wilkes.'

'You can shut up, too. Little witch? Isn't that what the others taunted you with? Little witch, little witch, little witch!' He barked out a laugh but it sounded strained now. 'See, I'm repeating what they called you!'

'You're too late, Wilkes.' Laura spoke with rock solid certainty. 'Jay's not like any other boy I've met. He's put a curse on you.'

'Curse?' The man's eyes darted from face to face. 'I can do better than curse. I've got this.' He fired the shotgun at the car's rear window; glass shattered in a spray of white. In the confined space of the vault the detonation was colossal. When Victor made a move toward him, Wilkes spun back to aim the muzzle at his chest. 'Don't you dare.' The man's composure had begun to disintegrate. His hands shook. Sweat dripped down his face. He barked at Laura, 'Stop that child saying my name!'

'I can't.'

'Make him stop!'

At that moment Jay did stop. He focused on Wilkes. 'I'm going to show you something.'

'Yes, yes! Show me some obedience. And shut your mouth.' A tremor ran through Wilkes' voice.

Jay sighed. 'It's something bad.'

Daylight burst through the wall, even though Victor knew it to be dusk outside. Through the light a large object rumbled. A moment later a car drove across the stone floor. From the car scrambled a younger looking Mayor Wilkes. He raced round to the passenger door, yanked it open, then dragged out the lifeless body of Ghorlan. The gold bracelet twinkled on the wrist. Clumsily, he managed to open the back door, bundled the body on to the back seat, then dragged a blanket over the corpse to hide it from view.

Present day Wilkes laughed. 'Is this the worst you can do? Well, do you want to see the worst I can do?' He swung the gun toward Jay.

Instantly the scene of Wilkes hiding the body vanished. In the corner of the vault a brilliant radiance appeared. This came from a light shining down on to a steel table. The floor around it was covered in white tiles – a stark, clinical appearance. There, a middle-aged woman in scrubs, and plastic apron, placed bloody organs on to a weighing scale. In a professional manner she crisply read off the readings into a microphone that hung from the ceiling. 'Spleen: one nine eight grams. Heart: three zero nine grams.'

Wilkes noticed that a naked figure lay on the steel table. 'This is an autopsy.' His once thunderous voice became a whisper. 'Who's that on the table? Who is it?' As if he had no control over his movements, the sight of the supine figure drew him a step toward it. He pointed the shotgun at Jay. 'He's doing this. Make him stop!'

With the man distracted, Victor took his chance. He swung a massive punch at Wilkes' head where it connected with a satisfying smack. With a grunt he crashed back to the floor. The gun clattered at his side. Laura was there in a second to grab the weapon.

Victor held out his hand. 'Laura, give it to me.'

She shook her head. 'No, you're not going to shoot Wilkes. This is going to be far worse for him than an easy death.'

Wilkes scrambled to his feet. A cut in the shape of a crescent moon opened the skin above his left eyebrow. But the man was too frightened to notice the pain. He held up both hands to block his view of the post-mortem.

'I'm not going to look – I'm not,' he yelled. 'You can't make me. If I don't see it then it can't be real.' Saliva flew from his lips. The man disintegrated into sheer panic. His hands shook, tears streamed down his face. 'I know you're trying to trick me. This is a projection. You've hidden the equipment! But it won't work, because I'm not going to look at it.' He began to shuffle away in the direction of the steps.

Jay intoned, 'Wilkes, you must look. I've brought this here specially for you.'

'No!' Again the force exerted itself. Wilkes lowered his hands. Try as he might to stop himself, his foot slithered across a stone slab, then he took another step. And another. By the fourth step he stood on the white tiles of the mortuary.

When his eyes snapped open he screamed. For there, lying on the coroner's table, lay the body of a man. Flesh wounds covered it. An angry graze denuded one elbow of skin. But, significantly, Victor saw the crescent-shaped wound he'd inflicted when he punched Wilkes.

Wilkes had gone to pieces. He squealed in absolute terror. 'It's me! How can it be me? I'm here. I'm alive!' Sobbing, he stared at his own naked corpse. A strangely pathetic and vulnerable figure on the cutting table. Its grey limbs were weak looking, lifeless. A pair of sad eyes had sunk into the sockets, while a huge cavity yawned in the chest, this made by the coroner in order to remove the organs.

'You've done this,' he screamed. 'It's a – a projection, a dummy. It's not real!'

Yet it could be seen by the way the man howled and wept that he knew it was true. He'd seen himself as he would be just hours from now. What lay ahead after the autopsy was the all-consuming fire of a crematorium furnace. Nothing more.

Laura's voice was measured. 'You've been thwarted again. That's what kills you inside, isn't it? To be thwarted. To be stopped in your tracks.' She nodded at the eviscerated corpse that dripped blood into a sluice. 'So now you will be thwarted for ever.'

The mayor screamed so hard that his legs buckled. In blind panic he fled up the stairs and out into the storm.

Forty-Seven

Wilkes ran. The only time he paused was to unlock the door in the castle wall. Then he raced pell-mell through the forest. By now a deep gloom had been cast over the island. Nightfall was drawing down fast. As winds roared through the branches so memories of what he'd just witnessed in the vault whirled through his mind. The pathetic, grey body lying on the steel table. The coroner intoning the weight of the heart. On the corpse had been his face. How was that possible? Then he remembered how Jay, repeating the name of the teenager, Max, had reduced the youth to panic. He'd leapt into the river in sheer terror. Moments ago, Jay had repeated Wilkes' name. Now Wilkes, too, ran in blind terror. A pain above his right eye nagged where Victor had punched him. The corpse had displayed an identical wound just above the right eye. Other injuries, too, had covered the naked body. Puncture wounds. And there had been a visible graze on the right elbow.

Wilkes panted, 'Get home . . . and stay there . . . I won't get those other injuries. Then it won't come true . . . I'll have won.' So far, the only wound he'd suffered was the cut above his eye. All he need do was avoid being hurt again.

Soon Wilkes joined the path that would take him back to the village. The Severn had the blackness of a river flowing right out of hell. Angry waves rose in jagged peaks. Turbulence ripped up the surface as if hungry beasts swam from the depths in search of fresh meat. Even though exhaustion made every limb ache Wilkes pushed homeward. Cloud broke on the horizon. The sun had almost sunk behind the hills but a splinter of it still burned brightly. Clouds racing across its face made it flash like a beacon. The light it pulsed out across Siluria was blood red. For all the world it looked as if a beating heart of gigantic proportions had been perched on the distant hilltop. Wilkes found himself distracted by the uncanny sight.

Shapes rushed him. He tried to stop, but his feet slithered on the wet path. When he hit the ground the pain flashing up his arm told him he'd taken the force of the fall to his right arm. He remembered the corpse on the cutting table. As well as the wound above the eye there'd been the graze on the elbow. Grunting, he pulled himself to his feet. So intense was the sting in his elbow he felt sick. *Two down, one to go.* He had to avoid those puncture wounds.

Then he saw what had caused him to fall. A dozen Saban Deer, after bursting from the bushes to startle him, now trotted along nearby. He searched the ground for what he needed. When he found a thick branch that would serve as a club he pursued the animals, screaming abuse. They were the cause of his woes, too. If it hadn't been for them he could have torn down the stinking forest and built houses there. The money he'd have made would have been phenomenal.

Cursing the animals, he chased them. However, they seemed strangely unperturbed. Without any fuss they cantered down the beach toward the water's edge. Wilkes followed. 'I'll kill you. I'm going to break your bloody heads!'

Shingle gave way to soft mud as he reached the water's edge. More than once he slithered on it, lost his balance and fell forward on to all fours. Sometimes it was so slippery he had to scramble on his hands and knees. Then, when he could get to his feet to run like a man, the yielding, sucking mud pulled off one of his shoes.

Right then, it seemed as if the beach was full of Saban. They trotted through the surf, or weaved round uprooted trees. In the light of the dying sun Wilkes saw the big root clusters still dripping with water; the branches were covered with seaweed, making them appear shaggy, like they'd sprouted green pelts. As he ran after the deer he aimed blows at them with the branch. Each time he missed. Fear and rage made his heart race madly. Exertion caused phantom bursts of purple light to flash along his retina. At times he was sure he saw the witch child. At every turn Jay stared at him. Those huge almond-shaped eyes. The uncanny gleam of his face. Wilkes yelled torrents of abuse. This time it was more fear than anger. Wildly, he ran toward the boy. An uprooted tree lay in his path. Being so eager to reach his victim, Wilkes scrambled through the branches rather than waste time by going round.

He found something snagged at his leg. Carelessly, he jerked his leg to free it. Instantly, a sharp pain flared up above his knee. Glancing down, he saw something in the blood red light that made him howl. A fish hook, still attached to a line, had embedded itself in his shin. Without thinking, he simply tried to drag his leg from it. But the line, entangled round a branch, pulled taut and the barbed hook slipped deeper into his skin. Desperately, he tried again. This time he lost his balance.

The instant he fell it seemed as if dozens of bees stung him all at once. From where he lay, face down on sopping branches, he saw fishing lines on which maybe a hundred fish hooks had been strung. Each hook was more than an inch long. And they were armed with wickedly sharp barbs of steel.

The pain made Wilkes thrash about wildly. This made each hook that embedded itself into his flesh sink deeper. The barbs held tight under his skin. Quickly, he explored his face with his fingertips. A hook had embedded into the soft flesh at the side of his nose. One had gone through his chin; two had speared his left cheek; at least half a dozen had gone through the skin on his throat. To his horror he realized that the full length of his body harboured more of the sharp hooks. None pierced deeply enough to be lethal. But they held him there. Held him securely. Irrevocably. Into his head flashed a childhood memory of a picture of Gulliver lashed to the ground by the little people of Lilliput. Only this time Wilkes lay face down. Instead of lines criss-crossing the body, he was secured to the fallen tree by hooks that were in turn fastened to strong fishing lines that were hopelessly knotted and tangled around the branches. Each fish hook was agony. In turn, the agony made him thrash, when he writhed the hooks worked ever deeper into his body.

Panting, he looked up. On the beach Saban Deer placidly regarded him. For a moment, he imagined Jay was there, too. Just standing. Watching. Knowing what would happen next to the man who'd once lorded his power over the island. When the strain of holding his head up grew too much he let it drop. In the last rays of the sun he saw that the pebble beach had vanished. Instead, water crept up the shore. The tide had turned.

Wilkes howled. Writhed. More hooks embedded themselves in his top lip, in his eyelid, in his fingers, and the soft flesh of his belly. When he imagined the intolerable pain could not possibly get any worse that's when it became even more excruciating. The waters of the River Severn rose inch by inch, wave by wave. For a while, he could keep his head above its surface by pulling back against the cruel barbs that worked so hard to hold him down. Eventually, as night at last fell, drowning the scene in absolute darkness, the tide covered his face. As he screamed a lungful of bubbles out underwater, he recalled images of the autopsy conducted on the grey-skinned corpse. The one with the cut above the eye, the grazed elbow, the dozens of puncture wounds. He wanted to scream again in absolute terror as he finally understood that those injuries now perfectly matched those on his own body, only by this time his lungs had filled with a water so cold it seemed to flow through his veins to freeze his heart.

Victor carried Archer in his arms, as Laura, bearing a lantern, led them out into the courtyard. Jay walked with them. Once more the boy appeared lost inside himself. His face lacked any expression whatsoever. Exhausted, they made their way toward the castle door that swung to and fro in the breeze.

Before they left the castle Jay stood in the doorway. His large eyes fixed on Victor. 'You're all evil. My reason for being here was to make you all suffer and then die. I am vengeance . . .' He frowned.

'But you don't believe that any more, do you?'

'I must punish.'

Softly, Laura said, 'Jay, I know you've realized that is wrong.'

Jay was deep in thought. He never even flinched when drops of water fell from the battlement on to his face.

Victor said, 'A man came all the way from Africa to tell us that the only way to stop you hurting people was to put you in danger. I've come to understand he was wrong. I reject his suggestion – reject it absolutely. Because I learned that you've changed, Jay, since you arrived on the island.

'When you were younger you didn't understand the power you have; you couldn't stop yourself using it to cause hurt. You thought you were getting revenge for the way your family and their neighbours suffered. Now, I truly believe you can reject that urge, just as I rejected the advice to make you suffer in order to kill this power you have. You are growing up, Jay. Just as children learn to control their temper, so you're learning how to control this destructive force inside of you. You tried to do good things for the islanders by making their dreams come true. Only it went wrong because you're not mature enough to know that when we wish for something to happen it isn't always a good thing if it does. We must be careful what we wish for. Even miracles can turn bad.'

He paused there with Archer sleeping in his arms. Laura had nodded her approval as Victor spoke, so taking a breath he pushed on. 'Probably one of the biggest challenges we face as we grow up is learning how to handle our emotions, and knowing how to take control of our actions, and accepting responsibility for the things that we do. Right now, your power is stronger than it ever has been before. It's time for you to be strong enough, and mature enough, to take control of that power. And then decide how you use it. Do you understand?'

Jay nodded. 'I thought everyone was evil, and they must suffer.' He sighed. 'But Victor isn't evil. Neither are you, Laura. Both of you risked your lives to help Archer and me.' The breeze whispered across the battlements.

Victor said, 'We did what we thought was right.'

'I took you to the sinking ship. On board the *N'Taal* you were prepared to die with the baby if you couldn't save her.'

Still holding the sleeping Archer in his arms, Victor said, 'So what now? More of the same? Are you still going to carry on hurting everyone you meet?'

'I want this thing to go. I want this power out of me.' Jay took a stuttering breath as if a pain had suddenly lanced through him. 'I'm trying to push it out!' He screamed.

Laura held up the lantern to light his face. 'Jay, what's wrong? Are you hurt?'

'It's leaving me . . . Laura, I can feel it going.' His eyes glistened. 'Get out, get out, get out!'

With that final screamed 'get out!' the boy sagged back against the door frame. His facial muscles went slack, his mouth hung open, while his eyes seemed to stretch impossibly wide. In the unsteady light it appeared to Victor that he beheld the features of an old African man, then they changed into those of a young woman, then morphed into youth, then a girl – all African. For maybe as long as a minute Jay's face strobed furiously as the faces of strangers raced from his head. Old men, old women, middle-aged, youthful – Jay disgorged images by the dozen.

The doomed refugees from the *N'Taal*? Victor didn't doubt it for a moment. Their ghostly residue was being ejected from Jay's frail body. As he used all his willpower to exorcize them from his soul they screamed out in dismay, frustration and rage. They knew that Jay, the vessel of their wrath, their vengeance weapon, had defeated the curse.

The last to leave was an old woman. Her face overlay Jay's like an ancient mask. Her bloodshot eyes glared at Victor. Her nostrils flared as her mouth yawned wide to reveal teeth so rotten they'd become yellow splinters embedded into crimson gums. That last scream, which erupted from her lips, was the sound of the stricken ship tearing in two, the howl of the soon-to-die passengers, the anger and the despair of the loss of innocent lives everywhere.

The sound shook the huge walls of the castle until stones were shattered by its violence.

Then . . . gone. Silence. Calm air filled the yard. A sense of peace.

Jay slumped against the doorway, utterly spent. His entire demeanour changed now he'd purged himself of that inbuilt craving to wreak terror and destruction.

There was nothing beyond that. For a moment Victor half expected to see shrieking phantoms stream away into the sky; however, the clouds had slowed until they moved above them in a way that could only be described as serene. When he examined Jay's face again, he wondered why he'd ever used the world 'elfin' to describe him. Jay was just a little boy. An eleven-year-old child who was so tired all he needed was to go to bed.

Victor's eyes met Laura's. He knew an understanding had passed between them. What the next few hours would bring he didn't know. Only it was time to get the children home. But as he carried Archer back through the forest in the direction of White Cross Farm he felt something leave him, too. For Jay what had left him had been the Vengeance Child – the demonic force that had possessed him from infancy. For Victor, what slipped from his mind now was the obstacle that had prevented him from grieving over Ghorlan. Tears came, but they weren't bitter. This was the release that he'd been waiting ten long years for. Despite everything, he could look into himself and see that an old wound had, at long last, begun to heal.

Epilogue

In warm sunlight Victor headed toward White Cross Farm. Jay walked alongside. They'd been to check on a colony of bats that roosted in the castle tower.

'The numbers are increasing.' Victor was pleased. 'And they're a rare species of horseshoe bat.'

The boy grinned. 'But no vampire bats.'

'Thankfully not. If we wind up with vampires we'll have to rename the place Dracula's Castle and start selling garlic ice-cream.'

Jay paused to appreciate this perfect September evening. Birds swooped high overhead as they picked insects out of the sky for their evening meal. After a moment he said, 'Tell me again what happened about the car in the dungeon.'

'I've told you plenty, Jay. All that's in the past.'

'But when I wake up on a morning I sometimes think I've dreamt it. I know I've got to make it real in here.' He touched the side of his head.

Victor watched the swallows, too, as he decided what should be told and what shouldn't. 'There was an epidemic on the island.'

'Caused by Mayor Wilkes, not me.'

'That's right,' Victor said. 'You were in no way to blame.'

'They said I caused things like that. Curses and bad stuff. They called me a "little witch".'

'But they don't any longer, do they?' The pair continued along the woodland path. A Saban Deer watched them from the shadows, its blue eyes like flashes of electricity. Victor shook his head. 'No, it was Mayor Wilkes. He tried to infect the herd with disease. Instead of making the deer sick the virus mutated then infected us.'

'How many died?'

'Nine died of the illness. Though there were others who died accidentally, or simply vanished. Anyway, once the doctors knew the outbreak was a strain of gastro-enteritis they could fly in drugs to treat it. And those big shots of vitamin B we were given every day.' Victor smiled. 'It was a week before I could sit down without shouting *ouch*.'

'Sometimes I dream that I see Mayor Wilkes lying on a kind of metal table and he's all red here.' Jay touched his chest. 'Was that real?'

'The night we found the car in the castle, Mayor Wilkes drowned.' Victor omitted reference to the fact that Wilkes was found entangled in fishing lines the next morning. In his body were forty-eight steel hooks. One look at the man's face told everyone that he'd died in terror. He also omitted mention that Ghorlan had finally been given her funeral. Or the days afterwards Victor had entered a dark despair that had been a long, uphill climb to emerge from.

As they crossed a meadow to the farm Jay scratched his head. 'I worry I'll have to leave White Cross. I get really scared.'

'We're running the farm as a place for children to stay as long as they want to.'

'It's a foster home?'

'That's the official title. But nobody can take you away from here if you don't want to go. You can live here until you're a grown-up. It's your decision.' Victor opened the gate. 'I did warn Archer about that goat.'

Jay tutted; it was a typical boyish thing to do when someone of his age saw a younger one making an apparent mess of things. 'Archer still likes Wilkes more than people, then Wilkes goes and eats his T-shirt.'

Archer was protesting, 'No, Wilkes, let go, it's mine.' At last he pulled the garment free, then joined Victor and Jay for the walk back to the house. Archer folded his arms as he called back at the goat, 'Do that again, Wilkes, and I'll smack your bottom!'

'Kids.' Jay sighed. 'Are you coming sailing with me later?'

'All right.' Archer examined the teeth marks in his sleeve. 'But don't splash me.'

After they entered the house Jay paused in front of the television, which showed footage of war in South-East Asia that left thousands of people facing famine.

Jay stared, his expression growing angrier by the second. 'You know what? It's wrong that governments don't do enough to help all those who are going hungry.' His voice grew deeper. 'One day someone will come along and make the politicians pay; they'll make them suffer for the bad things they've done.' Fury set his eyes alight. 'Maybe I . . . if I remember how . . .'

Archer cried, 'Wilkes has followed us back!'

The goat trotted into the lounge to hungrily eye the sofa cushions.

'Jay! Help me get him out . . . before he poops on something.'

As if by magic Jay's anger vanished. Both boys laughed happily as they helped one another tug the recalcitrant, four-legged Wilkes out of the house. As the pair giggled, and shouted advice on the best way to get the goat back to his pen without it eating any soft furnishings, Victor walked down to the broad waters of the River Severn.

On evenings like this, when the sun was low and golden, it made silhouettes of figures on the shore. So, sometimes, he found himself thinking he saw Ghorlan waiting for him by the water's edge.

Tonight, he saw a lone figure standing motionless on the shingle. The woman waited for him to approach before she softly spoke. 'Lou always insisted that this island could change how people think.' She smiled at him. 'Six months ago I couldn't have imagined my life would have changed so much. Especially that I'd be standing here, wearing a new ring on my finger.'

Victor smiled back. 'Sometimes, every now and again, we really do get what we deserve.' With that he kissed his wife . . . and he knew that everything was going to be all right.